SHOCK AND AWW

Blue Collar Bensons Book 2

Lilly Atlas

This one is for my wonderful mother-in-law.
There's a story later in this book that you might think
is ridiculous.

It's real.

<3

Other books by Lilly Atlas

No Prisoners MC
Hook: A No Prisoners Novella
Striker
Jester
Acer
Lucky
Snake

Trident Ink
Escapades

Hell's Handlers MC
Zach
Maverick
Jigsaw
Copper
Rocket
Little Jack
Joy
Screw
Viper
Thunder

* * *

Hell's Handlers MC FL Chapter
Curly

Bue Collar Bensons
First Comes Loathe
Shock and Aww

Audiobooks
Audio

Join Lilly's mailing list for a **FREE** No Prisoners short story.
www.lillyatlas.com
Facebook
Instagram
TikTok
Twitter

Table of Contents

Prologue

Summer 2020

He was getting too old for this shit.

And by this shit, JP meant muscling his way through a jam-packed crowd of drunk, sweaty bodies while Beyonce belted her heart out on stage.

Beyonce, really?

Sure, he appreciated her talent, and what hetero man didn't think she was hot as fuck? But he was a rock and roll guy all the way. Couldn't help it. It was in his blood.

And his name. His parents had called him John Paul for a reason, after all. Named him after the British rock star John Paul Jones of Led Zeppelin. They named all their kids after British rockers.

"'Scuse me, sweetheart," he said as he tried not to be a total creeper and drag his dick across the woman in front of him as he squeezed past her.

His buddy and favorite tattoo artist, Desmond, should have been the poor schmuck stuck at this overcrowded concert with his kickass wife, Jill. Desi had been all about a much-needed date night and time away from their kids. But the universe had different ideas, and poor Desi was home puking his guts out courtesy of a bug his two-year-old generously brought home from daycare. That was the problem with marriage right there. It led to scheduled date nights, which led to kids, who made more

1

date nights necessary, which led to more kids, and so on. Next thing a guy knew, he was hugging the porcelain throne all day.

JP shuddered. He felt for his sick friend, he really did, but the expulsion of bodily fluids was one of the many reasons JP never planned on having kids. One of the many, many reasons. Cock blocking, lack of sleep, and constant noise were a few others.

Being the stellar best friend he was, JP gave up a night of searching for his next hookup in favor of escorting Jill to the concert while her husband slept off his virus.

Desi owed him. Big time.

Now, he was on his way back to Jill, where she danced and sang with the rest of the floor-level ticket holders. It was a miracle that JP had managed to keep from spilling the margaritas in his hands all over some unsuspecting concertgoer.

"JP!" Jill shouted when he reached her. She threw her slender arms around his shoulders and squeezed the hell outta him. "Isn't this so much fun?"

He laughed at her enthusiasm, which came from the two margaritas she'd already sucked back. "The best. Here, sweetie," he said, handing over her drink.

"Oh, thank you! I'm so thirsty." She grabbed the cup and chugged as though it were a refreshing lemonade instead of a tequila-loaded drink. Being as thin as she was—which amazed him considering she'd had two kids in three years—those drinks hit her hard.

He, on the other hand, would be the exact right amount of pleasantly tipsy by the time he polished off his third drink. And that's where he'd stay for the night. Being entrusted with his best friend's beautiful, red-headed wife was a job he took seriously, so he'd refrain from getting smashed.

Twenty minutes later, the deafening roar of thousands of unattached women filled the arena as Beyonce strutted across the stage in a fierce silver bodysuit with her chest heaving as she sang *Single Ladies*.

Jill jumped up and down, screaming with the best of them.

She turned to him, short auburn hair plastered to her face as she yelled, "Are you regretting this yet?"

He took stock for a second.

Drinks, check.

Dancing, check.

Music, check.

Okay, it wasn't so bad, even if he felt like an old man. "Never. I've got the prettiest date in the place." He winked, then took her hand, spinning her around. They danced like fools, and he didn't give a shit because he wasn't searching for a woman to take home for the night. Scratch that, for a few hours. He didn't do sleepovers. Too domestic. Too…cuddly.

Yuck.

Why the hell would he stick around for all that extra bullshit when an orgasm was the reason he got naked with a woman in the first place?

By the time the Beyonce sashayed off stage after her second encore, his ears were ringing and his feet ached. Yeah, he was officially too fucking old for this shit. Or maybe he'd just been busy as fuck helping his brother Keith out at his auto shop over the past week. Tomorrow he planned to do nothing but eat, drink coffee, jerk off a time or two, then head outside for a long nap in the sun—perfect way to spend a summer Saturday.

As the arena brightened and concertgoers began to file out, Jill grabbed his arm. "Oh my God!" she squealed, pointing across the thinning crowd. "I know them."

Three women clustered about thirty feet away, gesturing with as much sloppy enthusiasm as Jill.

"They're all moms of kids in Lulu's daycare." After waving back, she started dragging JP over then seemed to remember he wasn't her husband. "Sorry, do you mind if I talk to them for a few minutes?"

Kinda, but… "Nah, sweetie. This is your night. Take your time. I'll wait for you over here."

She kissed his cheek then flounced off, slightly unstable on her feet. A high-pitched squeal of excitement from the women killed a few of his brain cells.

As he waited for Jill to get the socializing out of her system, he wandered toward the exit and propped his back against the wall. Typically, he'd have joined Jill and flirted until one of her friends showed interest. It'd been a solid week since he'd gotten laid, and his balls could use a good unloading. But these women came with kids, and he didn't fuck women with kids.

At least not if he could help it. One sweaty romp and a woman with kids got ideas in her head. Hearts and flowers kind of ideas. Stability ideas. Daddy-for-junior ideas.

Fuck that. Last thing he wanted now or ever was some rug rat running circles around him while its mom dreamed of rings and honeymoons.

His gaze snagged on a woman standing alone, talking into her phone. She was younger than him, maybe early twenties, with the most white-blond hair he'd ever seen. It barely grazed her shoulders and swung, sunny and shiny, as she gestured with her hand.

When she turned, he caught a glint of glitter covering her eyelids. Her expression was one of frustration, but it didn't disguise how adorable she was. Tight jeans, an asymmetrical black shirt that left one shoulder completely bare, and bright red heels. Simple, sexy, sweet. Probably too sweet for him. Women he classified as adorable tended to be too innocent for his tastes. Along with avoiding hooking up with moms, he shied away from virgins. Another group that got stars in their eyes the second a man made them feel special.

And what could he say? His brand of charm and physical skill made every woman feel special.

For a little while anyway.

As the woman hung up her phone, she glanced his way. As their gazes collided, her eyes widened, but she recovered so fast. Hell, maybe he'd imagined the flash of interest.

Her glossy pink lips curled up in a smile designed for one

thing and one thing only, seduction. Nope. Not his imagination.

And right on cue, his cock twitched. Huh, maybe Miss Adorable wasn't quite as sweet as he'd assumed.

Jill picked that moment to run back to him. "I'm so sorry for making you wait."

The blonde's smile flipped to a frown as she probably assumed Jill was his girlfriend, not just his friend. "Don't worry about it. I was enjoying the view."

"Oh really?" Jill made a slow turn. When she saw the woman he'd had his eye on, she hummed. "Cute. Well, that makes what I'm about to do to you seem a little less shitty." She spun back and bit her lower lip with a sheepish expression. The freckles she always claimed to hate seemed brighter than usual, thanks to the alcohol.

"Uh oh. What are you up to?"

"My friends are all going out to a bar afterward, and they want me to join them. I already ran it by Desi, and he's cool with it." She held up a hand as he opened his mouth. "Carmen is the DD and hasn't had a drop of booze all night. She'll get us all home safely afterward."

JP frowned at the group of ladies currently pleading with their hazy eyes. "I don't know…"

With a snort, Jill laughed. "You're worse than my husband. But lucky for me, you don't get a say." She winked. "I'm going. And you are now free to go pick up that little cutie." She rose on tip toes and kissed his cheek. "Have fun," she sing-songed. Then with a cheerful wave, she was hustling back to her girl gang while giving the *cutie* a thumbs up.

The poor woman across the way had a look of utter confusion on her face.

Well, the night certainly had taken an unexpected turn, but who the hell was he to look a gift horse in the mouth? Pasting on his most charming smile, the one that had his bedpost carved full of notches, he sauntered across the arena with his most confident swagger.

"I'm guessing that thumbs up means she isn't your girlfriend, wife, or baby mama?" the woman asked with a raised eyebrow when he was close enough to hear.

JP laughed long and loud. Shit, she was even cuter up close with a button nose, sparkling blue eyes, and a little freckle near the corner of her right eye. "No, she's the wife of a buddy who is home sick with his children. I am blessedly woman and child free."

Something indistinguishable flashed in her eyes, but it vanished as soon as it appeared. If he had to make a guess, it had seemed almost sad, but her personal problems were none of his business. Long as she was consenting, over eighteen, and some dude wasn't about to walk out of the bathroom and beat him bloody for flirting with his girl, they were good to go.

"You?" he asked.

"I also do not have a wife, girlfriend, or children." She smirked.

"Sassy. I like it. But please tell me you swing my way at least some of the time." He stuck out his lower lip in a pitiful pout, making her laugh.

"I swing your way all the time. What's your name?"

"John Paul, but for the love of God, please call me JP. You?"

She looked off into the distance for a moment, then faced him again. "Let's skip this small talk, flirty stuff, okay? I want to fuck tonight. And I want to fuck you. I have a car in the parking lot."

"Classy." Shit, a woman on a mission. No complaints about that. And probably not a virgin with that goal. "Lucky for you, I'm a classy guy. Lead the way…miss." Was she ever going to give up her name? Not that he genuinely cared, but it was fun to shout a name when he was coming.

She placed a hand on his chest, sending a tingle of sensation rippling across his skin. "I want an orgasm or two, and I'll return the favor. Nothing more. This isn't the start of…anything." Her eyes darkened with each word until the blue resembled turbulent waters on a stormy day. He'd always been a sucker for blue eyes, and these were no different.

"As I said, beautiful, lead the way." His voice dipped to a husky pitch as anticipation flooded his veins. He was gonna come tonight in the back seat of whatever the hell kinda car she had like he was a horny teenager hiding from his parents' notice. Not that he had a parent who'd given a shit what he did or didn't do when he was a rascally teen. Still, it'd be a fun fantasy to play out.

Smiling, she held a hand out to him. "It's Mary Anne, and I'd love to." Then she slicked her tongue along her lower lip in a sensual swipe that had him groaning in need.

No-strings, no-consequences, no-frills fucking.

The perfect way to end any night.

Chapter One

They were at it again.

Seriously, his brother, Keith, and Michaela, Keith's movie-star-turned-regular-person girlfriend, couldn't survive more than ten minutes without groping, kissing, or gazing at each other with the most revolting lovesick stares JP had ever seen.

He was all for the kissing and touching parts, but the I'm-peering-into-your-soul shit had to go. It gave him hives, and he had a "date" later that wouldn't end well if he showed up covered in red splotches.

And they were still going at it.

He groaned. "Seriously, you guys are like watching a Lifetime movie. It's disgusting. I think we would all prefer it if you gave us some porn instead." Pretty sure anyone in their family would prefer watching porn over a cheesy romance flick. Especially since their entire upbringing had been the opposite of anything Lifetime ever promoted.

A throat cleared from across the backyard. "Um, excuse me?"

The unfamiliar voice had everyone staring in her direction. A woman, probably in her mid to upper twenties, hovered near the open gate. She was cute, with a riot of curly black hair hanging past her shoulders. She wrung her hands at her waist and gnawed her lower lip.

Nervous.

He didn't recognize her, so she must be looking for one of his brothers. Ooh, unless he'd hooked up with her at some point. Shit, last thing he needed was a clinger sniffing around for promises he'd never make.

"I'm so sorry to interrupt, but I'm looking for someone named John Paul."

Huh. It didn't sound like she knew him either, so what the hell did she want him for? Maybe word about his prowess had spread, and she came for a few hours of horizontal fun. He did have a "date" later tonight, but there were many hours in between, and he had no problem showing this lovely creature a good time before then.

He sprang from his chair with an easy grin. Hopefully, he didn't have any corn stuck between his teeth—nothing worse than going in for some tongue action only to find a grill full of food.

He spread his arms. "Well, gorgeous, that would be me. What can I do for you? Do you need directions? Maybe to my bedroom?"

One of his older brothers, Jagger, groaned. "Maybe try not to be arrested for harassment before you know what she wants."

Chuckling, he walked around the table and made his way toward the mystery woman whose eyes had gone wide. "I'm just fucking with you. But I am JP. What's up?" There was a chance he came on too strong as she now glanced back and forth between the gate and him as though ready to bolt.

Up close, she was even prettier, with wide, brown eyes, smooth skin, and a curvy figure.

She eyed him then stepped back to the gate, where she reached for something. Two seconds later, a stroller rolled into his backyard.

"Um," she said as she swallowed. "My name is Bethany Rosen. I'm a social worker from children's services. This is—"

A stroller? Oh, hell no. He no longer wanted any part of this woman. Behind him, his siblings gasped and murmured amongst themselves.

"Whoa," he said, as he raised his hands and took a step back like the stroller was full of buzzing bees instead of someone's child. Same difference, really. "Maybe someone else should help you out here, Miss Rosen. I'm allergic to anything baby. Jag, you wanna tap in?"

He turned toward his uber-responsible and serious big brother. Jagger rose from the table, unsmiling.

"JP," he said in a disapproving tone. "I think she's trying to tell you something important."

Ugh, older brothers were the worst. He should know. He had four. Having a shit father figure meant the older brothers felt the need to step in and fill that role. Even now that he was in his fucking thirties.

Don't you want a real job, JP?

Aren't you tired of being with a different woman every night, JP?

Why can't you ever act like an adult, JP?

Of course, he knew he was a fucking adult. That didn't mean he had to settle for some boring-ass nine-to-five desk job, get a pinched look to his face, and become a lemming.

"Sorry," he said to the woman who was once again abusing her poor lip. She seemed more nervous than a virgin on her wedding night. What the hell was she so worked up about? "So, what's going on?"

She cleared her throat. "As I said, I work with social services. We've been trying to contact you."

"Yeah, sorry. Don't answer numbers I don't recognize." Did anyone anymore? He wasn't big on checking voicemail either, but wasn't that what text messages were invented for?

"Right, well, this is your daughter. Her name is Kayla." She spoke fast as though afraid she'd never get it out otherwise.

"Oh, my God," Mickie whispered from the table. Keith swore under his breath.

Jesus, this bunch was a fucking trip. "Okay, guys, very funny." He turned toward his siblings. This had to be payback for putting salt in the sugar bowl last weekend. His sister, Ronnie, had been pissed in a way only an uncaffeinated, non-morning person could be.

He'd learned his lesson quickly. Don't mess with a woman's ability to caffeinate properly. His shoulder still smarted from where she'd punched him. They didn't need to put on this elaborate little ruse, but he appreciated the revenge effort.

"You got me." He rolled his eyes. "Who is this? Mickie, a friend of yours? Someone you met at work, Jag?"

No one spoke. Wide-eyed, Mickie shook her head. Her mouth moved, but no words came out.

As he stared at what appeared to be genuine shock on his siblings' faces, his stomach twisted. None of them, except Mickie, could act for shit. If this was a joke, Jagger would have been snorting behind his hand like he always did. The guy spoiled every damn prank or surprise he participated in.

"This is not a joke, sir," the woman said.

He faced her with a brick in his stomach.

"She's your daughter. Her mother, Mary Anne, met you at a concert about a year and a half ago. I'm aware you didn't have a relationship, but Mary Anne was very explicit about wanting you to have full custody of Kayla when she passed."

He heard the words as though he stood at the end of a very long tunnel. They swirled in his head, not taking root. Except for one part. "Passed?" he asked with a thick throat. "What?"

Miss Rosen cleared her throat. "Yes, I'm sorry to tell you, Mary Anne died recently." She paused, then reached out and squeezed his arm. "There's a letter for you in the diaper bag. Along with quite a bit of legal paperwork to review."

Shaking his head, he took a step back. This wasn't real. Couldn't be real. For Christ's sake, he never fucked without a condom. Never. Not one single slip up. For this very damn reason.

No.

He wasn't ready.

He didn't want this.

He couldn't accept it.

His skin prickled as though wearing a wool sweater with nothing underneath. An invisible hand wrapped around his throat, constricting his airway. He grew ice cold and started to sweat in some strange paradox.

"This can't be right. I can't…I've never even held…" He lifted his hands and shook his head as words failed him.

Mickie stood from the table. "We'll help you, JP. We're all here to help you with your daughter."

A loud clanging made him jump so hard, his teeth clacked.

"Holy shit!" Everyone turned to find Ronnie standing near the table. She'd dropped the platter with the strawberry shortcake on the floor. "JP has a kid?" she asked in the most incredulous tone he'd heard from her.

Damn, he'd been looking forward to dessert.

"No! No, I don't." He took a few more steps back as the woman frowned, and panic entered her gaze. "I don't want it. It can't be mine. You're lying."

Mary Anne? Did he even remember a Mary Anne?

Damn his siblings for taking some random woman's word. Some woman who'd just busted in on a family barbecue and tried to destroy his life.

Fuck that.

The kid wasn't his. No way in hell. He was the last person on earth who should be trusted with another human being. He'd had nothing but horrid examples of parenthood throughout his childhood. An abusive drunk of a father who couldn't have paid a woman enough to take on him and five kids. A man who'd rather drink every dime he stumbled upon than make sure his family was fed. A man who spoke with his fists and currently sat rotting in a prison cell.

Great role model.

No, he couldn't accept this.

"Come on, guys. Let's finish eating." To the woman, he said, "You can see yourself out."

When he turned, he encountered the troubled stares of his siblings.

"But, it's—"

He tried to tune the woman out, but she was too damn close.

"Sir, I can assure you this is real. If you'll just—"

"Leave!"

Mickie rushed forward. When she reached him, she cupped his shoulders and smiled with sympathy. Or maybe pity. Then she went over to the stroller and gasped. "Oh, she looks just like a Benson. She's beautiful. Hi, sweet girl." She reached into the stroller. A huge smile broke out across her face.

He squeezed his eyes shut as he froze in place. Nausea churned in his gut.

This couldn't be happening. He didn't want this.

Didn't *want* it.

He was going to be sick.

"JP?" Mickie's impossibly soft hand circled his wrist.

Back at the table, his oldest brother stood and narrowed his eyes at JP in a subtle but firm warning. *Don't fucking upset my woman.*

"Just come look at her. That's all. For one minute," Mickie whispered as though speaking to a frightened animal.

He glanced down at her fingers, lightly tugging on his wrist, and nodded. If that was the only way to end this nightmare, he'd look at the baby. But there was no fucking way he'd touch it. Or claim it.

Because it wasn't his.

With a soft smile, Mickie led him over to the stroller. Miss Rosen stepped back to give him space but eyed him as if he couldn't be trusted.

After taking a fortifying breath, he glanced at the sleeping baby and nearly collapsed to his knees.

Jesus Christ, she could have been his twin as an infant. A tuft of dark hair, chubby cheeks, the same exact tiny nose.

"She's beautiful," Mickie whispered as she rubbed his back.

"She's you."

No. No. No! Inside he was screaming with all he had, but outside he stood motionless. Unable to speak, unable to breathe, unable to think.

"I know this is a lot." The woman said as she stepped forward. She reached into the diaper big and pulled out an envelope. "This will explain everything."

He blinked and reached for the envelope as though on autopilot. His arm moved without direction from his brain. Once he had the letter, he glanced back at his mini-me. She was real. A flesh-and-blood baby. A squishy little lump that terrified him to his soul.

"Would you like to hold her?" Mickie asked, still talking in a near whisper.

"What?" His head snapped up.

She smiled. "Do you want to hold your daughter?"

"No!" The shout startled Mickie and Bethany. The baby began to cry. He flinched as guilt joined his fear. "S-sorry." See? He'd scared the baby already. He couldn't hold her.

The woman shot him an angry glare then scooped the kid up.

"No," he said again. "I don't want anything to do with it. I have to go."

He fled into the house at full speed, ignoring the shouts from his siblings. Thankfully, no one followed him as he sprinted through the house then locked himself in his basement bedroom.

He dropped onto the side of his bed like a lead weight and sat gazing at the unopened letter for what had to be hours. Eventually, the sun set, and he found himself staring into darkness.

His insides felt heavy, as though he carried the weight of the world. Dread sat like a boulder in the pit of his stomach. He switched on the lamp next to his bed then went back to staring at the envelope. With trembling hands, he tore it open.

It contained multiple pages, handwritten in shaky, blue ink. In a few spots, a round stain had smudged letters.

Tears?

Had Mary Anne cried as she wrote this letter?

Had she really birthed his baby only to die shortly afterward?

Who the hell was she?

Though he knew deep down this letter was going to flip his entire life upside down, he took a deep breath and began to read.

Chapter Two

Dear JP,

Have you ever done something so wrong, so completely selfish, that it made you question the kind of person you were? Really wonder about the state of your soul? I mean, am I rotten at my core? Am I evil? Immoral? Tainted?

Sometimes I think I must be because what I've done is nearly impossible to comprehend without one of those labels.

I'm not talking about cheating on a test, swiping a shirt from a store, or deceiving your family. I'm not even talking about physically harming someone. What I mean is, have you ever known full well that what you were about to do would set in motion a series of events you couldn't undo? Events that would change and possibly destroy the lives of others?

Yet you did it anyway because something inside of you had shattered with no chance of repair?

You probably haven't. I imagine most people haven't sunk that low. Maybe broken is the most appropriate label to slap on me for what I've done. But it seems too kind. It gives me an out I don't think I deserve.

Regardless, I'm left with the insurmountable task of explaining why I committed such a sin. And the even more impossible task of making you understand and somehow not hate me when you have every right to. What makes it worse is that I've taken the easy way out. If you're reading this letter, I'm dead and will never have to face your wrath. I'll never have to see the shock on your face, watch you break down the *instant you realize your entire life has changed. I'll never hear you curse my name, though I've imagined it many times.*

I will never have to face what I've done. And, God, it's so much simpler that way.

Not only am I a sinner, I'm also a coward.

Once you're on the other side of a transgression like mine, the weight of it presses on your soul for the rest of your days. In my case, I'm not sure how long I'll suffer from the guilt of knowing I've caused an irreversible change in your life, but it won't be many. My days are numbered, and that number is low.

I suppose I need to get on with telling you what I've done, but even as I sit here with a pen in my failing hand, knowing I'll never witness your reaction to this letter, I'm finding it difficult to write the words. Maybe I don't know where to start, or maybe it's more of that cowardice.

Well, here I go. I'm taking a deep breath and starting at the beginning.

My parents adopted me when I was a baby. After that, I had what I would call a normal upbringing. Mom, dad, sister (also adopted), family pet, suburbs with a fenced-in yard, public school, not rich but not poor…you know, the basic American family unit.

If there was anything that set us apart from the rest of my peers, it was my parents' strict rules and close hovering over my sister and me. When my mother was a young teenager, one of her cousins passed in a tragic accident. My mom was there and tried unsuccessfully to save her.

She and my dad were high school sweethearts, so he witnessed the devastation that event caused my mother and her family. We've rarely spoken of it, but that event seemed to set off deep anxiety and fear of loss in my mother. Follow that up with long and heartbreaking years of infertility and miscarriages… More loss.

Eventually, they were able to adopt two girls within two years. She compensated for her fears by keeping very close tabs on my sister and me. No sleepovers, heavily censored television and books, nine o'clock curfew throughout high school, no sports, vetting our friends like they were FBI agents instead of shop owners, and absolutely no dating until we graduated high school. She hoped if they clamped down tight and put a bubble around us, we'd never get drunk with our underaged friends and get behind the wheel of our boyfriend's car as my mother's cousin did so many years before.

Unfortunately for them, no matter how many layers of padding they put between us and the world, there were some things they'd never be able to control.

My sister handled their structure and overbearing nature better than I did. She is a year older, always got straight A's, never broke a rule, and was generally the picture-perfect child. I struggled with the stifling inability to express myself, grow, and spread my wings. That struggle turned into rebellion.

Mind you, my form of rebellion was about ten times milder than most teens. I got B's instead of A's. I stayed out until ten at night—a whole hour past curfew. I had a secret boyfriend who I let get to second base. I even had a few beers before I graduated high school. I know, I was wild. My actions caused my mother countless sleepless nights and anxiety attacks when I'd probably have been a superstar child by any other family's standards.

When I turned eighteen, I wanted out of the house, but my mom was the master of the guilt trip and convinced me to attend a local college while living at home.

I hope you're still reading. None of this is meant to play on your sympathies or manipulate you into feeling sorry for me. I own what I've done and know you'll think poorly of me no matter what sob story I give you. My only goal here is to provide you with a sense of closure, so you don't spend your entire life wondering why I did something so outrageous.

After college, I put my foot down and informed my parents I was moving out no matter what they said. Dad yelled, Mom cried, and Saint Sister saved the day as she always did by offering to move into an apartment with me. Our parents still hated the idea but eventually agreed. I can only assume they hoped my sister would be a positive influence on me.

And she was. We got on great, worked jobs we both enjoyed, and reveled in our newfound freedom. Neither of us went wild as we still had the daily reminders from our mother of what could happen in the big, bad world if we weren't overly cautious.

When I hit twenty-two, I began having strange muscle twitches in my face and a few other areas. I ignored it for months, assuming I needed to drink more water or eat more bananas. Then, I mentioned it during a routine doctor's appointment, and my physician recommended I see a neurologist. In my never-ending quest for independence, I didn't bother taking anyone to the neurology appointment with me. The specialist ran a battery of tests and called me back into their office a week later.

Ever heard of Amyotrophic Lateral Sclerosis? Also referred to as ALS or Lou Gehrig's disease?

It's a nasty illness with a shitty prognosis. Most people who develop it are diagnosed in their mid-life years. Twenty-three is young, rare, and offers little hope for a lengthy life.

I left the neurologist's office in a fog with pamphlets, prescriptions, more appointments, and a whole host of rage in my gut.

Fifty percent of those diagnosed lived for three years.

Twenty-five percent lived five years.

The prognosis was even poorer at my age.

I'd spent my entire life so cautious, so careful, so sheltered, all for the purpose of surviving as long as possible. I'd never gotten a tattoo or been blackout drunk. Never hooked up with a stranger, never driven a hundred miles per hour in a car, never used drugs, and never woken up in the morning wondering why the hell I'd made the decisions I'd made the night before.

Sitting in that parking lot, I was bombarded by all the experiences and rites of passage I'd missed out on and might never enjoy. My clock was running out, and I'd never catch up with it.

I cried in my car for hours as I thought of all the things I'd miss out on if I died in the next three years.

Climbing the ladder in my job.

Falling in love.

Watching my sister fall in love.

Getting married.

Having a baby…

And that was the one to break me. I'd never hold my own child in my arms. Never feed him or her with my body. Never watch their little face as they sleep. Never know the exhaustion of a first-time mom. Never chase a precocious toddler around the house. Never feel the frustration only a sassy teenager could cause. Never watch my child get married and begin their own life. I'll never forget the crushing pain in my chest that followed the realization. For a moment, I worried I was having a heart attack.

Here's a fact about me. I'm a preschool teacher. I love children. Love them. I've always wanted at least four of my own. Being a mother has always been my ultimate goal in life.

And I'd had the chance ripped away from me on a beautiful July afternoon while I sat in a cold, sterile doctor's office alone.

I snapped. It's the only way of explaining what happened to my brain. All I thought of was how I could have a few years with my child if I got pregnant right away. And I wanted that more than I wanted to live those three years. So what followed was driven by desperation and despair.

I'd had tickets to that concert for months.

I got drunk.

I planned to find a man.

You caught my eye.

You made me laugh.

You were sweet.

You were hot.

I poked a hole in the condom I reassured you I had like some irrational soap opera villain.

We had sex in the very same car I'd sobbed in earlier that day.

The following day, I woke up shocked at myself for my reckless behavior. I remember pouring coffee and willing myself not to vomit. I'd finally broken all my parents' rules, woken up with regrets, and had a one-night stand. All it had taken to truly rebel was a death sentence.

Six weeks later, two little blue lines stared back at me from a pregnancy test, and I knew I'd become a monster.

Your daughter's name is Kayla. Her birthday is February 12, 2021. She loves peaches and yogurt, hates carrots, and drinks milk like it's her job. Her favorite toy is a stuffed elephant my sister bought her. She poops like a champ and is an okay sleeper. Also, I'm pretty sure she's a genius, but there's a small chance I'm biased.

She doesn't have a mother.

Not one who's living. But when she was living, Kayla's mother loved her more than she'd ever imagined loving anyone.

My parents want to raise her, but I've already done enough terrible things. Right now, as you read this, you might be thinking that giving Kayla to you is another of those awful things. It's not.

Because she's incredible.

And you are her father.

The best thing I've ever had came out of the worst thing I've ever done. How is that even possible? One of the universe's cruel ironies, I suppose.

I found you through social media. How else, right? Your family seems fun and messy; wonderful. I've read every interview Michaela Hudson did since she began dating your brother. The way she spoke about you and your family set my heart and mind at ease. I know Kayla will be loved.

I'm not going to beg you to love her because I know you will. It's impossible not to. And I'm not going to ask you to take good care of her because I know you will do that, too. You might not remember me, but I've followed you on social media since we met, and while you might have a healthy appetite for fun, I also see a deep love for your family. It's how I knew Kayla belonged with you.

There is one thing I ask of you, though I have no right. My hope is with time you'll soften and be willing to grant me this one wish. I'm shamelessly using the fact that I'm dying to get my way. If it's for Kayla's benefit, there is no depth I won't stoop to.

Please, someday, let her know her mother loved her. Still loves her from wherever she ends up in the afterlife. Please let her know that while she was created by a deceitful mistake her mother made, she never once considered Kayla a mistake.

She was the joy of my life, and I am grateful for every second I got to spend with her.

I owe you the biggest apology one can ever bestow, but I find it hard to write the words. If I apologize for that night, I'm apologizing for Kayla, and one day you will understand why I cannot do that. It'll hit you when you least expect it. This surge of love so strong, it's like a drug.

I am sorry for the circumstances, though. For the lies. For the shock. For the tough months ahead.

For my death.

But I'm not sorry for Kayla.

I can promise she will become the joy of your life. Just wait and see.

A beautiful rainbow after a raging storm.

Thank you for filling the final months of my life with love so pure and precious, I will carry it with me into eternity.

All my love,
  Mary Anne

Chapter Three

Hannah gaped at her parents with her jaw swinging. She blinked, then forced her mouth closed to swallow the lump in her throat. "I'm sorry, I can't possibly have heard you correctly. Say that again."

Silent tears coasted down her mother's distraught face. Ever since Mary Anne passed away two months ago, seeing her mother makeup free, red-eyed, and dabbing her face with a tissue had become the norm. Not long ago, Hannah couldn't have said what her mother looked like without freshly pressed clothes, makeup, or with her gray roots peeking out. Now, it was her daily uniform.

To say she wasn't coping well was the same as saying rain was wet.

"We need you to do this for us, Pickle," her father said in a defeated tone, using the dreaded childhood nickname. Apparently, she'd gone through a phase around two where she'd refused to eat anything other than pickles. A stage that haunted her to this day.

Her dad seemed to have aged ten years in the past six months. Where a thick head of silvery hair used to live, a bald spot shone in the light. He'd lost weight as well. Both her parents had. Getting them to choke down a full meal had been damn near impossible since Mary Anne died.

They'd known it was coming. All of them had, for months.

But while Hannah had been doing everything she could to mentally prepare herself for the loss while soaking up as many new memories of her sister and niece as possible, her parents had gone the route of deep denial.

Not that the loss of her sister and best friend had been or was easy for Hannah, but she was in a far better place than her parents thanks to counseling and the way she and Mary Anne spent those final months.

"We just l-lost our daughter. And now those people have taken our granddaughter." His desperate plea tore at Hannah's soul even as the request horrified her.

"Have you seen him?" her mother asked, voice trembling as though their grandchild now lived in the home of a serial killer.

Yes, she'd seen pictures of Kayla's father. She and Mary Anne had dozens of late-night chats about the man. Hannah had helped her sister research anything and everything about him and his entire family. Amazing how much information one could find with simply a name.

As soon as she'd seen the obvious love and connection between JP Benson and his siblings, her sister planned to give him custody of their child when she passed. At first, like her parents, Hannah had been horrified. Not because he was a man covered in tattoos with a different woman in every social media picture, but because she couldn't imagine not seeing her niece every day.

But it was the right thing to do. He was the child's father.

Please make sure JP gets to raise Kayla. She deserves her father.

It'd been Mary Anne's dying request, and Hannah would never break that vow.

Not only had Mary Anne put JP's name on the birth certificate, but she'd written a letter to their parents begging them not to fight for custody. The letter had been delivered by a lawyer a week after her passing as part of her will.

I've done so many things wrong. Please let me do one thing right.

Of course, the first thing her parents did was contact their own attorney to see what rights they had. But it seemed, thankfully, that all was above board, and unless someone discovered a legitimate reason to keep JP from getting custody of Kayla, he would be raising his daughter.

Hannah sighed. "I've seen him, Mom."

Seen him. Drooled over him. Committed the picture of the handsome man to memory.

His social media accounts suggested he was everything Hannah wasn't. Tall, inked, always smiling, carefree, surrounded by a big, boisterous family.

"He looks like a thug." She held out her phone as though Hannah hadn't just mentioned she'd seen him. A picture of JP filled the screen. "His whole family look like thugs. He looks just like the man who was driving the car when my cousin died! How can you possibly be okay with him raising your niece? Mary Anne was confused at the end. That's the only reason I can think of that she wouldn't have wanted your father and me to raise her baby." With shaking hands that had become so frail they were nothing but skin and bone, she pressed the soaked tissue to her eyes.

Her parents were older than her peers', having adopted her or Mary Anne in their late forties.

Hannah resisted rolling her eyes. "Mom, you can't judge him because he looks different. That's not okay. He's not the man who drove drunk and killed your cousin." They'd had this conversation a hundred times already, and, in their grief, her words had fallen on deaf ears. "He's Kayla's father."

"Yes! He's Kayla's father!" Her mother slammed her hand down on her knee. "And he hasn't done a damn thing for that little girl since the day she was born. He didn't support your sister during her pregnancy either. What kind of a man does that?" she yelled. "I'll tell you what kind. Someone unfit to raise my grandchild."

Pinching the bridge of her nose, Hannah fought for patience. How many times were they going to have this conversation?

"Mom," she said in a gentle tone as she reached for her mother's trembling hands. Experience had taught her to tread carefully here. One wrong word would send her spiraling down a dark pit of despair, resulting in days of bed-bound depression. "You know that Mary Anne didn't tell him she was pregnant. Until today, the man had no idea Kayla existed." She couldn't help but wonder how the man handled the shock. Had he embraced his new role of fatherhood, or would it take some time to warm up to?

Her mother's red-rimmed eyes narrowed. Since Mary Anne died, it was as though her sister had never committed any wrongdoings. Her mom suspended reality, letting her grief turn her daughter into a saint, and Hannah's father went along to keep his wife pacified. But Mary Anne had done something very wrong and hadn't shied away from discussing her regrets with Hannah.

"Yes," her mother spat out, "and what kind of man sleeps with a woman and never sees her again, huh?"

A normal man hooking up with a normal woman in an agreed-upon one-time thing. Something Hannah had never done herself. Nope, she'd always followed the rules, colored in the lines, stayed on track. Now she was left without her best friend, wondering if she'd missed out on opportunities she'd never have again.

A chilling thought.

But Hannah didn't say any of that. She'd tried it already, and it ended in hours of near shrieking sobs from her mother and her father slinking out of the house and disappearing for half the day.

As much as she loved her sister and as big as the hole in her heart had grown, part of her remained furious with Mary Anne for dying and leaving Hannah with this mess. For bringing Kayla into their lives only to have her gone months later. For abandoning Hannah to their mother's increasing mental fragility.

"I know this is hard to hear right now, Mom, but Mary Anne was the one who screwed up here. Not JP."

Her mother's mouth opened, and her gaze filled with fury.

Hannah spoke before her mother could lambast her. "I loved her as much as you did, and I miss her as much as you do, Mom, but we can't ignore the truth. Mary Anne made some terrible choices after her diagnosis. Conscious choices. She owned those decisions, and Kayla's father having custody now is her trying to atone for her mistakes."

"No." Her mother shook her head while her father stared off into space. "I can't accept that. Mary Anne was out of her head with fear and shock. She wasn't in her right mind when she had s—when she was with *that* man. We are the ones who love Kayla and want what's best for her." She slapped a hand over her heart. "Your father and I are the ones who should be raising that baby."

So you can smother it with ridiculously stifling rules?

So you can avoid facing your grief and get a redo for the child you lost?

Her heart ached. Hannah had no idea how to get through to them. She never had. It was always easier to give in and toe the line rather than fight against their overbearing nature. "I'm sorry. I know you're hurting, but I can't do it. I won't go to Vermont under false pretenses and try to take the man's child away. Finding out he has a seven-month-old daughter he knew nothing about must have flipped his entire world upside down. He deserves time to find his footing without someone trying to take his baby from him."

They'd actually asked her to befriend JP on the sly, then dig up any dirt on him to have him declared an unfit father. Her mother went so far as suggesting she set him up if she couldn't find any evidence to present to their attorney. Hannah found the idea as horrifying as having her toenails pried off.

What her mother failed to realize was that raising a rule-following, good girl who never once strayed across their inflexible boundaries meant she couldn't possibly pull off the devious plan they begged of her.

"Hannah, please. Our attorney says our hands are tied unless we have proof, physical evidence that JP is an unfit father or Kayla is being mistreated. We have no idea what they are doing to her right now."

Rolling her eyes, Hannah bit back a nasty retort. Her mother had always been dramatic in her worry, but this was taking it to the limit. "You know, no one has said you can't be in the child's life. You've seen the pictures; family seems very important to JP. I'm sure he will be thrilled to have Kayla's grandparents play an active and appropriate role in her life."

"Don't speak his name to me," her mother snapped. "That baby belongs with us here where we know she will have a good, safe, respectable upbringing. Not one where she'll be influenced to defile her body or act in countless immoral and dangerous ways."

Tattoos and piercings beyond a single hole in the lobe were defiling in her mother's opinion. A way to invite riffraff into one's life. A straight shot to drugs, overdoses, and death. And so much for their ability to mold their children into the perfect specimens of morality and safety. If they had, maybe Mary Anne wouldn't have tricked a man to get pregnant.

"Did you see who is in so many of his pictures? That actress. The one who has been in the news so many times for her philandering ways and drug addictions. What's her name? Scarlett? Is that the kind of trash you want influencing your niece?"

Michaela Hudson, known during her Hollywood career as Scarlett, was a woman who owned her mistakes and turned her life around in spectacular ways. That's who her parents feared? A hardworking woman with insight and drive to change her life for the better?

Seemed like a pretty good role model to Hannah.

"Please, Pickle," her father slid off the couch onto his knees as he grabbed her hands. "We're begging you. We'd never ask this if we weren't hurting so bad."

Her mother sniffed as she nodded. "Please," she whispered. "I lost my cousin. I lost my daughter. I can't lose my grandbaby, too."

Hannah turned away from their shattered faces and broken spirits. All her life, she'd done as they'd asked. Followed their rules. Gotten straight As. Never broken curfew. Never been drunk. Never had sex.

They'd wanted so badly to keep her safe from harm, but instead, they'd created a sheltered, inexperienced woman afraid to step outside her tiny box and terrified to truly live. Even greater than the anguish over the loss of her sister was this newfound realization of how empty her own life was. How many experiences had she missed out on because she'd been too worried about staying in line to grab life and run with it?

And here she was again, kowtowing because she knew they needed something only she could provide.

Blowing out a breath and ignoring the inner voice that told her this was a horrible idea, she said, "Okay." At least she would get to see her niece, who she missed so much it hurt.

Her mother choked out a sob. "Thank you. Thank you, Hannah."

She held up a hand. "Wait. I have some conditions. I will go to Vermont and meet JP. I will keep my identity a secret and make sure Kayla is well cared for and loved. But that is all I will do. I will not try to entrap him or his family and I will not dig around for anything to use against them. All I am doing is checking on Kayla."

Her mother's face fell. "But…"

Her father shook his head, no doubt thinking they'd convince Hannah to do their bidding once she arrived. Or that she'd come to her senses once she met the Benson family and be all too willing to rip Kayla away from her new home.

It wouldn't happen.

"Okay," her mother said. "Our attorney says we need more, but if that's all you're willing to do for us…"

She somehow managed to avoid rolling her eyes at the obvious manipulation. "While I'm there, you two need to do some soul searching and some serious healing. You can't go on like this. It's not healthy, and it's not what Mary Anne would have wanted. I also suggest you think about reaching out to JP as Kayla's grandparents so you can be in her life."

"We will," her father said, casting another look her mother's way.

No surprise, her mom didn't agree to anything.

They wouldn't adhere to any of the terms Hannah laid down. She'd left information on several grief counselors for them as well as book recommendations. She'd also invited her mom to accompany her to her own therapy appointment. But her mother always declined.

An hour later, when she returned to her achingly empty apartment, Hannah flopped down on the couch. This plan had disaster written all over it. Mary Anne would never want this.

"I'm sorry, sis," she whispered. "I don't know what else to do."

Of course, no one answered. She'd never had any kind of otherworldly experience or response though she spoke to her sister often. She closed her eyes and brought up an image of Mary Anne rocking Kayla to sleep. It was one of her favorite memories of her sister. Though her body had weakened, and she could barely walk, she had the most serene and joyous expression whenever she held her baby. Hannah always wanted to remember her with that happy smile.

"Well, Mar, guess I better get packing."

The only good thing to come of this farce was the ability to see her niece, who she missed as much as she missed her sister.

Chapter Four

How long had he been staring at the letter? How many times had he reread it? Long enough that his eyes were gritty, and his head throbbed.

A part of him that began deep in the pit of his stomach and radiated outward wanted to fly into a rage. He was tempted to shred the paper, rip apart his room, and howl at the unfairness of it all.

She'd tricked him. The adorable one-night stand he'd thought of fondly maybe twice afterward deceived him in the vilest of ways. Poking a hole in the condom, for fuck's sake. That'd teach him to trust someone else to provide it.

Who did something like that?

Someone in crisis.

The tiny voice in the back of his head spoke reasonably, but the other ninety-nine-point-nine percent of him couldn't see past the betrayal enough to let that nagging voice prevail.

Mary Anne.

Yesterday, he wouldn't have been able to recall her name for a million dollars. If someone offered him the world in exchange for the name of the woman he'd slept with at the Beyonce concert, he'd have been walking away with empty pockets. Now, he had her name permanently etched on his life in blood. Her blood and his, in the form of a fucking child.

His entire body began to quake. JP wasn't one of those men

who claimed they didn't want kids but might change his mind someday if he met a woman to settle down with.

He was a man who didn't. Want. Children.

Full stop.

Shit ran through his blood. Addiction, viciousness, greed, hatred, and the worst parenting skills known to man. Why the hell would he put more of that into a world already full of assholes and bigots? No, he was happy to keep his DNA from trickling down to future generations.

Or he had been.

Fuck.

Now he was the asshole who didn't want his own kid and hated her dead mother.

Hours ago, mere hours, he'd been enjoying a beer and a burger with his family. Not a care in the world beyond what he'd wear on his date and whether she'd let him finger her in a dark corner of the bar.

Oh shit, he'd stood her up. For sure, he'd find a slew of pissed-off messages on his phone. Dammit, he had a reputation to uphold. He was known for leaving the ladies happy, smiling, and very satisfied. Standing them up wasn't his style and wouldn't do him any favors in the future. Still, his evening was playing out far worse than hers. He'd love it if the biggest problem of his night was some jerk standing him up.

His problem trumped all. He was a single father.

Christ.

Would he ever be able to go out for a night of booze and mindless fucking again, or would he be changing diapers and wiping spit up until the kid was six or however old they were when they started potty training?

He dropped his head in his hands, letting Mary Anne's letter flutter to the floor.

His chest grew heavy as the trembling increased.

A single fucking father.

It couldn't be real. It had to be a cruel joke.

For the next eighteen years, a human being would be dependent on him. She'd expect him to be there every day. To support her. Go to dance recitals, help with homework, wipe her tears, and patch up her cuts.

The tips of his fingers began to tingle as his chest tightened even more. He tried to take a deep breath, but it lodged in his throat, unable to reach his lungs.

He'd have to keep her fed, warm, and safe. All things his father had never done for him. Where did he begin?

A soft knock on the door made him jolt. He wanted to tell whoever it was to fuck off, but the only sound that came out of his mouth was a high-pitched wheeze.

He couldn't fucking breathe.

The door flew open, and Keith rushed in.

"C-ca—" Another raspy whistle left him. "Br-bre—" Was this a heart attack? Was he dying? About to leave his daughter an orphan before he'd worked up the courage to even hold her?

"Shh, shh, shh." Keith sat on the bed next to him. "Don't try to talk." He shoved JP's head between his knees. "Just focus on breathing in and out. Slowly. Let's do it together. Breathe in, two, three, four. Breath out, two, three, four."

Keith counted over and over as he rubbed his large hand up and down JP's back. At first, nothing happened. JP sucked wind and made no progress toward getting oxygen in his system. But as the seconds passed, the repetitive sound of Keith's calm voice and his soothing touch helped JP relax one fraction at a time. When the first hit of air made it to his lungs, he nearly wept in relief.

Then he remembered why he had a panic attack in the first place.

"Better?" Keith asked when JP's breathing normalized somewhat.

He let out a harsh laugh. Better? Fuck no, but at least he was breathing.

Keith hauled him up and crushed him against his chest in a

mammoth hug. "We've got you, brother. Do you hear me? We've. Got. You. You are not alone."

But wasn't he? Sure, his family would help, but the responsibility was all his. And he ran from responsibility about as much as he ran from the idea of having children. Hell, he didn't even have a real job. He just flitted from family business to family business when they needed extra help. Jagger's contracting company, Keith's auto shop. He even manned the bar for Ronnie when she needed a night off. It worked for him, earning him just enough cash to have fun when he wanted without the repulsive thought of a steady nine-to-five life.

He closed his eyes and allowed his brother's strength to prop him up as he'd done so many times throughout his life. Oldest of the six kids, Keith was more a father than a brother sometimes. He'd had to take on the role. Their actual father was a piece of shit, and their mother passed when JP was very young.

JP pulled back after allowing his brother to support him for a few moments.

"You good?" Keith asked.

Again, JP laughed a harsh barking sound. "No."

Somber dark eyes watched him as though he were a skittish animal ready to flee. All the Benson siblings had the same near-black eyes and hair. JP had always found it funny to be on the receiving end of scrutiny from a gaze almost identical to his own.

"How about a drink? Think there's a bottle of that expensive vodka you like stashed somewhere in the kitchen."

"It's under the sink. Behind the cleaning supplies. But no, thanks." If he started drinking now, he wouldn't stop until he passed out, and this day would become nothing but a fuzzy memory.

"All right." Keith didn't speak again, just sat there. A silent, steady support.

After a few moments, he asked, "Where is it?"

"It?" The frown of disapproval on Keith's face had JP feeling like a scolded child.

Fucking up already.

"The, uh, my—the baby." He cleared his throat. "Uh, Kayla. Where's Kayla?"

Keith met his gaze. "Your daughter is asleep upstairs." Though he'd always have all his siblings' backs in any way they needed, Keith wasn't one for shirking responsibilities. Hell, the man spent years managing their abusive drunk of a father on his own so the old man's poison wouldn't contaminate his younger siblings. Yeah, Keith was a rock, but he'd also make sure JP understood he had a child he couldn't hide from forever. "Miss Lila from next door lent Mickie something called a Pack-n-Play. It's like a portable crib thing. She said you can keep it until you get a real crib."

Jesus. A crib? He'd need to get a ton of stuff, wouldn't he? Where did he even begin? Would he have to move out? Get a place where the baby wouldn't bother his siblings if it—she—cried? Did she have clothes and bottles and whatever else babies needed?

Oh God, what did babies even need?

"Hey," Keith said, squeezing his shoulder. "One task at a time, okay? How about you come upstairs and meet your daughter."

No!

The word was on the tip of JP's tongue, but he managed to keep it from bursting out. The only thing that prevented him from refusing was the hatred of disappointing Keith even more. His stomach cramped, but he nodded.

All of a sudden, Keith's face transformed. The smile he typically saved for his girlfriend lit him up. "She's damn cute, brother. Pretty sure I'm gonna be her favorite uncle, but I might have to fight Mickie for overall favorite. Also, prepare yourself, that little cutie of yours has done something weird to both Mickie and Ronnie." A look of confusion swept across Keith's face that JP would have found comical in any other situation. "They're talking about their ovaries exploding or some weird shit like that." He shrugged.

Keith had recently moved in with Mickie, who lived across the street.

JP nodded. "What happened to the social worker?"

Keith chuckled. "What do you think happened? Scarlett made an appearance. Swear to Christ, man, when Mickie is in Hollywood mode, she could talk a rock into doing her bidding. Scary how that woman can get whatever she wants. Bethany, the social worker, will be back tomorrow afternoon with the paperwork. "I'll give you a sec and meet you upstairs. We've set her up in my old room for now."

"Right behind you," he croaked.

When Keith disappeared, JP blew out a breath and then stood. Every movement felt like slogging through thick mud. His arms hung heavy as though weights dangled off his wrists, and a buzzing in his ears made it difficult to tell if all his siblings were talking upstairs.

He trudged up the steps with a brick in his stomach and a terrifying sense of impending doom. If he'd believed in demons, he'd have sworn one wrapped its wispy arms around his waist and tried its hardest to pull him back toward the basement.

He ran out of steps way too fast, finding himself on the main level of the house in under a minute. A harsh bark of laughter left him.

Everything looked the same. For some ridiculous reason, he'd expected something to appear different. For the house to reflect the way his entire life had changed. But it didn't. Someone had cleaned from the barbecue, but aside from the sparkling kitchen, everything was as it had been hours ago.

On feet that felt like lead blocks, he made his way toward Keith's old room. Whispers met his ears. He paused outside the door.

Keith and Mickie stood side by side, staring down into what appeared to be a small crib. The play pack or whatever Keith had called it.

"I love that she looks like a Benson," Mickie whispered.

JP's stomach turned. Hopefully, all she got from the Benson side were dark physical features. Dark eyes, dark hair. Unfortunately, many Bensons also came with dark souls and personalities. He'd fought it his entire life with an over-the-top carefree attitude, jokes, and a quick smile. Even still, he could feel it under his skin. A sludge of filth and hatred searching for a way out.

"She does, doesn't she?" Keith said, voice laced with amusement. "I'll have to dig up a baby picture of Ronnie because I'm pretty sure they could be twins."

JP cleared his throat, making his brother and Mickie whip around and face him. "Hey," he croaked.

The smile that had made Mickie a famous movie star bloomed across her face. "Hi, honey. Come on in." She reached for his hand, and he allowed her to pull him into the room. "I just can't stop staring at this beautiful daughter of yours."

His stomach lurched, and the acrid burn of bile tortured his esophagus. He couldn't do it. He'd mess this child up for sure.

"Come see her."

He stepped up to the little crib. Mickie wrapped her arms around one of his. Thankfully, Keith stood back and kept silent.

JP stared down at the sleeping infant.

Lying on her back with her hands up by her head as though in a stick-up, she slept in some sort of fleecy sack. They were right, she had the same near-black hair as the rest of the Benson crew. The same as him. He'd have to wait to check out the eyes. But her nose was all Benson as well. She had pink, pudgy little fingers. Actually, most of her was chubby in that way people seemed to go nuts over in babies. That was a good thing, right? A chunky baby meant healthy, didn't it? He thought he'd heard that somewhere.

She looked so peaceful, with her little chest rising and falling in a gentle pattern. So peaceful, yet the fear she brought with her had his knees knocking and his fingers trembling.

"Gorgeous, isn't she?"

Blinking, he nodded with robotic obedience. His throat was too dry to answer.

Mickie remained quiet, letting him absorb the moment. Who knew how long they stood there?

He was supposed to feel something, wasn't he? Didn't new fathers experience this intense surge of love and bonding? Wasn't he supposed to notice the similarities in their appearances and become instantly smitten?

Because he didn't. All he felt was…detached. Like he was hovering above the room, watching someone else's life, because he couldn't possibly be responsible for the living, breathing baby in that crib.

That had to be the Benson in him. The genetic predisposition to be a horrendous parent.

She moved, rolling her head from one direction to the other. A grunt came from her tiny lips. Her little legs flexed then kicked straight out.

"I think she's waking up," Mickie said, sounding as though she couldn't have imagined anything better in the world. "She's probably hungry. We gave her a bottle before she fell asleep, but Bethany said she typically wakes for a bottle once in the night."

Waking? No. The clock on Keith's old nightstand read two a.m. She couldn't be waking up to eat. At two in the morning, he was typically napping next to whoever's bed he'd stumbled into that night. Guess that part of his life was over. He'd still be spending the predawn hours with a female, but everything else had changed.

The damn elephant sitting on his chest began to jump up and down.

"Do you want to hold her and give her a bottle?" Mickie asked. For an Oscar-winning actress, she did a shit job of disguising the hope in her voice.

Did he want to hold her?

Kayla. His daughter.

The tiny baby whose fragile life now rested in his incompetent hands.

Her eyes popped open and locked with his.

His breath seized, and the fucking world stopped turning. He was experiencing intense feelings now. But none of them were good, and none of them were paternal.

He backed up, shaking his head. Every cell in his body rejected the idea of touching the baby. He couldn't. There were too many ways he could hurt her. Too many ways he could fuck up her life right from the start. "No. I—I can't," he spat out. Then he fled, ignoring Mickie's gasp and his brother shouting after him.

He was an unfit parent.

Just like a Benson.

Chapter Five

"Three days," Hannah heard the almost-whispered voice say from behind her. "It's been three days, Mickie, and he hasn't even touched the baby."

She froze. Were they talking about JP? He hadn't held Kayla yet? What the heck? How was that possible? Had her parents been right about him? Had she made a huge mistake allowing the social worker to take Kayla to her father? Should she have pressed her parents' attorney to do more, like they'd wanted?

"It's like he's pretending she's not even there. I'm starting to worry."

Her insides twisted. Maybe her parents had been wise in sending her. If JP was neglecting Kayla, she wouldn't hesitate to intervene. Heck, she'd raise Kayla herself before she let someone unfit have custody of her innocent niece.

Hannah was pretty sure that voice belonged to Ronnie. Michaela's had a familiar ring from all the movies she'd watched starring Scarlett.

A heavy sigh followed. "I know." That was Michaela. "I'm just not sure what to do about it."

A waitress had sat the two striking women in the booth directly behind Hannah.

As she eavesdropped, she clenched her menu so tightly her fingers creased the laminated pages.

The bout of nerves was ridiculous. The women didn't have a

clue in the world who she was. In fact, neither paid her a lick of attention as the waitress guided them past her booth. Still, she'd held her breath and stared at the menu as though trying to burn a hole in it with her gaze.

From all the creepy social media stalking she'd done both with Mary Anne and after her death, Hannah recognized Veronica Benson and Michaela Hudson, a former actress who'd turned her messy life around and moved to small-town Vermont. While Hannah's parents had been horrified to learn Hollywood's favorite former actress and tabloid sensation, Scarlett, was a part of the Benson crew, Hannah had been elated. If what she'd read in the media was accurate, Scarlett crashed and burned after a decade of drugs, men, and destructive behavior. Supposedly, she'd checked herself into rehab and walked out a new, sober, happier woman. After moving to a small Vermont town, she'd met Keith Benson, and the two had the type of storybook romance Hollywood lived for. Only now, the former actress rarely made headlines and lived as though she wasn't a mega rich actress.

Hannah found it admirable. Breaking bad habits and starting over in a new place wasn't easy. It was downright terrifying. Hannah would know. For years, she'd tried to build up the courage to move from Boston, where she and Mary Anne had grown up, but had never been able to walk away from the hold her family had over her. Then after Mary Anne got sick, the whole family moved from Massachusetts to Colorado, where a world-renowned ALS expert held his practice. Now, that's where Hannah lived as she couldn't possibly think of leaving her parents in the wake of Mary Anne's death.

"Are you ready to order, miss?" the waitress asked with an expectant smile. Had she been someone prone to giving into her impulses, Hannah would have shushed the woman so she could continue spying.

As it was, she hadn't read a word on the menu despite staring at it for five minutes.

"Um, I'll just have the pancakes." Seemed a safe enough bet. All diners had pancakes.

"How do you want your eggs cooked?" the waitress asked.

"No eggs, please. Just the pancakes."

"Okay." She cracked her gum as she wrote on her pad. "Sausage or bacon?"

"What?" Behind her, Michaela and Ronnie continued to talk. She was missing it. "Uh, neither. Just pancakes."

And leave so I can hear them.

"Okay, then. How about a biscuit or toast? English muffin?"

"No!" she snapped, then winced when the waitress raised an eyebrow. "Sorry. Just the pancakes, please."

"Got it." The waitress shot her an annoyed glare then stalked off to the kitchen.

Ugh, she'd be lucky if the woman didn't spit in her food. Hopefully, a big tip would make up for barking at the undeserving waitress.

Tuning back into the conversation behind her, Hannah tried to pick up on what they were talking about. Her shoulders slumped as she caught Michaela mentioning facts, figures, and budgetary items. They'd moved on from discussing JP and Kayla.

Crap.

The desire to see and cuddle her niece was so strong. Hannah's arms ached to hold her. She missed the adorable baby giggles she drew out of Kayla with silly noises and raspberries on her tummy. She mourned the loss of that soft weight against her as she rocked Kayla to bed. Going from caring for the baby daily to not spending any time with her over the past week had been agony.

"Here's the thing," Ronnie said. "We have no idea what we're doing. We're like two frat boys trying to take a class in astrophysics. Clueless."

Hannah's lips quirked as Mickie burst out laughing.

"Not sure how I feel about being compared to a frat boy,"

Mickie said through her laughter.

"I'm serious. I don't know how to create a reasonable budget, I don't know a damn thing about taxes and business finances, and all that shit. Do you?"

Mickie snorted. "Hell no. I pay someone a handsome sum to manage my money because I don't have the first clue. We should probably learn, though, don't you think?"

"Yeah, eventually. But I also think we need a professional to assist us. A CPA or something. Right?"

At the mention of a CPA, Hannah's ears tingled.

Mickie sighed. "I know, you're right. I don't want to use my guy out in LA, though. Actually, I'm looking to find someone new myself. He's the final tie to my acting career, and I'm ready to cut that last tether."

"Well, we might have to go into the city because the only CPA I know in town is old man Doolan, and I'm pretty sure he's eighty and might have retired last year," Ronnie said, with a hum of annoyance.

This was it. Her in with the Bensons. Could it really be this easy? Hannah's heart rate shot up like a racehorse bursting out of the gate. She closed her eyes and counted to ten as she breathed. The idea of meeting these women under false pretenses had her coffee curdling in her stomach, but if it got her close to Kayla, especially after hearing about JP's neglect, she'd do it. She'd do anything to ensure Kayla's safety.

"Well, that sucks," Mickie said. "I was hoping to keep this as much of project comprised of small local businesses as possible. I hate the idea of using some big-city financial firm."

"Me too, but maybe we can find a smaller firm in the city or a CPA who works solo and contracts out. Is that a thing?"

Hannah swallowed her natural introverted inclination and turned around as best she could. Not for the first time, she wished she had Mary Anne's outgoing personality. She draped her arm across the top of the booth as she came face to face with the back of Ronnie's head. "Um—" She cleared her throat.

"Excuse me?"

The ladies stopped talking. Ronnie looked over her shoulder with a raised eyebrow while Mickie leaned to the side to see around her friend.

"Yeah?" Ronnie asked. "You need our sugar or something?"

"Oh, uh, no, but thank you." She took a deep breath and smiled. "I promise I wasn't trying to eavesdrop"—*liar*— "but I couldn't help overhearing your conversation."

Ronnie's curious eyebrow raise turned into a suspicious narrowing. Made sense. Strangers probably approached Mickie all the time, and Ronnie wanted to protect her friend. Both women were beautiful, though highly opposite in their looks. Ronnie had thick, near-black hair that hung down her back. She dressed in casual clothing and wore little to no makeup. Mickie's hair was a softer brown and cut in a trendy bob style that made her look chic and expensive but fun. Her entire outfit screamed money but not in an in-your-face way. And her makeup was as perfect as her hair.

"Okay…" Ronnie said.

"I'm a CPA. I'm not locally based, but maybe I can help steer you in the right direction?"

Ronnie pursed her lips. "Where are you from?"

"Originally, Boston, but I've been living in Colorado for a little over a year, in a small town like this. I work for myself, mostly helping small businesses and personal clients. I needed a change of scenery after—" Crap. She'd almost said *after my sister died*. "After some family stuff. So I rented a house and escaped here for a few weeks. I'm happy to answer any questions you might have or even take a peek at your books." She cringed. "Sorry, I know this is super presumptuous of me. I just…well, I heard you guys, and I'm a huge nerd for this kind of thing, so I figured I'd extend the offer. But you can tell me to bug off. No hard feelings. Not that you'd care because we don't know each other."

Shut up, Hannah.

"Okay, I'm closing my mouth now."

Mickie laughed, and even Ronnie's lips twitched. The two shared a look then Mickie scooted farther into their booth. "Come on over," she said as she waved Hannah forward. "Bring your coffee."

Holy crap, had it been that simple?

A twist of guilt knotted her stomach as she slid onto the bench seat beside Mickie. She'd never deceived anyone in this manner before, and it didn't sit right. They wouldn't have invited her to join them if they'd known her parents had sent her to spy on Ronnie's brother.

You're here for Kayla. To make sure she's happy, healthy, and being treated well.

And selfishly to get close to her niece because she missed that baby so much. "So, what can I help you with?"

Their waitress arrived just as Ronnie opened the stark white binder on the table in front of her. After scowling at Hannah for the seat change, their server deposited a piping hot plate of pancakes that smelled mouthwatering.

"Be back with the rest of your meals in a minute," she said before heading back to the kitchen.

"Dig in," Ronnie said. "Don't wait for us. Those are better when they're hot as hell."

"Thanks." Hannah went about slathering the pancakes with the homemade honey butter and dousing them in the fresh Vermont maple syrup the restaurant boasted came straight from the forest out back. When she took the first bite, her eyes rolled back in her head. "Oh, man, that's good."

"Right?" Ronnie asked with a smile. "I got 'em too. Okay, let's get down to business, ladies." She flipped a few pages in her binder then spun it so Hannah could see it.

The paper before her had a simple map of what appeared to be a campground.

"We just purchased this property," Mickie explained, pointing to the binder. "It's an old campground partway up the mountain. The owners couldn't maintain it anymore. Actually, no one has used it in quite a few years."

"You want to run a campground?" Hannah asked, wrinkling her nose. The thought of the glamourous actress owning a rustic campground didn't fit.

Laughing, Mickie shook her head. "No. Can you imagine? That's not exactly my style."

"We want to renovate it and create luxury rentals," Ronnie said.

Now that she believed.

"And we mean *luxury*," Mickie added. "We're looking to attract a high-end clientele to bring some big dollars to the town. Those looking for a ritzy and glamorous winter getaway."

Huh, not a bad idea. Actually, it sounded like a lot of fun. She bet the property would be stunning by the time Mickie got through with it.

"One of my brothers owns a contracting company and will be doing all the demo and renos. We'd love to have all the work done by either local or small businesses along with purchasing all our décor, supplies, and furniture from small or locally run shops."

"I love this idea," Hannah said, and she meant it. Small towns and small businesses struggled in this day of online one-click mega shopping.

"Awesome!" Mickie's face lit up.

"Problem is, neither of us knows anything about the financial side of running a business, and we'd rather not involve my brothers there because they have a tendency to take over."

"Well," Hannah set down her fork. "As I said, I'm here for a few weeks, so I'm happy to help with anything you need."

"Eeep." Ronnie bounced in her seat with a big grin on her face, so opposite the skeptical look she'd given Hannah at first. "This is perfect. So, uh, what's your name?"

"Oh." They all laughed. "Sorry, I'm Hannah."

"Ronnie," Veronica said. "And that's Mickie." She used her fork to point at the once-celebrated actress.

"Nice to meet you both."

"You too." Mickie winked. "And thanks for playing it so cool and not asking me for a selfie or an autograph."

Hannah blushed. "I'm not really a selfie kinda girl. But, uh, how did you know I recognized you?"

With a snort, Ronnie said, "Everyone recognizes her. Now." They shared a look and snickered at whatever inside joke just passed between them.

For the next hour, they laughed, drank way too much coffee, and didn't get any work done. Hannah fell instantly in love with both these women. They were much more outgoing and extroverted than she was, but she found herself drawn out of her shell in their presence. How long had it been since she'd spent time laughing and enjoying the company of other women? Long before Mary Anne died. Probably not since she'd lived in Boston.

She had such a blast with them, she'd almost forgotten the real reason for approaching them.

Almost.

"Shit," Ronnie said as she looked at her phone. "We gotta get moving, Mickie. We're signing the closing paperwork in a half hour. And we got jack shit done here."

Mickie chugged the rest of her coffee, then nodded. "I'm ready. Hannah, would you be interested in coming by my house tonight to work with us? Like, actually work this time. We'll feed you dinner and ice cream."

"That's a terrible idea. You know you'll never be able to keep the rest of the family away, and once she meets the guys, she'll run screaming." Ronnie's eyes danced with mirth.

"You make a good point. Maybe we should meet somewhere else."

"No!" Hannah said, then cleared her throat. "Your house is fine. Takes a lot to scare me."

That was a huge lie. One of many she'd already told. She had no experience with loud, boisterous families and wouldn't have a clue how to handle it. They were right, she'd be inclined to run but would force herself to blend in if it got her to Kayla.

"All right. It's settled. Let's say six o'clock. That work for you, Ronnie?"

"Yep."

"Hand me your phone, Hannah."

She did as requested. What a surreal moment. One of the most famous actresses in the world was currently entering her phone number and address into Hannah's phone.

She shoved aside the wonder of it as they finalized plans. Who Mickie was didn't matter. What mattered was that she was getting closer to seeing her niece and finding out if JP was caring for her in the way she deserved.

If she was lucky, Hannah would meet him that night. If she was luckier, she'd see Kayla. Maybe even hold her. She closed her eyes, imagining her niece in her arms again. Of course, she'd have to maintain the charade of being the helpful traveler and random new friend of Mickie and Ronnie.

She'd have to lie her butt off all night.

But she could do it. If it meant even two minutes of cuddling Kayla, she'd do anything.

Even ignore the souring of her stomach at the thought of all those lies.

Chapter Six

The unmistakable howl of an unhappy child pulled JP from a fitful sleep. Shut eye had been an elusive goal for the past few days, only happening after hours of tossing, turning, and rioting emotions.

She sure did have some strong lungs. Even from his room in the basement, she sounded loud as hell. "What the hell?" he mumbled as he buried his head under a pillow. Sure, he'd heard Kayla crying over the past few days, but never so loud and never so close. Thankfully, the noise should quiet soon. One of his siblings would tend to her soon. They never let her cry for more than a few seconds.

Guilt hit him full force.

Kayla was his responsibility. It was his job to soothe her cries, feed her, change her, bathe her, and everything else his family had been doing. He was shirking those responsibilities in a huge way, forcing everyone in his life to pick up his slack. But he just…couldn't. Hell, he hadn't so much as held her since she'd arrived. Every time he walked into a room where she happened to be, he turned and fled back out as if she were a fifteen-pound bomb instead of his daughter.

My daughter.

God, he was some kind of asshole ignoring her like he'd been. But there was something off inside him. A mental block he couldn't push past. Thoughts of holding her, being responsible for her wellbeing, and having her depend on him sent him into the early stages of a panic attack, so he avoided her as he avoided most stressors in his life, by pretending they didn't exist.

He blamed his father. As one of the youngest of the six Benson kids, he'd had only a few short years with their mother before she died. His father sure never made up for the lack of physical affection and care. That had to be the reason for his emotional failings.

The crying didn't stop. It only grew louder and more desperate. "Fuck," he muttered. Guess that was the end of his night's sleep. As he sat up on the edge of his bed, he caught sight of the video baby monitor sitting on his nightstand.

The horrendous sound of Kayla screaming blasted throughout his room. No wonder she sounded so damn close.

Next to the monitor sat a pad of paper with a note on it.

Called to an emergency at a job site.

Time to man up, Daddy.

-Jagger

"Fuck!" he shouted, crushing the paper in his balled fist. He dragged his other hand through his hair. Jagger wouldn't have left the note if anyone else was home. The asshole had left him alone in the house with his daughter. And he was terrified.

JP laughed aloud even as he felt like he was splintering into a thousand pieces. If anyone on the outside heard what went on in his brain, they'd have him committed. Scared out of his wits to be left alone in the house with his own infant daughter.

The crying didn't let up.

He was going to have to do something about it. Jagger could be hours, and Ronnie had plans with Mickie for most of the day. Keith would be busy at the garage.

That left him.

He stood on legs that felt like they belonged to someone else. After sleeping all night, he had to piss but, fuck, that kid could scream. Emptying his bladder would have to wait. With each step, he took up the stairs and closer to what was now Kayla's room, the tighter his chest grew. His fingers tingled and his head spun. By the time he got to her crib, he was going to be in full-blown panic mode at this rate.

I can't do this.

Yet, he was the only one home, and someone had to see to the baby's needs, so he forced himself to breathe and keep walking.

He winced as he reached the doorway to her room. Damn, he should have grabbed some earplugs. Her cries were so loud and grating, they actually made him forget some of his nerves in his rush to make the noise end. By the time he reached the crib, he'd describe the noise as having hit the someone-is-being-murdered level.

One peek in the crib revealed his daughter lying on her back with her tiny fists balled, her face red and screwed up as she screamed the house down. No murder, no torture, nothing seemed immediately out of sorts. Just a pissed-off infant, letting the world know she wasn't getting whatever it was she wanted.

"Okay, drama queen, that's enough of the theatrics," he mumbled as he peered down at her. At the sound of his voice, her eyes flew open, and the crying stopped.

For all of five seconds, the universe blessed him with silence and the curious stare of his daughter.

Then she went back to demanding something. Loudly. Who the hell knew what this kid wanted? "Uh, that's enough crying."

Didn't work.

"Hey, kid, you're fine."

Shocker, none of that seemed to work. What did she want? A bottle? Diaper change? Was she hot? Cold? What was he supposed to do? Guess?

Damnit, at the very least, he was going to have to pick her up. His hands shook as he reached into the crib. Before he could touch her, he snatched his hands back.

Would anyone believe that as a thirty-year-old man, he'd never held a baby before?

What if he dropped her?

What if he grabbed her too hard and bruised all that soft baby skin?

What if he couldn't calm her?

What if she hated him?

What if he hated her?

What if she grew up to use drugs and prostitute herself because he sucked as a father?

JP swallowed a lump the size of a golf ball. He didn't do anxiety. Didn't do worry and what-ifs and self-doubt. He had fucking fun and played hard. Life was short and not worth it if he couldn't have fun.

But, shit, Jagger had been right. He needed to man the fuck up and take care of this baby because, like it or not, he had a daughter.

"Okay," he said out loud. "I'm just gonna reach in the crib and pick you up. And you're gonna stop crying and find a different way to tell me if I'm fucking it up."

Shit. Was it wrong to say fucking around a six-month-old baby, or were they too young to notice?

As though moving through molasses, he reached into the brand-new crib someone had purchased and assembled and gripped the baby under her arms.

He lifted her to eye level with straight arms as though holding a stinky trash bag. Thankfully, Kayla stopped crying and stared at him with wide eyes the same color as his. Her dark hair stuck out all over. On an adult it'd look ridiculous, but when combined with her chubby baby cheeks, it was kind of cute.

"Uh, hi," he whispered. "I think I'm your dad. I should probably apologize in advance for all the ways I'm going to fuck this up." He winced. "Like swearing in front of you all the time. Lucky for you, my siblings are much better role models. Well, some of them. Not so sure about Ian."

As he spoke, he brought the baby closer to his body. Seemed like he'd be less likely to drop her if she was flush against him.

After a few seconds, he had her snuggled against him as she rested on his chest with his arm banded under her bum. She still stared at him with watery eyes but hadn't cried since he picked her up.

Could she sense it? Some kind of blood connection they shared?

"If you tell anyone I said this, I'll deny it, but you're kinda adorable when you're not imitating a banshee." He wiped her damp cheeks with the back of his hand. "That's better, huh?" He found himself doing some weird bouncing for some strange reason, as though bopping to nonexistent music.

Kayla seemed to like it, though, so he kept it up no matter how unfamiliar it felt.

She grabbed his fingers with a slight squeal then brought them to her mouth.

"Ouch!" he yelped. "Shit, you got a sharp little tooth in there, you baby vampire."

Thankfully she moved his finger to a gummier part of her mouth before chomping down this time. It was…odd, to say the least. The moment he tried to pull his finger from her mouth, she whimpered, and her little lips turned down in the most pitiful pout he'd ever seen.

"Okay, okay. Here, it's your finger now. If it keeps you from crying, you can have it." He let her munch. "Guess this means you're hungry, huh? How the hell am I supposed to know what to do about that?"

He knew the stuff she drank from a bottle wasn't milk but baby formula, and that was the extent of his baby feeding knowledge.

"Let's see if we can figure something out in the kitchen."

With his daughter still on his hip, happily gnawing his finger, he walked into the kitchen. She was more solid than he'd expected. He thought she'd be floppy and super fragile, but she had some heft to her.

One of his siblings, Jagger it seemed from the shitty

handwriting, had stuck a Post-it on the handle of the refrigerator.

Formula maker on counter.

Wrinkling his forehead, he looked at the baby. "What the hell is a formula maker? You got any idea what he's talking about, Miss Kayla?"

She made a humming noise and continued chewing.

"Guess not. Okay, let's see." He scanned the counter. "What the…" On the far end of the counter was an appliance that looked exactly like a pod coffee maker. Another sticky note hung from it.

All set up. Just turn on and push start.

JP did as instructed, and the machine whirred to life. Seconds later, formula was streaming from the spout into the bottle beneath. "Well, shit. This thing is bougie as fuck, my girl. How much you wanna bet your Auntie Mickie is responsible for this fancy contraption?"

Kayla's ditched his hand and focused her attention on the bottle. She squealed as she kicked her legs and waved her arms.

JP laughed. "Seriously? You're that excited to drink this shit? Must be delicious." He screwed the cap on the bottle as best he could with one hand. "Let me have a taste?"

She squealed again.

Chuckling, he gave the bottle a little suck. As soon as the formula hit his tongue, he screwed up his face. "Ugh. I think we're gonna have to work on your palate, babe. That shit's nasty."

Kayla grabbed for the bottle, and he let her have it.

"Look at that, you're pretty good at holding that thing, aren't you?"

She shoved it in her mouth and went to work, greedily sucking away.

"Let's go sit outside." He'd spent the majority of the past few days hiding out in his room. Fresh air and Vitamin D were a necessity at this point.

He opened the sliding door and stepped out into the early

morning sun. Once settled in a chair, he glanced down at Kayla. She'd naturally slipped into position, cradled on his lap with her cheek resting against his arm as she guzzled her meal. Two dark eyes watched him with an intensity he hadn't expected.

He couldn't tear his gaze away from her. Everything she did was alien to him but fascinating. The way her tiny fingers held the bottle and her cheeks worked as she drank. The soft grunts she let out every so often. The way her chubby legs kicked continuously.

Her weight against him felt…nice. Weird as fuck, but nice. Cuddly.

All around them, birds chirped, flowers bloomed, and the air swirled with summer warmth. Same as it always did. But inside him, something changed. Maybe everything changed.

He'd never be able to look back and say he fell instantly smitten with her. Never be able to share one of those tales of immediate love and bonding, but at that moment, he felt something shift inside him.

Warmth spread through his chest. This little baby, his baby, knew nothing about him. She didn't know the man he was. Had no idea he ran from responsibility, hated serious shit, and fucked his way through life. She had no idea she wasn't planned or conceived out of love. All she knew was that she was warm, fed, and comfortable. That was enough for her to trust him.

It was a heady feeling. A huge responsibility to keep that trust.

Could it be enough for him to trust himself?

He had to try.

"I'm going to mess up," he whispered. "A lot. I have no idea what I'm doing, and I'm pretty sure I'm too selfish to be a father. But I'm going to try. And I'm sorry for ghosting you the past few days. I'll do better. I'll do more. For you. For us."

Most men had months to wrap their minds around having a child and prepare for its arrival. He'd had nothing. Hopefully, taking a few days to process the monumental life change didn't make him the worst father in the world.

They stayed out back until Kayla drained the bottle. He chatted to her about their family and what she had in store for her as part of the Benson crew. When she finished drinking, she dropped the bottle on the ground, making him laugh out loud.

"It's gonna be like that, huh?"

Her milky mouth curled up in a gummy smile.

"Damn, girl, you are some kinda cute. That could be a problem when you get to be a teenager. Trust me, men fucking suck." Good Lord, one day he would be raising a teenaged girl on his own. And he thought he was scared now? "Think maybe you could be interested in girls? Not sure I can promise not to murder some horny teenaged boy sniffing around you."

A loud gasp had him looking over his shoulder.

Mickie and Ronnie stood in the open sliding glass door. Mickie her hands pressed to her chest while Ronnie stood with her jaw on the floor. Both had tears in their eyes.

"Jesus, ladies. It's like you've never seen a man hold his fucking daughter before."

Snickering, Ronnie walked outside and straight to him. She still appeared seconds from crying, but now a smile replaced the shock. She stroked a hand over Kayla's soft head. "I can see we're going to have a problem with your language in front of her."

If his laugh was a little hysterical, Mickie and Ronnie let it slide. After all, he'd made great strides in his fatherhood journey today. He'd held his child. Fed her, too.

"Pretty sure we're gonna have a lot more problems than just my language," he said, looking down at his daughter. He still didn't have a clue how to raise a child or even what to do with her next, but he was ready to try. That was miles above what his own father did, and he'd survived. "But neglecting her won't be one of them."

Now he just had to dig deep and find a way to embrace this monumental responsibility, so he didn't break that promise.

Chapter Seven

From the outside, Mickie's home was lovely. Nothing like what Hannah would have expected from a mega-millionaire actress whose over-the-top LA mansion had been splashed across dozens of style magazines. She'd owned a house with massive square footage, a minimalistic contemporary style, and zero warmth. Hannah recalled wondering where the star sat when she wanted to curl up with a fuzzy blanket and spend an evening bingeing her favorite TV shows. All her furniture had been stiff, tiny, and white.

This Vermont house was large, but not by Hollywood standards. Vibrant flowerbeds adorned the front yard, along with a sprawling lawn of lush green grass. The wraparound porch had a swing with plush cushions and a wooly throw.

Mickie kept the exterior perfectly maintained. Everything from the landscaping to the siding gave off an expensive impression, but not in a showy way. It was clear to Hannah that Mickie was a woman who enjoyed luxury but in an understated, comfortable manner. This home fit with the woman she'd met at the diner, whereas the Hollywood mansion seemed to be part of a persona Mickie had played to maintain her celebrity image.

"Miss, I'll take a few boxes of the Thin Mints," a deep voice spoke from the porch.

Hannah jumped. Heat rushed to her face. What a creeper she must look like loitering around, gawking at the place. "What?"

Holy crap, the guy was gorgeous. She recognized Keith from JP's social media, but the photos hadn't done the man justice. Sex oozed from that half smile and those tattooed muscles peeking out beneath the sleeves of his shirt. He had a dark, closely cropped beard and the hair to match.

"Nothing. Just being an ass." He waved her over. "You must be Hannah. Come on in. The girls, sorry, ladies—they both give me dirty looks when I call them girls—they're inside having a drink."

"Thanks." She climbed the few steps up to the porch. "And yes, I'm Hannah."

He held out a large, callused hand. "Keith. Mickie's worse half."

Chuckling, Hannah shook his hand. The man could probably crush every bone in her hand with one squeeze if he wanted, yet he gripped with a gentle hold. "Nice to meet you."

"Follow me. I'll show you where the troublemakers have congregated. Can I get you a glass of wine? I think Ronnie is drinking a Sauvignon Blanc or some shit. Mickie is just having soda if you prefer something non-alcoholic."

For sure, she needed a little liquid courage to ease her nerves. Not enough to cloud her judgment or make working a challenge, but something to calm the jitters. A large part of her wanted to skip all these pleasantries, and demand Keith inform her where JP and her niece were. Being so close to Kayla and not seeing her could be considered torture. But she was there to play nice, make friends, and then get the details on Kayla. "I'd love a glass of wine, thank you so much." Never in a million years would she tell him she didn't even know if the kind he'd mentioned—she'd never been much of a drinker and had already forgotten the name—was red or white.

"Hey, Hannah! You made it. Come sit." Mickie smiled from her spot on a beautiful cream-colored sofa. The wide cushions looked soft and inviting. Another change from how the public viewed this woman. Like the outside, her interior décor was beautiful, cozy, and expensive.

"Hey, guys," Hannah said as she walked into the large living area. She glanced down at her feet then back at the door. Should she have taken her shoes off? The light area rug looked like it cost more than her rent.

"Make yourself at home," Keith said with a wink. "We're not formal, promise. Be right back with your drink."

As he turned and made his way into a stunning kitchen, Hannah risked it and joined Mickie and Ronnie, still wearing her shoes. They had binders, two laptops, and an iPad spread out on a coffee table in front of them, along with various pens, highlighters, and colorful labels.

"Hi, Hannah," Ronnie said. Like Mickie, she wore jean shorts and a T-shirt, but hers had a band logo, whereas Mickie's was a simple pale blue. She'd gathered her long hair up a high ponytail. As earlier, Mickie's short bob didn't have a strand out of place, her makeup was flawless yet understated, and everything about her screamed money. But in a surprisingly approachable way.

Chic was the perfect word to describe the woman.

"Hope you don't mind if we dive right in. We wanted to get as much done as we could before dinner. Two more of my brothers will be joining us, and once JP gets here with my adorable niece, it'll be hard to focus on work."

The women shared a smile.

Hannah's breath caught. JP would be there with Kayla. Not much longer now, and she'd see her niece. Maybe even hold her. How the hell could she be expected to focus on accounting tasks when Kayla would come through that door at any time? Her stomach fluttered as she worked to keep the thrill off her face. "That sounds great. Let me know if I can help with dinner in any way, too."

Mickie waved away her offer. "We're good. I've got Keith on kitchen duty tonight."

Hannah blinked. The man was that gorgeous and could cook,

too? Mickie had won the lottery. "Oh, gosh, I hope you didn't make him go to any trouble on my account."

"No trouble at all, seriously. I was going to—"

Ronnie snorted.

"Excuse me?" Mickie shot her friend a narrow-eyed look. "You got something to say, Veronica Benson?"

"Uh, yeah, just that you can't cook to save your life, so don't try to pretend you were going to do it."

"I wasn't going to, you ho," Mickie responded with sass. "I was about to say that I was going to order out, but Keith offered to grill some salmon." She shot Hannah a worried glance. "Hope you like fish."

"Love it." She grinned what she hoped wasn't a sad smile. The way Mickie and Ronnie were with each other, half making faces, half laughing at each other, reminded her so much of her relationship with Mary Anne. Not only had they been sisters, they'd been best friends, despite their vast personality differences.

"I apologize for Ronnie and her childish behavior. She can't help it. She's a Benson, and a high level of immaturity runs through their blood."

"I heard that!" Keith called from the kitchen as Ronnie mimicked Mickie with mocking hand gestures and facial expressions. All three of them burst into laughter.

"Sounds like you're really working hard," Keith shouted. "Do you think you'll get this place opened by the next century?"

"Hey," Mickie yelled back, "Keep your trap shut. Your job is to cook and keep me satisfied in bed." She winked at Hannah, whose face burned while Ronnie made mock vomiting sounds.

Would she be able to talk so freely if she had a gorgeous man who worshiped her?

"Okay, let's get to work." Mickie straightened and grabbed a binder.

Since moving to Colorado, caring for Mary Anne and Kayla had consumed all Hannah's non-working hours. She hadn't had time to get out and make new friends. Growing up in Boston, her friends had been more like she was. Rule followers who didn't rock the boat and always colored inside the lines. Mary Anne had been the rebel of the bunch, and even she only stepped a few feet outside their steel-reinforced mold.

Well, until her diagnosis.

God, she missed her sister and friend. Hannah swallowed her grief. This wasn't the time or place to break down about how unfair life could be.

"Okay," she said with a slightly forced smile. "I'll be the task master. Let's focus so we can relax later."

They dove into work, casting jokes and playfulness aside. Both women had a lot to learn about the financial aspect of running a business, particularly when it came to tax law, but they were quick studies, and more importantly, eager to soak up whatever knowledge Hannah could impart.

Within two hours, she'd gotten them up and running with her favorite bookkeeping software, reviewed their profit and loss projections, as well as assisted in designing a budget plan to match the scale and scope of the project. Money wasn't an issue for Mickie, but the two were adamant their goal was to create a profitable business. The resort wasn't merely a passion project for either of them, so they had no plans to go hog wild on the spending.

With each passing minute, Hannah enjoyed the company of Mickie and Ronnie more and more. Both worked hard but knew how to have fun and didn't take themselves too seriously. They meshed well and spoke of their budding business with contagious enthusiasm.

If Hannah had three thousand dollars per night to spend at their resort, she'd stay in a heartbeat. Everything they spoke about sounded luxurious and fabulous, from the plans for food to the high-end linens on the fancy beds.

Before she knew it, the front door swung open, and another tall, bearded man strode into the house as though he lived there.

Jagger. He wore black slacks and a charcoal gray button-up with the sleeves rolled to his elbows, revealing a tattoo on each forearm. These Benson siblings sure did like their ink. Even Ronnie had a few visible tattoos.

"Sup, fam?" Jagger asked as he dropped his worn messenger bag on the floor next to the door. A cloud of dust wafted from the bag. The casual way they treated Mickie's expensive home had Hannah snickering.

"Hey, Jag," Mickie said without looking up from the note she'd been jotting. "Please tell me you aren't bringing a whole construction site's worth of dirt into my house as usual."

He gave a sheepish grin then shrugged. "Okay, I won't. Sorry, I didn't bother to go home first. Keith in the kitchen?"

"Yup." Ronnie tossed her pen down and stretched her arms over her head. "Jag, this is Hannah. Hannah, this is another brother, Jagger. Hannah is helping us with some financial planning for the resort."

"Nice." A smile transformed his face from handsome to stunning.

Geez, these men were potent. She had a few male friends, but not ones built like these Bensons. Not ones that made her eyes bug, her tongue dry up, or her heart skip a beat.

"Good to meet you.," Jagger said with an easy smile. "Hope Frick and Frack here aren't driving you nuts. They tend to get a little silly."

Ronnie flipped him off.

Hannah swallowed nothing since her mouth had gone bone dry. "No," she croaked before clearing her throat. "They've been great."

"Yeah, asshole, we got a shit-ton accomplished," Ronnie added, after sticking her tongue out at her brother. "Seriously, Jag, you should be thanking her. We were getting so desperate, we thought about asking you for help."

His eyes widened. "Shit. Thank you, Hannah. You're my new favorite person."

She couldn't help but laugh as Mickie and Ronnie scowled at him. "Well, this is right up my alley, so I'm happy to help." They made her feel so comfortable, it felt as though she'd known them for months instead of hours. Usually, she needed longer to warm up to new people, but the Bensons and Mickie had a natural friendliness and acceptance that made it easy to be herself around.

Well, not herself, since she was there under false pretenses. Her conscience tried to burst through the fun of the evening, but she fought to keep it out. Later tonight, she could let the guilt in until it made her sick, but now she had to stick with the plan, so no one grew suspicious of her motives.

God, she was a terrible person.

"Hey, Jag." Keith strolled into the living room with a beer in each hand. After passing one off to his brother, he wandered over to the couch. "You gir—ladies about done?"

"Yeah," Mickie said. She lifted her chin to accept a kiss from Keith. "I think we're at a good stopping point. If I look at too many more numbers, my eyes will cross."

"Agreed." Ronnie hopped to her feet with her wine glass in hand. "I'm gonna grab a refill. Hannah, you want one?"

Usually one glass of wine was her limit as she didn't have much drinking experience, but she was having fun and wanted to fit in. Plus, she'd finished her drink a while ago, and the one glass hadn't stemmed her nerves. Every few seconds, she found her attention drifting toward the front door. Where the heck was her niece? What if JP didn't come? Was he alone with Kayla? Hadn't Mickie and Ronnie made a point of how he hadn't even held his daughter? The thoughts wouldn't stop, threatening to overtake the ease she'd found that evening.

"Yeah, sure. I'll have another. Why not?"

"All right," Jag said as he plopped down next to her. "I like the sound of that." He stretched his arm along the back of the couch behind her head.

She stiffened. Across the coffee table, Mickie's eyebrow rose, and a half-smile quirked her lips. "He's single," she mouthed, or at least that's what Hannah assumed.

She widened her eyes and gave a subtle shake of her head. A peek at Jagger let her know his focus was on a conversation with his brother and, thankfully, not Mickie. "Stop," she mouthed back.

The complications that would cause were mind-boggling. Plus, what the heck would she do with a man like Jagger? Hannah had been on a fair number of dates, but she'd only had one long-term boyfriend, and it'd been a few years ago. He'd been very dedicated to his church and planned to save himself for marriage. While Hannah wasn't overly pious, her parents' rigid control and sheltering of her meant she had limited experience when it came to the opposite sex. Particularly the physical side of relationships.

A man like Jagger probably found a twenty-six-year-old virgin laughable. And it was in some ways, but it was also her reality.

Mary Anne lost her virginity at eighteen. At the time, she'd teased Hannah to no end about being a year younger and more experienced. Hannah had no illusions about leaving sex for marriage, but she rarely went against her parent's wishes. Even if they'd never find out. Whether it was a lifetime of preaching from her parents about abstinence, STDs, unplanned pregnancy, rapists, and murders, or her internal hesitancy, she'd never gone much beyond heavy petting and giving a man a hand job.

After Mary Anne became sick, Hannah had often wished for a boyfriend. Someone to share her fears and struggles with. Someone to wrap his arms around her and let her cry out her grief over the unfairness of the situation. A few times, she'd even contemplated a hookup app just to get rid of her pesky virginity and feel something besides worry and duty for a night. But instead of indulging in those naughty fantasies, she'd gone in the opposite direction, doubling down on responsible behavior. Mary Anne's reckless actions and her unexpected illness brought so much heartache and despair to their parents, Hannah felt the unspoken obligation to ease their minds in whatever ways she could. If that meant giving into their ridiculous demands even more than usual, then that's what she'd done. Hence flying to Vermont and deceiving an entire family of really decent, kind, welcoming people.

"Hannah?"

She blinked. Ronnie stood before her, holding out a fresh glass of wine. Shoot, when had she come back in the room?

"You okay? You kinda zoned out there."

Shaking her head. Hannah accepted the glass. "Sorry, I got lost in my thoughts. Thanks for this." She brought the glass to her lips. The wine was cool and tart with an underlying sweetness. Refreshing.

"No worries. Just wanted to introduce you to another brother —there are too many—and my adorable baby niece."

Hannah followed Ronnie's gaze toward the front door. Oh, my God, JP stood there with Kayla in his arms. She sucked in a breath then began a violent coughing fit as the wine slipped down her windpipe.

Jagger pounded her on the back. "Whoa. Easy there, hon."

She lifted a hand to ward him off. The man was going to send her flying across the room.

"Jesus, Jag, don't beat her to death." Ronnie pulled the wine glass from Hannah's lurching hand before the liquid sloshed all over Mickie's lovely couch.

Finally, she was able to take a breath. "Sorry," she croaked as she lifted her gaze.

After anticipating his arrival so vigilantly, how on earth had she missed it?

She stared at Kayla as though frozen in blazing headlights. Had the baby grown in the time Hannah hadn't seen her? It was hard to be sure since she looked so tiny in the tall man's arms. Her heart squeezed. God, she'd missed those chubby cheeks.

"I know I'm shockingly handsome, but I didn't mean to kill you," JP said, his voice laced with humor. The comment yanked her gaze from Kayla's to his face.

It was like being punched in the stomach, or at least what she assumed it would feel like. Air rushed from her lungs in a whoosh as her insides clenched.

The man was…stunning. Tall, lean but muscular, and heavily tattooed. Standing there with her niece in his arms, he was the most attractive man she'd ever met.

And that was a huge problem.

Chapter Eight

This was the woman Ronnie and Mickie had hounded him about all day? The one they wanted him to meet? The one saving their asses from the overwhelming world of business financing and accounting? The woman Mickie described as *his type*? He nearly snorted. His type was tits and a pussy. No one could accuse him of being picky.

Fine, he'd admit those big blue eyes, golden hair, and her sinfully sexy, plump-lipped mouth held a particular draw. He'd even go so far as to admit he'd always had more fun with blondes, but why the hell did they think he'd go for this one? From the moment he arrived, she'd been gaping at him and Kayla like she'd never seen a tiny human before. Well, after she got over that choking episode.

Hello, awkward.

Did he have something on his face? Fuck, for all he knew, he'd gotten a smear of baby shit across his forehead after changing Kayla's last diaper. That nuclear bomb had been horrifying.

Horrifying.

The child probably needed a digestive specialist. That amount and stench of the toxic sludge that came out of her couldn't be normal. Wasn't there something in the baby rule book about going easy on a first-time father?

Apparently not.

Thankfully he'd been alone for the first few diaper changes.

No one would ever have to know he'd watched no less than four YouTube tutorials and still had to change his clothes a few times. It was a secret that would stay between him and Kayla forever.

"Hannah, this is John Paul, but call him JP. Unless you want to annoy him, which is always fun," Ronnie said, oblivious to the way her new friend gawked at him.

Such a comedian, his sister.

"JP, this is our new best friend, Hannah." Ronnie walked to him and tickled Kayla's round tummy. "And this little cutie," she said in that high-pitched voice women loved to use on babies, "is Miss Kayla, the sweetest baby girl in the world. Oh, yes, she is."

Hannah smiled, but it didn't reach those baby blues. "Nice to meet you." Though she spoke to him, her attention had shifted back to Kayla. What was her deal? Fuck, she better not be the type to judge a man with lots of tattoos as an unfit father by the way he looked. He had enough internal doubt and didn't need some Karen judging him.

Maybe she was one of those baby fever women who dreamed of nothing more than popping out a hundred kids. Or, perhaps she viewed him as a fish flopping out of water. One who had no idea what the hell he was doing and hadn't spent more than a few hours holding his seven-month-old daughter. If so, she'd be wise to buy a lottery ticket.

His vote went for the baby-fever chick. There was too much mushy softness in the way she watched Kayla. Hell, if he wasn't careful, this one might try to scoop him up, marry him, and shackle him to her for the rest of their miserable days.

He shuddered. Fuck that. No way he was risking ending up like either of his parents. Mom, miserable and abused, or Dad, miserable and abuser.

Could you be more dramatic?

"Uh, yeah. Same. Nice to meet you." It was as much enthusiasm as he could muster. Just enough to keep Ronnie from hounding him later about being rude to their guest.

"Shit, brother," Jagger said with a grin from across the room. "You're holding the baby. That's progress. Before you know it, you'll be wearing a *Dad of the Year* apron as you mash puréed sweet potatoes."

JP shot Jagger the finger as Ronnie thwacked their older brother on the shoulder.

He cast a glance at Hannah's way to find a fierce frown on her face as her attention ping-ponged between him and Jag. Last thing they needed was some stranger thinking he wasn't taking care of his kid. That's how fucking CPS got involved. He'd know. They'd been called because of their father's bullshit a dozen times throughout this childhood. Though he probably didn't need to worry. If the system hadn't removed JP and his siblings from their drunken mess of an abusive father, he wasn't at any risk of losing Kayla.

Not yet, anyway.

"So, uh, we eatin' or what?" Normally, he was the life of the party. The one his family turned to when they needed the mood lightened, wanted a laugh or were craving fun. In the days since Kayla dropped into his life, he'd felt off his game. His carefree personality had suffered, and he didn't like it. Mustering the energy to make dirty jokes or keep up the happy-go-lucky façade felt like a Herculean task he couldn't accomplish without a nap.

Was this parenting? Was he doomed to settle into a new, boring as fuck existence for the next eighteen years? One in which he thought of nothing but what Kayla ate, how much she pooped, and how many hours she slept? No more clubs. No more bars. Maybe an occasional fuck here or there when he could swindle one of his siblings into babysitting.

His stomach cramped. In the blink of an eye, his life had become everything he'd always dreaded and more. Suddenly, Kayla felt like a hundred-pound weight in his arms instead of a fifteen-pound baby. Before he lost his shit, he needed a break. "Someone take her," he blurted, holding Kayla out with straight arms.

Hannah rushed forward with a look of concern. "I ca—"

"Don't mind if I do," Ronnie said, snatching her from his arms without seeming to notice his distress. She gathered Kayla close and babbled nonsense.

"Uh, let's have some grub," Keith said as he rose, shooting JP a glare. "Everything is ready. I'll grab the salmon off the grill. Figured we'll eat inside since it's supposed to rain in a bit."

"Great, let's do it," he said, earning a curious look from Ronnie at the false cheer in his voice. He opened and closed his hands, trying to get the blood flowing back into his tingling digits.

From her perch on Ronnie's hip, Kayla squealed and flapped her arms. As everyone oohed and aahed over the baby noises— he had to admit they were kind of endearing—JP couldn't help but notice Hannah's gaze still fixed on his daughter. Funny thing was, Kayla seemed fascinated with the newcomer, making wild screeches and smiling a big gummy grin in Hannah's direction.

As they all made their way to Mickie and Keith's enormous dining table. Hannah had no choice but to shift her focus from Kayla, but the second they made it to the dining room, she was back to staring.

What the hell was this chick's deal?

"JP, I bought a highchair so Kayla can sit at the table with us," Mickie said, beaming as though she'd just told him she'd found the cure for cancer.

He shouldn't criticize because he sure as hell hadn't thought of any such thing. Fuck, he probably had a shit-ton of baby crap to buy. How would he afford everything? Crap he'd never even heard of would consume his life now.

His dad-life.

Still didn't seem real.

"Awesome," Ronnie said. She deposited Kayla back in his arms without warning. Reflex had him pulling her close, but he tensed and couldn't relax into a comfortable hold.

"Better watch yourself, Keith. The way Mick keeps going on about that baby, she's gonna be begging you for one before too long," Jagger said as he winked at Mickie.

That got everyone laughing. Well, everyone except him. Their typical Benson sibling banter kicked into full gear. They all teased and ribbed as though nothing had changed. As though he wasn't holding a fifteen-pound explosive that had detonated all over his footloose and fancy-free life. None of them noticed his absence from the conversation. Though his brain knew it was only a matter of time before someone clued in and asked him what the fuck was wrong, he couldn't bring himself to participate in his usual fun-loving manner. For him, everything had changed due to the child in his arms. Hell, he didn't even feel like the same person he'd been before her. But everyone else acted the same.

It was the ultimate mindfuck.

Aside from him, only Hannah stayed quiet, seeming somewhat dazed by his siblings' loud and brass nature. She really was pretty, even with a wide-eyed gaze that reminded him of a kid experiencing a circus for the first time.

With a sigh, JP walked Kayla over to what he assumed was the so-called highchair, a plastic monstrosity with a large white tray and smiling ducks all over a padded seat. As he stared down at it, the panic he'd been battling the past few days began to creep up his spine once again. For a million bucks, he wouldn't have thought to purchase this ridiculous contraption.

How the hell was he supposed to get Kayla in this torture device?

He grabbed the tray to pull it out so he could fit the baby in the seat, but the thing didn't budge. "What the hell?" he muttered as he gave the tray another tug. On the third pass, he added a jiggle.

Maybe just was supposed to shove her in the small space between the tray and the seat? He frowned as Kayla grabbed a handful of his hair and yanked.

"Ow, fuck!"

Christ, what the hell was he doing?

He wasn't cut out to be a father. It felt as though all eyes in the room were fixed on him, waiting for him to fail at one of his very first fatherly tasks.

A throat cleared softly beside him. "Need a hand?" Hannah stood next to him with a sweet smile.

"Oh, uh, yeah. You know how to work this thing?" he asked as he gently pried surprisingly strong baby fingers from his scalp.

Hannah nodded. "I do. I can get her settled for you."

"That'd be great. Thanks." Anything to keep him from looking like even more of an idiot.

With a high-pitched squeal, Kayla wrenched her body and practically launched herself toward Hannah.

"Shit!" he cried as he lost his grip on the squirming sack of potatoes.

"Yikes, cutie," Hannah said with a laugh, catching Kayla as though she'd anticipated the daredevil move. "You're a little young for cliff diving. How about you try not to give your d-daddy a heart attack tonight, huh?" She spun away from him, bouncing Kayla on her hip as she cooed at the baby. She appeared so comfortable, as though she handled babies every day, while JP felt like a wooden statue whenever he picked her up. Afraid to hold her too tight and crush her but terrified of not having a solid grip and dropping her.

"Okay, let's get you settled in here, pretty girl. You must be hungry." Within seconds, she had the tray pulled out, Kayla strapped in the seat, then the tray back in front of his daughter. "There you go," she said, bopping Kayla on her teeny nose. "Bon appetit."

JP blinked. "Wow, I'm gonna need a tutorial on that before you leave. Maybe a PowerPoint with videos and shit."

A soft chuckle left Hannah. "I'll see if I can schedule you in, but I'm pretty booked up with other clueless dads, so you may have to wait."

The moment the words left her mouth, a horrified expression crossed her face. "Oh, my God. I'm sorry. I can't believe I said that. I didn't mean to imply you're clue—"

For the first time in days, he laughed. "Trust me, sweetheart, you may not have meant it, but you hit the nail on the head. You're a natural, though. You got kids?" He took the seat next to Kayla's highchair then gestured for Hannah to settle into the chair on Kayla's opposite side.

A pretty blush formed over her cheeks.

Okay, his sisters were right. She was his type. Sue him, he loved shy girls. That little nugget of information surprised most people since his personality was extroverted and over the top. Often irreverent. But he loved a girl who blushed. One who seemed all reserved and timid but turned into a wildcat once the lights went out. There was something about taking a sweet girl and making her all dirty that cranked his gears.

"Ah, no. No husband, no kids." She set a napkin over her lap as though in an upscale restaurant instead of a friend's house. "I, uh, have a niece though. She and her mom lived with me when she was a newborn, so I gained a lot of baby experience. There's a pretty steep learning curve."

He grunted. "You ain't kidding." He grabbed a bottle of wine from the center of the table, then froze as he caught sight of all his siblings quiet and gawking at him. "The fuck? I can have some. I'm not breastfeeding."

Mickie blinked and pressed her lips together as Ronnie let out her patented inelegant snort. That girl would need to find herself a special kind of man who could handle her brash energy. His three brothers just stared at him.

"What? I got something in my teeth?"

"Nah," Keith said, shaking his head. "Just weird as fuck to see you sitting there next to a baby. And you're not even hyperventilating. It's like an alternate universe. Or maybe I'm dreaming."

Mickie pinched his forearm.

"Ow! Fuck!" Keith scowled at his girlfriend as he rubbed his arm.

"Nope," she said in a cheerful tone. "Not dreaming."

Hannah's soft chuckle had JP glancing her way to find her curious gaze on him. He cleared his throat. "I, uh, only recently, very recently got custody of her. Actually, I didn't even know she existed until a few days ago. Her mom never told me."

"Wow," Hannah whispered. "That's…that's…" She shook her head as though unable to put the shock of it into words.

"A total mindfuck? Yeah, you're telling me."

She swallowed, and her face took on a wary look. "You must have a lot of…complicated feelings about her mother."

He raised an eyebrow at her, and her cheeks turned pink.

"Gosh, sorry. That is so none of my business. Forget I said anything." She rubbed her forehead. "I don't know what's going on with me. I'm not usually this blunt. Or nosy." A slight wince and shrug only made her cuter.

People were going to be curious. He'd have to get used to it. And most, especially those who knew him and his family history, wouldn't be as sweet as Hannah with their inquiries. "Nah, it's okay. Complicated is a good way to put it." So complicated, he had yet to sort those emotions out even though he'd thought of nothing but Kayla and her mother for days.

Kayla chose that moment to smack her tiny palms on the tray of her highchair as she let out a window-shattering shriek.

"Shit!" JP jumped and looked at her. What the hell did that wretched sound mean?

Was she hurt?

Did she need her diaper changed again?

Was she ill?

How the hell did anyone figure out what a baby wanted?

Hannah laughed. "I think someone is hungry. Aren't you, sweetie?"

This time, Kayla smiled a big ole one-toothed grin as she

whacked the tray again. "Mind if I give her some mashed potatoes? She should be able to handle them fine. I mean, uh, as long as she doesn't have any allergies."

He shook his head. "No allergies." At least not according to the medical documents that had arrived with Kayla. He watched in awe as Hannah plopped a small blob of mashed potatoes directly on Kayla's tray. Guess plates weren't something a baby cared about. Kayla attacked the food as though starving, shoving her little fingers through it and then lifting them straight to her mouth.

From across the table, Jagger laughed. "What are you fucking starving the kid, JP?" He laughed again. "Shit! Look at her go. That is one hungry lady."

"Now we know where those thighs come from," Ronnie said as she snickered.

Seriously. Since he'd taken over caring for her earlier in the day, he'd only given her the bottles as Jagger had instructed. How the hell was he supposed to know she could eat real food too?

Goddamn, he had a long way to go.

"She's a fucking mess," Keith said, laughing. "Have fun cleaning that up."

As though responding directly to him, Kayla squealed then rubbed a filthy hand all through her hair, making the entire table laugh.

After wiping Kayla's hands with her napkin, Hannah frowned at the group. "You know," she said, sounding like a teacher lecturing their class. "You all are gonna need to start watching your language soon. Won't be long before she's repeating every word out of your mouths."

All around the table, Benson jaws dropped. His family wasn't exactly known for their delicate tongues or modesty. Nor were they used to near-strangers putting them in their place. Not this group of rough-and-tumble brutes. Ronnie included.

His respect for Hannah grew.

Ronnie, in particular, seemed stricken by that news. She'd always been brazen and ballsy, having to keep up with five rough-and-tumble older brothers. She huffed out a sigh. "Well, fuck me."

He couldn't have said it better himself.

Chapter Nine

Hannah woke much the same way she'd fallen asleep the night before—with thoughts of Kayla on her mind. If she was honest, Kayla wasn't the only one she'd been thinking of. JP had taken up much of her brain's square footage as well.

Okay, fine, she'd been ruminating over JP even more than her niece, which was saying something because she'd been over the moon to see Kayla. And hold her, which she'd gotten to do after dinner. In fact, that little girl never touched the floor. Her aunts and uncles couldn't get enough of her and spent the evening bickering over who got dibs on her next.

Who could blame them? Kayla was the sweetest, most wonderful baby in the world.

She wasn't biased at all.

JP had defied all her expectations. After overhearing Ronnie and Mickie's concerns about him, she'd prepared herself for the worst. A deadbeat dad who didn't give a crap about his child. She'd expected a dirty, cranky kid and pissed-off man who'd rather be anywhere but with his child. What she'd found was an overwhelmed father who had no experience or idea what he was doing. But what first-time parent did? Mary Anne certainly hadn't known what she was doing in the beginning. Neither had Hannah, and she'd been the one doing more of the work than Mary Anne at times. It'd been exhausting for all of them. Long, sleepless nights, worry, and plenty of messing up. Where she'd expected to be critical of JP, she found herself empathizing and rooting for him.

JP acted attentive, though clueless, and willing to learn. He also had terrific support in that crazy family of his. Though she'd been concerned when she'd learned he hadn't even held the baby for a few days, she had to cut him some degree of slack. Who knew how they'd react in a situation like his until faced with it?

As much as it pained her to admit, she had to remember Mary Anne was the one who'd done wrong. So many things wrong. And that was a detail her parents struggled to accept. So much that they'd rather send their other daughter to spy on the man trying his best. Believing JP to be a no-good manipulator who'd seduced and impregnated their innocent daughter was more palatable than the truth. Finding dirt on JP would only strengthen their conviction that their infallible daughter had been hoodwinked by a no-good Casanova.

But the truth was their daughter did a horrible, deceptive, straight-up immoral thing. And her actions had a high cost, forever altering the lives of many people. As much as she loved and missed her sister, Hannah couldn't shed the small amount of resentment she felt at the way all their lives had been upended without consent.

What a mess.

Her phone rang just as she decided to pull the covers over her head and try for another hour of sleep. With a resigned sigh, she sat up. The fluffy comforter pooled at her waist. Lying on the empty side of the queen bed, her phone rang and rang with the word Mom flashing at the top.

"Here goes nothing," she whispered as she lifted the phone to her ear. "Hey, Mom."

"Hello, darling," her mother responded. "I've got you on speaker. You're dad's here with me."

Great. For whatever reason, her dad's grief and agony gutted her more than her mother's.

"Hey, Dad."

"Catch us up, please," her mom ordered, speaking over her father when he tried to give his greeting. "We're so eager to hear what you are learning. I imagine it's unpleasant having to interact with any of those Bensons."

Sitting in the middle of the bed, Hannah rolled her eyes. *No how are you,* or *we miss you.* Just straight to the point.

"Well, I got to meet JP last night. Looks just like he did in the photos online." No point in commenting on how the man was the furthest thing from unpleasant when it came to his appearance.

Her mother gasped. She could imagine her dad rubbing his hand up and down her mom's delicate spine. There'd been a time when Hannah thought her mother's stringent parenting a sign of strength. Once she'd hit adulthood, she realized it was the opposite. All the suffocating rules and over-the-top limits to her social life hadn't come from a woman trying to instill unshakable values in her children. It'd been one hundred percent driven by fear.

Fear of the unknown.

Fear of things she did know.

Fear of failure.

Fear of pain.

Fear of loss.

Now, that wasn't fair. Her mother learned the horror of loss at an impressionable age. She'd also struggled to get pregnant for years, suffering numerous losses and heartbreak. But maybe if she'd agreed to therapy to work through her grief, they all could have lived a happier, more typical life.

"Tell us everything," her dad said in the gruff voice that had comforted her so many nights as a child. Now edges of sadness and heartache had taken over and made it difficult to speak to him.

"Yes," her mother agreed. "Everything. I can't imagine how hard it was for you to keep from ripping Kayla from his hands and running back to Colorado."

Great. This should go over well.

For crying out loud, she hadn't even had a sip of coffee yet.

After massaging her forehead, she took the plunge. "I know this isn't what you want to hear, but the Benson family is…"

Soften the blow or rip off the Band-Aid?

"They're wonderful."

Band-Aid it is.

Neither of her parents said anything. If she didn't know them better, she'd have assumed the call dropped.

"Um, we had dinner at Michaela Hudson's last night. Mom, she isn't anything like you read or see on television. She's warm and kind and loves Kayla. The entire family does. They're just smitten with her."

"And the father?" her mother asked, ice dripping from the question.

A half-smile tilted Hannah's lips as she recalled the flustered way he'd tried to figure out the highchair. "He's in over his head," she said with a chuckle.

Her mom sucked in a breath. "I knew it. We have to get Kayla awa—"

"Like any first-time parent, Mom. He's tired and overwhelmed and has no idea what he's doing. But he's trying." She left out the part about him not holding the baby for days after she'd arrived. They didn't need to know. While she didn't fully understand his initial reaction either, the man she'd seen last night was dedicated to his daughter. "He's a good man, Mom. They're a good family. And they love her."

A strangled sob came through the phone.

Hannah closed her eyes. Her shoulders drooped as grief squeezed her heart.

Damn, you, Mary Anne.

All this pain and sadness. All this confusion and hardship. All these heartbreaking moments came from a conscious decision Mary Anne had made. How many times over the past few months had Hannah shouted to the heavens and asked her sister what the hell she'd been thinking?

Too many to count.

But then, her sister's choices, however convoluted and wrong, led to Kayla. And there wasn't a person on earth who would condemn the choices that led to the precious child's existence.

What a mess. What an absolute disaster.

"Look," she said over the sound of her mother's sobs and her father's murmurs of comfort. "I think we need to cut JP and his family a little slack. Give them some time to settle in and get their feet under them. Then I think you should approach them as Kayla's grandparents. Mom, from what I've seen of this family, they will welcome you with open arms."

"I can't. Hannah, I just can't. She belongs with us. Not with those people. How can you not understand this? Michaela Hudson lived a life of debauchery and drugs. She's a substance abuser. The others are crass and vulgar. The father looks like a hoodlum. And his father is in jail, for goodness' sake! Is that the kind of environment you want your only niece to grow up in?"

"Mom, once you meet them—"

"No!" her mother said with heat. "You need to think about that child, Hannah. Really think about her and the type of people you want influencing her development and caring for her. Do you want her to end up on drugs? Or in a gang? Or… selling herself?" She whispered the last part.

Hannah sighed. "Of course not." Her mother needed therapy. Probably medication, too. Her anxieties and fear of something happening to those she loved had always been over the top, but since she got sick, it'd become pathological. She could barely function outside her home because she was constantly worried about everything from a gust of wind to a shooting ten states away.

"Look, Mom, I'm going to stick around here a little bit longer."

"Yes! Yes, that's good. You'll find something, Hannah. I know it. The only way we can make sure she grows up safe and the right way is if she's with us. Just document anything suspicious that you find. Check the house for drugs and unsecured weapons. Michaela Hudson's, too. I'll just bet she has some illegal substances stashed somewhere. Our attorney said those are great details to have."

Hannah's heart hung like a heavy mass in her chest, pressing down on the rest of her organs. She shook her head, letting it fall forward. "Mom, I'm not staying for that reason. I'm staying so I can see my niece. So I can get to know the family. At some point, I'll have to tell them who I—"

"No! Please, Hannah. Please don't. I can't…" Her mother sucked in a wheezy breath then coughed.

"Patricia, it's okay. Sit down. Breathe slowly. There you go. I'll get your inhaler." Her father's calming tone and endless patience floated through the phone. "Hannah, that's enough for today. We'll talk another time." The line went silent.

"That went well," she mumbled into the quiet room.

With a weighted sigh, she flopped back against the soft bed. Then pressed a pillow over her face and let out a scream that would have rattled the windows.

As if she didn't have enough guilt over deceiving the Bensons swirling in her gut, now she could pile on the remorse of sending her mother into yet another panic attack. If only there was a time when she could catch her father without her mother around. Maybe then he could be convinced to seek professional help for Patricia. The demons living inside her head grew stronger all the time, and if something wasn't done about it soon, her mother would cease to be functional.

Her mom's mental health was another reason she'd avoided pursuing a long-term relationship. How could she subject a man to a woman who'd question every move he made? Who'd constantly fear he had ill intentions toward her daughter? Who'd invade his private life looking for dirt?

After another muffled scream, she let her arms drop to her sides. The pillow remained on her face. Releasing a little pent-up tension felt great, but didn't do squat toward erasing her problems.

She couldn't tell JP who she was. Not yet. Not until she was certain her parents' attorney wouldn't be able to have Kayla taken from him. Once the Benson's found out who she was, they were sure to kick her straight out of their lives. She wouldn't be able to protect Kayla or them from her mother's delusional goal of getting custody of her granddaughter.

Despite it all, she wanted to protect her own family as well. Her mother wasn't a bad woman, but she needed help. Professional help she refused to seek. If they sued for custody of Kayla, they'd be ruined. Hannah and her family would never stand a chance against the resources someone like Mickie had at her disposal. Her family had spent tons of money helping Mary Anne in the end, and now poured the rest of their savings into this attorney. Frequent anxiety attacks kept her mother from working, and her father retired a few years ago. Hannah had a small amount saved and invested but hadn't been working in a professional capacity for long enough to have developed a significant nest egg.

Money was tight.

Mickie had millions at her disposal and would no doubt use every dollar to ensure Kayla stayed with JP. She could make it so Hannah's family never laid eyes on the sweet girl ever again.

And who could blame her?

A dying woman tricked JP into getting her pregnant, and now the woman's sister misled him again.

One more strike, and Hannah's family would be out.

So, no, she couldn't tell them who she was. Not now. But she could stick around town for a while and make as many memories with her niece as possible. The fact JP intrigued and attracted her had nothing to do with her desire to stay.

Nothing.

Her phone chimed. Then chimed again.

Without removing the pillow from her face, Hannah felt

around for the offending device.

"Please don't be from Mom," she whispered as her hand made contact. After what felt like the hundredth sigh of the morning, she sat up.

A few texts from Ronnie awaited her.

"Oh, thank God."

Found a necklace on M's couch. Not mine or Mickie's. Yours? At my house now. Stop by whenever.

She lifted a hand to her neck where her favorite necklace typically rested. It wasn't there. A picture followed the text. Yep, that was her necklace.

Looked like she'd be swinging by Ronnie's. Her lips curled at the notion of having another chance to catch a glimpse of Kayla. Too bad a giant storm cloud hovered above her head, just waiting to unleash a bolt of lightning and fry her for her lies.

Maybe later, she'd find the strength and courage to work on a way out of the mess she'd created. But for now, she'd concentrate on memorizing every detail about her darling niece.

Be there in 30.

Chapter Ten

The universe fucking hated him.

Why else would someone ring the doorbell the second JP got the yogurt-covered, slippery-as-hell baby into the bathtub when he was the only one home?

He hopped to his feet then started for the bathroom door. After one step, he glanced back at the tub where Kayla sat in a few inches of water, happily splashing away.

"Shit, I can't leave you in here, can I?" he grumbled to her smiling face. Over the last twenty-four hours, he'd learned she could sit on her own but every so often lost her balance. Combine the instability with the wet tub, and she'd most likely topple over and drown if he left.

Score one point for a sliver of parental instinct kicking in.

Finally.

Maybe she would make it to her first birthday without some catastrophic injury.

The doorbell rang again, this time followed by a knock. How the hell did people manage all this shit at once?

"Dammit."

His child was going to be the one who dropped the f-bomb in preschool, for sure. He snatched her towel off the counter then lifted her out of the tub. Water sloshed all over the floor. Kayla gave a squawk of protest, but as soon as he started running for the front door, her anger turned to giggles.

Damn, that sound really was too cute for words.

"Coming!" he shouted as water soaked into his shirt and jeans. He hadn't even begun to wash Kayla when the visitor arrived. Gooey vanilla yogurt covered her hands and face.

Not that she cared.

Another knock.

"Keep your pants on," he muttered as he yanked the door open. His eyes nearly popped out of his head at the sight of the gorgeous woman on his doorstep. "Or don't."

"What?" Hannah blinked up at him with the most adorable furrow in her brow. "Did you say something?"

Holy crap, the universe sure as fuck hated him. She looked too yummy for words standing there in a snug coral tank top, short denim cutoffs, and flip-flops. Pink tipped toes peeked up him. And those smooth, bare shoulders just begging for his mouth?

JP bit off a groan. "Sorry, no. I didn't say anything." Though she wasn't tall, her legs were shapely and looked as silky as the rest of her skin. The kind of skin he'd love to run his tongue all over from ankle to thigh.

But of course, there'd be no licking as he was soaking wet and holding a filthy baby. A baby who chose that moment to let out a happy but ear-piercing shriek.

"Hello, sweet girl," Hannah said, shifting her attention to his daughter. She laughed. "You seem like you enjoyed your snack, huh?"

And just like that, he no longer existed. All Hannah's attention went to the baby, flapping her arms and legs as though she could fly out of his arms.

His daughter, cockblock extraordinaire.

"Yeah, don't get too close, she's gooey as hell. I was just getting the firehose to blast her clean."

Hannah held out a finger to the sloppy Kayla, who immediately brought it to her mouth.

"Oh, shit, sorry. Kayla, no biting." Christ, it sounded like he was scolding a nippy puppy.

With a laugh, Hannah waved him off. "She's fine. Babies chew. No biggie. We need to get you some teething toys, don't we?" As though she realized how strange it was for her to say we, Hannah took a step back. "Looks like you shared your snack with your daddy, too."

"Yeah, she's generous like that." He ran a hand through his hair, wincing when he felt a crunchy clump. Yogurt, no doubt.

Sexy.

Not that he was trying to hit on the little hottie on his doorstep. He didn't have time for women these days. Maybe not for the next eighteen years.

Oh, God…

He might as well face it. His days of hitting the bars and making his dick happy were behind him. Maybe he should have a funeral for the poor thing. Give it the proper send-off if it wasn't ever going to experience the hot clasp of a wet pussy ever again.

He might cry.

"You okay?" Hannah asked.

He tore his eyes away from her glossy lips and forced his brain to keep from wondering what they'd look like wrapped around his—

Really, tears were coming.

With a shake of his head, he said. "I'm good." Then he cleared his throat. "So, uh, were you looking for Ronnie? She ran out about fifteen minutes ago. Kayla and I are the only ones here right now."

"Oh." She frowned. "She texted, saying I left a necklace at Mickie's last night and that she had it here. Said I could stop by anytime."

With a snort, he gestured for her to come in. "That's Ronnie for you. Responsible as the day is long."

Not that he could talk. Responsibility gave him fucking hives.

Kayla squealed and squirmed in his arms.

Unfortunately for him, responsibility was his new middle

name. Looked like he'd be mainlining Benadryl until the end of his days.

"You wouldn't happen to know where she left it, would you?"

"She didn't mention anything to me, but come on in." He stepped aside to give her room. "You're welcome to poke around the kitchen while I get this little rug rat cleaned up. Ronnie probably set it on the counter somewhere."

"Thanks. And thank you, Miss Kayla, for being the cutest baby ever." She stepped into the house and followed his hand, pointing toward the kitchen.

JP snorted. After shutting the door, he turned and caught sight of Hannah's retreating form as she disappeared into the kitchen. Her shorts weren't overly tight, but they molded to her ass just enough to tease him with a hint of how plump and bitable it was.

He groaned.

Kayla cooed and stared up at him with wide, curious eyes. Dark eyes, the same color as every one of his siblings. Benson eyes. Poor kiddo. "You know," he said in a hushed tone as he made his way back to the bathroom, "If it wasn't for you, I'd be working on getting that delicious treat on legs into my bed right now."

She made another one of those charming sounds. He frowned down at her as a horrifying thought popped into his head.

One day she was gonna be old enough to date. To meet men. Men like him who wanted nothing more than a hookup and a few hours of fun.

Hell. No.

"Listen to me, baby cakes." He set her back down in the warm bathtub. Instantly she went back to smacking the water with her little palms. "If a man ever calls you a delicious treat, run, don't walk. Run away. Got it?"

All he got in return was a splatter of water across his face.

"Snarky already, huh? Guess you really are mine."

A throat cleared behind him. He peeked over his shoulder to

find Hannah hovering in the hallway.

"Found it," she said, wearing a necklace she hadn't had on when she arrived. Pink tinged her cheeks.

"Great."

"Um, I was thinking that you might like to take a shower."

What? Oh, hell yeah! Damn right, he'd like to take a shower. Slick his soaped-up hands across her skin. Over those perky breasts. Down her ass. Between her legs. His dick began to fill. A little morning shower play was exactly what he needed to get him back on track. It'd been way too long since he'd had that kind of fun.

"I would like that. How'd you know?" he asked in a flirty tone.

Hannah's nose wrinkled. "Well, I don't want to embarrass you, but you have some yogurt in your eyebrow. Looks like it dried and probably not too comfortable." Her lips twitched, and her eyes sparkled as though trying to keep from laughing.

"What?" Yogurt in his eyebrow?

He ran a hand over his crunchy eyebrow. "Fuck." How could he have missed that?

Hannah giggled. "I can sit with Kayla while you jump in the shower." She stepped into the room. "I've got plenty of experience with h—with babies. I'll have her squeaky clean in no time."

That hopeful smile of hers made it impossible to decline the offer. Even if he'd be showering alone. Rising to his feet, he stepped forward until she had to crane her neck to look up at him. "Thanks," he said.

Her cheeks flushed, her eyes warmed, and she swallowed. Shyness? Lust?

Whatever it was, he couldn't resist running a finger over the soft skin of her cheek.

Hannah sucked in a breath.

"She sits pretty well," he said. "But she loves to splash, so you may get…wet."

Her eyes flared wide. "I, uh, that's fine. Don't worry about me." She looked everywhere but at his face. "I'm just glad I can, uh, help out."

After tapping Hannah on the nose, he turned back to Kayla, who was still sending water flying all over. "Be good for Miss Hannah, you hear me?"

All he got in return was a string of baby babble.

As he jogged down the stairs toward his room, he chuckled. "Miss Hannah?" he mumbled. "Jesus." A week ago, he'd have been more than happy to call her Miss Hannah himself. Maybe they could have done a little professor and naughty student role play. Hell yeah, he could imagine her in a tight pencil skirt with her hair tied in a prim knot on the top of her head and librarian glasses on the tip of her nose. Maybe a set of heels to accentuate those sexy legs.

Instead, he was calling her Miss Hannah, so his infant daughter would eventually learn to use the title as a sign of respect. Shit, what the hell had happened to his life? It'd become unrecognizable in a matter of days.

And wasn't that depressing as fuck.

He stepped into the bathroom he was lucky enough not to share with any of his siblings, peeled his shirt off, and tossed it on the floor. Next went the pants. Then he turned the shower to warm.

Had he brushed his teeth that morning? Who the hell could remember when he'd been awakened at five by a hungry baby? He cupped a hand over his mouth and breathed out. Not bad. At least he wouldn't have killed Hannah if he'd been lucky enough to get his mouth on her.

By the time he finished brushing and flossing, steam rose from behind the fogged shower door. He groaned as the hot water hit his tired body. Whoever said having kids was exhausting hadn't been shitting anyone.

As he let the water unknot the tension in his back, he allowed his mind to take a journey back in time.

He called up a memory of a night only two weeks ago. After working a long day at his brother's garage, he'd met up with friends at a bar. They'd laughed and drank without a care in the world. The actual events of the night faded away, replaced by a fantasy in which he'd met Hannah at that very bar.

Damn, that would have been nice.

He wouldn't have hesitated to buy her a drink if only to watch those cheeks turn pink. She'd have thanked him in that reserved way she had about her. He'd have winked and asked if he could take the seat next to her.

Would she have bitten that bottom lip of hers and nodded? Yeah, that's precisely what she'd have done.

His cock sure liked this scenario. It'd plumped and practically begged for attention. Not one to ignore his favorite body part, JP wrapped a fist around his dick and gave a few rough tugs. Hannah's face stayed front and center in his mind, only now they'd left the bar and were on their way to her Airbnb.

Would they have made it to her bedroom before tearing each other's clothes off?

Nah, he wouldn't have been able to keep his hands off her. She'd be hungry for him too. The shy ones always were.

He imagined her sinking to her knees, taking his jeans with her, a half shy, half adventurous gleam in her eyes.

"Shit," he cursed as he thought of the intense pleasure of that first touch of her mouth to his cock. His hand flew over his dick, jerking with harsh, uncoordinated strokes. His balls tightened as a coil low in his belly drew them up and prepared them to unload.

Fantasy Hannah opened her mouth and drew him deep inside.

One good, hard, imagined suck was all it took.

"Fuck," he shouted as he sprayed all over the shower floor. His knees wobbled, and his thighs quivered with the force of his climax.

"Jesus." Lightheaded, he turned into the spray to clean his

dick. Hopefully, Hannah hadn't heard him cry out. Last thing he needed was for her to know he was twenty feet away behind a shower door whacking off to her like a horny teenager.

After drying off and throwing on fresh pair of sweats and a T-shirt, he jogged back upstairs.

Hannah sat on the floor in the den with Kayla between her splayed legs.

"How big is Kayla?" Hannah asked. "So big!" she sing-songed as she lifted Kayla's pudgy little arms. "How big is Kayla? So big!" This time Kayla lifted her arms herself when Hannah cued her.

"Yes!" Hannah said with a laugh. "What a smart little girl you are."

A smile curled across his face as he watched his daughter interact with Hannah. She made it look so easy, playing with the baby. Would he ever get to that point? To a place where caring for his child became second nature and he didn't question every move he made?

The two made a sweet pair. One dark-haired, one fair. Mary Anne had been blonde too, but his Benson genes won out.

Kayla repeated her trick again as Hannah praised her.

Pride filled his chest. She was a smart little cookie.

He froze, unable to take a step.

Well, shit.

He was thinking like a real father.

Chapter Eleven

For the first time in many months, Hannah's heart was full. Yes, there was still an acute ache from the recent loss of her sister, but as she played with Kayla, she couldn't stem the rush of happiness and pure love. Even though it hadn't been much more than a week since she'd seen Kayla, she'd missed her niece with a vengeance.

Not only could Hannah feel her sister's presence, the baby fascinated her. So much joy, so much curiosity. Every little thing was new, exciting, and something to be celebrated, from a pulled thread on the carpet to Hannah's ankle bracelet.

"Why are you so stinkin' cute?" she asked as she tickled Kayla's tummy. The little girl burst into giggles. God, that sound shot straight to her wounded heart. Mary Anne should be the one sprawled out on the floor with her daughter. The one enjoying that delighted sound and the pleasure of holding the soft weight of the baby. Swallowing, Hannah shoved the grief aside. Her time with Kayla was precious and wouldn't be spent mourning. She'd save that for later when alone.

"We have to show your daddy your new trick, huh? Show him how you're so big!"

"He saw it. Pretty impressive there, you two."

"Oh, hey." Hannah looked to her left and nearly swallowed her tongue. Fresh from the shower, his wet hair lay perfectly across his head. Tattoos had never really been something that interested her, but JP's fit him. He was muscular but not bulky, and had a bit of an edge. The ink complemented the attitude and made for a mouthwatering picture.

Mouthwatering? Since when did she describe men as mouthwatering?

"Hope I didn't take too long," he said as he joined her on the floor. He sat diagonal to her with his back against a plush chair and his long legs stretched out. His feet were bare, clean, and decorated with various tattoos.

Sexy.

"Nope," she said with a shake of her head. "We just finished up a few minutes ago."

Why on earth was the sight of his bare feet so attractive? Maybe it was time to get serious about finding herself a boyfriend to keep her from doing weird things, like drooling over random men's feet.

Only JP wasn't random, was he? He was the man who fathered a child with her sister. Her niece's father.

Even worse, her niece's father, who had no clue Hannah had any connection to his daughter.

What a mess.

Why couldn't he have been a troll?

She almost laughed out loud. Mary Anne would never have had a fling with a troll. Her standards for looks had always been over the top.

Kayla lurched forward as though she wanted to crawl to her father. She landed on her hands and knees, but not more than a second later, she collapsed out flat on her tummy. After a few seconds of unsuccessful wiggling, she let out a loud, dissatisfied wail.

"Come here, baby girl," he said as he reached for her. "Looks like we gotta work on this crawling thing, huh?"

Hannah watched, transfixed as he cradled the baby against his chest. Kayla settled after a minute, resting her head on those strong muscles. He kept one large hand splayed over her diapered bottom to keep her in place. With the other, he rubbed soothing strokes up and down her back.

Lucky girl. She wasn't sure who she envied more. JP for getting to hold the niece she ached to hold every day or Kayla, who got to experience the safety and comfort of his arms.

"You're great with her," Hannah said as Kayla's eyes fluttered shut.

JP snorted. "Thanks."

"What?" Tilting her head, she studied him for a moment. "You don't agree?"

"Truth?"

She nodded. "Always." Despite being there under false pretenses, honesty was important to her.

After sighing, he gave her a twisted grin. "I don't know what the hell I'm doing ninety-nine percent of the time. Hell, I almost left her in the tub by herself when you rang the bell. And have you heard my potty mouth? Pretty sure dropping the f-bomb every few minutes isn't something I'm going to come across in the eight million parenting blogs I now subscribe to."

He'd subscribed to parenting blogs? What a sweet man. He might not realize how his willingness to learn and do right by Kayla made him a great father, but Hannah had no doubts. Her parents were wrong. Kayla needed her father, and JP deserved to raise his little girl. She needed to find a way to prevent them from filing a lawsuit and to help them come to terms with Kayla's living arrangements.

"But you didn't leave her," she said with what she hoped was a reassuring smile. "Your instincts kicked in, and you did the right thing. Look at her. She's totally passed out. That wouldn't happen if she didn't feel comfortable and safe with you. And I know I said you guys need to curb your language, but I'm pretty sure you have a little time before you have to worry about the swearing."

He gazed down at his daughter. Hannah stared, transfixed by the expression on his stubbled face. A combination of awe, love, and uncertainty. "Thank you," he said as he shifted his attention back to Hannah. "I needed to hear that. I'm feeling pretty overwhelmed almost all the time these days." He struggled a bit to get to his feet with Kayla in his arms but managed with nothing more than a grunt or two from her. "Give me a few minutes to lay her down, or try to lay her down without waking her up, then I'll treat you to some lunch as a thank you for your help."

"Oh, no," Hannah said as she also scrambled up. Spending time with him without Kayla sounded like a recipe for poor choices. "That's not necessary. You probably want to enjoy a little quiet time, and I'd hate for you to go to any trouble."

He cocked his head. "Actually, I'd love to spend time talking to another adult who isn't in my family. And a beautiful woman at that. Besides," he said with a shrug. "I was gonna heat up a frozen pizza. Not exactly a backbreaker."

This was such a terrible idea. "Okay. That sounds good." Too good. She genuinely liked the guy. He was sweet and funny, kind, and seemed to be working very hard to care for Kayla.

"Great. Be right back." He winked and darted off.

She sat down on the couch and let her gaze roam the den as she waited for him to return. Photos of the Benson crew throughout the years littered the walls. All but a very few excluded the parents. A couple of snapshots showed their mother, but not a single image of their father had made its way to the collection. The smiling faces and silly poses depicted a story of a close-knit family despite the challenges they'd faced with an alcoholic father and a mother who'd passed early.

Hannah experienced a pang of jealousy as she stared at one particularly endearing picture. A young Ronnie sat on teenaged Keith's broad shoulders, clutching a snowball in each hand. On the ground, Jagger, JP, and two other boys lay in the snow laughing. Whatever they'd been doing, they had been having a ball.

From what little she'd been able to discern off social media, she knew their childhood hadn't been easy. Still, growing up having that kind of fun with their siblings couldn't have been all bad. Her mother would have passed out if she'd seen either of her daughters sitting on someone's shoulders at that age. Mary Anne would have defied their mother, of course, but not Hannah. She'd have watched on and longed to join the fun, much as she did now, gazing at those pictures. God, she missed her sister. How unfair was life to rob years from a young woman with so much of the world left to experience?

"All right, think we are good to go. Thankfully this little girl came to me a champion napper."

"That is lucky," Hannah said as she turned.

JP frowned at her. "You okay?"

Her momentary burst of grief must have shown. Then, forcing a cheerier expression, she nodded. "Absolutely."

JP walked until he was once again in her personal space. Hannah tipped her head back. Those dark eyes, that nearly black hair, the sun-tanned skin, and all that artwork inked on him. The man was the epitome of tall, dark, and handsome. For the first time in her life, she had to clench her fists to keep from reaching for a man. The temptation to shove the hem of his T-shirt up and learn where else he had tattoos nearly sent her to her knees.

JP brought his lips to her cheek and brushed a chaste kiss there before whispering, "Thank you for helping out with my daughter."

A shiver ran straight down her spine, settling between her legs.

He drew back with a chuckle, running a hand through his wet hair. "Never thought I'd be saying those words to a gorgeous woman. Come on, follow me for some grub."

As he headed for his kitchen, Hannah allowed herself a moment to regroup. How was it possible to be so affected by such an innocent gesture, especially when it hadn't fazed JP? There she stood in the middle of his den like an idiot with what might as well have been a brand on her cheek, while he whistled a jaunty tune in the kitchen.

She was so in over her head.

Kayla. Keep the focus on Kayla.

And cue guilt for lying to the man about to feed her as a thank you for her kindness.

"Grab a seat," he said over his shoulder as she entered the kitchen. He stood bent, peering in the fridge.

Hannah forced herself not to notice the way his dark sweatpants stretched over his buttocks. Okay, she took a tiny peek. And spared a second to wonder if he had any tattoo there as well.

"Want a drink? Your choices are soda, diet or regular, iced tea, water, or formula." He straightened then faced her with a wink.

Hannah laughed. "Sure. I'll take a regular soda. Thanks."

The smile she received should not have lit her up the way it did. None of this had anything to do with Kayla and everything to do with her curiosity about the man in general. That and her enjoyment of his company so far. She needed to steer her thoughts back to Kayla and off the man making her stomach all fluttery.

"Grab a seat." He handed her a can before plopping into a chair at a large round table.

"Thanks."

Silence thickened the air between them, making Hannah hyper-aware of the way his gaze tracked the movement of her can to her lips. She loved soda but didn't let herself drink it too often. Usually, she reveled in the treat, but today she barely tasted it. Her senses were already overloaded with awareness of JP and couldn't process the added input.

As the seconds ticked by, Hannah couldn't help but wonder what he knew of her sister. Or what he thought of her at this point. He'd liked her enough to…make a baby with her. But now? It didn't really matter since Mary Anne wasn't alive, but he had to have strong feelings where she was concerned considering the situation he now found himself in after a one-night stand more than a year ago.

After swallowing a few more bubbly sips, Hannah mustered the courage to ask, "So, um, is it okay if I ask about Kayla's mother?"

JP stilled with his can halfway to his lips. A deep freeze settled over the kitchen, coming from the block of ice formerly known as JP.

Oh, my God, she shouldn't have asked.

She'd be lucky if he didn't tell her to mind her own business and toss her out of his house.

He cleared his throat as though to talk, but she leaned forward, pressing a hand over her racing heart. "I am so sorry. That is none of my business whatsoever. We aren't even friends. Sorry. I don't know what I was thinking. You don't owe me any kind of explanation about your life." Her words tasted sour, knowing how many lies she'd already told to get close to him. "Crap, I'm sorry."

She shouldn't be allowed near people.

With a huff of laughter, he ran a hand across his stubbled chin. She'd have thought he would have shaved when he showered but had to admit the dark shadow gave him a roguish appearance. A strange urge to test if it was soft or scratchy overtook her with so much strength, she had to clench her drink to keep her hand in line.

"You're fine, Hannah. It's a normal question. One I'll have to get used to, I guess. Shit." He straightened then set his can down, staring at it as though it held the solution to all his newfound problems. "Kayla's mother is dead."

She bit her lip to keep the whoosh of air from leaving as his words hit like a punch to the gut. Yes, Mary Anne was dead. Gone. Never coming back. She stared down at the table to give herself a moment. Would hearing those words ever stop hurting?

After clearing her throat, she lifted her gaze. "I-I'm so sorry." Tears sprang to her eyes, but Hannah blinked them away. How awkward would it be for her to break down at his table over a woman she wasn't supposed to know? "Were, um, were you together long?" Sickness twisted her belly. What kind of person asked these questions when they already had the answer? But she had to know how he felt about her sister.

He snorted then grabbed his bottle again. After three long gulps—in which she did not stare at his throat while he swallowed—he set the drained bottle on the table with a loud clunk. "We weren't together at all. I met her at a concert, fucked her once, then put her out of my mind."

Hannah cringed at the crude description his time with Mary Anne, but she wasn't naïve enough to dispute it. That's what it'd been on both sides, confirmed by Mary Anne. At least he didn't shoulder the blame for an ulterior motive.

"Oh, wow. Well, I'm sorry to hear she passed. I imagine it's been hard for you to be on your own with a baby."

With a grunt, he stood then slapped both hands on the top of the table. "Know what's hard?" he asked in a disgusted tone.

She didn't bother replying. He didn't want her to. Clearly, the man needed to unload some pent-up resentment.

"What's hard is when you're at a barbecue with your family, and some random chick shows up, toting a seven-month-old baby she claims is yours. What's hard is reading a letter from that baby's mother that describes how she knew she was terminally ill but wanted a baby, so she picked you as the sucker to knock her up. What's hard is reading that she poked a hole in the fucking condom, had my baby, and fucking died without giving a single shit about the number of lives she destroyed or the people she fucked over."

Hannah's eyes widened. Oh God, was that how he saw it? That Mary Anne didn't care about the repercussions of her actions? If only he'd known how many nights Hannah had held her sister as she sobbed her regrets and fears for both her unborn child and JP.

Yet, how could she begrudge the man his thoughts on the matter? Despite multiple promises that she'd contact JP, Mary

Anne never had. She let her nuclear-level secret fester until she died, leaving the mess for everyone else. His anger was appropriate and justified, yet it still cut her to the core to hear him spew hatred for her recently deceased sister.

The urge to tell him, to ease his troubles in some small way, grew so strong it was a physical ache inside her. But she couldn't. Not without exposing herself and making his suffering worse.

"I'm so sorry, JP."

"Don't be. You're not the fucking liar who saddled me with a lifelong responsibility I never asked for or wanted."

Hannah swallowed. That statement hit too close to home.

Shoving away from the table, he crossed the kitchen then turned to face her again. with tense, jerky movements, he stalked back to the table. "Ask anyone in my family, and they'll tell you I'm the exciting one. The you-only-live-once carefree schmuck who's allergic to commitment. I don't even have a real fucking job, Hannah. I flit between my siblings' businesses, earning enough money to live and have some fucking fun while I'm doing it. I didn't want kids, a house, a retirement fund, or any of the shit that weighs people down and makes them boring as fuck nine-to-five lemmings in miserable marriages, raising a pack of brats, and mourning the youth they lost because they didn't take advantage of their freedom." He took a deep breath. "I'm a selfish asshole who likes my life without any strings."

Her hands started to shake, so she set the soda down. Were her parents correct? Was JP the wrong person to raise Kayla? This impassioned speech sure made him sound like it. Like a man with no interest in putting his child first. Or even claiming the child.

His face twisted into a mask of pain. "Now I'm bound by rope so tight, there's no way of cutting free. I'm raising a baby alone, with no job and no savings. I live with my siblings and don't have the first fucking clue about babies, toddlers, or kids. In a matter of minutes, my entire life flipped on its ass and will never,

ever be the same again. No nine months to prepare for this guy." He jammed a thumb into his chest. "Just a 'Here's your baby.' And a 'By the way, the mom was a selfish con artist who tricked you then up and died, so you're on your own.'"

He pushed away from the table again. "So yeah, it's fucking hard, Hannah. It's really fucking hard." Blowing out a breath, he gripped his hair with both hands. "You know what? I'm not hungry anymore. Sorry about all this. You can see yourself out."

With that, he stormed out of the kitchen. The heavy clunk of his footsteps on the basement stairs mimicked the hammering of her heart.

Damnit, MaryAnne.

Guilt had become her constant companion. Guilt for adding to her parents' grief. Guilt for deceiving JP. Guilt for being so angry at her deceased sister.

She dropped her head to the table, sick to her stomach.

Now what?

And she'd thought things were a mess before she came over.

Chapter Twelve

Three hours.

JP had three whole hours to himself.

This was his life now. Stealing seconds or minutes of baby-free time to live his own life. Mickie had been more than happy to babysit, but when would that offer end? At what point would his siblings grow tired of him always begging for help and relying on them?

The craziest part of it all? Well, he felt weird as fuck being away from Kayla. How was that for a kick in the balls? When he was with her, he felt like a bird falling from its nest before its wings fully developed. Nervous, incompetent, overwhelmed by the task. Flapping around and occasionally catching some air but careening to the ground in the end. And now that she was safe and sound in Mickie's capable arms, he had an uncontrollable urge to check in every few minutes.

Shit, for the past few days, all he'd wanted was some time to himself, and now that he had it, he was spending it obsessing about the baby. Shaking his head, he climbed out of the piece of shit car he'd owned for over fifteen years. At some point, he'd need to get something a little better suited for a car seat. Maybe something that had a safety rating. And that meant he needed steady money.

And a real job.

He tugged at the neck of his T-shirt as the fabric suddenly felt shrink-wrapped to his skin.

What the hell was happening to him?

As he walked up the short path to Hannah's small, rented house, the front door opened, and the woman herself strolled out looking cute as fuck in a simple teal sundress. Her long hair had been pulled up in a high ponytail, giving him all sorts of naughty thoughts about wrapping his fist around it. She had her attention on her purse, but the second she looked up, her feet stopped moving.

"JP." She looked around. "Are you here by yourself? Is everything okay?"

With what women told him was a charming smile—might as well get a leg up on the apologizing—he nodded. "Yes, to both. Kayla is spending time with her Aunt Mickie."

Hannah broke out a brief smile before her eyebrows drew down. "Okay, so, uh, what are you doing here?"

He stepped closer until a waft of something sweet and citrusy nearly made him groan. It wasn't enough she looked good enough to eat in a flowy sundress that showed off her shoulders and legs. She also had to smell like an orange creamsicle. His fucking favorite dessert. "I got your address from Mickie. I owe you an apology for my freak out the other day, and I was hoping to give it to you over ice cream. My treat. What do ya say?"

She stared at his car as she gnawed her lower lip then sighed. "I don't know."

He'd never admit it out loud because his siblings gave him enough shit about his "womanizing ways," but women didn't turn him down. It just didn't happen. It'd been well over a decade since he made his intentions known and had a woman reject him. Jag constantly told him his good looks got him out of more trouble and into more beds than the rest of them combined. What could he say? He was a delightful fucker. Whether it was the tattoos, the way he didn't take life too seriously, or his snarky wit, something was working for him.

Until now.

Sure, he'd fucked up the other day, but he'd seen the flare of heat and interest in her eyes before his meltdown. Hadn't he? Surely one dickish act couldn't have blown his chances out of the water.

Chances for what?

What the hell did he think he was going to do with this girl who gave off heart and home vibes for days?

For today, he'd settle for adult conversation. "Just ice cream and an apology," he said as he lifted his hands in surrender. "That's all."

She didn't budge.

"What if I promise not to be an asshole this time?"

A soft chuckle escaped her. "You weren't an asshole."

He cocked an eyebrow, making her laugh grow.

"Okay, maybe a little bit. But I never should have butted into your business, so the apology isn't necessary. I should be the one apologizing to you for the inappropriate questions."

So, they were doing this here. Damn. He'd been hoping to plow halfway through an Oreo sundae before diving into the tough shit.

"Hannah, you didn't do anything wrong." He stepped closer and took one of her hands between his. Her name felt good on his tongue. Sounded good to his ears too. It'd sound even better if he was shouting it while her mouth—

Not going there.

"Asking about Kayla's mother is a normal question and one I'm going to have to come to terms with." He sighed. Her neighbors were probably plastered to their windows, ready to feed the town gossip mongers. Sure enough, a curtain fluttered in the house next to her rental. "Look, were you on your way somewhere right now?"

"No, not really. I was just going to find a park. Take a walk. I've been working a ton the past few days, and the walls were beginning to close in on me."

"Please let me buy you an ice cream." Then, a genius idea

struck him. "How about we get them to go and take them to the campground?. We can wander around, and you can see the land you're helping the ladies develop."

Her eyes lit with interest. He had her.

With a slow nod, she said. "Okay. Let's do it."

"Perfect." He held out an arm as though about to escort her to a ball while gesturing to his old Corolla with the other. "Your chariot, m' lady."

She giggled but didn't make eye contact as she looped her arm through his.

"Now, you may be confused as to how I can afford to drive such a luxury vehicle, but I assure you, it's not as nice as it looks on first impression."

Though she remained tense as she strolled next to him, she did laugh. Guess he could call that a point in his favor. Was she uncomfortable because of how he'd acted the other day? Maybe she just needed some time to warm up to new people. She'd seemed perfectly at ease at his house the other day, but it was hard to stay distant around Kayla. Maybe he should have brought the baby.

When they neared his car, he released her then opened the door with a flourish.

After flashing him a shy smile, she took a seat.

"Nice, huh?" he asked.

"Mm-hmm. Not sure I'm worthy of such extravagance." Her eyes sparkled with mirth.

There we go. Much better.

"Trust me, I know how you feel. I felt the same at first. But you'll get used to it. We all deserve nice things occasionally." With a wink, he shut her door and jogged around to the driver's side.

Seven minutes and some stilted small talk later, he parked outside of his favorite place in the world, Coop's Scoops. Once again, he'd opened her door, if for no other reason than to enjoy the flush it brought to her cheeks.

"Oh, my God," she said as she stepped out of the car. "What is that smell?"

"Drool-inducing, right?"

She closed her eyes and inhaled, then let out a little moan.

JP shifted as his pants grew a little tighter. Christ, the woman seemed oblivious to how pornographic that sound was.

"Drool-inducing is right." She licked her lower lip. "My mouth is literally watering."

Mine too.

"Cooper, the owner, makes all the toppings and add-ins from scratch. Brownies, different types of cookies, cake pieces, all of it. The ice cream is all handmade on site as well."

"Okay, now I'm seriously excited," Hannah said as she bounced on the balls of her feet. This was the most animated she'd been since he'd met her. "Ice cream is my weakness."

"Good to know." He winked, and she blushed. "Well, let's get that cute ass in there so we can sugar you up."

Her steps faltered as though she'd never had anyone tell her how fine that ass was.

Impossible.

The overhead bell jangled as he pulled the door open for her.

"Thank you," she said as she passed. Her eyes widened. "Wow. This is incredible."

Coop's wife decorated the shop to look like a classic, old-fashioned ice cream parlor. Everything from the white-and-red awning out front to the black-and-white checkered flooring and bowties worn by staff transported visitors to a simpler time.

"John Paul Benson!" Cooper yelled from behind the counter. "Get your dumb ass over here." He came out from behind the counter and opened his arms wide.

Hannah's slack-jawed, gaping stare had him snorting.

"Coop!" With a laugh, JP embraced his oldest and largest friend. At six foot five, with an equally large wingspan and the broadest chest known to man, Cooper was a mammoth. Add to it his fiery red hair and handlebar mustache, and no one could ever forget the man.

Coop slapped him on the back so hard, he nearly lost his breath. "Damn, JP, it's been too long. You better not be cheating on me with that chain ice cream shop."

Laughing, he pounded his friend just as hard then pulled away. "Hell no," he said as he ran a hand down his stomach. "Just trying to keep my sexy figure."

Cooper snorted, then slung an arm across JP's shoulders. "Sexy as a raccoon," he said in his deep boom. "But forget you. Who is this lovely lady you brought to my palace?"

"Hannah, this is Cooper Manning. Coop, this lovely lady, as you said, is Hannah."

"Welcome, Hannah, nice to meet you." Cooper dropped his arm from JP's shoulders then extended a hand to Hannah.

She watched with fascinated eyes as her small hand disappeared into Coop's giant mitt.

JP stepped back over to her. "All right, hands off. What would your wife say?"

Cooper let out a loud laugh. "She'd call me smart for recognizing a beautiful woman."

With a snort, JP rolled his eyes. "Shit, man, could you maybe try to tone it down a bit. I'm working on apologizing for being a dick, and it won't happen if your game is better than mine."

"An apology, huh? Well, you've come to the right place. Step on up to the counter and pick your poison."

"Thank you," Hannah said, finally speaking. "And it's so nice to meet you. This is a wonderful shop. You must be so proud."

Coop puffed out his chest like a preening peacock.

"Now you've done it," JP muttered.

"Heard that. Want your usual JP?"

"You know it."

"Coming right up. Take your time perusing that menu, hon," Cooper said as he went to work.

"What's your usual?" she asked, staring up at him.

"A cup of strawberry cheesecake ice cream with hot fudge and about six pounds of whipped cream. He makes the cheesecake fresh in house for the ice cream. Seriously it's the most amazing thing you'll ever put in your mouth. Well, maybe the second most amazing."

She blushed, of course, which had him chuckling. He'd always liked the shy ones, but her actions were beginning to make him wonder if she wasn't inexperienced on top of the shyness. That had never been his thing, but for some insane reason, the thought of it had him growing hard.

In the damn ice cream shop.

"JP, don't be crude," Coop yelled from where he was scooping ice cream with ease as though it was melted instead of rock hard.

"Just keeping it real."

And hoping he didn't get a full-on boner. Cooper would never let him live it down.

Cooper snorted.

"I like him," Hannah said with a smile.

Within seconds, Cooper delivered a giant cup of JP's favorite treat. Favorite food treat, that was. "Have you decided?" he asked Hannah.

"I have. I'll take the classic brownie sundae," she said. "Small."

"My personal favorite," Coop said. "And you'll be getting a medium at minimum. Be right back."

"What? I can't eat that much."

"Just go with it. Coop's ultimate goal in life is to give everyone he meets diabetes."

Snickering, she gazed around the shop. "This place is so great."

Nodding, JP said, "Sure is. It's been open about seven years now and has always done incredible business. Coop worked as a pastry chef at some fancy-schmancy restaurant in Boston for a few years. Eventually, he got sick of the pretentious patrons, shitty hours, and even shittier pay. So he came home, he opened this place, and the rest is history."

"That's right," Cooper said as he returned with a jaw-droppingly large sundae. "Now I'm my own boss. I make what I love, work when I want, and life is pretty damn good."

They chatted for a few more minutes until a group of moms came in with their toddlers. As usual, Coop refused to allow him to pay, so he slyly shoved a twenty in tip jar before they took off. Business might be booming, but Coop also had four little ones at home. The crazy man.

Now that I'm a father—

Holy shit.

He was one of them now. Only there was no mom to join that group. He'd be doing it all alone. Terrible Twos. Threenagers or whatever he'd heard Coop call it one time. Jesus Christ, sometimes the magnitude of the responsibility smacked him so hard it nearly bowled him over.

JP stopped walking before he reached the exit.

Hannah bumped into him from behind. "Oops, sorry!"

Shaking his head, he said, "No, my fault."

"You okay?" Her mouth turned down but seemed more a look of concern rather than displeasure.

"Uh, yeah, I just had a crazy thought." He started walking again, pushing the door open for her as he reached it.

"Anything you want to share?" She took a bite of her ice cream then made another of those obscene moans.

JP willed his dick to ignore the sound. Of course, it ignored him instead. How was it possible for her to be so unaware of her effect on him? Once again, he had to do a little discreet shifting to keep her from noticing the growing bulge in his jeans.

"Nah, it's nothing important. Let's head to the resort. Well, the future resort."

A quick drive was all it took to arrive at the campground. The property belonged to Mickie and Ronnie now, so campers were no longer permitted.

"Oh, wow, it's beautiful here."

As he shut the car's engine, JP nodded. "It is. You should see it in winter, all covered in snow. It's breathtaking." Located partway up the mountain, the property stayed snowy and stunning throughout winter.

"How many cabins are there?" She asked, peering through the windshield.

"Ten, I believe. Let's go sit outside. There are some picnic tables over there."

"Sounds good."

This time, she was out of the car before he had a chance to grab her door. Damn, that meant a missed opportunity to see her pretty blush. They walked toward the picnic area in silence, taking in the serenity of nature.

When they reached the picnic tables, Hannah climbed up and sat on the tabletop instead of the bench. She faced the cabins and the mountain. JP sat beside her, far enough that she wouldn't feel crowded even though he had the insane urge to plaster himself to her side. If she were any other woman, he wouldn't think twice about it, but Hannah would most likely get shy and scoot away.

For a few moments, they ate their ice cream in silence. After a while, Hannah turned to him with a smile on her face. "You know, I can see it. Their vision."

"Yeah?"

"Yes. This will be the perfect spot for luxury rentals. Mickie mentioned they were going with a modern cabin theme. I can just imagine a grand lodge over there." She pointed to where the main offices for the campground were. "Then a spa and ten luxurious cabins. Maybe some gardens. An area for bonfires. This has some great potential."

He'd felt the same way ever since Ronnie and Mickie presented the idea. He'd been coming to this very spot at least once a week and letting his imagination run wild. His brother Jagger's construction company would be handling the demo and renovations. Ian and Jimmy, two of his other brothers, were overseas with the military. Ian planned to get out soon and would join in on the renovations. Jimmy was due some time off and did something with electrical components for the army. He'd be taking care of the wiring. Keith would pitch in whenever he had time off from working at the garage. When they'd presented the idea, Mickie and Ronnie told everyone they wanted it to be a family affair. A business created by and run by all of them.

Where did that leave him? Sure, he had skills, but he flitted from business to business, helping his siblings out. He worked construction sites when Jag needed help, fixed cars when Keith was overbooked, and helped Ronnie out at the bar when she needed it. He also worked at a friend's landscaping company when his siblings' workload slowed.

"You're quiet," Hannah said. She bumped his shoulder with hers.

He gave her a long, assessing look before saying, "Can I show you something?"

Her brow creased, but she nodded.

Blowing out a breath, he set down his ice cream. His literally shook as he reached into the back pocket of his jeans and pulled out the wrinkled piece of paper he brought with him every time he came here.

"I haven't shown or talked about this with anyone, so I'd appreciate it if you keep it to yourself. I'm not ready for Ronnie or Mickie to see it."

Hannah swallowed her spoonful of ice cream, set the cup down on the table next to her, then brushed her hands together. "Of course. I'd never break your confidence."

JP didn't do vulnerable. He didn't get deep with anyone, especially a woman he found immensely attractive. Usually, he flirted, bedded them, then moved along, keeping things light, fun, and hot. Something about the sincerity in Hannah's crystal eyes had him wanting to reveal his secrets to her, even if it put him at risk for ridicule.

"So, they want to create a 'peaceful oasis.' I think that was the phrase Ronnie used. A European winter sanctuary. They want to focus heavily on nature and the outdoors while keeping the place extremely lavish and fancy. One time, I saw an Instagram post from a travel blogger who visited a lodge in Finland in winter. It was the most beautiful spot I'd ever seen."

"Okay," Hannah said as she nodded. "Tell me more." He had every ounce of her attention, which both bolstered his confidence and terrified him. It felt as though he was about to reveal his soul, not just a silly idea he had for the resort.

He handed over the folded paper. There was no way she'd miss how his fingers trembled, but she was kind enough to pretend she hadn't noticed.

"I can open this?"

"Yeah. Please."

With her face scrunched in concentration, she unfolded the paper. JP looked away as she studied his drawing. He'd be sketching it out for weeks, building upon a seed of an idea until he had something that truly excited him.

"JP, did you draw this?" she asked in a slightly breathless voice.

"Yeah. It's just, you know, kinda scrawled out from my thoughts."

She chuckled. "If this is scrawled, I can't imagine how amazing a final draft would be." She faced him. "Tell me about it."

"Uh, okay." He scooted closer until they could both see the paper. His hip came to rest against hers as her bare shoulder pressed into his upper arm. Heat immediately traveled to his dick as though they were naked. Did Hannah feel it too, or was he losing his mind?

She grinned up at him with excitement in her eyes, but not the lustful kind. The same buzz of exhilaration he'd felt when he'd come up with his idea.

Disappointment swamped him. Christ, when did he pine over a woman? Maybe the lack of sleep was finally getting to him.

Or the lack of sex.

Shaking off the insane thoughts, he pointed to the paper. "So, I basically sketched out my ideas for landscaping the entire property." He went through section by section, outlining his ideas for outdoor hot tubs behind each cabin, firepits also behind each cabin, and through the property in general as well as the foliage and flowers. He'd gone a little crazy with the designs, making elaborate plans and not letting financial implications derail his vision.

"All these areas of flowers will look so beautiful in the summer."

He nodded. "They will, but I've also planned it out with a ton of winter-blooming plants."

"Really?" She bent over the paper.

"Yep, see here?" He pointed to the top corner of the paper.

"Yeah."

"Those are called Christmas roses. They are gorgeous in winter. I also deliberately picked trees that will be perfect for twinkling lights once they lose their leaves in the fall."

Hannah blew out a breath. "Oh, imagine how magical it will be when this entire place is blanketed in snow with fires burning, lights twinkling, and flowers blooming. It will be like a snowy paradise."

Holy shit. She got his vision.

He huffed out a laugh as his insides warmed. "That's exactly what I was calling it in my head."

She stared up at him with wonder and appreciation in her gaze. But appreciation for his mind, not his body, for once. "You are really talented. Are you sure you're not a landscape architect or something?"

"Nah." He shook his head. "I work with a friend's landscaping company when I need some extra cash, but this is just doodling."

"Well, you should think about it because this is unbelievable. I think you'd be perfect for a career like that." She shrugged then blushed as she glanced up at him. "Wow, sorry. Look at me telling you what to do with your life. Didn't mean to overstep. I just think this is so great, and I can see you loving a job like this."

And just like that, with a few words, Hannah was able to do something no one had ever done for JP before.

She sparked a small ember of curiosity about an actual occupation.

Landscape architecture.

A real job. A career. A car. Insurance. Eventually, a house. He needed all those things now that he had Kayla to think about.

Was that something he could do? Should do?

He loved being outside. Always had. He'd also been drawing and doodling for most of his life. With a mother who passed when he was just a child and a piece of shit father, JP hadn't had assistance from his parents in exploring interests or options for his future. But he loved the outdoors and had notebooks full of random sketches and drawings. Most of the artwork inked into his skin had been designed at least in part by him.

Shit, inventing elaborate outdoors designs for a living?

That just might be the perfect career for him.

Chapter Thirteen

The man was a creative genius. This was a side of JP she hadn't seen and wouldn't have expected. That'd teach her to judge. He had an out-of-this-world eye for aesthetics and had been able to capture on paper precisely what'd been in his inspired mind.

Whatever he was doing for work, he was wasting an incredible talent.

She glanced up to find him staring down at her. An intensity entered his gaze, chasing away some of his usual playfulness but making him no less appealing. In fact, seeing him without his typical lighthearted personality gave him a depth of character she found herself drawn to. He was multidimensional. Someone who could laugh and have fun but also had a serious side, especially when it came to something he had an obvious passion for. Combine it all with how attracted she was to him physically, and it made an extremely tempting package.

"Did I overstep? I don't mean to tell you your business."

"No. Not at all." Gone was the playful teasing JP she was coming to expect. This wasn't the angry JP from the other day either. This was a pensive, serious version, and the way he seemed to stare into her mind made her shiver with awareness. It was as though she'd been laid bare and open for him to discover.

He sat so close their sides touched. As soon as his body had come in contact with hers, tingles of pleasure erupted across her skin.

God, how on earth was she supposed to maintain her distance and keep the focus solely on Kayla when the most attractive man she'd ever been around licked his lips like he was about to devour her?

All she had to do was lean in and stretch her neck up a bit, and their lips would touch. Would be a gentle kisser? Or a hungry one?

How long had it been since a man last kissed her?

Well over a year. Ugh, maybe even two. She missed kissing. The feel of a man's lips on hers. The heat of his body radiating against her. The firmness of muscles under her hands. She hadn't had much of it, but JP was opening a well of craving for the things she had experienced and everything she hadn't. She'd spent too many hours wondering about all the things he could show her if their situation wasn't so complicated.

"I'm sorry," he whispered, making her blink and draw back.

Had she been drifting closer to him?

She frowned as she shook her head.

"For the other day."

Right. The reason he'd invited her there. To apologize. Not to kiss her.

She straightened as though a bucket of melted snow fell right over her head.

Kiss him? Was she out of her mind? He was the father of Mary Anne's child, for crying out loud. She needed to keep that fact at the front of her mind at all times. "Don't worry about it. Really."

He placed a hand over hers where it rested on her thigh, and she nearly swooned from the scratchy feeling of his calluses.

"I only found out Kayla existed about ten days ago. It was also the first time I'd heard from Mary Anne, her mother, since I met her. I had no idea she was sick, no idea she was pregnant, and no idea she had died. In case you haven't picked up on it, I've been having a little trouble adjusting. But that's no excuse for taking my frustration out on you. I was out of line."

Ugh, a man who genuinely apologized for his mistakes. The guy was a unicorn. "JP, it's really okay. Besides the fact that it isn't any of my business, you're more than entitled to be upset about the situation. I can't begin to imagine how it would feel to be in your shoes. You received life-altering news with no time to prepare and no choice on what to do moving forward."

And that was the truth. For so long, she'd listened to Mary Anne's perspective and prepared with her sister for Kayla's arrival. JP had no time to prepare. Look at how Mary Anne reacted to the news of her diagnosis. No one would think running out and purposely getting pregnant was a healthy response to life-altering news. But no one knew how they would handle something as terrifying as their own mortality until it crashed into them. As shocked as she'd been by what her sister had done, and as wrong as it had been, watching JP struggle through his own shock was helping process her sister's actions. Her heart hurt to imagine how scared and alone Mary Anne must have felt when she received her diagnosis.

"JP, I have no right to judge you and forgave your reaction almost as soon as I left your house."

"Well, I'm not so sure I deserve such quick forgiveness, but thank you. Reality is, people are going to ask about Kayla's mother, so I need to come to terms with it."

Unfortunately, he was right about that. Though she'd forgiven him and even empathized, one thing had been on her mind the past few days. "Can I ask you something?"

He smirked. "Sure. I even promise not to lose my shit."

"You said you never wanted children. Okay, that's not really a question, but…" She shrugged. "You're good with Kayla."

"Yeah." He blew out a long breath then scrubbed both hands over his face. As he stared out over the gorgeous landscape, he sighed, and she felt the weight of it in her own heart. "It's not like I hate kids or anything. And I'm not an unreliable loser. I keep my promises and fulfill my commitments. I had a shitty childhood. My mom died when I was young, and my old man is garbage. Abusive, neglectful, your basic horrible husband and father. Wasn't willing to see if I'd turn out the same, so I stayed away from relationships and children. I decided to live my life the opposite way. No full-time job, no relationship, no responsibility. It's fun, and no one gets hurt. Or so I thought."

No wonder he'd had a hard time adjusting. "I'm sorry that choice was taken from you."

He shrugged. "When I say it out loud, I realize what a selfish prick it makes me."

"No." Now it was her turn to rest her hand on his. "A selfish prick would shirk the responsibility right in front of his face. You may not have been looking for Kayla, but you're giving her your all."

With a snort, he shook his head. "No. I'm not. I still don't have a job. I live with my siblings. I drive a death trap."

"Didn't you say it'd only been a week or so? Cut yourself some slack. No one can expect you to have all your stuff together already."

He grunted. "You know I didn't hold her or acknowledge her for the first few days. Mickie and Keith did everything for her."

"Hey." She squeezed his hand, which caused him to meet her gaze finally. "I stand by what I said. Cut yourself some slack. You needed a minute to breathe. To process. It's okay, JP. You didn't abandon her. She wasn't neglected. She was in good hands with your brother and Mickie. So many kids have it much worse when a parent dies. Trust me.When M—uh, my friend's sister passed away and, um, left a young child, that baby had it much worse."

Oh, my God. What the hell was wrong with her? She nearly blurted out how difficult it had been when Mary Anne died, and she was left caring for Kayla with her parents. "Anyway, uh, you stepped up."

Please don't notice my screw up.

His brow scrunched, but she nodded. After an extended silence, he turned his palm up and interlaced his fingers with hers. Hannah tensed, then forced herself to relax. It was nothing but hand holding. He didn't need to know about the ridiculous sensations coursing up her arm or making her belly flutter. The man needed support. An understanding ear.

What he didn't need was Mary Anne's sister lying to him day after day, but that ship had already sailed. She had no choice but to continue with the lie despite the shame she experienced when she laid her head down each night.

"For a few days, I thought about searching around to see if Mary Anne had any family that would raise Kayla."

Hannah's ears burned, and she held her breath. This was it. A moment she could push her parent's agenda. She could sway him. Convince him the best choice for his daughter would be Mary Anne's family. His daughter would be raised by two people who loved her. Two people who could provide for her financially. And Hannah would be there every step of the way.

But then he said, "In the end, I dismissed the idea."

"Why?" Was that her voice? That gravelly croak?

When he looked at her, the conflict was clear as day in his eyes. Love for Kayla combined with resentment for the drastic changes in his life. "Because she is my daughter. My flesh and blood. What kind of man would I be if I walked away from her when she'd already lost her mother? I might have a shitload of growing up to do, but she is my daughter. For Christ's sake, she has my eyes. My hair. She's mine. I made her. And as overwhelming and terrifying as this all is, it's also pretty fucking spectacular, you know?"

Her throat thickened. "Yeah," she whispered. "It is." If only her sister had the chance to know this man. To see this mix of fear and determination in his eyes. To witness the transformation as he went from stressed and uncertain to smitten with his daughter. And he'd get there. He was already well on his way to falling head over heels in love with Kayla.

Some might criticize him for not experiencing an instant connection. For not taking one look at her and developing an unbreakable bond born of paternal love. But not Hannah. Maybe before Mary Anne had told her the whole story, she'd have judged him with a harsher eye, but Mary Anne was the perfect example of how extreme shock could lead a person to make out-of-character decisions. He hadn't even gone that far. JP took a few days to get his head screwed on right, then jumped with both feet into the heavy responsibility of raising a daughter on his own.

She was so screwed. She straight-up wanted him. The man who'd had a child with her sister. He'd been with her sister. Why, oh why did it have to be him who woke these feelings and desires in her? The reasons she could never have him counted into the thousands with the fact that he'd slept with her sister at the very top. Being adopted, they weren't blood related, but still, they'd been more than family. They'd been best friends.

"Fuck," he said with an awkward grunt of laughter. "I didn't mean to make shit so serious. I just wanted to apologize." Then he shrugged. "Guess I might have needed to talk, though, because it feels really fucking good to get that all out. So, thanks for listening."

"I'm glad I was here. I'm sure a lot is going on inside your head right now. It can't be good to keep it bottled up. But you have a great support system in your family. I'm pretty sure any one of them would be more than willing to listen."

"Yeah. I know. For some reason, it was easier to talk to you. You don't have any preconceived opinions of me. Well, maybe you do after my outburst the other day." He squeezed her hand but didn't release it.

It felt nice, the simple connection of her hand in his larger, stronger one. Between work, Mary Anne's illness, and helping when Kayla was a newborn, Hannah hadn't spent much time out of the house in the past year or so. Finding a boyfriend hadn't been on her radar for even longer as she'd been focusing on her degree and wasn't one to put herself out there anyway.

Boyfriend?

Was that how she saw him? As boyfriend material?

She risked a peek at him. He'd shut his eyes and tilted his face up toward the sun. Summers in New England never heated to overly stifling. The temperature rose just enough for her to be comfortable in a sundress. Like her, JP seemed to enjoy the warmth of the sun on his skin.

He seemed more relaxed than he had the few times she'd met him previously. Relaxation looked good on him. Heck, anything looked good on him. His tattooed skin had a deep golden tan that complemented his toned muscles. Stubble dotted his jaw. Not enough to be considered scruff, but he'd obviously skipped the shave that morning.

She liked him like that. A little rough around the edges and wild, as if he were unable to be tamed. However, that description seemed to hit his internal conflict right on the head. There he was, free and uninhibited, only to be wrangled in and weighed down by the unexpected task of raising a child.

As a single father, no less.

"She regretted it," he said, startling her out of her thoughts.

By the time she blinked and returned to the conversation, he'd opened his eyes and focused on her.

"I'm sorry?"

"Mary Anne. Kayla's mom. She left me a long letter where she apologized profusely and told me how much she regretted not telling me when she found out she was pregnant."

Yes. She had. Her biggest regret in life. The words were on the top of Hannah's tongue, but she bit them off. This wasn't the time to confess her own sins. Not when he finally seemed to be finding some peace.

"But she didn't regret the night we met. The night that led to Kayla. She said Kayla was the best thing she'd ever done."

Hannah's eyes began to water. She swallowed a hard lump and willed herself not to cry.

"I thought she was crazy at first. How could she not regret getting pregnant? We'd created a little person who was going to be raised without a mother and with a shitty father. How fucking selfish was that?"

Even though a small part of her agreed with JP's assessment of her sister, hearing it hurt. He'd never known the real Mary Anne. The version he'd met so briefly was in crisis mode. Panicked and dealing with the very horrifying reality of her own mortality. He'd have liked the true version of her sister. They had a similar zest for life and a fun personality. Messed up as it was, she wished she could talk to him about Mary Anne. To share stories about her personality and give him insight into his daughter's mother.

"But I think I'm starting to understand it. Kayla smiled at me today, and something happened in here." He rubbed a hand over the left side of his chest. "At the end of her letter, she asked me not to let my anger at her color my feelings for Kayla."

Oh, the heartache...

She pressed her lips together, unable to form a response without sobbing.

He stared at her as though trying to see into her soul. She felt sliced open, laid bare, and vulnerable before him.

"You ever done something like that? Something you knew was indefensible, but you did it anyway?"

"Once." She was doing it right then. God, he'd been screwed over by her family in so many unforgivable ways.

"Hmm," he said. "Me too. Were you in your right mind when you did it?"

And the hits kept coming. For someone who didn't want to get deep, he sure knew how to twist the knife in just the right spot without even knowing it. "I'm not sure," she answered. "I think so. But I didn't realize the magnitude of my decisions or actions until it was too late."

Until she'd developed an enormous crush on the man she'd deceived. The one man she could never have and shouldn't want. The one who'd impregnated her sister. The one her parents would never forgive her for befriending.

He sighed, then rolled his shoulders. "I should get you back. I promised Mickie I'd be home by two. She has something going on in a bit."

Disappointment had her wanting to cry for an entirely different reason. "Yeah, sure. Of course."

Without releasing her, he hopped down from the table then helped her do the same. Hand in hand, they strolled toward his car at a lazy pace and without talking. It shouldn't have been as comfortable as it was. As though they'd done it a million times before and had an easy vibe between them.

When they reached his rusty old car, he turned her and gently backed her against the passenger's side window. "Thank you for today. For letting me talk and for being so quick to understand and forgive. Not sure I deserved it, but I'm selfish enough to grab onto it."

Forcing a smile through mounting guilt, she said. "Thank you for the ice cream. And I enjoyed talking to you. A lot." She meant it. Even if it jacked the temperature on her guilt up to near boiling. "Um, if you need any help with Kayla over the next few weeks while I'm here, I'm more than happy to spend time with her."

Understatement of the century. She could feel her time Kayla slipping away and only hoped to have more days with her.

"Thank you. I might take you up on that."

He stepped closer then. So close, not more than a sheet of paper could have fit between their bodies. A bead of sweat rolled down the back of her neck. She could blame it on the sun. Or the warmth of the car pressing against her, but both would be a lie. And she'd done enough of that for one lifetime.

It was all JP, and how he made her feel on fire with a need she couldn't fully identify. All she knew was that his eyes had darkened, and he moved in as if about to kiss her.

Danger. Danger.

Everything inside her brain screamed at her to dodge his advance. But her lips tingled, and her stomach tightened with need. Even her knees quivered, and he hadn't done anything. If this was it, her one chance to be kissed by a man who invoked this kind of desire in her, she was going to take it. Consequences be damned.

And he'd asked if she'd ever knowingly done something epically wrong. If he only knew how she was drowning in the results of her poor decisions.

He came closer and closer still, until the soft puff of his breath drifted across his face. She smelled the sugary goodness of sweet strawberries and cream.

Their eyes met.

Hannah sucked in a breath and held it.

The next thing she knew, his lips were less than an inch away, and her heart was pounding like a stampede of wild elephants. She clenched her fists to keep from reaching for him to close the distance.

At the very last second, he angled his head and pressed his lips to her cheek. They lingered, warm and soft against her skin.

"Thank you," he whispered in her ear. "You're kind of amazing."

Hannah closed her eyes, finally letting out the breath she'd held. Why did an innocent peck on the cheek from JP feel more intimate than any other kiss she'd shared? How did it reach into her and jumble her insides more than they were already twisted?

She needed to end this before one or both got hurt.

It'd be her heart to bruise or worse when he found out who she was and sent her away. For him, her actions would only compound the damage done by her sister at a time when he was discovering new and wonderful parts of himself.

And if, by some miracle, he didn't banish her from Kayla's life once her secret got out, her heart could still shatter. JP wasn't the man for her. He wasn't even the man for her right now.

She was a boring, homebody CPA who followed the rules and rarely colored outside the lines. He was a wild stallion who wouldn't be fully domesticated no matter who came into his life.

This entire situation had heartbreak written all over it, and the only way to stop it was to cut it off before she let herself get sucked in any deeper.

But did she listen to her brain's logical advice?

No.

Instead, she climbed in the car, laughed at a ridiculous story, and agreed to join him and his family for a movie night in a few days.

She was so screwed.

Chapter Fourteen

"Hey, JP!" Mickie burst through his front door without knocking like she always did. Not that he minded. She was as much family as the rest of them by this point.

"Hey, Mick. What's up?"

"Not much." She bent down to kiss his cheek. Less than a second before her lips landed, she caught sight of Kayla. "Oh, hello, sweet baby!" She changed course and beelined for Kayla, who was lying prone on a blanket with a barrage of toys around her while he worked on a laptop. Most of the toys had come from Mickie and were things JP hadn't known existed.

The baby flexed her arms and legs as though trying to swim to Mickie. A wide gummy smile transformed her face from cute to downright adorable. Until the drool came.

Ugh. The drool was out of control.

"Man, she is such a chick repellent, I can't even get a kiss on the cheek anymore," he said as he rolled his eyes.

Laughing, Mickie scooped up his daughter. "Oh, how can you say that?" She kissed a chubby cheek.

"See? The goober gets all the sugar. It used to be mine, but now I get nothing." He pouted.

Mickie smiled at him. Even after months of getting to know her, her down-to-earth personality and love of a quiet life surprised him. She'd graced movie screens across the world, earned millions upon millions of dollars, and lived in the glamorous world of an A-list movie star. Now she settled on the worn carpet with baby dribble soaking into her silk blouse and a cheesy grin on her impeccable face.

"You know," she said, letting Kayla grab onto her necklace and tug for all the little monster was worth. "I'm pretty sure if you take this smoosh out with you, you'll attract every woman within a five-mile radius. You think Kayla repels them, but I have it on good authority that women can't resist a sexy man with a cute baby." She winked one of those perfectly made-up eyes.

He snorted. "Yeah, but the minute I go to make a move, she'll have a shit explosion. Or she'll spit up all over my face. Or scream like a fucking banshee. Did you hear her last night?"

Man, the previous night had nearly killed him. After drinking an entire pot of coffee this morning, he finally felt awake enough to function at half capacity, but, fuck, this baby-raising shit wasn't for the weak. He was trying his damnedest but doubted himself at least two hundred times each day.

With a laugh, Mickie shook her head. "I don't think even this loud mouth's lungs are powerful enough to wake me across the street." Then she turned her attention back to Kayla. "Did you keep your daddy up last night? Were you singing to him all night long?"

It was still such a mind fuck to hear someone refer to him as daddy. Well, someone fully clothed and not looking for the fun kind of spanking.

"What's that?" Mickie held Kayla up to her ear. "It's all lies? Hmm. That's what I thought." She frowned at JP. "Why are you making up stories about this perfect little angel?"

"You're lucky you're so cute," he grumbled.

"Thank you," Mickie said with a smirk as she set Kayla down on her stomach.

Who the hell ever heard of something called tummy time? Apparently, it was a thing, and Kayla needed to be doing a lot of it to help develop her muscles for crawling. At least that's what the blogs claimed.

"I was referring to the baby. You are too intimidating to be cute." As Mickie burst into laughter, JP clicked a link he'd been debating opening since before Mickie distracted him. A quick perusal of the page confirmed what he'd read elsewhere. He could pursue a degree in landscape architecture online by taking either full or part-time classes.

But it'd take years. And more money than he had to spare. He shut the computer with a grunt. "Probably not worth it."

"What are you mumbling about over there?" Mickie placed a soft toy just out of Kayla's reach.

The baby stretched her chubby little arms and kicked her legs. He had to admit watching her attempt tasks and progress toward achieving them gave him a thrill. For example, yesterday she'd spent fifteen minutes trying to use a sippy cup. He'd cheered along with her gleeful squeals when she mastered the task.

"JP?"

"Sorry. What?" He tore his attention away from the little girl whose entire life was reliant on him and his ability to provide for her.

"What were you looking at on the computer?"

For the first time in his life, his face heated. Usually, he loved the spotlight. Being the life of the party, working the crowd. Now he felt like a bug under a microscope as he endured Mickie's assessing stare. "Nothing. Just looking at some options for the future, but it was probably a dumb idea anyway, so I scrapped it."

"Tell me."

"Nah, like I said, it's dumb."

"Tell me anyway. I've had plenty of dumb ideas in my day. Some of them even turned out to be amazing. Like that time I gave up my career in Hollywood to move to a small town in Vermont."

Smirking, he shook his head. Stubborn woman. "Touché."

Kayla pushed up on all fours and rocked back and forth. She'd been doing that a lot over the past few days, but fell within seconds.

And down she went with a frustrated shout.

"Come on. Lay it on me."

"Anyone ever told you you're annoying?" He asked as he shifted from the couch to the floor to join Mickie and his daughter.

Holy shit, you have a daughter.

Maybe if he reminded himself more, it'd stop freaking him the fuck out.

He tapped the carpet in front of him. "Come on, Kayla-girl. Crawl to Daddy. You can do it."

You're a Daddy. A real life father.

He closed his eyes, inhaled, then blew out slowly. When his heart steadied and he looked up, Mickie was beaming at him. "What?"

"Well, first of all, yes. Plenty of people, your brother included, have called me annoying. And second, you're a daddy!" she sing-songed.

"Jesus. If I tell you what I was looking at on the computer, will you promise to never sing *daddy* to me again?"

Mickie nodded, but he didn't believe her for a second.

"Okay, fine." What the hell. He reached behind him and grabbed the paper with his sketches. "Here."

Mickie accepted it from him, then studied it with a frown of concentration on her face.

He held his breath for the three solid minutes it took her to peruse his sketch. Had time ever ticked by so slowly? Why the hell wasn't she saying anything? Did that mean she hated it? Was she trying to think of a polite way to tell him it sucked?

"JP, what is this?" She finally glanced up with wide eyes and her mouth in an *O* shape. "Did you draw this?"

Now he was a bug under a microscope being stuck to a board by a long pin. "Uh, yeah. Just some ideas I had for the grounds of the resort."

Tucking her knees under her, Mickie shook her head. "I can't
—I didn't know you could do this. JP, it's stunning."

"Yeah, uh…" He tugged at the ends of his hair at the back of
his neck. Shit, it was time for a haircut. Beyond time. "I showed
that to Hannah the other day. She mentioned something about
landscape architecture. You know, as a potential career option."
His palms were damp, so he wiped them on his jeans. Her gaze
might as well have been a laser beam, burning a hole straight
through him. "Anyway, I was just looking into it. For fun, I
mean. Not seriously." He barked a laugh. "There are a variety of
online degrees, but they take years and cost a shit load more
than I make."

"Wow." She held the paper in one hand and gaped as though
she'd never seen him before.

"Dumb, right? I mean, how would I pull off something like
that? I'd still have to work so I could pay my bills and provide
for Hannah. Then I'd have to squeeze in time for classes. But I'd
have to make extra money to pay for the degree. And hire
someone to care for Kayla while I'm doing all this working and
schooling."

He grunted. Saying it out loud really drove home how
ludicrous the idea was. His life was complicated enough without
adding an expensive and intense education to the mix.

Mickie handed the paper back to him. "I had no idea you
were considering a formal career," she said.

He shrugged. "I'm not, really. It's just…" With a sigh, he
shrugged. "Look, I know what you all think of me. The fun one.
The irresponsible one. The one who doesn't give a shit about
anything and can't be bothered to get a real job. I don't take shit
seriously or act like an adult."

Straightening, Mickie said, "JP, we don't think that—"

He held up a hand. "Maybe, *you* don't, but Keith does. And so
do the rest of them." When she went to argue, he said, "I'm not
angry about it. I deserve it. They're right. I've enjoyed working

when I want, where I want. Not having a normal nine-to-five job is great. It gives me the freedom to do whatever the hell I want." He gestured to Kayla. "But that's all changed now whether I like it or not."

They both watched Kayla in silence as she rolled from her tummy to her back and over again. It seemed to be one of her favorite moves.

"She's real," he said. "And she's here. And she's mine to raise, apparently." He shot Mickie a self-deprecating smile. She didn't fall for his lame attempt to lighten the mood, just continued to watch him with a pensive expression. "You know we grew up with a shit father figure. One of the things I remember about him was how he never had any real employment. He flitted from job to job, earning just enough to keep himself liquored up. I can't— I won't—be anything like him as a father." Fuck, that got dark, fast. Shrugging, he added, "But whatever, there are plenty of jobs I can do without throwing money I don't have at a degree that will take years to earn."

Mickie scooted across the carpet until she was able to grab him and hug him tight. "God, I'm so proud of you, JP," she whispered. "You're stepping up for her in ways many people wouldn't. It's admirable."

"Ha. Have you already forgotten how I didn't even look at her for the first few days?"

She waved away his concern. "Eh, water under the bridge. She never has to know. And you more than earned the right to have a freak out."

As she drew back, she gripped his shoulders and stared him straight in the eye. "I'm going to say something, and I do not want you to respond with anything but, 'I'll think about it.' Okay?"

He arched an eyebrow. "Not sure I can make that promise."

"Then my lips are sealed." She made a show of mashing her lips together, then mimed locking them and throwing away the key.

JP rolled his eyes. "How the hell did you ever win an Oscar?"

"Hey!" She slapped his arm. "Just for that, I'm deciding I heard you promise." The teasing expression morphed into a serious one. "If a degree in landscape architecture is something you want, I want to pay for it."

What? His chin hit the floor. Was she out of her mind? "Mick—"

"Nope!" She mashed a finger to his lips. "All you're allowed to say is, 'I'll think about it, Mickie,'" she said, mimicking his voice. Then she smiled the charming smile that won over millions of hearts in her final drama. "JP, I have a stupid amount of money. More than anyone person deserves. You're my family now. What the hell is the point of having that money if I can't use it to help my family?" She held one of his hands between hers. "To help the people I love? You guys have given me so much. You've given me a life I love and never thought I could have. I wake up happy every single morning, and part of that is because of you."

Keith felt the same way about her, and it warmed JP's stony heart to know these two had found each other and were making it work despite initial challenges. She and Keith were perfect, and JP was so fucking happy to have her in his family, not only for his brother's sake but because she was an incredible human being. His throat thickened with emotion.

Damn, this baby was stealing his edge and making him soft.

"Please let me do this for you. Not because I feel the need to pay you back, but because I can. If I play a part in making it so you wake up happy every morning too, then I want to do that more than anything."

"Just let her do it, man. She won't give you a moment's peace until you agree."

JP glanced up to see his brother standing behind the couch with hearts practically floating out of his eyes as he watched Mickie. He rubbed a hand over his fluttering stomach. Damn, he better not be turning into some mushy romantic. That shit had to stop.

"I don't even know what to say. I never expected—shit."

Mickie squeezed his hand. "I know. And I told you what to say." She winked. "I'll try one more tactic, though. If it's too much to think I'm doing this for you, tell yourself I'm doing it for her. So you can give her the childhood I know you want to."

No one had ever made him such a selfless and generous offer. His eyes fucking itched, and if he wasn't careful, he'd start crying and put Kayla's wails to shame. To honor Mickie's generosity, he'd do what she asked and give the idea some serious consideration.

"I'm waiting," she said, cupping a hand around her ear.

He snorted. "I'll think about it, Mickie."

"Yay!" She clapped her hands as though he'd agreed to take her to Disney World instead of borrowing tens of thousands of dollars from her.

"Thank you." He lost the sarcasm and playfulness. Mickie deserved to know how much he appreciated her and the offer.

"Sweetie, you are so, so welcome." She squeezed his hand one more time, then hopped up and rushed over to play tonsil hockey with Keith.

Wait until he told Hannah. Would she be as shocked by Mickie's offer as he was? Would she be thrilled to know he couldn't get her idea of school out of his head.

Wait...

Wait until he told Hannah? Why would he tell Hannah? What the hell was he thinking? They were barely friends, barely even acquaintances. Why the hell would she care what he did with his life. And why did he itch to hop in his car and drive to her rental so he could see the look on her face when he told her?

Was this what happened when someone didn't get laid for too long? Did they start having insane thoughts about sharing feelings and news with beautiful women they hardly knew?

Gross. That was a disgustingly domestic thought.

His gaze tracked to Kayla as she once again pushed up on all fours. Maybe it wasn't Mickie's offer that had him thinking out of character. Perhaps it was the influence of the tiny human who'd turned his life ass over elbows in the blink of an eye. That had to be it. Had to be the reason Hannah had been on his mind so much. Had to be the reason he'd kissed her cheek two days ago instead of taking her sweet lips like he'd have done if she were any other woman. This baby was scrambling his brain the same way she scrambled the rest of his life, and he needed to clamp down and get a hold of himself and his wayward thoughts before he did something insane—like develop feelings for a woman.

With a sweet babble, Kayla rocked back and forth on her hands and knees a few times. Then she moved one hand forward, followed by the opposite knee.

JP straightened.

She did it again with the alternate limbs.

He held his breath.

She did it again.

"Holy shit!" he shouted, making Kayla startle and collapse onto her stomach.

"Did you see it?" He glanced up at Mickie and Keith, who were just coming up for air.

"See what?" his brother asked.

"She did it! She crawled!" Holy shit! She'd actually done it. For days she'd been doing that rocking back and forth thing without any forward progression. Once in a while, she'd tried to advance but always crashed. "Look, there she goes again!"

She was back up and moving forward. This time she made it a solid five feet before flopping.

"Oh, my God!" Mickie cheered and clapped while Keith said, "Damn, she's motoring."

JP scooped her up and lifted her into the air. Her smile and shriek of delight lit him up inside in a way he'd never experienced. When had he ever felt a warmth like this in his chest? It could only be pride. He'd created this beautiful baby girl, and now he had the privilege of watching her grow and learn to find her way through this world. Bizarre as it was, it also sent a joy like he'd never experienced rushing through him. Who knew he could take such pleasure in watching his daughter learn a new skill? He felt like she'd won a Nobel Prize.

When he hugged her close and smooched her loudly, he caught sight of Mickie wiping beneath her eyes. In such a short time, Kayla had become the heart of their entire family.

"Who is the bestest girl?" he asked as he kissed his daughter again, this time on the tip of her tiny nose as he held her up. She patted his cheeks with her hands and babbled away.

Wait until Hannah heard about this. She'd freak.

He froze.

There he went again, thinking of Hannah before anyone else.

What the hell was going on with him?

Chapter Fifteen

A chill night watching movies with a fun group of new acquaintances was exactly what Hannah needed to shake off the stress of the afternoon. She'd spent the day working with clients remotely, and one of the newer businesses she worked with had an archaic accounting system that took her hours to sort through. One pounding headache and three cups of coffee later, she'd been able to decipher their shorthand and sloppy records. Now they were set up with a cloud-based system they'd find much more efficient and organized.

She hoped.

Sometimes people who'd been running their businesses for decades refused to accept technological advances to their old-fashioned bookkeeping. Much as she hated to admit it, she understood the trepidation accompanying the new and unfamiliar. For her, it wasn't technology, but stepping outside her tiny comfort zone when it came to social situations that took a boatload of effort.

Situations like inserting herself into a close-knit family she had no business messing with.

Ugh.

A few ibuprofen killed the headache, but her back ached from hunching over the computer all day, and she hadn't fully relaxed. Hopefully a few drinks and laughs with new friends would dissolve the rest of her tension. As long as she could keep the guilt at bay.

The giddiness making her stomach flutter as she parked in the Benson sibling's driveway had nothing to do with JP and everything to do with seeing Kayla.

It was eight p.m. Kayla was most likely sleeping.

What's your next excuse?

"It's just a stupid crush," she mumbled as she stepped out of the car. "Nothing will come of it. Nothing can come of it."

"You know, talking to yourself is one of the first signs of insanity."

She glanced at the door to find Jagger standing with his arms folded across his chest and a smirk peeking through his dark beard.

"Does that mean I shouldn't mention the unicorn I saw showering in my bathroom earlier?"

He threw his head back and laughed long and loud. Like the other Benson men she'd met, he was exceedingly handsome but also had a great personality. Hannah didn't have many male friends, so hanging with a mixed group was a fun change.

"That was pretty good. You here for Ronnie?"

"Uh, no." She faltered, almost stumbling over an invisible crack in the driveway. Had JP not mentioned he'd invited her? Oh, God, what if he'd forgotten, and she looked like a needy loser showing up where no one expected her?

"JP invited me to movie night earlier in the week." He couldn't have forgotten, could he? No. He'd texted her yesterday with the time and an adorable picture of Kayla with macaroni and cheese all over her face. He'd also asked if there was a way to keep the baby from becoming a disaster zone each time he fed her, and she'd reassured him it was inevitable. Actually, he'd texted numerous times over the past few days, typically with concerns about his parenting skills. She was certainly no expert but helped as much as she could. The way he automatically assumed he was doing everything wrong hurt her heart, and she always rushed to reassure him the chaos was normal.

"Oh, sweet! Come on in." He waved her up to the front door. "Sorry. Didn't mean to make you feel unwelcome. I've had an insane work schedule this week and have barely seen JP at all. I think Kayla's been giving him a run for his money the last few days, too."

"No, you're fine," she said as she stepped into the house.

"Hannah!" Ronnie shouted. "I'm so glad you made it. Now we have an even number of girls and boys. Want a glass of wine?"

She started to say yes, but Jagger pulled Ronnie's long ponytail, making her smack his arm and Hannah laugh.

"How come when I call you a girl, I get a twenty-minute speech about being a misogynistic pig and how you're a woman? Then you go and call yourself a girl? And us boys? Doesn't that kinda make you a man-hating bit—"

Ronnie shot him a glare that could have melted an iceberg.

"Person," he finished.

Hannah giggled. This family was just so damn fun.

Don't get used to it.

Pointing the unopened wine bottle at her brother, Ronnie scowled. "Because I can say whatever I want. And you are a pig. It's that simple."

Jagger rolled his eyes before opening the refrigerator. "Well, at least you have solid logic behind your reasoning," he said as he pulled out a beer.

"Exactly," Ronnie replied, winking Hannah's way.

"You have any siblings, Hannah?" Ronnie asked. "If so, I hope they're not half as annoying as mine."

The question, innocent as it may have been, hit her like a horse kick to the stomach. It was then she realized it'd been weeks since she'd had to tell anyone about her sister's death. And now that she was, she'd be telling half-truths and twisting the story. It seemed disrespectful to the memory of her sister and the daughter she left behind.

The words wouldn't pass her lips.

"Hannah?" Ronnie said in a soft voice.

"Yeah?"

"You okay? You kinda spaced out for a second."

"Uh, yeah, sorry." Shaking her head back into the moment, Hannah found the courage to voice the painful words. "I, uh, had a sister. A little younger than me."

"Had?" Ronnie's tone held profound sadness. Even Jagger watched her with sympathy in his gaze.

"Yes. She passed away not long ago. Part of the reason I'm taking some time away from home." Not a complete lie. And growing truer by the day. She'd found being removed from the suffocating grief of her parents helped her personal healing journey.

"Shit. I am so sorry, Han. I did not realize I was stomping on a sensitive subject." She set the bottle down and walked over with her arms outstretched.

Before she knew it, Hannah found herself wrapped up in a surprisingly strong embrace. She was the worst person in the world for lying to such kind people. "Please don't feel bad," she said. "It's just hard to think about sometimes."

"All right, the baby is out cold. Let's—Hannah?" JP rushed into the kitchen. "You okay?" He turned toward Jagger with a ferocious scowl. "You do something to upset her?"

"Whoa, there, papa bear. Simmer down." Ronnie released her and went back to opening the wine.

JP took her place. He cupped Hannah's shoulders. "What's wrong."

She sniffed and shook her head. "Nothing. Really, I'm okay. Ronnie was just asking about my family, and I mentioned my sister passed away not long ago. Just kinda stirred up some painful memories."

"Shit."

Now he was the one hugging her, and as much as she'd appreciated Ronnie's kind comfort, JP's embrace brought things to a whole other level. His firm body pressed all along the length of hers. She wanted to wrap her arms around him and sink into his warmth.

"I had no idea."

His deep voice stroked over her nerve endings, igniting a tingly need she'd rarely experienced. Forget sinking into his warmth; she had the senseless urge to rip off her clothes and rub herself all over him like a cuddly cat. And beg him to do the same. What would he look like under that plain black T-shirt? More ink? Tanned skin or paler than his arms and face?

Ugh. Dangerous thoughts!

"It's okay. Just catches me by surprise sometimes."

Kind of like this foolish crush she'd developed. More than foolish—plain stupid. She didn't belong here in JP's world. Not after all the damage her family had caused. He'd never accept her as part of his life after all the lies she'd told. And he shouldn't.

JP kissed her cheek then stepped back. She tried hard not to react to the feel of his lips on her skin but failed. Her stomach quivered, and her heart fluttered with silly hope.

"Let's get you a drink," he said, voice thicker than usual.

Did her pain affect him?

No, how silly. She'd probably imagined the change in his inflection.

"Okay, no more sad talk allowed," Ronnie said as she held a glass of wine out. "Drink this. I'll keep an eye on you and refill when you're low."

"Thank you."

JP slung an arm across her shoulders. She stiffened then forced herself to relax. Her own family hadn't been overly demonstrative, and neither were her friends. This group was constantly hugging, roughhousing, kissing, and generally being affectionate with each other. While she enjoyed their vibe, it took some getting used to. With each embrace, she grew more comfortable with their demonstrative ways. By the time she returned to Colorado, she'd miss it.

And so many other things.

Mary Anne would have loved them. If she hadn't passed, would she have been the one here with the Bensons at some point? Would she have eventually sought out JP and formed a small family unit?

Her stomach lurched.

What kind of person was jealous of a nonexistent relationship their dead sister had?

Being in Vermont was messing with her head and heart.

"Yo! Where is everybody?" Keith's voice came from the den.

"Kitchen," Ronnie shouted back.

"Hey!" JP grabbed an orange off a bowl on the counter and threw it at his sister. It bounced off her shoulder.

"Ow!"

"Stop fucking shouting. Kayla's asleep."

"Oh," Jagger said with a laugh. "Daddy's gonna send you to your room if you're too loud, Ron."

"Jesus," JP mumbled under his breath before he dove for Jagger. They mock wrestled while Ronnie shook her head.

"Come on," she said as she weaved her way around her brothers. "Let's claim a seat." She looped her arm through Hannah's. "They'll be along in a few minutes."

With a final peek over her shoulder, Hannah allowed Ronnie to lead her away. By the time they reached the den, Mickie and Keith had already claimed a corner of the couch and were locked in a passionate kiss.

Hannah couldn't help but stare while Ronnie made vomiting noises. They were gorgeous together. So clearly in love and always wanting to be close.

Sigh.

"Oh, sorry," Mickie said as she pulled back. Her face turned pink, and she wiped lipstick off Keith's mouth. "Didn't hear you come in."

"Cleary," Ronnie said with a huff.

Hannah was somewhat in awe of Mickie, and not for her prior

news-worthy status. It took incredible strength to walk away from something that had such a strong hold. For Mickie, it'd been drugs, fame, and glory. For Hannah, it was her parents' expectations and the fear of causing them harm. The guilt trips and worry over her parents' wellbeing was as powerful a chain around her neck as any drug. Somehow Mickie had found the courage to walk away from her captor, and Hannah found that more admirable and inspiring than any award she'd won or the millions she'd made. Maybe someday, Hannah would be lucky enough to learn more of Mickie's story and how she changed her life.

Someday?

There she went, weaving a future where none existed.

These people weren't her friends. At least they wouldn't be when they found out who she really was. Lied to by the Briggs sisters. Tricked, deceived, and had their lives blown apart. Yeah, this close-knit family would boot her out on her rump as soon as they found out, which had to be sooner rather than later. The more time she spent with them, the more the guilt of deception ate at her. Yet on the flip side, she was so terrified of losing Kayla, she hadn't mustered the courage to confess her identity.

Her reticence had nothing to do with the way JP looked at her sometimes.

The way he was looking at her now as he stood in the opening to the den. As though he wanted her.

Nothing to do with that.

Liar.

Her damn conscience had always been overactive. Hence the reason she'd shown up in Vermont in the first place. Her parents were masters of the guilt trip.

"Move your ass, Ron. That's my spot," JP said as he strode into the room. He had a beer in one hand and a bowl full of chips in the other.

"No way. I was here first. Get your own seat."

"Suit yourself." He plopped down right onto Ronnie's lap.

The cushion next to Hannah sagged with the weight of two grown adults, sending her careening into the siblings.

"Jesus, get the fuck off me," Ronnie said as she shoved JP's back.

Hannah giggled then pushed off the ridiculous pair.

"Ahh." JP wiggled around as though settling in for the long haul.

"All right, you can have the damn seat. Just get your bony ass off me. You're such a child. Like, seriously, did your brain stop maturing at thirteen?" Ronnie gave him one last push, which had him hopping off her. She grabbed her wine glass, stood, then stuck her tongue out at him before taking a seat in an overstuffed chair.

Barking out a laugh, JP sat down. "Cuz you're a prime example of adulthood."

Ronnie flipped him off.

Hannah watched, enraptured as always by the banter between them.

"Are you sick of our shit yet, Hannah?" Keith asked. Of all of them, he was the one who intimidated her the most. A perpetual scowl lived on his bearded face unless Mickie was in touching distance. Then he softened, but only towards her. To the rest of the world, at least in Hannah's opinion, he had a resting growly face. But beneath the mug, he'd been as kind as the rest of them.

"I'm good," she said with a smile. "I love hanging out with you guys. You're a ton of fun."

"Don't take this the wrong way, but there's a chance you need to get out more."

They had no idea. "Fair enough."

"Hey, I'm shit loads of fun." JP stretched his arm across the back of the couch then tucked her into his side. No one seemed to find the move surprising.

Well, no one but her. She had no idea how to react to such a touchy-feely person. As she sat there, stiff as a board, she peeked at each of the Benson's faces. None of them paid her any attention. They all continued to rib each other and joke as though it was normal to see JP snuggling on the couch with a woman.

Maybe it was.

God, she hadn't even considered that. Clearly, he left her in the dust when it came to experience with the opposite sex. Was she sitting there analyzing his every touch, every thought, every smile when this was just another Saturday night for him?

And she'd started to think she was special.

"You good?" he whispered as Jagger walked into the room and claimed the last chair.

Hannah smiled and forced herself to relax against him. "Perfect."

He squeezed her shoulder. "Great." Then he called to Ronnie. "We gonna watch this shit or what?"

"Keep your pants on, I'm getting it," Ronnie shot back as she scrolled through the streaming channel. They argued back and forth, finally settling on a popular slasher movie.

Concentrating on the cheesy movie was almost impossible, though she seemed to be the only one struggling. The rest of the group laughed, commented on the dialogue, and asked Mickie questions about the actors. Hannah couldn't focus on anything beyond the feel of JP's body against hers.

Once she'd let her tension bleed away, she practically melted into him. His lean muscles made the perfect cushion. Warm, cozy, and supportive. Her eyes grew heavy, and her head began to droop from the ultimate comfort. The combination of an attractive man and two glasses of wine had her fighting to stay awake. If she were smart, she'd make her excuses and leave before she embarrassed herself by passing out on him.

But he felt so good. Too good. She found it physically impossible to move away.

"Rest your head on me if you're tired," JP whispered about halfway through the movie. He gently pressed her head to his chest.

She went willingly, nearly purring when she settled against him.

She'd leave soon. And she'd tell him who she was. This madness had to stop.

Tomorrow. She'd tell him tomorrow.

For now, she'd enjoy a few more minutes of being close to this man. At least she'd have this sweet memory to call upon once she was back in her apartment in Colorado.

All alone.

Chapter Sixteen

The low sound of Kayla's fussing pulled JP from a deep, restorative sleep. He rubbed his eyes and sighed. In a matter of seconds, those frustrated grunts and occasional whimpers would turn into full-on screaming as his little piggy of a daughter demanded her midnight meal.

But, damn, he didn't want to get up. This was the most comfortable he'd been in ages, and he owed it all to—

JP's eyes popped open.

Shit.

He was in the living room slouched on the couch with his bare feet on the coffee table. Someone had killed the overhead lights but left a nightlight glowing near the entrance to the kitchen. After tripping over Jagger's shoes on her way in from work late one night, Ronnie had purchased the nightlight.

Based on Kayla being awake, he guessed it was somewhere around two in the morning, which meant the movie ended *hours* ago.

He glanced down at the reason he felt so much more cozy than usual. Hannah lay with her feet curled under her and her head on his chest, snoozing away. Hopefully, she wouldn't have a crick in her neck from hours of napping in an awkward position.

Kayla's cries grew in volume, indicating she was reaching her limit. Thankfully his siblings never gave him grief for her nocturnal singing routine. He'd read that babies her age could sleep through the night without eating, but she attacked the bottle with almost ravenous hunger, so cutting it out might have to wait a bit.

"Hannah, honey, I need you to wake up," he said as he gently shook her shoulder. If she felt this good draped all over him on the couch, he could only imagine how amazing she'd feel naked and under him in bed.

"Hannah?"

"Hmm?" She shifted then blinked a few times.

JP knew the second she realized where she was because she shot up and gasped.

"Oh, my God. I fell asleep." She rubbed a hand over her face. "I'm so sorry. How embarrassing." She scrambled to her feet and began searching around the dark floor. "Where the heck is my purse?" she mumbled.

"Hey." JP grabbed her hands. "Please don't be embarrassed. I didn't mind at all. In fact, I kinda loved it. The only reason I woke up is that Kayla is singing the song of her people."

"What? Oh, she's crying." She blinked then glanced toward the hallway with longing in her gaze. "Go see to her. I can let myself out."

Maybe this made him a shameless asshole, but he didn't want her to leave and wasn't above using the only weapon he knew would keep her around a little longer. "Wanna come with me? Give her a bottle? You didn't get to see her tonight."

The way she lit with pleasure twisted him up inside. Hannah wasn't like the women he usually hung around with. She was sweet, genuinely kind, and didn't play games. Since, typically, he only ever wanted a fun time and a few orgasms, he wasn't picky about personality or character.

Hell, half the time, he barely knew the women's names. Not in a sleazy way. Everyone knew the score, but what the hell was the point of memorizing someone's name when they'd be in and out of his life in an hour or two?

"Um, I'd love that. Yes, please."

"Ok." Her eager reaction gave him pause. Maybe he shouldn't be encouraging her to help with Kayla. It wasn't as if he planned to date Hannah and find a mom for Kayla. Is that how she'd interpret a night like this? Was she there with the hopes of snagging a ready-made family? One look at her happy smile had him chasing away those ridiculous thoughts. Hannah wasn't the type to play games. She was honest and sweet.

"Why don't you grab her while I get the bottle ready? You know where her room is?"

"Yeah, I got her dressed after her bath the other day. Remember?"

He grinned. "I do." They locked eyes. Something passed between them. An electricity that was a combination of desire and a budding friendship. Though there was a good chance he was the only one experiencing it. Lack of sleep and stress had been fucking with his brain.

Kayla let out a godawful screech, making him wince and breaking the spell.

"I'd better go get that bottle before she shatters the windows."

With a nod, Hannah dashed down the hallway.

After not staring at her ass while she hurried off, he made his way to the kitchen to prepare a bottle. Aside from his daughter's wails, the house was quiet. Keith and Mickie had most likely retired to her house. Ronnie was probably asleep and who knew about Jagger. Work had been rough for him lately, so he might be asleep as well.

By the time he'd grabbed a clean bottle and stuck it under the formula maker, Kayla had quieted. He worked quickly, shaking the prepared bottle as he made his way toward his daughter's room. When he arrived, he froze at the door, struck immobile by the sight that greeted him.

Hannah sat in the rocking chair Mickie had purchased. She didn't notice his arrival as she rocked back and forth with Kayla in her arms, humming the same song she'd sung Kayla a few days ago. Soft light glowed from the nightlight, casting a hypnotic glow over the room.

JP swallowed as unfamiliar emotions bombarded him. The scene was entirely too domestic for him, yet he couldn't tear his gaze away. The serene smile on Hannah's face mesmerized him. Kayla, too, if the way she stared at Hannah without blinking was any indication.

"Oh, I didn't realize you were there," Hannah whispered.

He grinned. "Just watching you two beautiful ladies."

The room was too dim to tell, but he'd bet a hundred bucks Hannah blushed.

"Here." He handed the bottle to her.

"Thank you." She took the bottle then laughed as Kayla practically ripped it from her hands to get it in her mouth. "Somebody's hungry, huh?"

"Yeah, the kid can eat, that's for sure. If I had any lingering doubts about whether she was mine, her appetite put an end to them." He pushed a button on the music box Jagger had purchased. A soft lullaby filled the air.

"Ha. I'm pretty sure you took one look at her and knew. She has the exact same hair and eye color as you. Same nose too. Not blond like—" She coughed. "Uh, like some babies."

"Yeah. Both my parents had dark hair. All us kids, too. We have two other brothers. Not sure if you knew that. Both are in the military and overseas right now. They're all dark-haired, too."

"Yeah, I noticed in the pictures in the den."

They fell quiet with only the sounds of Kayla's eating and instrumental playing of Rock-a-bye Baby in the background. Oddly enough, he didn't feel the need to talk. Didn't feel like he had to make jokes or provide a fun, jovial time. He was perfectly content to sit there in silence while Hannah fed and rocked his daughter back to sleep.

Was this what real families did? Did parents get up together in the wee hours of the morning and marvel at the wonder of the life they created?

His sure hadn't. According to his siblings, his mother had done it all while their father drank himself stupid every night. Thank God, the man was in prison and out of their lives for the next eighteen months. Would he be able to keep himself from becoming the horrendous father he'd had? He sure as hell planned to try.

Would a partner help? Would having someone like Hannah by his side make that easier? Or would he destroy her and his child the way his father had? He'd never been willing to take the risk with a woman, and after years of flitting from bed to bed, he wasn't sure he could be monogamous.

"You can't be comfortable down there," Hannah said after a few moments, tearing him away from his confounding thoughts.

"I'm good." Too good. "So, I mentioned what we talked about the other day to Mickie."

"Oh yeah? About your ideas for the rentals?"

He nodded. Nerves skittered through his stomach. He fucking hated that feeling. Putting himself out there, making himself vulnerable to criticism or ridicule. But Hannah hadn't done either of those things when he showed her his ideas.

"Yeah, and the idea of getting a degree in landscape architecture."

Hannah beamed. "What did she say?"

"She was blown away by my ideas."

"Ah, I knew she would be. See! I'm so glad you showed her." Her genuine happiness was contagious, and he found himself smiling along with her.

"She also offered to pay for the degree."

Hannah gasped. "JP, that's incredible. Wow. Will you take her up on it?"

After shrugging, he drew his knees up and wrapped his arms around his legs. "Dunno yet. There's a lot to consider. More than just the money. Plus, I'm not comfortable taking that much from her. I'd feel like I'd owe her forever."

"Hmm. I could see that, and I'd probably feel the same way, but Mickie seems like a woman who knows her mind. I don't think she'd make the offer if she didn't mean it or really want to help out."

He chuckled. "That's pretty much exactly what she said."

"See? She's very smart." She glanced down at Kayla, who'd almost finished the entire bottle. "So, what are you thinking?"

With a sigh, he shook his head. "I'm starting to think I want it. It's a little overwhelming, though. So much is changing in such a short time. My head is spinning a bit."

"Well, you hide it well. You seem calm and like you're handling all of this with no problem."

He grunted. "I'm not usually one to freak out, but trust me, I'm stressed." He should get up and take Kayla from her so she could head home. But instead, he kept talking. She was easy to talk to, and he just didn't want to be out of her presence yet. Why? Who the hell knew? He hadn't even kissed the woman, for Christ's sake. All he knew was that she listened, didn't judge, and made him feel...important.

"So, I called a guy I know who is a landscape architect and asked if I could meet him for coffee tomorrow to ask some questions."

"JP, that's a great idea!"

"Yeah, well, I might have to cancel. Mickie was going to watch Kayla, but she forgot she had an appointment."

"I'll do it!" Hannah practically shouted. Then, with a wince, she glanced down at Kayla. "Sorry, sweet girl," she whispered. "I'd love to watch her for you. I have nothing going on tomorrow."

"I couldn't ask—"

"Please let me. I enjoy spending time with her. If you're nervous about me—"

"No," he said with a shake of his head. "That's not it. I guess I was looking at Mickie canceling as some kind of sign I'm not meant to move forward with this."

"Nah, that's just fear talking."

"Fear?" He raised an eyebrow.

Hannah laughed. "Yes, JP. Men can have fears. Even big, strong men covered in sexy tattoos."

The rocking chair stopped moving, and her mouth moved without sound as though shocked by her own words. So she thought his tattoos were sexy.

Good to know.

It took every remaining ounce of energy he had—which admittedly wasn't much since he was exhausted—to keep from jumping on her slipup and asking for more details. All the details. Which ones did she think were the sexiest? Did she want to see the ones hidden under his shirt? Touch them? Lick them, perhaps?

He shifted as his interested cock protested his curled-up position.

Hannah cleared her throat. "Anyway, the offer is on the table. I'll hang with Kayla as long as you need."

"Thank you. I think I'll take you up on it. Shouldn't be more than a few hours. I'm meeting him at five tomorrow evening."

"Perfect. I'll be here at four-thirty so you can show me where everything is." She peered down at Kayla with a smile.

Though she probably made the same sweet expression at all babies, he'd swear she gazed at Kayla with love in her eyes.

"I think she's asleep. And I should probably go get some sleep as well."

Asking her to stay was on the tip of his tongue, but he bit it off. No woman had ever slept in his bed. Ever. Hell, he rarely even brought a woman home to fuck—only if there weren't any other viable options. With how many of his siblings lived there, someone was always ready to ask questions or be annoying as hell to a "guest."

No, he'd see Hannah to the door and wish her a goodnight like a proper gentleman. Then he'd head to his bed to rub one out before his balls got so blue, they up and died from lack of blood flow.

The thought had him shivering.

Seriously, when had he gone so long without sex? Had to be more than a decade. By the time he got laid again, he'd forget how it worked.

"I'll put her down." He rose from the floor then made his way to the rocking chair. As Hannah handed the sleeping baby over, her arms brushed the length of his. Electricity skittered across his skin.

Christ, maybe he just needed to fuck her and get it over with. He'd been holding back both because of Kayla but also the confounding feelings Hannah stirred up in him. But maybe all those feelings only arose because it'd been weeks since he'd touched a woman. With anyone else, once he'd had them a time or two, he lost interest. That's what he needed here. To fuck her out of his system as was his typical MO. His cock certainly liked that idea.

He turned from her and laid Kayla down in her crib on her back. At some point, she'd roll to her stomach, but he'd read the morbid statistics on SIDS and it'd terrified him, so he was careful to always set her on her back.

When he turned back, Hannah was no longer behind him. After a final peek at Kayla, he shut her door and made his way back to the den. Hannah stood near the door with her shoes on, and purse slung over her shoulder. Well, there went his chance for an orgasm. At least one not provided by his hand. Asking his siblings to watch Kayla so he could go out and hook up felt shady, even for him.

"Thanks for letting me stick around and feed Kayla. I loved it," she said in a low voice. Her blond hair seemed to glow in the low light of the den. "I guess I'll see you tomorrow?"

JP was struck with an almost overwhelming urge to touch her. To taste her. Even if only this one time. He strode forward, nearly cheering at the way her eyes flared when he got close. It wasn't fear. Uncertainty, maybe, but definitely interest.

He cupped her face between his hands. She immediately grabbed his wrists but didn't push him away. She held on instead. "JP," she whispered as she sucked in a breath.

God, those lips. Those pink, unglossed lips that had been tempting him for days. Fuck it. He deserved a taste for being such a damn gentleman around her.

She let him pull her close until their mouths met. Christ, she was as soft as she looked. Hannah gasped, and he took full advantage, sneaking his tongue between her lips. Sweet wine and a hint of chocolate hit his tastebuds and overwhelmed his senses.

Her grip on his wrists tightened as though to keep him in place. They explored each other in a kiss unlike any other. This wasn't a prelude to ripping each other's clothes off for a quickie. They had time. No one would interrupt them. So they each took it.

He played with her, teasing his tongue against hers then darting away, so she had to give chase. He nipped her lips with gentle brushes of his teeth, and he tasted every corner of her mouth.

Delicious wasn't strong enough a word to describe her flavor; intoxicating was more accurate. He felt drunk off her yet craved more. His skin tingled, and sparks of pleasure zinged along his nerve endings. His cock filled and ached with a fierce desire to get in on the action, but he kept his hips apart from hers and enjoyed this for what it was.

A first kiss.

Maybe an only kiss.

Hannah let out a small mewl of pleasure, maybe frustration, then moved closer. She pressed against him, torso to torso, and he lost the ability to keep from grinding his cock into her soft stomach. She squeaked but didn't pull away. Instead, the kiss grew hungrier until they were all but devouring each other.

Her blunt nails dug into the tender skin of his wrists, but he didn't give a fuck. He'd wear her brand with pride. Hell, maybe he'd get those crescent gouges tattooed into his skin to remind him of the hottest kiss of his life.

They writhed against each other, still making out like it was their last night on earth. Hannah pushed her hips forward and up, the perfect move to stroke directly over his cock. He groaned into her mouth, and she did it again.

Shit. He had to put a stop to this. If he didn't, he'd have her stripped and on her back in the foyer before she knew what hit her. Though they hadn't spoken about it, and as hot as their kisses were, he had a feeling Hannah wasn't prepared to sleep with him tonight.

With a heroic show of strength, he ripped his mouth away and tugged his wrist free of her grasp. He stepped back, needing to physically separate himself from her, or he'd dive back in for another taste.

Hannah stood there, chest heaving, pupils blown, and lips swollen from his mouth. Her face had a gorgeous pink glow to it.

They should probably talk about this. About how he just changed the nature of their relationship with one kiss. Well, more than one, but one impulsive decision on his part. But instead of dissecting every move, complicating things further, or possibly screwing up the best night he'd had in ages, he smiled.

"Have a good night, Hannah."

Still wide-eyed and shocked, she nodded as she pressed a hand to her lips.

Hopefully, her shock didn't outweigh the pleasure. Hopefully, she wouldn't get in her car, bang her head against the steering wheel and regret kissing him. Hopefully, she'd come back tomorrow.

Then she gave him a soft, yet satisfied grin. "Goodnight, JP," she said, then turned and slipped out the front door.

He watched her as she got in her car and drove away. After shutting the door, he sagged against it.

Damn, that had been a kiss like no other. Would he get a shot at a second? Or third? Reason tried to work its way into his mind. Emotion threatened to cloud his thinking, but he shoved both away.

Tonight had been fun in a way he hadn't expected and never wanted, but it'd been fantastic all the same. Laughing with his family and Hannah, sharing the late-night tasks of caring for Kayla with another person, opening up about his future, kissing a woman he couldn't stop thinking about. So many simple pleasures he'd never allowed himself but feared he'd want again and again.

What did any of it mean? Was he beginning to think in terms of a relationship? Admitting he wanted Hannah was the easy part. Confessing to wanting more than just her body terrified him. There were so many ways it could end in utter disaster for her. For him. For Kayla.

With a heavy sigh, he shoved the deep thoughts from his weary mind. He deserved at least the rest of the night to enjoy the taste and feel of Hannah before reality, logic, or feelings blew it all up.

Chapter Seventeen

"Hey, man, thanks for meeting up with me," JP said as he extended a hand to a buddy he ran across from time to time while working with Jagger's contracting company.

"JP! How's it going, brother?" Mark stood from the table and grabbed JP's hand, giving it a hearty shake. "Been a minute."

"Yeah, it has. I'm doing well. How about you?"

"Good, good." Mark sat and pointed to the empty chair. "Wife's pregnant with our fourth, so life's good, man." He grinned like the happy father and husband he'd been since he got married to his high school sweetheart two months after graduation.

At the time, JP thought he was batshit crazy for locking his shit down at such an early age. He vividly remembered hearing when they'd gotten pregnant with their third and how fucking relieved he'd been not to walk in Mark's shoes.

Life was a funny bitch.

"Congrats," he said with a grin. "Happy for you, man." And he meant it. With a new perspective on parenthood came the realization that he might have been a bit of an uncongratulatory ass to his friends who already had children.

"Congrats?" Mark raised an eyebrow and pursed his lips. "Pretty sure the last time I told you we were having a kid, you said I better get a vasectomy this time, so I don't keep making 'crotch goblins.'"

Ouch. "Yeah, about that…"

"What?" Mark asked, cocking his head.

A waitress came to their table with a perky smile and even perkier tits. Her bright smile, short skirt, and gleam of interest in her eye would have had JP jacking the charm up to full blast, but he placed his order, and that was that.

"Okay," Mark said when after ordering a coffee and snack for himself. "What the hell is going on? First, you congratulate me on the pregnancy, then you don't flirt with the hot waitress who stripped you bare with her eyes and practically begged you to ask her out."

JP scratched the stubble he hadn't bothered to shave that morning. He'd planned to shave, but Kayla had a different idea. She'd fussed for hours, turning the volume up to ear-splitting every time he set her down. His new best friend, Google, suggested it could be teething. By the time he'd given her a chilled teething toy to chomp on, he'd completely forgotten about his unkempt appearance.

"So, um, turns out, I've got a kid."

If he'd told Mark he was an alien from planet lightyears away, his friend couldn't have had a more shocked reaction.

Mark's jaw dropped, and he blinked. "Wh—I'm sorry, I think my head just exploded. Wanna tell me that again?"

"I'm a father," JP said with a straight face.

Mark ran a hand down his face then looked over his shoulder. "This is a joke, right? Some kinda prank you're pulling to get your sick jollies? Is someone gonna pop out with a camera? You, Mr. kids-suck-and-I'll-die-before-having-them has a child? No fucking way. Not buying it."

JP bristled even though he deserved the reaction. "Yes, fucking way, and you're gonna feel like a douche when I tell you about it."

Lifting his hands in surrender, Mark sat back in his chair. "All right. I'll pretend to believe you. Give me the details."

The waitress dropped their coffees off. If she noticed the

heavy blanket that settled over JP, she pretended not to. Instead, she winked and practically snapped her spine, arching her back so her tits were on display. Unfortunately for her, JP's body and brain were a total fucking shit show now. The only things that had been able to get him hard over the past few days were thoughts of Hannah, smelling Hannah, dreams of Hannah, and now the memory of how goddammed sweet she tasted.

"Not many details, really. Met a girl at a concert, fucked her in her car, knocked her up. She didn't tell me. Then she had a baby and died a short time ago. Now I am a single father to a seven-month-old infant."

With each word out of his mouth, Mark's eyes grew wider. "Ho-ly shit," he said once JP finished talking. "That is a lot, man."

JP grunted. "Yeah, you're telling me." He sipped his coffee. Hot and strong. The only thing keeping him awake these days.

"How're you handling it?"

How was he handling it? Who the fuck knew? "Better now than the first few days. I kinda freaked. Checked out. But we're working our way through it, one bungle at a time."

With a laugh, Mark nodded. "Just like every first-time parent out there."

"Really?"

"Uh, yeah. You think just because we planned on our children that we have any idea what the fuck we're doing?" After sipping his coffee, Mark chuckled. "Hell, no. We try our best and hope we don't kill them or fuck them up too bad. That's about it as far as parenthood."

Ridiculous as the advice was, it made JP feel better than any suggestions he'd read or been told. Knowing he wasn't alone in feeling as though he was dangling off the edge of a cliff by one weakening fingertip helped lessen the angst he'd been living with since Kayla came into his life. There were countless ways he could break her or ruin her life, and he always felt as though he were one wrong decision away from doing just that.

"Thanks, Mark. You have no idea how good it is to hear that. You've always seemed like such a natural with your kids. Like they came out with a step-by-step instruction guide you memorized in a day."

"Don't I wish?" With a snort, Mark shook his head. "Fuck, no. I was on morning duty yesterday. I sent our youngest to preschool with her dress on backward, her shoes on the wrong feet, and her teeth unbrushed. Getting three kids ready for school in the morning is no joke. I also burned my arm on the toaster, then yelled 'fucking piece of shit' which, apparently, Mark Jr. repeated in his kindergarten class when he tripped over a block. Needless to say, I'm pretty sure I lost my shot at father of the year."

Laughter burst from deep in JP's gut. "Damn, that's rough. But I gotta admit it makes me feel better hearing it. I keep wondering when someone is gonna turn me in for having no fucking clue what I'm doing."

Mark waved a hand. "Nah, you're good, man. You got this shit."

"Thanks." Not that he fully believed it, but this conversation bolstered his confidence in his parenting skills. "Anyway, that's not why I asked to meet with you. Well, it's related, but now that I've got Kayla in my life, I've been thinking I need to get serious about my career."

"Look at you, growing up before my eyes." Mark lifted his napkin and dabbed the corner of his eye.

"Fucker," JP said.

"Kidding. What can I do for you?"

"I'm thinking, well seriously considering, shooting for a degree in landscape architecture. Wanted to pick your brain about it for a bit."

"Yes!" Mark slapped the tabletop. "Dude, you'd be amazing at it. I told you that years ago."

"You did." And JP had rebelled at the thought of college or a steady job that ate up his days and tied him down.

But life was different now. His world no longer revolved around him but around a fifteen-pound, cute-as-hell potato.

"All right, let's do this." Mark rubbed his hands together then launched into a detailed description of life as a landscape architect. He covered everything from schooling to day-to-day work life, and even starting his own company. JP hung on every word, taking notes when necessary.

If his siblings could see him then. Taking life more seriously than he ever had before. They'd flip their shit if he went to school. They'd probably tease him until he changed his mind and dropped out.

By the time they finished chatting, and Mark had answered a whole slew of JP's questions, it was almost seven o'clock. He said goodbye to Mark and promised to make plans soon so he and his wife could meet Kayla.

Just as JP climbed into his car, his phone chimed with a text. As soon as he saw Hannah's name, the goofiest grin spread across his face.

Ugh, what the hell was wrong with him? Why did the sight of her name have hearts floating from his eyes?

He opened the text to find a selfie of Hannah and Kayla. Hannah smiled at the camera while his daughter shoved a little fistful of food into her mouth.

Your daughter can eat as much mac-n-cheese as an adult man.

That had him chuckling. Not only was Hannah beautiful, but she had a fantastic personality and sense of humor as well. Being more reserved than him didn't mean she wasn't as fun. She just went about it in a less obvious way.

He glanced back at the photo. Kayla had food spread out all over her highchair tray.

"What the…" He brought the phone closer to his face. "What the hell is that?" After zooming in, he began to chuckle, but it soon turned into a full-on belly laugh. "Oh, my God."

What the hell did you feed her?

Three dots appeared, then disappeared, then reappeared a few times before Hannah's text came through.

Mac-n-cheese. I thought you said it was okay. Oh, God, did I screw up?

He couldn't control his laughter now. This would go down as one of his favorite stories, and he couldn't wait to tell his siblings. Hannah was enough of a friend by now to be teased mercilessly by them.

Take a closer look at the box.

Her response did nothing to help him stop cracking up.

Oh nooo! I fed your baby penises. I'm never going to be allowed around children again for as long as I live.

Tears streamed down his cheeks as he laughed so hard his stomach cramped.

Without responding, he put the car in gear and sped home, beyond eager to see both his girls.

HANNAH STARED IN horror at the food spread out across Kayla's tray. Not only had she made a box of Mac-a-weenie and cheese without realizing the pasta was shaped like penises, but she'd fed it to an infant. Then sent pictures to the father.

Had she ever been more mortified?

Nope. That was a very quick and easy no.

She'd be lucky if JP didn't call the cops and have her arrested for child endangerment.

Kayla grabbed up another fistful of the pasta with her uncoordinated grip.

"Oh, no, baby, no! Don't eat any more of that!" Hannah squealed just before it got to the baby's mouth. Her shriek startled Kayla so bad, she dropped the food and began to cry.

What was worse? Taking food from a hungry baby or feeding one penis-shaped pasta?

"Okay, here you go. I'm sorry." She took a step back and let Kayla resume her meal. She'd already eaten most of it. What was a little more?

JP hadn't responded to her last text. Should she apologize or wait until he came home?

Was he mad?

Ugh.

Her shoulders slumped as she dropped into the seat next to Kayla's highchair. The baby gave her a gummy, cheesy smile. "Pretty sure your daddy's gonna kill me."

Maybe this was for the best. If she ruined this friendship with her stupid mistake, at least she wouldn't spend another night pining away for a man, she shouldn't have ever allowed to kiss her.

A man she sure as hell shouldn't have kissed back.

And rubbed herself against.

Could this day get any worse?

She pulled out her phone and stared at the picture she'd taken of her and Kayla. How on earth had she not picked up on what the pasta was shaped like? Now that she knew, it was glaringly obvious.

After setting the phone down, she folded her arms on the table and dropped her head onto them. Kayla giggled.

"You think that's funny?" She picked her head up, then let it fall again, this time with a little more flourish.

Kayla giggled again, so Hannah repeated the action. By the time she'd done it at least seven times, Kayla's laugh had become so loud and infectious, Hannah laughed right along with her.

And that's how JP found them. Giggling in the kitchen like a pair of loons.

He cleared his throat, making Hannah jolt so hard, she nearly toppled off her chair. Kayla squealed and held out her arms to him.

It filled her heart to capacity to see how much Kayla had taken to her daddy, yet at the same time, an equal amount of sadness crushed her because she wasn't an actual part of their life here. This was all a fantasy. A wonderful reprieve from her empty life.

Something she now wanted but could never have. She couldn't help but wonder if things would be different had she come to Vermont in a different manner. Would she be here enjoying JP and Kayla if she'd been honest from the start? Or would he have sent her back to Colorado without the opportunity to get to know him or her niece?

And which fate would have been worse?

JP walked straight to Kayla, picked her up, and blew a loud raspberry on her cheek. Of course, Kayla started giggling all over again.

Her heart squeezed.

He settled the baby on his hip and turned to face Hannah.

With a wince, she asked, "How mad are you?" She held her breath.

Laughing, he shook his head. "Not mad at all. I laughed so hard I think I gave myself a hernia."

Air rushed out of her lungs. "Really? I figured you'd be furious."

"Why? It's pasta, and Kayla has no idea what the hell shapes are."

Well, when he put it like that…

"You may have a point."

"Of course, I do." He winked. "Now, let's get this cheesy monster cleaned up and ready for bed."

Together they gave Kayla a quick bath, got her in her jammies, then JP fed her a bottle. It was a simple, routine kind of night, but Hannah had more fun than she would have had on a fancy date with any other man. Not that this was a date.

Kayla passed out before finishing her bottle, making bedtime a snap. Hannah watched from a spot on the floor as JP laid the baby in on her back in her crib. After she was settled, he straightened and turned toward Hannah.

"Done with dad duty for the day. Now it's time for fun. Come here," he said as he crooked a finger at her. His voice dropped lower, almost gravelly, and his eyes smoldered, making his intentions perfectly clear.

If she went to him, he'd kiss her again.

So she was staying right where she was. No matter how much she wanted it.

Muscles acting of their own accord made her rise to her feet. Then they took control of her legs and walked her straight to him.

When she reached him, he gave her a half grin that shouldn't have been as sexy as it was. With his tattoos and that smirk, he looked like every guy her mother warned her off her entire life.

"I didn't ask if I could kiss you last night. Today, I'm trying to be a gentleman." The pitter-patter of her runaway heart nearly drowned out his voice. Still smirking, he bent down until only a millimeter separated them.

"May I kiss you, Hannah?" he whispered just a breath away from her lips.

No, no! Say no!

Now was the perfect time to set boundaries. Establish this was only friendship. Take a step back.

But, no, her head moved up and down in a nod her brain hadn't approved. She didn't try to stop him, though. Despite all the logical, smart reasons allowing anything physical between them was a terrible idea, she wanted it. She wanted it more than she wanted to appease her family, more than she wanted to make a wise choice, and more than she wanted to keep being the responsible sibling.

So, she looked him in those heated, mesmerizing eyes and let herself be wild for once, "Please," she whispered.

And then he was kissing her, and she couldn't have drummed up a single intelligent reason to resist if she tried.

Chapter Eighteen

This wasn't Hannah's first kiss. Not by a long shot. Sure, she hadn't had dozens of boyfriends and no random hookups or one-night stands, but she'd been kissed. Or at least she'd thought she had. Friendly kisses, exploratory kisses, even some passionate, frenzied kisses. But never had she experienced this scorching heat suffusing her from the tips of her toes to the roots of her hair. As though her entire body erupted in flames the moment their mouths met. And only one thing could extinguish the burn.

More JP.

Her skin prickled with the need to have his hands on her, and the man didn't disappoint. He hauled her as close as she could possibly get with their clothing between them, then slid his hands under her shirt. As soon as those large, rough palms coasted over her back, electricity blazed across every surface of her skin.

She shivered as waves of energy pulsed from beneath his fingers.

"God," he whispered against her lip once they came up for air. "You taste so fucking good."

She tasted good? Kissing him was like tasting the sun, so hot it scorched, yet she couldn't get enough. Instead of answering, she reached up, threaded her fingers through his hair, and pulled him back down to her. A split-second before their lips crashed together again, she flexed her fingers against his scalp, loving the way the strands of hair felt between her fingers. His eyes rolled back.

"Fuuuck," he whispered.

Hannah smiled that secret, proud smile she imagined all women smiled when they made a man like JP moan in pleasure.

With his mouth still firmly attached to hers, he walked them out of Kayla's room and down the hallway. At one point, her back met the wall, and JP took full advantage of the position.

He pulled her hands from his hair and held them against the wall at her sides.

Unable to use her hands, she arched into him. The hard ridge of his erection pressed into her core.

They both groaned at the same time before JP jerked his lower half away. "Too good," he mumbled. "Can't have you doing that just yet, or I might come in my pants like I did that one time I was fourteen."

She giggled, but it quickly morphed into a low moan as his lips found a sensitive crevice on her neck.

"Oooh, a sweet spot," he said as he sucked right where he'd made her tremble seconds before.

Her knees buckled, she gripped his hands so tightly her knuckles ached, and she canted her head to the left to give him all the access to that spot he wanted.

"Greedy," he muttered on a chuckle.

"Mmm."

He kissed up the side of her neck, leaving a trail of goosebumps. When he reached her jaw, he nipped, making her yelp. The barrage of new sensations overwhelmed her. She'd stepped, no jumped, so far out of her neat box of rules and caution, she wasn't sure she'd ever find her way back inside.

She turned her head, and their eyes met. Her breath caught in her throat at the brazen lust staring at her. Having an experienced, sexy man like JP want her was a thrill like no other. Before she knew it, they were kissing once again.

That look in his eyes made her confidence soar. She might not have a fraction of his experience, but he didn't seem to care about that at all.

Before long, the restraint of her hands grew maddening. Wriggling, she tried to pry free of his grip, but he held her firm. "Please," she ground out on a frustrated sigh.

He gave her a smirk that made her thighs quiver. "Please, what?"

"I want to touch you, too."

"Long as you don't complain if I shoot off like it's my first time." He grinned like a sly fox.

First time. God, he had no idea it was hers—if sex was where they were headed. And she was pretty sure it was. Would she hold up to his expectations? Could she dare hope to live up to his previous experiences?

He released her, and she shoved her hands under his shirt, needing to feel the warmth residing there. His stomach was flat, with ridges of muscle. Not a six-pack—he was too lean for that—but the man still had visible strength.

"Jesus," he bit out as she stroked her hands all over his abdomen and chest. "I need you fucking horizontal, now." He kissed her once, twice, hell they made out against the wall before he grabbed her hand and led her down the stairs to his room.

She hadn't been there before and would have stopped to soak in JP's space at any other time. But right then, she was too needy for more of his heated skin.

"On the bed," he said. "Clothes on. I want to peel them off you."

That confirmed where the night was heading. For the first time, a zing of trepidation ran through her. How far was she willing to take this? As Hannah, the twenty-five-year-old virgin, or Hannah, the sister of Kayla's mother and the woman lying to JP? Either way, she needed to put an end to this no matter how far down this rabbit hole she'd already fallen.

Stopping now might kill her, and not only because her body

was dying to feel him inside her. To have this incredible man be her first. But because she felt a connection to him that she hadn't had before. Physical, yes, but something more. Something deeper.

Something terrifying and exhilarating at the same time.

Something so wrong given their circumstance.

He's Kayla's father. Think of Mary Anne. Think of your family.

And there it was. Typical Hannah voice of reason cutting through her bold actions and reining her back in.

As she opened her mouth to slow things down, way down, JP grabbed the back of his T-shirt and yanked it over his head.

Hannah's mouth dried up.

Reason once again fell straight out of her head.

She gawked at the man as though he were a prized animal at the zoo.

JP's lips quirked. He dropped the shirt at his feet and strolled over to her as slow as could be while fingering the button on his jeans. "I take it you approve?"

Nodding, Hannah licked her lips. Ink covered his chest and stomach. Not so much that she couldn't see the tanned skin of his nearly hairless chest, but enough for her eyes to feast on and her hands long to explore.

He was so different than any man she'd spent time with. So much so, she felt as though the guys of her past had been mere boys.

JP was all sexy, mouthwatering man. But he was also fun and kind and deeper than anyone gave him credit for.

He was also off-limits. But she'd already crossed a million lines and couldn't bring herself to stop from charging past this final one. She stood on the edge of a cliff, and if she jumped, that was it. Her world would change once again. There was no climbing back up the rock face she was about to fling herself from.

Guilt over the mountain of lies she rested on threatened to destroy the moment, but even that wasn't strong enough to stop her. She wanted him too much.

"I tend to render most women speechless," he said with a wink.

Hannah laughed. Leave it to JP to bring the levity while she was battling an internal war between her conscience and her body.

"I've just never..." She waved a hand at him. How did she even describe what he did to her?

"Never seen someone so sexy? So fucking impressive? So perfect?" The smirk remained, and he arched an eyebrow.

Hannah smiled. God, this man was everything she wasn't. Amusing, lighthearted, snarky. The fun to her typical responsibility. It was liberating and terrifying all at the same time.

"Yes," she said as she closed the distance between them. "All of those things." She lifted her hands to a particularly intricate tattoo of a bird soaring on his chest. A hawk, maybe? "Can I?" she asked before touching it.

He nodded. "If you don't, I might beg."

She ran her fingertips lightly over the gorgeous inkwork. His muscles danced beneath her fingers as though responding to her touch. Being able to affect him with nothing but the tips of her fingers had her dying to know how else she could make his body respond. An exhilarating power flashed through her. One she wanted to explore until she made him beg.

"Feels so damn good," he whispered.

"It's beautiful," she whispered back. "What does it mean?"

He tilted his head and watched her with dark eyes. "How do you know it means anything? Maybe I just like birds?"

Shaking her head, she said, "No. It's too perfect. And over your heart. That's a special place."

He swallowed as though struggling to decide if he should share with her. Though they were no longer groping each other, this quiet moment of conversation didn't lessen her desire in the least. In fact, it only made her want him more. There was something so intimate about standing in his dimly lit room, running her hands over him while they spoke. The anticipation of what was to come hung heavier in the air, but she no longer felt rushed. They had time. All night.

They did not need to hurry, especially if this was to be one of her only—maybe the only—night with him.

"This was my first tattoo. It took more than one sitting, but I got it as soon as Keith bought this house. We all moved in and out of the double-wide we lived in with our piece of shit father. I was underage but had a friend whose older brother was a tattoo artist. He knew my family and the shit our dad put us through. It's a falcon soaring and symbolizes freedom. No chains holding me down. No more abuse, no more bullshit. Freedom."

She frowned. No relationship. No permanent job. No desire for children. All the things he'd claimed to want before Kayla.

Pieces of JP were falling into place, and instead of scaring her away with his truth, he drew her in even more. Because this man who valued his freedom above all was adapting his entire life to raise his daughter. It wasn't easy, and she knew he struggled, but he did it. Did he even realize how wonderful that made him?

Her parents would look at his past and lose their minds. They'd worry themselves sick, fearing he'd repeat the vicious pattern of his father. But she only saw his devotion to Kayla and willingness to step up to the plate as strengths of his character.

"I've never had that," she whispered, giving him a piece of her soul. "I envy you that freedom. But I admire you so much for giving it up for Kayla." She'd lived in an invisible prison created by her adherence to her rigid parents' desires, whereas he'd chosen his own way. Yet their paths had merged, bringing them both to this point. Bonded by deception, obligation, and family loyalty.

But she couldn't tell him any of those things. Not without destroying the moment. So she flattened her hands on his chest, lifted onto her toes, offered him her mouth, and tried to ignore her conscience.

He met her halfway with a kiss that reached into her very soul. Sweeter than the others, she reveled in the light, almost reverent kiss. The tenderness didn't last too long, thank God. It made her think dangerous thoughts about futures and promises. Impossible dreams.

She wasn't sure which of them ramped it up. It could have been either of them. She felt too raw, sitting on her mountain of lies, to allow such softness from him. She didn't deserve it. Keeping this hungry and turbulent was far safer.

He groaned into her mouth and guided her to his queen-sized bed. When her legs hit the mattress, she broke the kiss and scooted on her back toward the center of the headboard. He followed, crawling over to her.

Hannah swallowed. This was it.

JP grabbed the edges of her shirt and lifted. She sat up, allowing him to remove her top. For a moment, she stared at him as he stared at her breasts encased in a simple magenta push-up bra. Her heart raced. She hadn't been this vulnerable with a man in a very long time and had barely gone beyond this point.

"Damn," he whispered.

If she hadn't known better, she'd almost believe he hadn't slept with many, many women. His expression, his tone. It all came across as so sincere. As though he was truly awed by her body when he probably said the same to every woman he'd been with. She'd be smart to remember that.

Though it all muddied in her head the second he bent forward and kissed the swell of one breast.

Hannah gasped and fell back onto his pillows. He moved with her, pressing his weight onto her. She wanted to cry at the delicious feeling of his body lined up along hers, but she barely had time to process the new sensation before he added another to the mix.

With a low growl, he shoved her bra up and off her breasts. Cool air hit her nipples, puckering them instantly. Or maybe it was the deep desire coiling her belling that made them bead up and ache like never before.

"I want to taste every inch of you," he said in a voice she'd not yet heard from him—rough, gravelly, full of need.

For her.

His mouth closed around one nipple, pulling it with a hot, wet suction that curled her toes.

She grabbed for his head, catching his hair in her hands. While she'd meant to push him away to give herself a moment to catch her breath, she held him closer instead. He used his tongue to play with her nipple until she had to bite her tongue to keep from crying out. Then his fingers went to the other breast, treating that nipple to pinching and little tugs that had her squirming beneath him.

"JP," she finally said on a gasp when the tension in her grew too tight.

He chuckled as he lifted his head.

She'd done a number on his hair. It stuck out in all directions. His mouth had a shiny glow to it and a smug smirk.

Keeping his gaze on hers, he kissed a slow, torturous trail down her stomach. It quivered beneath his lips. Every kiss wound her insides tighter with anticipation.

Hannah clenched her fists at her sides then squeaked when he tongued her belly button. New sensations bombarded her from all angles. She tried to rein in her response and get her brain to kick in. With each kiss, he drew closer to her leggings and an experience she'd never had. He'd been so incredible, she owed him the truth before he found out in an awkward way.

Part of her worried he'd call it quits, and she'd be forced to drive back to her rental frustrated and humiliated. Still, she needed to reveal her secret.

Well, one of them.

I'm a virgin.

Say it.

Tell him.

I'm a virgin.

He reached for her waist band with a wicked gleam in his eye. "You have any idea how many times I've jacked myself off to thoughts of this moment since I've met you?"

Oh, God.

Tell him!

"Mary Anne was my sister!"

Hannah stopped breathing.

JP froze with the tips of his fingers curled into her pants. His expression reflected utter shock, then morphed into disbelief, and finally fury.

No. Those were not the words that fell from her mouth. They couldn't be.

But his face told her all she needed to know.

She'd said it.

And she'd ruined everything.

Her chance at a bond with her niece.

Her parents' shot at a relationship with their granddaughter.

Her friendship with the Bensons.

Her chances of ever touching JP again.

Chapter Nineteen

What the fuck just happened?

How did he go from worried about busting a nut too early to the second biggest shock of his life in a matter of seconds?

JP's body flushed hot, then so cold he had to fight from breaking out in a storm of violent shivers.

"What the fuck did you say?" he asked as he withdrew his hands from where he'd been about to yank her pants down and taste her in a whole new way.

He had to have heard wrong. There was no fucking way.

Hannah sighed a defeated sound. She sagged into his pillows and gazed up at him with deep sadness in those pretty eyes.

"I'm so sorry," she said, making his stomach dive. "I didn't mean to blurt it out like that. I just…I was feeling so much, and then the guilt took over, and—"

Screw her guilt. "Say it again. Fucking tell me again." How the hell was he managing a calm, even voice?

She swallowed. "M-Mary Anne is, *was*, my younger sister."

"Mary Anne," he said as the gravity of her statement worked its way under his skin. "The woman who tricked me into knocking her up then didn't bother to tell me she had my kid before she up and died, leaving me a single father to a baby I didn't know existed. That Mary Anne?"

She flinched at his cold description of her death, but at that moment, he didn't care. Twice, these women had tricked him.

"Y-yes," she said with a tremor vibrating her voice.

Still straddling her, he gaped down at her, trying to reconcile the information and deception with the woman he'd been spending time with. She'd been lying to him. Every fucking second of every fucking day.

"Was this all a big game to you? Have you been part of it from the beginning?" He ran a hand through his hair, gripping the strands hard to ground himself as he felt the world spiral out yet again. "Did you all have a good laugh at the stupid chump whose sperm she used for her selfish purposes?"

Hannah's eyes widened in horror. "No!" She folded her arms over her chest, hiding her naked breasts from his view. She needn't have bothered.

There was no way in hell he'd touch her again.

"No, JP, not at all. I had no idea what she was planning until she found out she was pregnant. Then she broke down and told me the whole story."

A grunt was all he could manage. How the hell could he trust a word out of her lying mouth now? The one and only time he'd opened up and given a woman more than just his cock, and she'd been lying to him the entire time. He was a stupid fool.

"Can, um, can I please have my top?" She reached around him but couldn't grab it.

"What the fuck are you doing here? Why the lies? What's your angle?" Her comfort wasn't his high priority right then. Understanding why he'd been chosen for this nightmare was. Figuring out what she wanted from him and Kayla.

And getting rid of her.

Suddenly, he couldn't stand being so close to her. Still touching her. She represented everything wrong with this fucked up situation. The fabrications, the tricks, the confusion, the disbelief. All the feelings he'd been working to process and move past since Kayla dropped into his life came roaring back with a vengeance.

How could he have been fooled so easily twice? He hadn't

protected his daughter from the first liar that came their way. How could he be trusted to keep her safe from other threats and dangers? His chest tightened, and fingers tingled in the familiar warning signs.

He sprang off the bed as though burned by her naked skin.

Hannah scrambled to sit, then fished around for her discarded shirt. While he paced his room, she jerked the top over her head. Once in place, she drew her knees up to her chest and wrapped her arms around her legs as her eyes tracked his agitated movements.

"I begged her to tell you," Hannah eventually whispered in a tiny voice. "Before she had Kayla, and then after. I begged her every single day. Even when she was too weak to h-hold a phone."

He stopped walking and stood at the foot of the bed, staring at her. "Is that supposed to sway me? Is that sad little hitch in your voice when you talk about your dead sister supposed to make me feel like an asshole for getting angry at you? For fucking hating you and her?"

She recoiled as though he'd smacked her, but aside from glassy eyes and a trembling lower lip, she didn't lose her cool. "No," she whispered. "Not at all. I'm just trying to explain. To be honest with you."

He refused to allow the genuine devastation in her expression to make him feel guilty. She was the bad guy here, not him.

With a snort, he resumed prowling the room. Somehow, he had to expel the troubled energy flowing through him, and it was either pace or punch a hole in the damn wall. "Honest? That's rich."

"She showed me who you were on social media. You and your family." A tragic smile curled her lips. "She loved you guys. Thought you were so great. So different from our family." Her throat worked as she swallowed. "Uh, she knew…" Hannah blew out a breath. "She knew her prognosis wasn't good. And as she got sicker and w-weaker she knew she wasn't going to be around long…"

A single tear rolled down her right cheek. Even wrecked, she was so damn pretty. JP stared at a spot on the headboard six inches above her head. He was the wronged party here. No way would he allow her tears to sway him. Even if they made his chest ache.

"Um, as she got sicker, I tried, JP, I really tried to get her to contact you or allow me to. At the very end, I took care of Mary Anne, and my parents were taking care of Kayla. We were all just trying to make it through the day. There was so much pain and sadness. So much heartache. And then there was Kayla. One bright shining spot in all the anguish. Despite the lies and sadness, she's perfect."

She pressed a hand over her heart. Tears flowed in rivers down her face now. He'd die before admitting her story tugged at his heart. Imagining Hannah tending to her ailing sister and a new baby, giving up her own life, well, it fit with the woman he thought he knew.

But he'd been wrong. Hannah was as much a liar as her sister.

"I'm sorry," she whispered. "I love my niece, and I'm sorry I couldn't convince Mary Anne to tell you."

Her niece. Jesus. Kayla was Hannah's niece. If that wasn't a mind fuck, he didn't know what was. What the hell would his siblings think? They'd be as disgusted as him.

The weight of reality became too heavy on his shoulders. He sat on the edge of the bed, cradling his head in his hands much as he had after reading Mary Anne's letter.

"Why are you here?"

When she didn't answer right away, he turned his head and let his gaze bore into her. She still sat huddled in as small a package as she could compact herself. Her lower lip rested between her teeth, and her face had a sickly pallor to it. Whatever she was about to say, he wasn't going to like it.

"Why?'

"My parents—" The words came out strangled and barely

audible. Hannah cleared her throat. "My parents are struggling with Mary Anne's death. Um, more than I think is healthy." She tugged at a loose string on her leggings, staring at it as though it had the power to whisk her away from this conversation. "They're overprotective. In a bit of a pathological way." She shook her head. "I'm sorry. I'm not making sense."

No shit.

"There's just so much in my head right now." With a heavy sigh, she lifted her gaze to his. "Might as well tell you all of it. When my mom was sixteen, she and her cousin snuck out of their house in the middle of the night. They wanted to go for a midnight drive to meet some boys. Her cousin was driving. About halfway there, a drunk driver hit them head-on. My mom tried to save her cousin but couldn't get either of them out of the car. She almost died, and her cousin did die. When they cut the car open with the jaws of life, they found my mom wrapped around her cousin, sobbing. I'm convinced she never processed that trauma properly, and it became the compass for the rest of her life.

"Then my parents spent over a decade trying to conceive a child. Mom suffered multiple miscarriages before they finally gave up. Mary Anne and I were both adopted, which is why we didn't look alike. After all she suffered and lost, our mom was constantly afraid of something happening to Mary Anne or me. Or even our father. We were locked in a cage made of our mom's fear, guilt, and anxiety. We had so many rules and were kept on the shortest leash imaginable. Mary Anne pushed back a little, but I always followed every rule." She gave him a sheepish, half-smile.

He tried hard not to care. Tried not to imagine a lonely and compliant Hannah missing out on life's experiences because of her mother's neurosis.

"Uh, anyway, despite spending her entire life trying to minimize all risk and avoid disaster or loss, her youngest daughter not only got pregnant out of wedlock, but she died young of a disease completely out of my mother's control. Afterward, she turned all her focus to Kayla, and when she found out that Mary Anne listed you on the birth certificate and granted you full custody in her will, she broke."

Much as he tried to harden his heart, the damn thing had softened in the short time he'd had Kayla. His bicep twitched as he imagined gathering Hannah up in his arms and promising everything would be okay.

A beautiful fantasy, but not a wise one. He still didn't understand why she'd been lying since she arrived. Why not tell him who she was? "That sounds extremely shitty, but, Hannah, what does that have to do with the lies? I'm not going to bar them from her life. I wouldn't have kicked you out. Any of you. I'm not a monster. If you'd wanted to see her, spend time with her, you only had to ask."

An agonized sob left her lips as her legs flopped to the bed. She dropped her head to her hands and wept.

JP clenched his jaw. This woman and her lies, her tricks, and games—shit, he'd been about to have sex with her—she was not the victim here.

She lifted her head, staring him straight in the face with ravaged eyes. Her bleak expression had his blood running cold. "They wanted me to come here to find dirt on you and your family so they could petition for custody. They planned to say that Mary Anne wasn't in her right mind at the end and that you aren't fit to be her father. They have an attorney ready to file a petition for custody as soon as they have solid evidence against you."

Ice filled his veins.

He couldn't possibly have heard correctly. "Excuse me?" he asked in a lethal tone as he rose to his feet then backed away from the bed. "You're here to try to take my daughter?"

The one good thing to come out of this conversation was the complete realization of how much he loved Kayla. The thought of someone taking her was as painful as a knife to the gut.

"You're here to take my daughter." The words ripped a deep hole in him as he realized Kayla wasn't the only one he'd become attached to. Hannah had slipped past his decades-old defenses and wormed her way inside, only to set off a bomb in his chest. It hurt his heart and his head to know he'd been played by a convincing vixen with malicious intent.

"No!" she cried, shooting to her knees. "I told them no. I refused. I saw your family on social media, JP, and I thought they were wonderful. Now I know firsthand just how wonderful you all are. I told my parents I wouldn't do it." She shook her head and held out her arms as though pleading with him to understand.

Too bad.

"They begged so hard. My family is a disaster right now. My mom is broken, and I don't know how to fix her. She refuses to get help. And my dad is just lost. He blindly follows her lead no matter how toxic." She grabbed his hand with both of hers. "I told them I would come here to check on Kayla and hopefully ease their minds that she's in a loving home, but I wouldn't try to take her from you. I wouldn't. You have to believe me."

He blocked out the desperation in her voice and jerked out of her hold. "Why? Why the hell would I believe you? All you've done since you've been here is lie. All your sister did was lie. I don't have to believe a goddammed word that comes out of your deceitful mouth."

"JP," she said, reaching for him again.

He lifted his hands out of her reach as he backed away. The sounds of Kayla crying came over the baby monitor and made him jump. Shit, had his yelling awakened her?

Another thing to hate Hannah for.

"You need to get the hell out of my house and the hell out of our lives."

"No," she cried, large tears cascading down her cheeks. "You can't mean that."

"Go back home and tell your parents you failed. Kayla and I

never want to see your face again."

With that, he left her there crying on his bed to jog up to his daughter's room.

How many ways could one man be taken for a fool?

Tricked into getting a woman pregnant. Check.

Shocked to within an inch of his life to find out he had a seven-month-old daughter. Check.

Deceived by his daughter's aunt who might or might not be trying to take his child away. Check.

And the worst of all…

Spending all his free time thinking about a woman who was out to con him. Check.

This was why he steered clear of relationships altogether. People fucked each other over if given an inch of leeway.

Well, screw it all. He had his siblings, he had Mickie, and he had Kayla.

He didn't need anyone else.

Chapter Twenty

Hannah couldn't bring herself to leave Vermont.

Four days, an embarrassing amount of ice cream, a shameful number of wine bottles, and countless hours spent staring, unseeing, at the TV screen, and she still hadn't left her rental house.

Why? Who the hell knew? After four days of no contact from JP or any of the Bensons, Mickie included, she should have gotten the message. They didn't want anything to do with her.

Big surprise there. What had she expected? Open acceptance and understanding of her lies and all the ways her family had wronged his? She sure as hell wouldn't have opened her arms to someone who'd caused so much turmoil to her family.

"Ugh," she said aloud to the textured white ceiling. "It's time to go home." The thought of it had her stomach roiling. Not only had she been deep in pity-party mode since her confession to JP, but she'd also dodged every call from her parents. And there had been multiple attempts to contact her. Voicemails, texts, missed FaceTime calls. They'd have made everything that happened about them, and she just hadn't been able to deal with them on top of everything else.

With a groan, she sat up and ran a hand through the rat's nest that had formed on top of her head. Shit, when had she last taken a shower?

Time to stop feeling sorry for herself. This was exactly what she'd known would happen and what she deserved. She knew JP would ban her from Kayla's life once he'd found out the truth. The man was a good father who protected his family from scheming liars.

There was one consequence she hadn't expected, though. How deep she was mourning the loss of JP in her life along with Kayla. Heck, all the Bensons had become important to her in a short period, but JP was special. He'd gotten under her skin in a way no man had before. He'd also been close to getting under her clothes in a way no man had before him, but she refused to let herself dwell on that.

Too depressing.

And frustrating.

Along with the ice cream and wine, she'd spent a startling amount of time with her vibrator recently. Hence the refusal to think about JP shirtless. Or JP touching her. Or JP kissing her.

It was a new resolution. One she was failing at because now she was all hot and bothered again.

"You're pathetic," she mumbled. "Put on your big girl panties and move on with your life."

She grabbed her phone and rang her parents' house before she could talk herself out of it again. As far as she knew, they were the only people alive who still had a landline in their house.

"Hannah? Oh, my God, you're alive!" Her mother's frantic voice filled her ear.

Hannah rolled her eyes as an image of her mom standing in her kitchen clutching the phone to her ear popped into her mind. "Hey, Mom. Yes, I am just fine."

"Oh, I'm so glad you called. Your father is the only reason I haven't called the police to file a missing person report."

The drama!

"For God's sake, Mom." Thankfully, her father had a modicum of sense. "I texted twice and told you I'd be out of touch for a few days." Not that her texts had stopped her mother from calling at least ten times over the past four days.

"Yes, honey, but how did I know it was really you texting? You could have been kidnapped and forced to type that."

Because that often happened to twenty-five-year-old women in rural Vermont. Same worries, different day. Hannah endured these inflated fears from her mom her entire life. Every time she missed a phone call, she was presumed kidnapped by her mother. Didn't matter if she was in the middle of a final exam, at a doctor's appointment, or on a date. It was exhausting. "I'm fine, Mom. Just had a rough couple of days."

"Those Bensons, right? I knew it. You can tell me, honey. We'll figure it out together. We'll work out a way to get Kayla home to us where she belongs."

Pinching the bridge of her nose, Hannah squeezed her eyes shut. "Mom, is Dad around?" He needed to be on the line as well to keep her mother from going off the deep end when she caught them up to date on what had happened between her and JP.

"No. He ran to the hardware store. But he's been gone a while. I'm getting worried." Her mom's voice shook with the truth of her words.

Poor guy was probably sitting in the parking lot, enjoying a few moments of solitude.

"Well, how about I call back later when he's home and fill you both in then?"

"No!" Her mom screamed into the phone as though Hannah had just ripped Kayla from her arms and ran off with her. "Tell me now, Hannah. Please tell me now." She started to cry. "That baby belongs with us. Not with that trash. Please, it's what your sister wanted."

Wow. This was going to go over even worse than she'd expected. Mary Anne wanted JP to raise their daughter, hence putting him on the birth certificate and explicitly stating so in her will. No way would she say that to her mom, though. It never failed to send her into a rage.

What now? Hang up or keep talking? Screw it, might as well get it over with. There wasn't any point in sugar-coating it. She'd learned when it came to her mother, giving the information in a neutral tone without excitement or emotion was best. Dealing with the fallout in the same unaffected manner worked as well. Or, at least, worked better. If Hannah cried and let her mom know how destroyed she felt inside, it would only fuel the drama to come.

After clearing her throat and straightening her spine as though that would steel her against the impending outburst, she said, "Mom, I told JP who I am. I told him I'm Kayla's aunt."

Crickets.

"Mom?"

"Hannah Lauren, this better be some kind of sick joke."

Rubbing a hand across her forehead, Hannah said, "No, Mom. It was time. Things got…complicated. They are an incredible family who love Kayla and take wonderful care of her. Lying to them isn't right." It had never been right.

"He is covered in tattoos, Hannah."

"Yes, Mom, I know. And you know that doesn't speak anything to his character at all. It's ink on his body." She picked at a stray thread on the comforter. It was either that or pull her hair out.

A disbelieving sniff met her ears.

"Kayla's grandfather is in jail."

"I know, Mom. It has nothing to do with JP or any of them. I'm pretty sure he doesn't know about Kayla's existence."

"And that sleazy actress Scarlett has influence over my grandbaby," she said as though Mickie was the devil instead of a thinking, feeling woman.

Same drama, different day.

"Her name is Michaela, Mom, but everyone calls her Mickie. And you'd like her if you gave her a chance. She has worked extremely hard to turn her life around. She's down-to-earth, warm, and loves Kayla to pieces. Mickie is nothing like what you see of Scarlett in the media."

Another sniff or maybe more of a snort of derision. "Please

don't tell me you're falling in with these people. Don't break my heart like that, Hannah. They took my grandbaby."

"Mom, you know that's not tru—"

"I will not let them take you, too. My heart cannot take another tragedy."

Because becoming friendly with the other side of her niece's family would be tragic? Her mother's performance was getting out of control. The theatrics had been compounding since Mary Anne revealed her diagnosis.

Now came the part that made Hannah apprehensive. "Listen, Mom, what I'm about to tell you might be a little difficult to hear. I think it'd be best if we wait until Dad is there with you." Someone to absorb the blow and provide the comfort and attention her mom would require.

"I know you're an adult, but I'm still your mother, and you will treat me as such. Tell me now."

Her head began to throb between her eyes. Coffee would have been a smart idea before this conversation, but then she'd made plenty of stupid decisions lately, what was one more?

"All right, as I expected, the Bensons were extremely upset to find out I'd been lying to them. JP is rightfully worried about our intentions toward Kayla. I—"

"Good. Let him worry. He should be worried. I will be the one to raise that baby no matter what I must do. I'll call our attorney as soon as we're done. Wait, why aren't you with her right now? You need to be around her as much as possible, Hannah. You're the only one I trust to keep her safe." The tears were gone, and her mom's voice hit the high notes she reached when frantic.

Hannah closed her eyes. "Mom, they kicked me out of their house and won't let me see Kayla right now. I'm sure, with time, they'll—"

"What?" her mother screeched so loud Hannah yanked the phone from her ear with a wince. Her mother railed and wept. "Something bad is going to happen to her, Hannah. I can feel it. Please go back. Please go back to her."

"I can't do that, Mom. I have no right to be there. Nothing bad is going to happen. You have to stop worrying." Advice she'd given thousands, maybe tens of thousands, of times throughout her life. "She's perfectly safe and well cared for. They are good people. I'm hopeful that after the dust settles, they'll let us spend time with Kayla."

"Spend time? Spend time?" her mom repeated, louder each time. "They do not get to decide that, Hannah. She is *my* granddaughter. My deceased daughter gave birth to her, and I should be raising her. I've lost so much already." Her outrage turned back to sadness, and she began to sob in a near-violent manner. "I can't handle anyone else leaving me, Hannah. It hurts so bad."

Her heart sank. She understood the all-consuming pain of missing Kayla and Mary Anne. all too well. "I know, Mom. I know." And there was the reason Hannah had never distanced herself from her mother even when she knew it'd be healthier for both of them. Whatever untreated mental illness her mother was suffering from, she was doing just that, suffering. Experiencing very real pain.

And it killed Hannah to witness it. Even more to know she had a part in causing it.

"Have you given any more thought to talking to someone? It helped me so much while Mary Anne was sick and right after she died. Maybe—"

"I am not crazy, Hannah."

"I know that." She hesitated. They'd gone this far, they might as well keep pushing. "I don't think you're crazy, but I do think you're sick."

Silence.

"It's nothing to be ashamed of," she rushed on. "There are so many treatments. So many ways for you to feel better and live a happy life."

"Live a happy life?" her mom said in an incredulous tone. "My youngest daughter died a few months ago. My grandbaby has been stolen from me. And my oldest daughter betrayed me."

Hannah's shoulders slumped as hope for a positive outcome to this conversation disappeared.

"How am I supposed to be happy, huh? Answer that."

She opened her mouth to tell her mom that she wasn't the one to ask. That professionals spent years of their life learning to balance different therapies and come up with an answer to that heavy question. But her mom beat her to it.

"You're not welcome at home until you have my granddaughter in your arms. That's a promise."

What? After all, she'd done for them? Taking care of Mary Anne, helping with Kayla, traveling to Vermont, and lying to a man she liked very much? This was how her mom thanked her? Anger bubbled in her veins. "Your house isn't my home anymore, Mom. I've lived on my own for years."

"Then you can continue to be on your own because you aren't allowed in my house until I know Kayla is away from the Bensons and safe with me. It is the only way I can be sure nothing bad will happen to her."

As much as her mom's words cut into her heart, Hannah couldn't resist one last chance to bring reality to this conversation. "Mom, bad things can happen no matter how hard we try to protect the ones we love. There are no guarantees in life. Look at what happened to Ma—"

"Don't you dare say her name to me right now," her mother spit out. "You dishonor her memory, allowing her daughter to remain with those animals. They are disgusting, and if you can't see that, then I don't want to see you! I need to call our lawyer."

The line went dead.

Mouth agape, Hannah stared at her phone.

"What the?" She put it back to her ear. Yep, her mother had hung up on her. No matter the circumstance, her mother never left in anger. Her deep-rooted fear of her loved ones dying wouldn't allow her to walk away from an argument before a resolution had been reached.

"You don't want ugly words to be the last thing you say to someone you love." How many times had Hannah heard that throughout the years? Hundreds, if not more.

But she'd apparently upset her mother so badly, she'd forsaken her favorite rule.

Hannah glanced around the quiet bedroom.

No sister. No parents. No Kayla. No Bensons.

No JP.

Her mother obsessed over everyone she'd lost. That obsession ran her life, yet Hannah was the one sitting all alone in a rented house while everyone she cared about pulled away from her. She had no one to turn to, nowhere to go and nothing to do.

She dropped the phone to the bed then covered her face with her hands as the hot tears she'd been holding off for four days finally burst free. Maybe she should have stayed safely locked up in her lonely box instead of taking a risk and letting herself get close to JP. At least then, she wouldn't have gotten a glimpse of what she was missing out on.

Chapter Twenty-One

A light tap on the door had JP glancing up from where he sat on the floor with Kayla. Since his daughter had crawled for the first time, life exploded into a new phase of gates and babyproofing.

She'd gone from inching three feet forward to cruising around the entire house with the speed of a NASCAR driver in a matter of days. The first time she'd wonked herself on a piece of furniture, JP had a heart attack and bought out the entire stock of babyproofing supplies at the local Walmart.

For now, she was content to sit in one spot and play with the laces on his shoes while he applied for college courses online. Anything to keep his hands and mind busy and away from thoughts of Hannah.

"Hey, Jagger. You need something?" he asked his brother.

"Nah, bro. Just checking in to see how you're holding up?"

"I'm great." The lie slipped off his tongue too easily.

Jagger shot him a disbelieving look then switched his focus to Kayla.

"And how is my niece? The cutest baby in the world." Jag moved in and scooped her up. She squealed as he hoisted her in the air then brought her to his massive chest. Jag had the bushiest beard of all the Benson men, and Kayla couldn't get enough of tugging on the thing. Thankfully, Jagger was also the most mild-mannered and handled it like a champ. JP knew from experience how fun it was to pry little fingers from his hair. "Did you work with Keith today?" Jag asked.

"Yeah," JP answered, as he saved the application and closed the laptop. "Ronnie and Mickie split the day taking care of the princess." He settled back and smiled at the sight of his brother and his daughter. Exhausted as he was—Kayla had been a little fussier than usual since he got home—he found himself feeling more satisfied than he'd ever expected.

Unless his mind drifted to thoughts of Hannah, then he felt nothing but anger, betrayal, and frustration.

Fine, he also felt loss. He'd convinced himself what he was feeling was merely lust, yet he found himself missing her at the most random times of the day. Hell, they barely knew each other, but he'd come to enjoy spending time with her more than almost anyone. Had to be more than lust because he hadn't fucked her yet. If he had, he'd be over this stupid crush on the woman who lied her ass off for weeks. He glanced at his daughter in Jagger's arms. Did she notice the change? Could she be missing Hannah, and did that account for some of the crankiness?

Probably not. Most likely, he was projecting his complex feelings on the munchkin.

A yawn took him by surprise, cracking his jaw and making his eyes water.

"Shit, JP, you look wrecked. Why don't I hang with Kayla until bedtime? I'll get her down for you, and you can try to hit the sack early."

Shaking his head, JP reached out and bopped Kayla on the nose. She gave him a one-toothed grin then went back to trying to tear Jagger's beard off. "Nah. I got it. My responsibility."

With a frown, Jagger gave him one of those big-brother glares Keith was known for.

"Dude!" JP said with an exaggerated shudder. "Stop looking at me like that. It's way too Papa Keith."

Over Kayla's head, so she couldn't see, Jagger flipped him off, making JP laugh.

"Seriously, JP, you are doing an amazing job with her. None of us are questioning your devotion or how much you love her. But this shit is hard, and you're exhausted. Take the help where we offer it. Promise we don't think you're shirking your duties."

JP scratched his chin. He could really use a long, hot shower, a good shave, and a solid eight-hour sleep. Though that last one wasn't likely to happen with the way she'd been fussing on and off all evening.

"All right. Thanks, Jag."

Grinning, Jagger climbed to his feet with Kayla secure in his arms. "My pleasure. It's never a hardship to have a date with such a beautiful lady." He blew a raspberry into Kayla's neck, setting her off on a fit of baby giggles. Jagger laughed. "That seriously the best sound ever."

"I know," JP said, still sitting on the floor. It'd probably take him a few minutes to work up the motivation to move.

"You talk to her at all?"

The *her* didn't need further clarification. With a murderous glare for his brother, JP shook his head. "I knew there was a fucking catch."

Jag raised his free hand. "No catch. Just checking in. You guys seemed to get close fast. No one would fault you for missing her or wanting to call her."

Fuck. "We're really going there?"

Jag shrugged. Kayla yawned then settled her chubby cheek against her uncle's chest. JP noticed she loved to cuddle like that, all snuggled up to his or his siblings' chests. He liked to think it was because she found their heartbeats soothing under her ear, but who knew?

He sighed then let his head drop back on his bed. "Fine. I liked the woman. A lot."

"You bang her?"

He scowled, and Jagger laughed.

"Shit. You really did like her, huh?"

Embodying an angsty teen, JP shrugged. "Whatever."

"Eloquent, brother." Jag swayed back and forth, rubbing a

hand over Kayla's back. Her eyes began to droop.

"I don't know what you want me to say, Jagger. This entire situation has been fucked up from the moment I found out I was a father. Did I like the woman? Yes. A lot. So much that I'm finding it nearly impossible to stop thinking about her. Okay. But do I know what the hell any of that means? No. Beyond that fact that it fucking hurt to find out she was lying to me, I don't know a damn thing. I'm just trying to make it through each day without losing my mind or having someone call CPS on me."

"Jesus, JP, why haven't you mentioned any of this before. Brother, no one is calling CPS. You're doing a fu—" He eyed Kayla. "Freakin' amazing job right now."

"Can't stop swearing around her," he grumbled.

Jagger chuckled. "Yeah, well, she doesn't know what the hell you're saying, so it's all good."

Sighing, JP watched his daughter fail in her attempt to fight sleep. Her cheeks were a little flushed, but he'd read that can happen with teething, along with the fussiness. "I don't, Jag. I feel like I'm living someone else's life right now. It's all still so surreal."

"I'm sure it is. Gotta say, though, I love this uncle thing. Look what a natural I am." His teeth shone white through his beard.

"You're like her personal teddy bear."

"I don't know. I'm sure it's easy for me to say since I'm not her parent, but so far, I think it's been damn special having a little Benson crawling around here. I know you've been thrown in the deep end, but you're keeping your head above water pretty well. I'm impressed and proud of you." He held up a hand as JP opened his mouth. "Please don't think I'm being condescending. Lotta people wouldn't have stepped up to the plate like you did."

Well, shit. Normally, he'd make a joke or shy away from the heavy conversations, but he'd already changed most of his life, might as well work on his emotional maturity as well. Wasn't often someone said they were proud of him. Felt nice. "Yeah, well, a lotta people don't have the support I do. You guys are pretty amazing."

"We are, aren't we?" Jagger asked with a wink, making JP laugh. "Last thing, then I'll go get this one ready for bed so you can have some peace. It's like you said, this whole situation was fu—uh, fracked up from the start. So maybe cut her some slack. She lost her sister, had her niece go from living with her to across the country, and it sounds like her family is a hot mess right now. Not to minimize what you're going through but remember you're not the only one affected by the decisions Mary Anne made. Maybe she's just trying to slog through it the best she can. Just like you."

He kissed the top of Kayla's head then nodded at JP before heading out of the room.

JP let his brother's words sink in as he rested against the bed.

Hannah had lied. For God's sake, her parents wanted to take his daughter away. The crazy thing was, if they'd approached him in the first few days of learning about Kayla, he might have agreed to let them raise his daughter.

Jesus. That was a sobering thought.

Would he have done it? Let someone else have custody of his baby?

The question wasn't worth analyzing since it hadn't happened, but maybe it proved Jagger's words were true. They were all just trying to deal with the aftermath of Mary Anne's choices. Even from beyond the grave, she was the puppet master making her dolls dance on the ends of strings she'd crafted.

"Fuck," he said as his head began to pound. It wasn't exactly fair of him to think of her that way. He couldn't imagine receiving a terminal diagnosis in his early twenties. Chances were his poor choices would have put Mary Anne's to shame. He could understand her not wanting to die without experiencing her greatest wish.

With a sigh, he rubbed his aching temples. He needed a shower and a few hours' sleep, in that order.

He was too tired to even grab his dick and jerk off to thoughts of Hannah, naked from the waist up in his bed, as he'd done every night since he'd kicked her out of his house.

God, he was a sick fucker. Booting her from his life then creeping on her in his mind each night. And mornings in the shower.

With a disgusted grunt, he dragged himself into his bathroom. One long, hot shower later, he crashed facedown onto his bed with nothing but a towel around his hips.

Sometime later, he was jolted awake by a heart-wrenching cry coming through the baby monitor. He'd always thought people had a few screws loose when they told him they could tell the difference between their baby's cries but it turns out they weren't crazy. In the short time Kayla had lived with him, he'd learned to differentiate between her hungry cry, her frustrated cry, and her sorrowful cry. But this one he hadn't heard before.

Within seconds, he was charging into the hallway while trying to shove his feet in a pair of underwear at the same time.

JP ran into the room to find Kayla on her back, thrashing around as she screamed bloody murder.

"Hey, baby girl, what's wrong?" he asked as he scooped her up. "Holy shit, you are hot."

Burning hot.

He stared at the crying baby with absolute panic in his heart.

She was sick. His baby was sick. What was he supposed to do?

Thick yellow gook ran from her nose. She coughed, and the sound rattled his bones. "My God," he said as he grabbed a burp cloth and wiped away the snot.

His heart raced as he cradled her to his chest. "Shhh," he whispered. "It's okay, honey. Daddy's here." For all the good that would do her. He literally had no clue what to do with a sick child. Did he give her medicine? Could he give her medicine? And what kind? How much? He'd barely mastered the art of feeding her correctly. How the hell was he supposed to manage this?

Should he take her to the emergency room?

Or was he totally overreacting, and she'd be fine?

Another scream rent the air, making him wince in sympathy. Being sick sucked ass even when you understood what was going on. How awful must it be for a helpless baby?

"Okay, what do I do?" he muttered. Ronnie was at work, and Jagger had probably gone out. Not that they'd be any help in this situation.

Just as he was about to say fuck it and drive her to the emergency room, he caught sight of a small stuffed unicorn Hannah had brought for her last week.

"Hannah," he whispered out loud. She'd lived with Kayla and helped take care of her for months. Maybe she'd know.

With Kayla snug in his arms, he ran back downstairs and grabbed his phone. After sending up a quick prayer that she'd take his call, he pushed her name.

"JP?" She asked in a groggy but hopeful voice.

"Something's wrong with Kayla. I think she's sick, and I have no idea what to do. Hannah, I'm freaking out. Please tell me what to do."

"I'm on my way," she said, then the line disconnected.

"Oh, thank God," he whispered as he gently bounced Kayla, who hadn't stopped crying.

Her little body felt like a fireball in his arm. Should he give her something to drink? Would that make everything worse? How the hell was he supposed to know?

Time crawled slower than when he was a kid stuck in detention during high school. And he'd spent many an afternoon staring at the clock while Mrs. Westin read her book and ignored the classroom full of delinquents. To be fair, detention beat going home to his father most days, but still, time dragged.

It was nothing compared to this, where each minute that passed ramped up his anxiety and Kayla's distress.

What the hell was taking Hannah so long? A quick peek at the clock revealed only eight minutes had passed. Probably not even enough time for her to get dressed and drive over.

Kayla's cries turned to whimpers as she finally began to drift off in his arms.

"Thank God," he muttered, rocking her as he stood in his room.

Unless that was a bad thing. Should he force her to stay awake, so he knew she wasn't dying or something?

His stomach cramped so hard he nearly doubled over.

To think he'd been growing confident in his ability to take care of his daughter. Fuck, he should not have been allowed to reproduce. What the hell did he know about anything?

Kayla let out a weak, pitiful cry that broke his heart.

"Hannah will be here soon, baby," he said as he left his room and headed back up the stairs to meet her. He prowled around the house with Kayla in his arms. She dozed in fitful bursts of unhappy sleep. Hopefully, the constant motion would keep her from the full-on screaming. "Hannah's com—"

Wait. He stopped walking.

Hannah was on her way over.

He'd kicked her out of his house four days ago.

Kayla must have noticed the lack of motion. She stirred in his arms, so he resumed the pacing.

Why was Hannah still in Vermont?

Chapter Twenty-Two

Hannah drove like Satan himself was hot on her tail.

Her heart pounded so fast, she felt it hammering in her throat. If something happened to Kayla, she'd shatter into a heap of broken pieces. That little girl had to be okay.

She just had to.

By the time she made it to JP's house—only fifteen minutes after ending the call—she was a trembling mess of worse-case scenarios and what-ifs.

What if Hannah was seriously ill?

What if she should have told JP to drive her straight to the emergency room?

What if she took too long getting there?

What if Kayla di—

"No!" She shouted out loud as she ran up the driveway. She could not, would not, allow herself to think along those lines. She needed to stay calm, rational, and coherent to assist JP and her sick niece.

JP wasted no time throwing the door open before she reached the porch. One look at his alarmed face and all her fears evaporated, replaced by a calm countenance. The man was a wreck. Bloodshot eyes, disheveled hair, and an aura of complete panic met her at the door. Shirtless, he clutched Kayla to his chest. "Thank God, you're here," he said as a greeting. "I'm freaking the fuck out. She's so hot."

"Come sit on the couch," she said as she put a hand on his arm to usher him back inside. He listened and headed straight for the couch as though on auto pilot. As she followed, she realized he wasn't wearing anything other than a snug, *snug* pair of boxer briefs.

The universe hated her.

As they sat, she set the bag of supplies she'd stopped for down on the coffee table, then held out her arms. "May I hold her?"

"Yeah. Yes, of course." He handed Kayla over but scooted closer as though he couldn't bear to be away from his baby when she wasn't feeling well.

Hannah lost a little piece of her heart right then.

Their knees bumped and a zing of electricity buzzed across her skin. Only the needs of her burning-up niece could have distracted her from a nearly naked JP's so close to her.

"Gosh, she really is hot." Her little chest moved up and down in a rapid rhythm as she thankfully slept in Hannah's arms. Heat radiated from her, and a yellow crust had formed around her nose. "Poor baby," Hannah whispered. "We're gonna get you feeling better."

"Okay," she said, focusing on JP. "Does she have a pediatrician?"

He ran a hand through his hair. "Uh, yes. I took her to one a few days ago. I had medical records but, you know, wanted to make sure she was healthy on my own."

Well, that was smart.

"Great," she said. "They will have an answering service and an on-call doctor they can connect you to. Why don't you give them a call? Tell then exactly what you've seen and done so far."

"The pediatrician." He slapped a hand to his forehead. "You're right. Christ, why the hell didn't I think of that?" Frowning, he snatched his phone from the back of the couch and quickly scrolled through his contacts.

As he held it to his ear, Hannah turned her attention to Kayla.

The baby slept, but the occasional whimper slipped out, nearly making Hannah want to cry along with her. She'd gotten sick twice when Mary Anne had been alive. Once with an ear infection and once some kind of stomach bug. Hannah had been the one to deal with both episodes due to Mary Anne's weakness.

The first time, she'd been just as panicked as JP. Who knew an ear infection could give a baby a fever and make them scream like a banshee? The second time around, she'd promised herself she'd remain calm and rational. That decision lasted as long as it took for Kayla to vomit up everything she'd ingested in the past day. Having a sick baby was truly terrifying and had given her a new definition of helpless.

Poor JP seemed out of his mind with worry as he nodded along with whatever the doctor said. The phone call only lasted a few minutes, and when he hung up, JP no longer looked seconds from fracturing.

He set the phone down then rubbed his scruffy chin. "Thank you so much for staying calm and thinking of that. Um, could I ask you one more favor?" He didn't meet her gaze as he asked.

No matter what went down between them a few days ago, she'd do anything he needed for Kayla. No questions asked. Truth be told, she'd probably do anything he needed for him as well. Or his siblings. Even knowing them for such a short time, she felt the loss of them in her life like a physical ache. "Of course, JP. Whatever you need."

"Um, okay." He blew out a breath, which seemed to expel most of his anxiety. "The doctor said it sounds like nothing more than a simple cold. I can take her in tomorrow to get checked out, but for tonight she said to give her acetaminophen for the fever and make sure she's drinking some pedia-something to keep her hydrated. She also recommended some bulb thing to clean out her nose as well as a vaporizer in her room. She also said we could run a scalding hot shower and hang out in the steamy bathroom for a while before we put her back to bed. If the fever rises despite the medication, then we should take her to the emergency room."

Nodding, Hannah said. "Okay, that all sounds doable. What do you need from me?"

"I have nothing. No medication, no bulb snot thingie, and none of that drink she mentioned. Would you mind running to the drugstore for me? I'm so sorry to ask you to do this so late. I think there is one close by that's open twenty-four-seven."

Hannah smiled at the frazzled man. How was it that even in his most freaked out state, he was more attractive than any other man she'd met? She pointed to the bag on the coffee table. "I'm one step ahead of you, actually." Her face burned, and she averted her gaze. "Uh, she got sick twice when Mary Anne was alive. I had to give her all those same things."

It'd been one time she thanked her worrywart of a mother. Even before Kayla was born, she stocked up on every pediatric medication, safety device, and first aid item on the market.

"I did a mad dash through the drugstore on my way here. It's why it took me a few minutes longer than usual."

Mentioning Mary Anne felt akin to dropping a bomb in a peaceful park, but JP seemed to have forgotten all about their awkward situation. As soon as Kayla was feeling better, he'd probably toss her out on her ass again, but for now, he was able to put it aside for the sake of his baby.

JP held out his hands for his daughter. After reluctantly handing Kayla over, Hannah grabbed the bag and pulled out the items he'd mentioned. She'd purchased a few other things as well, wanting to make sure she didn't miss anything they might have needed. "Okay, let's get the medication in her first. I'll get the shower heating up while you get her some of this electrolyte drink, then you can sit in the bathroom with her for a while."

He blinked at her, relief written all over his face. "Jesus, you're an angel," he said as he settled Kayla in the safe and strong cradle of his arms. "I could kiss you right no—"

Their gazes met. Hannah sucked in a breath. The world

seemed to stop rotating as they stared at each other. Was he recalling the way they were together? How desperate they'd been for each other's kisses. It'd been on her mind every hour since she'd last left this house.

Kayla cried out. As though a bucket of ice had been dumped on them, the spell broke.

"Um…" Hannah cleared her throat. This man affected her in ways she struggled to deal with. "How much medicine did she say to give her?"

JP glanced up from Kayla.

"She said to follow the chart on the back of the package. She's about fifteen pounds, so go by that."

"Right." She knew that. Being so close to him was short-circuiting her brain. Hannah followed the chart and dosed the medicine into the dropper. Together they managed to get most of the medication into Kayla and only a small amount on her. Afterward, Hannah turned the shower on while JP worked on getting Kayla to drink a bottle.

As she waited for steam to fill the bathroom, she sat on the closed toilet lid and let herself breathe for the first time since JP called almost an hour ago.

So many emotions bounced around inside her, colliding and trying to take over.

Fear, worry, trepidation, relief. All the expected feelings when one was dealing with an unfamiliar situation and someone with whom they had a strained relationship. What took her by surprise and seemed to come from nowhere was the lust, longing, and loneliness that hit her just being in JP's presence.

The man hated her, and there she was pining for him, wishing he would kiss her and wanting to pick up exactly where they'd left off right before she blurted out Mary Anne's name four days ago. If all she'd wanted was something physical, these feelings would have been easier to deal with, but JP appealed to her on so many levels. Though his life was in a season of transition and growth—one of the many reasons she shouldn't be thinking along these lines—JP made her smile. He made her feel light and fun.

And sexy.

He cared about his daughter so much more than he realized. He'd changed his entire life around for her already. One day, he'd wake up and realize what an incredible man he was. Too bad she wouldn't be around to witness it. Hopefully, whatever lucky woman he ended up with would be deserving of him.

Hannah wasn't. He'd made that perfectly clear.

With a small groan, she dropped her head to her hands.

JP cleared his throat, making her jump and then whip her gaze in his direction.

He stood in the bathroom with his back to the door, holding Kayla and still wearing nothing but those damn black boxer briefs. They outlined his assets in a way that had her fingers itching to explore—an urge she'd never experienced with another man. Something about him made her want to burst out of her safe box and soak up every part of life she'd missed. Starting with his naked body.

The steam had to be going to her head. She wasn't the type of girl to ogle men's crotches. Then again, she wasn't typically sharing a small, enclosed space with a gorgeous man wearing only his underwear. What had happened to her life? It was almost unrecognizable compared to this time last year, as was she.

A huge part of her loved it. Too bad she screwed it up with lies.

"Sorry," he said. "Didn't mean to scare you. You all right?"

"Uh, yeah. I'm good. I was just resting for a second." She rose and gestured for him to take her place on the closed toilet.

He eyed her as though deciding whether to press the issue but ultimately let it drop. Thank God. Hannah lacked the energy for a conversation about their extremely complicated relationship.

"How is she?" she asked as she slid to the floor with her back against the wall. Warm humidity filled the bathroom, giving his skin a damp glow. She must look like she'd stuck her finger in the electric socket. She could feel her hair growing frizzier by the second.

"Okay, I think," he answered, looking down at Kayla, who was once again sleeping. "I got her to drink about four ounces."

"Good."

They sat in silence, not an easy one, but not overly uncomfortable either. At least three times, Hannah almost made conversation, but bone-deep exhaustion kept her from speaking up. If she was tired, he had to be completely drained.

After a while, JP stood. "She's out cold and seems to be breathing a little easier. Can we check her temperature again?

"Sure." Hannah darted back to the living room and grabbed the thermometer. She found JP standing in Kayla's room near her crib. "Let's see," she said as she ran the thermometer across Kayla's forehead. "Yes! Ninety-nine!" She grimaced. "Sorry. Ninety-nine point two," she whispered this time.

He sagged. "Oh, thank God. Okay, I'm gonna put her down. Wanna say goodnight?"

He held her sleeping niece toward her.

Hannah's throat thickened. "I do." She bent down and pressed a light kiss to Kayla's forehead. "Night, sweet girl," she whispered. Inhaling, the sweet scent of baby powder and the same tearless soap she'd used overwhelmed her senses. Tears filled her eyes. JP's call had terrified her to her very core. She couldn't imagine losing Kayla to an illness in her infancy.

On some level, she understood her mother's desire to put everyone she loved in a protective bubble. Wouldn't anyone do everything in their power to protect their family?

The problem was her mother tried to control the things outside of her ability as well, taking it to a level so extreme it became pathological.

God, how she hoped that wouldn't be the last time she kissed her niece for a while. She'd find out as soon as JP set her in the crib.

Suddenly she couldn't be there for a moment longer. Couldn't witness the bond JP and Kayla already shared and that she wasn't a part of. "I'll be in the hall," she said as she practically ran from the room. Once out, she leaned against the wall and breathed a few times.

The sound of the door snicking shut had her turning her head JP's way. He faced her, then scratched his flat stomach. His gaze followed his hand. "Oh shit," he whispered on a chuckle. "I was so freaked out I didn't realize I wasn't dressed."

When he looked her way, a sheepish grin gave him a boyish, playful look.

She shrugged. "It's okay. I barely noticed."

Liar.

His hum sounded disbelieving.

"Well, um, now that Kayla is doing better, I should get back." Ugh, things had gotten thick and tense in a matter of seconds. The giant elephant standing between them in the hallway wouldn't budge, and she didn't have the emotional reserve to deal with it right then. Running back to her rental house seemed the wiser choice.

As she turned to leave, JP caught her hand. "Stay," he said, without a trace of insincerity.

"What?" she whispered. After he'd practically thrown her out the door? What was his game? "I don't think that's a good idea."

"I know everything is super fucked up right now. And I know we need to deal with it. But it's late. I'm exhausted, and you must be, too. I'll worry about you driving back, and I can't leave to take you. Sleep with me. In my bed. Just sleep." He glanced away, then back at her. "I just…please stay." Pleading eyes begged along with his words.

Hannah must be a hundred different kinds of fool. With a nod, she allowed him to lead her down the hallway to the stairs. She was doing this because it was late, she was tired, and she didn't want to risk falling asleep at the wheel on the drive home. It was the sensible, logical, most restful choice.

That's all.

Once in his room, he crawled under the covers on the right side of his bed, closest to the door. Holding the navy-blue comforter peeled back, he said, "Climb in."

He hadn't so much as put on a shirt. She'd have all that skin lying inches away. Close enough to touch. How would he react if she stripped her own clothing off so she could feel his heat?

Too risky.

Instead of following that instinct, she kicked off her shoes and laid down on her back next to him. His arm went around her waist, and he dragged her close until she had no choice but to shift onto her side and fit like the perfect little spoon to his big one.

"Thank you," he whispered in her ear. His warm breath tickled her skin and caused an eruption of goosebumps. He sounded tired but relaxed, whereas her body felt like a guitar string strung so taut it would snap at one pluck. How could he lie there exchanging pleasantries like he wasn't one step away from being naked?

Unless he didn't want her the way she wanted him.

How humiliating.

"You're, uh, you're welcome."

"Sleep. Forget everything else for one night and sleep."

He was warm and comforting, all curled around her. Under normal circumstances, that kind of cozy cocoon would lull her to sleep, but there was no way in hell she'd get a wink tonight. Too many thoughts ran through her head.

What did this mean?

What would happen in the morning?

Would Kayla be okay?

What would his siblings say if they found her in his bed?

How would she feel if he woke up unhappy to see her?

The only thing that would have made the moment more perfect was if they were skin to skin.

A rogue, dangerous thought.

Chapter Twenty-Three

JP woke with a start at the first crackle from the baby monitor. Curled up against his front, Hannah stirred but didn't wake up. Quick as he could, he silenced the monitor, then slipped out of bed. A clock on his nightstand read five in the morning. Pretty typical wake-up time for his early bird, but who knew if today would be normal or if Kayla would still be feeling miserable.

Man, he'd love to soak up a few moments of enjoyment next to Hannah's soft, warm body, but with the drama of last night, he was too worried about his daughter to let her cry more than a few seconds.

He tip-toed upstairs and toward Kayla's room. As he entered the kitchen, he froze at the sight of Jagger sitting at the table with a bagel and an oversized mug of black coffee.

"Well, well, well," Jagger said with a smirk. "Looks like you had a fun night."

"You're kidding, right?" JP snarled as he stomped past his nosey brother.

Of course, Jagger didn't take the hint and followed him to Kayla's room. "What? Do you think I'm blind? Or stupid? Hannah's car is in my parking spot, for God's sake. You made up, then got down."

JP turned in the hallway. "Made up and got down? How long did it take you to come up with that one?"

"'Bout two seconds. I'm quick like that."

With a grunt, JP continued into his daughter's room. He found Kayla sitting up in her bed, nose runny, face not nearly as flushed as the night before. "Hello, my pretty girl. Are you feeling better?"

"Feeling better? What do you mean?" Jagger nearly crashed into JP's back as he peeked into the crib.

"Mm-hmm." JP scooped Kayla up and hugged her to his chest. Thank God, she simply felt warm from sleep. Not feverish as she had the previous night. "I woke up around midnight, and she had a fever."

All teasing fled Jagger's face as he reached for his niece. "Shit. Give her to me. Should we take her to the hospital?"

After handing her over, JP fetched the thermometer from Kayla's changing table. She felt cooler, but better to know for sure. "I almost did. Shit, Jag, I totally panicked." He ran the thermometer across her head. Ninety-eight point eight. His shoulders unknotted, and a lightness entered his chest for the first time in hours.

Thank Christ.

"I would have too." Jag pointed to the medicine bottle sitting on the changing table. "How did you know what to do?"

"I called Hannah."

As though a light switch flicked on, Jagger nodded. "Ahh. That was a good call, brother."

"Yeah, she stopped at the drugstore and bought all this shit on her way over. We called the doctor, and she advised us on what to do. I'll take her in to get checked out today, but the pediatrician said it sounded like a cold."

"Fu—fudge, I'd have been scared out of my mind." Jag kissed the top of Kayla's head, and of course, she went right for his beard.

"Believe me, I was." More scared than he could ever remember being. "I lost my mind."

Jag squeezed his shoulder. "You and Hannah work things out?"

With a sigh, JP scratched his face. It itched when he didn't shave for a few days, even though he liked the way it looked. He'd also liked the way Hannah had shivered when he rubbed his stubble across her neck a few nights ago.

"No. Not yet. It was so late, and we were both drained from the stress. We just crashed." He stroked a finger over Kayla's soft cheek. "I didn't want her to leave. How fucked up is that?"

"It's only fucked up if you let her leave today without working your shit out," Jag said.

"Yeah." Hopefully, Hannah wouldn't wake and sneak out of the house before he had a chance to apologize. Hell, before he had a chance to figure out what the hell he was going to say to apologize. No matter how much brain power he'd dedicated to her since the last time they'd spoken, he hadn't sorted it all in his head. Looked like he'd be winging it.

If she hadn't snuck out already.

He wouldn't blame her if she did.

"How about this. You go down and talk to her. If it goes well, take as long as you need to…make up." Jag winked. "I'll hang with my best girl. Get her breakfast and dressed. Ian is supposed to be checking in this morning. I know he'd love to see her. She can FaceTime him with me."

JP frowned. Ian had just called a few days ago and typically only checked in every couple of weeks. "Everything okay with him?"

"Not sure. His text was a little cryptic. I'll find out soon."

"I don't know if I should be away from her today." What if she spiked a fever again? What if she cried the whole time? What if she felt sick?

"You'll be one staircase away, JP, not across the state. I'll come get you if anything changes or if I have concerns. Trust me, I'm not about to try to handle shit myself if she seems sick."

Biting his lower lip, JP watched his daughter. She seemed fine. A little snotty, but she was acting normal, trying to chew on Jagger's shirt and yanking his beard. "Okay." He lifted a finger.

"But you find me the second anything changes or if you even have a small inkling that something might not be right. Like if you're questioning anything. Got it?"

"Got it." A smug grin crossed Jagger's face. "Never thought I'd see the day you turned into a mother hen."

JP flipped him off.

With a gasp, Jagger covered Kayla's eyes— well, her whole face—with his huge hand. "How dare you use such a vulgar gesture around my niece. What kind of father are you?"

What kind of father was he? Right now, when she was a baby, that question wasn't hard to answer. He was a father trying to survive. Later, he'd be responsible for teaching her morals, politeness, street smarts, kindness. So many heavy topics that would help shape the way she viewed the world and her place in it. How the hell was he supposed to manage such an important job when he'd never had a positive father figure in his own life?

"Hey," Jag said, snapping him out of his thoughts. "You know I'm kidding, right? You're doing an amazing job."

"Thanks." They didn't often speak of their father, who was currently serving an eighteen-month sentence a few hours away. Nor did they speak of their shitty upbringing, the abuse and neglect, or the untimely death of their mother. "You know, I look at her, and I would do anything. Any goddammed thing in this entire world to keep her safe, warm, and fed. It's gonna be hard not to helicopter her because the idea of her being sad or hurt by the world is devastating, even knowing in some cases it will be best for her to muddle through situations on her own. But I'll always be there if she needs me. With all the scary things in this world, the one constant will be me. That she'll never have to fear me. Not a single second in her life."

Jagger frowned. "JP, I know all this. No one wonders this about you. You don't have it in you to hurt the ones you love."

"But how did he?" He rubbed a hand over his chest where an ache formed in his heart. "How did he look at his five children and not give a single shit whether we were hungry, safe, warm, educated, even fucking alive?"

Understanding dawned in Jagger's eyes. "He's a special kind of asshole, JP. And you're not going to become that kind of father."

"I'm trying. I just...now that she's in my life, I can't understand how a father becomes one like ours. I never wanted this because I was so afraid I'd become him." He shrugged. "I'm still petrified of being a shitty father, but I'm at the point where the abuse and hatred is baffling."

"That's because you're a good man, JP."

"Well, I owe that to you and Keith. You did all the things he should have done."

Jag smiled at him but didn't say anything.

"Anyway. I'm gonna head back downstairs. Thanks for hanging with her this morning."

"My pleasure."

JP kissed his daughter's cheek once, twice, then a third time for good measure. She giggled and grabbed his nose with that surprisingly strong grip. After a few tickles and more laughs, he slapped Jag on the shoulder then started out of the room.

"JP?"

"Yeah?"

He turned in the doorway.

"Don't let those questions of yours take root in your mind. You'll never understand that man because you are nothing, *nothing* like him. Don't give him any space in your head. He's not worth it and doesn't deserve it."

"Thank you," he said, and meant it for so much more than just a few hours of babysitting.

Jag nodded then turned his attention to Kayla. After watching them interact for a few seconds, JP jogged back down the stairs to his room.

Now that he had time, he spared a moment to admire the woman sleeping in his bed. She really was beautiful in a way that came from deep inside her. Sure, her blond hair, piercing blue eyes, and delicious lips got his dick hard, but his dick wasn't exactly picky. This desire he'd developed for Hannah wasn't only about getting off. He wanted that and wanted to do every dirty thing imaginable with her, but he also wanted to laugh with her. He loved having her there for his family's movie night. He enjoyed eating ice cream with her. Hell, he had more fun hanging around and talking with her than he did with anyone else. And when she loved on his daughter? Shit, that did all kinds of strange things to his insides. Was this what it had felt like for Keith when he first met Mickie?

There were so many reasons they shouldn't explore anything between them. First and foremost was the fact that he'd kicked her out of their lives only a few days ago. Then there was the family connection. She was Kayla's aunt, for fuck's sake. The sister of a woman he'd slept with. And she'd lied to him. It sounded like her family would never accept him in their lives. He was also a thirty-two-year-old man with no real job or education, trying to survive as a single father living with his siblings.

Christ, what a catch.

Best case scenario, they'd date a little and fuck a lot while letting the attraction run its course. Worst case, they'd let messy emotions get involved and be left with deep battle wounds. Either way, it wouldn't last. The odds were stacked too high against them.

Yet despite all the reasons he shouldn't, JP crawled back under the covers, ready to apologize his ass off so he could get back in her good graces and hopefully have the chance to touch her again.

"JP?" she asked, in a voice thick with sleep as he wrapped an arm around her waist and pulled her close. Her round ass fit perfectly against him, making him hard in an instant.

"Mmm." He couldn't help himself; he nuzzled his nose into the crook of her neck and inhaled the clean, fresh scent of her hair. "You smell so fucking good."

She stiffened in his arms, making him sigh. They had to talk this out.

"I know," he said even though she hadn't spoken. Closing his eyes, he pressed his forehead to the center of her back and counted to ten. Didn't do shit to kill his erection.

He lifted his head, kissed the back of her neck then released his hold on her.

She flipped his way then gazed up at him with confusion in her eyes.

Time to pay the piper.

Hannah didn't pull out of his arms.

That had to mean something, didn't it?

"JP, what's going on? I understand why you called me last night, but I don't understand why I'm still here. You made your feelings about me very clear the other day."

"Why didn't you leave Vermont?"

She blinked. "What?"

"When I called you last night, I thought I'd just be asking for advice. I thought you'd gone back to Colorado. But you didn't leave Vermont. Why?"

Her cheeks pinked, and she averted her gaze to something over his shoulder. Whatever it was, it must have been fascinating because she stared at it as though it'd save her from this conversation.

"I don't know."

"Hannah," he said though it sounded more like a plea.

Whatever she heard in his voice, she sighed and met his gaze. "I couldn't. I thought maybe...well, I hoped..." She shrugged, and her mouth turned down. "I just couldn't leave. No matter how many times I tried."

"Because you didn't want to leave Kayla?" He held his breath as he searched her gaze.

Her blue eyes held a world of turmoil. "Why are you asking me this? I don't blame you for hating me. I lied. I came here, met you under false pretenses. If you feel guilty for getting angry, you don't have to."

Even when he'd wronged her, she gave him an out. He didn't deserve a woman like her, but he was selfish enough to grab whatever scraps she allowed him while working for more. Jagger had been right. Like him, Hannah was just trying to swim through the shark-infested waters of Mary Anne's actions without drowning or getting eaten alive.

"I fucked up," he said. "I was shocked. More than shocked, really, and I reacted without thinking."

"JP, I understood your reaction. I can't say I wouldn't have done the same. I lied to you for weeks then blurted it all out at the worst possible time. The one thing I want you to know, though, is that I never came here with the intention of taking Kayla away from you. Never."

Even though only a few inches separated them, the distance seemed too far. He had to touch her. So he cupped her face, stroking his thumb across the smooth skin of her cheek. "I believe you, Hannah. Jagger said something to me the other day that really resonated. He said that I'm not the only one trying to settle into my new normal after the consequences of your sister's choices and her death. You are, your parents are, all of us are doing the best we can with the circumstances we were given. None of us are going to handle this perfectly or without screwing up on occasion. I'm sorry I lost my shit on you the other day. Kayla needs you in her life, Hannah."

And I think I might need you in mine.

"JP, thank you," Hannah said on a rushed exhale as she nuzzled into his palm. She closed her eyes and placed a hand on his bare chest. Heat seared straight to his balls as though he'd been zapped with a cattle prod.

"Hannah," he said in a strained voice as he fought to keep from grinding his now hard as fuck dick against her.

"Sorry," she started to pull her hand back, but he pressed his over it, keeping her touch on his skin.

"I'm not. Christ, Hannah. I'm so fucking hard for you right now."

Her eyes flared. "Y-you are?"

"I want you. I wanted you the moment I saw you, and that desire has grown each time we've hung out. Not just because I think you are the sexiest woman I've ever met. Hannah, you're kind, you're fun, you're amazing with Kayla, you're sweet, you're intelligent. Every time I'm with you, I learn something new about you that makes me want you even more. I've never given a shit beyond getting off. I'm in so far over my head I can't see the surface, but I don't think I want to. Fuck, I'm rambling."

If she ran in the opposite direction, he wouldn't blame her. But now that he'd opened his mouth, the words wouldn't stay in. He needed her to know how he felt.

"I know there are a million reasons I should stay away and keep my hands to myself, but I can't. Not anymore. I want you more than I want to breathe."

And he did. At that moment, he worried he'd die faster from unrequited lust than if all the oxygen suddenly disappeared from the room.

"JP," she said, flexing her fingers against this pec muscle.

He bit his lip to keep the frustrated groan inside. God, how he wanted that hand wrapped around his needy cock.

She blinked up at him with a shy smile. "I want you, too. The same way. It's intense and unfamiliar, and I'm getting so tired of fighting it." Clouds drifted into her gaze, giving her eyes a stormy, almost gray hue. "Kayla isn't the only reason I couldn't leave Vermont."

Those words made his heart soar.

"But there is one other confession I have to make before we can move forward."

Well, fuck, what bomb was she about to drop now?

Chapter Twenty-Four

Hannah's insides shook worse than they had when she met JP for the first time. And she'd been beyond nervous then.

Earthquake-sized tremors rolled through her stomach now.

Please don't throw up on him.

JP frowned. "Hannah, you're shaking." Tension had his back straightening. "Is it that bad?"

"No." Yes? Maybe. Who the hell knew how he'd react, but she'd opened the box and now she needed to let the contents out.

"Tell me." His hands roamed up and down her back, along her arms, over her hips. The touch was equal parts comfort and agony. Not for the first time, she wished she'd tossed away her virginity in her teens, so she could come to him as his equal, without the nerves and with knowledge and experience. Unfortunately, wishing was a waste of time. She'd learned that years ago. All she could do now was embrace her new life outside the box, be honest, and wait to see if her news killed his desire.

She kept touching him as well, running her fingers over the tattoos on his chest. Someday, she'd love to hear the stories and meaning behind each one. "I was trying to talk myself into admitting this to you the other day when we were, um, you know, but I blurted out the wrong thing."

Why did her face have to get so warm when the spotlight

shone her way? The reaction ruled out any chance for a poker face.

One of JP's eyebrows twitched as a wry smile curled those lips she'd die to kiss again. "When we were about to fuck?" he whispered in a gravelly voice, making her shiver.

"Yeah. That." Her cheeks were so dang hot it'd be a miracle if they didn't melt off her face.

Well, he gave her the perfect lead-in. Time to reveal her secret. She stared at the tattoo beneath her palm. A symbol she didn't recognize. At least the ink wouldn't judge her. "So," she said in a near whisper, "I've never actually done that before."

"What?" he asked in a teasing tone. "Blurted out the wrong thing at the wrong time? I know we still have a lot to figure out, but we're moving past that. And I pretty much do that once a week."

"No. That's not what I meant." Crap. She was going to have to spell it out for him, wasn't she?

Suddenly, he sucked in a breath and grabbed her shoulder. His dark eyes searched hers. "Wait, are you talking about fucking? You've never had sex?" Surprise showed all over his face, so she went back to watching his chest.

Where was a good lightning bolt when she needed one? Something to strike down from the sky and vaporize her, so she didn't have to endure the humiliation of telling a man she cared for that she was a twenty-five-year-old virgin. When the heavens remained calm, and JP continued to stare at her as though she was an alien from another planet, she nodded. "Yes. That's right."

As soon as the words were out, she wished she could suck them back in. She'd rather die a virgin than see disgust or ridicule in his eyes. Or even worse, pity.

But JP had other plans. He grasped her chin between his thumb and forefinger, lifting her to meet his gaze. "But you want to? With me? Or at least you wanted to the other day?"

She couldn't have lied straight to his face to save her life or spare her further humiliation. "Um, yes. Yes to both." God, did she want to. Like him, even the potential for disaster didn't dampen her desire or change her mind.

"Fuck. Me," he whispered. Then he closed his eyes and took a deep breath as though fighting for control.

Her heart sank. Did knowing how inexperienced she was turn him off? Surely, he was used to practiced women who knew how to please him and what they wanted in return. Maybe she should have thought her admission through better and told him when they weren't lying in his bed. Then again, she never thought she'd get the opportunity to be this close to him after he'd ordered her to leave.

"I'm sorry," she whispered back. "You have to be disappointed. I just didn't want any more secrets between us." She started to pull away, shame heavy on her heart. "I can go. I promise this doesn't change how I feel about Kayla or how I'll act around her. It's a totally separate issue."

He grabbed the front of her shirt, holding her in place. "Hannah," he said with his eyes hot and dark. "Are you telling me I would be the first and only man to be inside your sexy body?"

She swallowed and nodded. "Yes."

His gaze bored into hers with an intensity that left her weak.

"The only man to hear you scream as you fall apart around my dick?"

"Um, yes," she squeaked.

"I'd be the one to show you how good a cock, my cock, feels? To have your nails rake my back as you try to pull me closer, deeper? To see your face as pleasure takes over and consumes you?"

Heat flashed through her, no longer from embarrassment but longing. "What are you doing to me?" Her need for something she didn't fully understand ramped up to incendiary levels. If he didn't touch her, didn't do something to ease the tension coiling low in her belly, she'd implode.

"Hopefully, I'm making you want me as much as I want you. Thank you for telling me." He brought his hand up to her face and stroked a finger across her lips. "If it's what you want, I'd love to be your first. Hell, I'd fight for the chance."

"Really?" The urge to nip his finger bombarded her, so she did just that. Caught it between her teeth and licked the tip. Who the hell knows where the instinct came from? But it hadn't been willing to be ignored.

"Christ," he said on a groan. "Really." After tugging his finger from her teeth, he grabbed her hand. Their eyes met as he pressed it to his groin.

The second her palm encountered a very hard, very prominent bulge in his shorts, she stared down at him. "I was worried you wouldn't want me if you knew I've never been with anyone."

"I'm a little surprised myself," he said. "At how fucking hot it's making me to think of corrupting you. Of ruining you for all other men."

He might have already done that, but she didn't say it out loud. Whatever they had, however they felt... In the long run, this wouldn't be more than physical. Couldn't. A relationship with JP would destroy the last remaining parts of her family, and she couldn't shoulder that burden.

The sun hadn't risen yet though the sky was no longer completely dark. The first traces of dawn peeked through his small rectangular windows, casting a romantic glow around the room. For a short time, she'd allow herself to exist in this bubble with him. To pretend the outside world would never intrude. To forget they were connected by her sister's child and that her parents depended on her to deliver something she never would.

"Can I kiss you now?" he asked.

The simple, gentlemanly question had her heart flipping over in her chest. "Please," she said.

He slid a hand around her back and up into her hair. When he gripped the back of her head in a firm hold, she shivered. "I want you to tell me when you like something I do and when you don't. If something feels good, I'll do it over and over and over until you're a needy mess, begging me to fuck you. I want you out of your mind by the time I get my cock in you."

"God," she said, as a shiver ran over her sensitive skin. She wasn't sure she'd be one to beg, this time or ever. It seemed so out of character, but the idea of getting that desperate for him thrilled her.

"Not yet, but you might be calling me that by the time I'm through with you."

She giggled as he kissed her, part nerves, part humor, but it quickly turned into a low moan of pleasure. Oh, how she'd missed this over the past few days. The hungry way he took her mouth. How he made her feel like the only woman on the planet when he focused his attention and his mouth on her. No one had ever tilted her world's axis with just a kiss.

He took complete control, holding her head where he wanted, plundering her mouth, and making her insides all swoony and tingly. The longer they kissed, the more her confidence grew. Or perhaps it was just her need. After long minutes passed, her fingertips itched to touch him the way he was touching her. Hands smoothing all over skin. Learning, exploring, playing.

She flattened her unsteady hands against his hard stomach, eliciting a grunt from him. His grip on her hair intensified, and his tongue grew more aggressive in her mouth. She could barely breathe at this point but didn't care about oxygen.

She had JP.

Slowly, she flexed her fingers, testing the flesh beneath them. "Yes," he said against her lips. Touch me, baby. Touch me anywhere you want. Any way you want. With you, I don't have a single fucking limit."

Why was that so hot? Given the green light, she allowed herself to play. To feel all that warm, tattooed skin. To learn the spots that made him squirm, suck in a breath, or groan. He bit his lip when she ghosted over his nipples, and he grunted when she raked a fingernail over one. His exuberant reactions gave her the courage to explore further.

Her mouth had been watering for a taste of him since the moment she saw him shirtless. Now was her chance to take a taste. She kissed him just above his collar bone, where his shoulder sloped into his neck.

He groaned and fisted his hands at his sides. Encouraged, she did it again and again, growing bolder with each kiss. After a few, she let her jaw relax and opened her mouth. Soon she was sucking his skin with each kiss and traveling all over his chest and torso. His tortured sounds only made her want more. His skin tasted slightly salty and a little spicy. He was warm on her tongue, and there was something so erotic about licking over his tattoos.

"Christ, you didn't mention you were a sadist," he said as he arched into her. His erection nudged her thigh, thick and hard.

Would she get to explore it next?

Never having been very outspoken or overly extroverted, Hannah always assumed she'd be an anxious wreck the first time she had sex. With each year of celibacy that passed, she assumed the trepidation would be worse. She guessed she'd be a timid lover, afraid to take the lead and preferring to follow.

There were nerves, but his easy acceptance and chill personality chased away her fear. The strong desire to touch him made her brave. She reached for his pants, only to be intercepted before she could touch him.

"Nuh-uh," he said, wagging a finger at her.

His smirk let her know she hadn't overstepped.

"You touch me, and I'll most likely make a mess all over you. I think we'd both rather I come in you. So, while I love how curious you are about touching me, and we'll definitely come back to that, I'm gonna need you to leave these here and let me have a turn first." He flattened her hands to the bed up by her shoulders. "Keep 'em there," he said with a wink.

Oh, God, he was about to torment her, wasn't he?

"Now," he said as he lay his weight on top of her.

It felt wonderful. If he went no further, she'd be more than happy. The feel of him, strong and heavy, anchoring her to the mattress was enough to make her month.

He scooted down until he lay between her legs. Then he began to work her shirt up her torso. "I've already met and made friends with these gorgeous tits." He shoved her shirt and bra up to her neck without much finesse, leaving her exposed to the chilly air-conditioned air and his perusal.

She'd have felt ridiculous if it wasn't for the appreciation in his gaze. She bit her lower lip as she waited there with her hands raised and her upper body bared.

"So I'm just gonna say a quick hello for now." He rubbed his thumbs over both nipples at the same time.

Hannah gasped and arched her back. It felt great but also created a frustrating throb between her legs.

Grinning like he knew just how he was affecting her, he pinched, plucked, and rolled her nipples with his skillful fingers.

Her teeth were going to puncture a hole in her lip if she wasn't careful.

"Look at you, getting all squirmy. You need something, sweetheart?"

Did she need something? She needed a lot of things. She needed use of her hands. She needed him to quit toying with her, and she needed him to yank her pants down and do something to ease the ache.

"Yes."

"I know exactly what you need." He released her breasts then kissed each nipple before slowly kissing his way down her stomach.

Her skin pebbled beneath his lips. Her muscles quivered, and her sex pulsed. She was so wet she felt it soaking into her panties and possibly through her sweats.

"I believe this is right where I was last time before things got messy. Can't tell you how fucking happy I am to get another shot. Bend your knees and lift that sexy ass for me."

She obeyed without question.

A wolfish grin stayed on his face as he worked her sweatpants and panties over her hips and down her thighs. She barely noticed as he pulled them completely off because she was too busy being aware of just how exposed she was. She had the insane urge to cross her legs to keep him from seeing how soaking wet her sex was.

"I don't think so," he said as she started to shut her thighs. He pushed them wide before settling in between once again. Only this time, he was eye level with her sex.

She swallowed.

"Damn," he said on an exhale. "That is a pretty pussy."

"Um, thanks?" Pretty?

He chuckled. "Look at you. So wet for me, huh?" Before she had a chance to squeak out an answer, he said, "Please tell me I can eat you."

She sucked in a breath so fast, it caught in her throat, making her cough. JP chuckled again. He seemed to get a thrill out of flustering her. For days, she'd been fantasizing about him like this even though she didn't have the experience to know exactly what to expect.

It was just so...intimate. He was about to be all up in her. There was no way to hide. Nowhere to run.

"I've jerked off to thoughts of my mouth on your pussy."

No one had ever spoken to her in such crude, raw language. She'd be lying if she said she hated it. Quite the opposite. The primal way he talked, as though he didn't have the patience to find fancier words, made her feel wanted, sexy, powerful.

"Yes," she finally said. "Do it."

"You're gonna fucking love this," he said. He dipped his head then popped it up again. "And, Hannah?"

"Yeah?"

"Stop biting that lip. I wanna hear you."

Hannah let her bottom lip slide from between her teeth,

unable to speak around the thickening in her throat.

Hear her? Why did she think that sounded so hot? In the past, when Mary Anne had regaled her with stories about guys she'd hooked up with, Hannah could never imagine herself acting in such an uninhibited way when at her most vulnerable. Now she understood. This man awakened a side of her she hadn't known existed under mountains of obligation and responsibility.

She stared, transfixed, as he lowered his head between her legs. Before anything happened, she pressed the back of her hands into the bed, bracing.

JP's nose brushed her in her inner thigh, making her jump and yip.

"Shhh." His hot breath tickled her skin. "Settle, baby."

Baby? No man had ever called her that. It shouldn't send a kaleidoscope of butterflies fluttering through her stomach, but it did. Another quick brush of his nose along her inner thigh followed by a deep inhale. Did he just smell her?

A deep rumble came from him the second before his tongue licked the crease where her thigh met her pelvis. Hannah gasped. Her fingers curled into fists. Nails dug into her palms, but she barely noticed the prick of pain.

"Mmm," JP murmured.

Then he licked right where she was wet and most needy.

She cried out as a burst of electricity shot through her limbs. Over and over, he teased her with little, playful licks, like a cat lapping at a bowl of milk. Each one in a different part of her sex. She never knew where his tongue would land, only that it would feel incredible.

After a few moments of trying to process all the new and overwhelming sensations, JP's actions became less flirty and more intentioned. He licked, sucked, and even used his teeth to drive her out of her mind.

Before she knew it, she was lifting her hips off the bed to increase the pressure of his mouth.

He grabbed her butt with both hands, holding her to his

hungry mouth. Then, as he ate her, he kneaded her cheeks with those strong fingers.

Hannah moaned out loud. God, she sounded like a porn star. She felt like one, letting him do whatever the hell he wanted without a single word. But she couldn't quell the noises coming from her or think of a single reason to stop him.

Hannah watched every move he made. She couldn't have looked away for anything. She'd never seen a sight more erotic than his dark head working between her legs.

They'd crossed a line she could never return from. She loved every second of her time with him. And with this added layer of a physical relationship, she was likely to start stalking the man.

How would she eventually return to Colorado? To a quiet apartment? To suffocating grief, a dysfunctional family, and crushing pressure to live her life as dictated by someone else?

Now that she discovered just how good JP made her feel both in and out of bed, how would she ever leave?

Chapter Twenty-Five

She tasted like fucking sunshine.

Bright, warm, intoxicating; her flavor lit up every cell in him. And those noises she made? Damn, he wanted to record them and listen on repeat every time he got the urge to rub one out, which was damn often since Hannah walked into his life. He hadn't gone after his cock so much since he was a teen and got hard every time the clock ticked.

As soon as her ass lifted off the bed, he had to get his hands on it. Those cheeks filled his hands perfectly, giving him something to squeeze as he held her up and feasted.

His cock was so hard, he could barely stand the pressure of his shorts holding it hostage.

If he didn't make her come in the next few minutes, he'd embarrass the hell out of himself by unloading inside his drawers.

Time to take this to the next level.

He flicked his tongue over her clit, eliciting an adorable half gasp, half squeak from Hannah; the same sound she made every time he changed things up. For a few moments, he kept up the assault on her clit, licking, sucking, and playing until she was trembling and thrashing her head back and forth on the pillow.

He could live and die a happy man, right there. Between her legs, ready to pleasure her on a moment's notice.

After torturing her clit, he licked down and straight into her pussy. Hannah shouted and jammed her hips upward. His nose bumped her clit. Her juices coated his face, and her scent bled into his pores.

He'd never been happier.

"J-JP," she said on a gasp as he tongue-fucked her damn good. "Please, JP."

"Please what, baby?"

"I don't know!" Desperation tinged her voice. Her head rolled back and forth on the pillow, making a mess of her hair. Sweat dotted her stomach and tits. Her face flushed with a healthy glow. She kept her hands exactly where he'd placed them, by her head.

Damn, she was a fucking sight. The picture of erotic surrender.

Sometime soon, he'd have to shoot a few photos of her in this needy frantic state.

"I think I'm gonna come," she said, breathless. "God, I think I'm gonna come soon."

"Fuckin' do it," he growled before diving back into the most delicious treat he'd ever had.

No more words were spoken for long moments. Just moans, shouts, and unintelligible hollers. JP wanted nothing more than he wanted to give her the strongest orgasm she'd ever experienced. It even trumped his own desire to come, which was a first.

He drove her on like a man possessed, pulling out all his tricks. After a few minutes, he felt her pussy flutter around his tongue. Trying to curb a triumphant cheer, he pulled out, then wrapped his lips around her clit. One gentle suck was all it took to have her hands flying into his hair and her pelvis grinding against his face.

"Holy crap," she shouted as her legs clamped down on his shoulders. "Oh, my...fuck." Her head flew up off the pillow, and she shook as she rode the orgasm out against his face. For a short while, he was completely smothered by her smooth, creamy thighs, her soaked pussy, and her heady scent.

And he fucking loved it.

Eventually, she released his hair and flopped back onto the bed. JP crawled up her body, settling along the length of her. She had a slightly dazed look about her with glassy eyes, flushed cheeks, and lax muscles. He couldn't keep the smug smile off his face. "I made the good, sweet Hannah curse. Does that mean I blew your mind?"

She let out a weak chuckle and gave him a shy smile. "I'm pretty sure my brains melted, yes."

"God, you're beautiful when you come. You know that?"

Her face flushed deep, ruby red. "Thanks."

Always so sweet. "Can I kiss you?"

Her eyes widened and focused on his mouth. "After, uh…"

He nodded and forced himself to keep from laughing. "Yes. With the taste of your pussy on my tongue."

"The things you say," she said with a shake of her head, but her attention remained on his lips. "Okay."

He leaned in and captured her mouth in a slow kiss. Much more tender than any they'd shared before. Hannah was tentative at first, probably due to the unfamiliar flavor, but she quickly took the lead.

When he ground his poor, neglected cock into her thigh, she gasped against this mouth and shifted so she cradled him between her thighs. Then she rocked into his dick, and he saw stars.

"Shit!" He broke the kiss and rested his forehead against hers. "You trying to kill me?"

"No," she said with a giggle that made his insides dance.

Making her light and happy was a pleasure. One he was finding as addictive as her body.

"Not trying to kill you at all. But maybe, give you a hint?"

A hint? Ohh. He grinned. "Are you saying you want me to fuck you?"

She nodded. "Yes. That's what I want."

Usually he'd make a sexy quip or jokey comment, but the moment felt heavy in a good way. Important. Significant. And not only because it was her first time, but because it was Hannah. So instead of letting his knee-jerk reaction burst out, he said, "There is nothing I want more than to be inside you, Hannah. As long as you're sure."

"I am. Very, very sure."

Keeping his gaze locked with hers, he pushed up to all fours then reached for his nightstand. She turned her head and watched as he grabbed a condom from the drawer. Then she tracked him as he shucked his shorts and knelt over her in a straddle.

"Wow," she said in a reverent whisper.

He gripped his cock and gave a few strokes. "You're good for my ego."

The open way she studied him with open curiosity and heated desire only made him hotter. But when she reached for the condom and said, "Can I put it on you?" he nearly came right there.

"Jesus Christ, I hope I have the strength to endure that."

He handed over the foil packet and clenched his teeth. Hard. They groaned under the strength of his jaw.

With a fierce frown of concentration, Hannah sat up, ripped the condom open, and pulled it from the packet.

She placed it over the head of his dick and began to roll it down with mildly trembling fingers. The second she touched him, his cock twitched, and he hissed out a pained breath. There wasn't really anything sexy about it. It was her first time, and she was nervous, so she fumbled a bit, but it didn't matter. She was touching him, and it was the best feeling in the whole damn world.

Once she had the condom in place, she wrapped her hand around him and smoothed up and down the latex. "So hard," she whispered.

He'd never get to feel her come around him if she kept up the curious exploration. JP groaned and grabbed her wrist in a gentle grip. "Another time."

He pushed her to her back and nudged her thighs wide. "Ready?"

She nodded. "Please." Everything about her relayed trust. From the open way she looked at him, to the way she lay beneath him, allowing him to take the lead. He wanted to do right by her in every way. To make this first time not only great but fucking spectacular. He wanted any and every guy who came after him to have a ridiculously high bar to reach.

Thoughts of another man having what he was about to threatened to deflate his hard-on, so he shoved them out of his head with force.

He took his time, positioning his dick at the opening of her pussy, loving the way her eyes flared, and she bit her lip again as she squirmed against him. Then, as slowly as he could bear, he pressed inside her. Her chest rose and fell faster as he slid deeper. She winced once or twice but didn't ask him to stop. Instead, she nodded her encouragement.

"You okay?" Last thing he wanted was to hurt her, even if a little discomfort was expected the first time.

She nodded. "I'm good. So good. Don't stop."

Their gazes locked in an intense stare he felt in his soul.

Their powerful connection scared the piss out of him, but he didn't dare break it. He couldn't. She'd ensnared him in a vortex he couldn't escape.

He breathed through his nose and fought for control. With each inch that sank into the tight, hot-as-hell clasp of her pussy, he struggled to keep from coming. He gripped her hips so tight she'd wear marks tomorrow. Fuck, he'd love to see. Fingerprints along those sexy hip bones.

"JP," she said as he bottomed out inside her. "JP, you feel so good. So good. Please don't ever pull out." She wriggled around his cock, testing the fit and feel.

"Jesus, you're the tightest fucking thing I've ever felt. Christ, baby."

"I-I think I need you to move," she said.

"I can't." He spoke through clenched teeth, fighting the powerful need to detonate already. "If you want your first time to last longer than two point three seconds, I can't move yet."

Hannah laughed. The movement caused her pussy to clench around his cock.

Damn, he'd swear he saw heaven.

"You're right," he said as stars danced in front of his eyes. "I've gotta move." He had to fuck. Now. "Shit, baby, this is gonna be too fast, but I promise to make it up to you next time. And every time after that." Hopefully, he could keep that promise. Chances were he'd be on a hair trigger any time she allowed him inside her.

Dragging his cock out, he watched as it left the perfect clasp of her body covered in her arousal. Right before he completely exited, he changed course and thrust back in.

Hannah cried out, practically levitating off the bed. "Oh, my God, that feels so good. Do it again. Please."

Only a fool could resist a sweet demand like that. He did it again and again until he worked up a steady rhythm, gentler than his usual fucking. Hurting her or scaring her off by being too rough wasn't an option.

Hannah's eyes darkened, and she met him thrust for thrust. After a few moments, she grabbed his ass and hauled him into her with a strong tug. "Harder," she said, gasping with wide eyes and flushed skin. "Um, faster, harder."

"Hell yeah." He slammed into her this time, loving the way she arched and shouted his name.

Her hands remained on his ass, nails scoring his skin as she helped him fuck her harder.

The hot slide of her pussy down his cock was like nothing he'd ever felt. How was it possible to be thirty-two and have slept with more than his share of women but never felt something so damn perfect? So life-changing?

Her whimpers and harsh breathing echoed in the room alongside his fierce grunts. The orgasm he'd been fighting since the first stroke tightened his balls, threatening to burst forward whether he was ready or not. At the very least, he had to hold off until Hannah came again. Not only because he was trying to embody a gentleman, but he needed to see it again. To watch that flicker of surprise and ecstasy cross her face the second before she flew.

"Come for me, gorgeous," he ground out as he pounded into her. "Give me one more."

They'd never been out drinking and dancing together, but he imagined she'd look much the same. Dazed eyes, flushed skin, a dewy glow. Damn, they needed to make that happen. Drink, dance, then come back and fuck the night away.

"N-not p-possible," she managed between heavy pants.

"Oh, baby, challenge accepted."

Her tits bounced and swayed with every pump of his hips, begging for another lick of his tongue. Never one to ignore such a sexy sight, he bent forward and caught her tit between his lips. He sucked hard as he thrust into her. Then, putting his skills to use, he wormed his hand between their bodies and found her clit. As soon as he circled his thumb around it, Hannah mewled and squeezed his ass so tight, it hurt.

In the best damned way.

A war started in his mind between the desire to continue feasting on her tits and the equally strong need to watch her find her pleasure. In the end, his need for the visual won out, and he released her tit.

Hovering just inches from her face, he worked her clit without mercy as he thrust them up the goddammed bed. "You're getting close, baby. I can see it."

Thank God. His own balls ached with the fierce need for release. This orgasm was going to drain the life from him.

"JP," she groaned as she squeezed her eyes shut tight and held on for dear life. "Oh shit, JP!"

There it was. *Dayum*, he'd never seen anything sexier. Her head pressed hard into the pillow, baring her neck to him. He'd love to lean down and take a nip but couldn't promise he wouldn't fucking bite her when he went over. She dug her nails into his ass, holding their hips together with surprising strength. Even if he'd wanted to, he couldn't have pulled out.

"Oh!" she cried in a surprised tone. "It's so much."

Without her saying, he knew she'd never given herself an orgasm this intense, and that knowledge had him feeling like the fucking king of the jungle.

She called his name again as tremors began to roll through her. Her pussy rippled around his cock, giving it the most intense massage. With a harsh shout, he yanked his hand from between their bodies and grasped her shoulder, doing anything possible to press them even closer. Forceful contractions seized his muscles. With a roar he didn't try to stem, he sprayed into the condom and lost his fucking mind to the pleasure.

Continuing to hold himself up on his arms became impossible, so he dropped down onto Hannah. Between the heat and the sweat, they might never peel themselves apart.

Long moments passed where their chests heaved against each other, they sucked in gulps of air, and their muscles twitched with lingering shocks.

Hannah's hands lay limp at her sides on the bed as though she didn't know what to do with them now.

With a groan, JP forced his muscles to function, pushing his heavy body up onto his elbows. A shower followed by hot coffee and a huge breakfast would be the perfect way to round out the epic morning.

But first, time to check in and make sure Hannah didn't have any regrets. If she did, he had no idea what the hell he would do. As far as he knew, no woman regretted her time with him, but he wanted her to stay for that shower, coffee, and breakfast. Then maybe she could stay for the rest of the day as well. And the night.

An alien had invaded his brain. It was the only explanation for these kinds of thoughts, but right then, as she stared up at him with a shy, satisfied smile, he loved that alien almost as much as he lo—liked Hannah.

Shit, where the hell had that near disaster of a thought come from?

"Hi," she whispered. Damp hair stuck to her cheek and forehead.

JP pushed it back then cradled her cheek. The urge to leave, the need to run before any awkward conversation could occur, hadn't hit yet. Typically, he didn't even stick around until awkward. Now, he wanted to fill every second of his day with Hannah. "Morning." He kissed her softly.

"That was, um, well…" Her eyes darted everywhere but never lingered on him.

"It was perfect," he said.

Finally, she met his gaze. "Yeah. It was." She stroked soft fingers over his stubble. "I love the way this feels. Uh, not just on my fingers."

"Really?" he asked with a wink, pretending he hadn't noticed already. "Not to self. Don't shave and be sure to rub my face all over Hannah's stunning naked body." As he spoke, he brushed his cheek against hers, drawing a giggle from her. It quickly morphed into a gasp when he gave her breast the same, scratchy snuggle.

With a small shriek, she pushed his face away then laughed. "I guess I should go so you can get on with your day."

"Or you could stay and spend the day with Kayla and me. We might not do anything exciting if she feels crummy, but we'd love to have you hang out with us."

"Really?" Her face lit up like it was Fourth of July night. "You sure that's not too much…well, me? Please be honest."

"Hannah?"

"Yeah?"

Something flowery, bordering on romantic, hovered on the tip of his tongue, but he bit it off. Despite the new and unfamiliar feelings wreaking havoc on him, anything beyond sex had disaster written all over it. Even friendship. So instead of letting her know just how much he wanted her to stay for the day and maybe every day until she left, he said, "It's not too much you. Promise. I'm not sure I could get enough of you."

"Okay. Then I'd love to stay." Her smile could have powered the entire block in a nor'easter blackout. As it was, her delight made his heart flip over in his chest.

A few times.

Maybe he could convince her to cancel the rest of her rental and crash with him until she returned home.

Right then, he realized he was screwed. No matter how much he pretended he didn't want something real with Hannah, the thought of her returning to a life in Colorado made him sick to his stomach.

Chapter Twenty-Six

The next three days passed faster and with more bliss than Hannah could remember experiencing in the last decade. When they weren't laughing, she and JP were at the very least smiling. Unless they were kissing. They shared many, many kisses. So many, her lips looked a little swollen.

JP claimed to love it. Any mark he left on her, whether it was the small hickey on her collarbone or the beard burn on her neck, he said he wished he could brand every part of her body. As insane as it sounded, the statement made her shiver in delight.

She'd left a few brands on him as well. That first morning, after he'd talked her into taking a shower with him, she'd nearly died when he climbed out of bed, and she saw the ten little bloody scratches she'd gouged into his backside. When she gaped at them in horror, he'd just laughed and shaken his butt around like being mauled by her was a trophy he'd proudly wear.

Okay, maybe she got it a little bit.

JP turned her into a woman she barely recognized. A woman who craved his touch, couldn't get enough of his mouth, and looked forward to the nighttime more than any part of the day.

Not that the daylight hours weren't amazing as well. They were. JP made everything fun, from brushing their teeth to feeding Kayla to grocery shopping. The time she spent with her niece was precious and filled her heart right alongside JP.

But the nights. Those blew her mind in a whole other way. Hours spent exploring each other culminating in earth-shaking orgasms—typically more than one for her.

She'd never been happier, and that was before she even thought about how much she loved his entire family and how they accepted her as one of their own despite her initial lies.

Only one black cloud hovered over her happy bubble and was the continued criticism from her parents. They wouldn't budge on their stance against all things Benson and had even gone so far as to stop answering her phone calls. However, they weren't above sending passive-aggressive texts all day every day about how she was breaking her mother's heart, ripping the family apart, and dishonoring her sister's memory.

Pre-JP, those texts would have sent her running home to fix every problem she could for her parents out of guilt, worry, and obligation. Now that she'd had a taste of true happiness and independence, she realized how toxic their relationship had become. Something needed to change before it dissolved completely.

All those worries were getting put on the back burner until tomorrow. Or maybe the next day. Whenever she could talk herself into dealing with it. Tonight, she and JP were headed out on a double date with Mickie and Keith.

Jagger and Ronnie offered to babysit Kayla, who had nothing more than a lingering sniffle at this point. A few moments ago, Mickie had kidnapped her under the guise of helping her get ready for their night out. She now sat on an enormous bed and waited while her friend searched for a dress she'd claimed would be perfect for Hannah to wear.

"Mickie, don't go crazy looking for it. I can run to Target quickly and grab a dress or something."

Behind her, Ronnie snorted.

"Ew! There is no way in hell I'm letting you wear something from Target," Mickie called out as she rifled through one of her closets. *One* of her closets. The woman had more clothes than

Nordstrom.

"Hannah, meet Mickie, the clothing snob," Ronnie said with a snicker.

"I heard that, bitch!"

Hannah raised an eyebrow. This was a side of Mickie she'd yet to see.

"I meant for you to." Ronnie yelled back. "And my whole outfit is from Target."

"Yeah, well, you're a lost cause. There's still hope for Hannah."

Frowning, Hannah glanced down at her lavender ribbed tank top and denim shorts. Her style wasn't bad, but she certainly didn't have the eye for fashion Mickie did. Or the budget to back it up.

"JP is going to flip his shit when he sees you in this outfit, lady. So you're gonna suck it up and wear it. I just have to remember where I put it," she muttered from out of sight.

"She's not your dress-up doll, Mick," Ronnie called back, but she was laughing. They teased each other as much as the guys did. "Better you than me, Hannah. She's scary when she's like this."

"Ah-ha! Found it." Three seconds later, Mickie emerged from the closet with a scrap of black material. "Put this on." She thrust it at Hannah. "I only wore it once. It was too short, even for Scarlett, but it should work for you since you're shorter."

To be honest, she was excited to wear a designer dress. The most glamorous piece of clothing she owned was a two-hundred-dollar pair of jeans she'd purchased for half off at a Black Friday sale. To wear something once worn and probably captured on camera by the spectacular movie star Scarlett gave her quite a thrill.

"We'll give you a minute of privacy. Come on, Ronnie." Mickie grabbed her friend's hand and tugged her out of the room.

"Hey!" Ronnie called as she was yanked without ceremony

into the hallway. "I never agreed to give her privacy. What the hell does she need privacy for? It's just us. We all have tits!"

"Shh, quiet. Help me pick out the makeup." The door shut, leaving Hannah alone in Mickie and Keith's guest room, where Mickie had decided to give her a makeover, apparently. She peeled out of her clothes then put on the strapless bra as instructed by Mickie. A tiny thong followed only because she refused to go without panties, as her foolish new friend suggested. After getting a lecture and finger shake about panty lines, she'd gotten Mickie to agree to a seamless thong. Both the bra and thong had been purchased for her by Mickie earlier that morning.

Heavens, it'd been a long time since Hannah had worn one of these damn thongs. After a few false starts, she managed to shimmy herself into the slinky black number Mickie swore would make JP's "tongue loll out then crawl across the room to lick her all over."

Whatever that meant.

After tying the halter straps behind her neck, she glanced down. Wow. More cleavage than she'd ever shown stared her in the face. The dress had a keyhole cutout right over the tops of her breasts, which crossed into the halter straps. Other than the cleavage and a bare upper back, the dress didn't have much pizzaz. Black and fitted. Nothing sparkly or overly eye-catching. Simple and sexy. She loved it.

Hannah slipped her feet in the very tall heels Mickie had claimed were accidentally sent to her by a designer, thus not her size. Hannah had a feeling that was bull. Over the past few weeks, she'd gotten to know Mickie, and the woman was nothing if not generous with her money. Most likely, she'd purchased the shoes for Hannah and this very outing.

"Can we come in yet?" Mickie yelled through the door.

"Yep. I'm dressed."

The door flew open, and Mickie dragged reluctant Ronnie in much as she'd lugged her from the room.

"Look, Mick, I love you, but if you pull my arm out of the socket, we're gonna fight," Ronnie said as she rubbed her wrist. "All right, let's see this—damn, woman."

"I knew it!" Mickie clapped while beaming. Then she smacked Ronnie's arm. "Didn't I tell you this dress would be perfect?"

With a sweet smile, Ronnie whacked Mickie back with a little too much force.

"Ouch!"

"She might be crazy, but she is so right, Hannah. Have you looked at yourself yet? You look like a fucking supermodel."

A supermodel. Not likely. A nervous laugh escaped her. Had she ever been on the receiving end of so many complements on her looks and appreciative stares?

No. And she had no idea how to take it without feeling like a bug under the microscope.

"I haven't looked yet."

"Well, let's change that right now." Mickie grasped her shoulders and propelled her into the walk-in closet. She cupped her hand over Hannah's eyes then positioned her, presumably in front of the full-length mirror hanging from the wall. "Okay, ready?"

Maybe?

"Yes."

"One…two…"

"Jesus, Mickie, just let the woman look at herself."

"Three!"

Mickie yanked her hand away with a flourish, then took a step back.

"Wow," Hannah said as she took in the sight before her. Who the hell was this woman? She looked…hot.

"Sexy AF, right?" Mickie asked.

"Actually, um, yeah." Hannah twisted right and left, unable to keep from checking out her own backside. The dress hugged her in all the right places. Her stomach looked flatter than usual, her breasts perkier, and her butt rounder and higher. All things her mother would lose her mind over convinced Hannah would be drugged, abducted, and trafficked to some pervert, never to be heard from again.

She wasn't worried. JP would be by her side all night.

"What is this thing made of?" she asked as she continued to check herself out.

"Honey, trust me when I say the dress is just the icing on the very yummy cake. This is all you. We just put some pretty wrapping on you. Now let's get to hair and makeup."

"Kill me now," Ronnie muttered, but she dutifully followed Mickie into the bathroom.

Hannah took a few more moments to gawk at herself. A shiver ran up her spine as she imagined JP's reaction. Would he like it? Probably. Her breasts were on display, and the dress was tight as anything. Would he touch her tonight while they danced? Pull her close? Run his hands over her body? Grind against her?

The thought of being out with him, of dancing, losing herself in him and letting the music take over thrilled her. No matter how many other women watched him, lusted after him, or wished he'd talk to them, JP would be going home with her.

Other women would be jealous. There was no doubting that. She'd never admit it, but that notion gave her a secret thrill she should probably feel embarrassed about.

But she didn't. Not tonight. Not in this dress. Instead, she felt powerful, sexy, beautiful.

All things she'd rarely allowed herself to feel because of her upbringing. So many things had changed in her life over the past few weeks, and she owed it all to the Bensons. They were terrific, accepting friends who'd introduced her to the fun side of life.

Her mother would need a sedative if she knew, but Hannah's desires trumped the guilt over causing her mother anxiety for the first time in her life.

"Hannah! Get your hot ass in here."

"Coming." She dashed out of her closet, wobbling her way

into the bathroom on the four-inch stilettos.

Making it through the night without breaking an ankle would be the real challenge.

"YOU BE A good girl for Uncle Jag and Aunt Ronnie. Okay?"

Kayla wiggled her arms and grabbed for the toy giraffe JP held.

"Quit nagging her. She's always the best girl," Jag said as he strode into the room. "Aren't you, my perfect niece?"

Kayla squealed and reached for Jagger.

Little traitor. She'd barely been in his life longer than a month, and he had already lost his spot as favorite adult.

"Changed my mind. Make sure you have a diaper blowout, spit up all over Uncle Jagger, and scream all night long."

With a snort, Jagger came and plucked Kayla from his arms. "Pfft, she would never. She's always a perfect angel baby for her favorite uncle." He lowered his voice and whispered, "But if you want to give Aunt Ronnie a hard time, feel free."

The front door swung open. "I heard that," Ronnie said as she ran into the house. "And I'll make you pay for it as soon as I pee."

A Ronnie-shaped whir blew through the den and down the hallway.

"Why is your auntie so weird?" Jagger asked Kayla in a high-pitched voice. "Can you tell me that? Please don't turn out like her."

Snickering, JP turned as he heard the click-clack of high heels coming up behind him. "You ladies just about ready—holy fuck."

Instant boner.

In-stant. The blood fled from his limbs and brain, straight to his cock. He didn't even bother to be discreet as he adjusted himself. Maybe he should have worn a loser pair of jeans.

"Classy, bro," Jagger said as he covered Kayla's eyes. "Hannah, you look gorgeous."

"Hey!" JP snapped. "Don't look at her. In fact, go to another room. What I'm about to do to her might not be appropriate for little ones. Or grown men with the intelligence of an infant."

"Classy and clever. You're a lucky woman, Hannah," Jag said as he rolled his eyes. But he turned and made his way into the kitchen.

Hannah stood behind the couch with wide eyes and pink cheeks. And more makeup than he'd ever seen on her. She looked downright sinful with a dark smoky shadow around her eyes, ruby-red lips, and those damn delicious tits taunting him.

"Christ, woman, you are sexy as fuck. Tell me you know how smokin' hot you look. Shit, I'm gonna be fighting assholes all night, aren't I?"

With a shake of her head, she walked closer. "No. My attention couldn't possibly be diverted from you. You look amazing as well."

He'd gone with a pair of dark jeans and a slim-fitting charcoal button-up made from a satiny cloth. Rolled sleeves, some hair-styling time in front of the mirror, and a spritz of his favorite cologne completed the outfit. He was vain enough to notice he looked good.

"Thank you, beautiful, but I've not nothing on you. Seriously, every man in the club is gonna be hard as hell the moment they set their beady eyes on you."

"Thank you," she squeaked, smoothing the front of the unwrinkled dress.

Aww, his girl was nervous and maybe a little shy. Crazy considering how hot she was, but so fitting with the Hannah he'd come to know.

He walked around the couch until he stood in front of her. Unable to keep from touching her for a second longer, he rested his hands on her waist and put his lips to her neck, nibbling his way up to her jaw as he walked her back toward the wall.

A breathy sigh left her as she tilted her head to give him better access. Getting to watch Hannah discover her sensual side and teaching her all there was to love about sex was turning to be one of the highlights of his life. She embraced everything with an open mind, eager to experience it all with him. Underneath her curiosity and responsiveness lived a hint of apprehension and modesty he found endearing as hell. Especially since she lost all bashfulness as soon as the pleasure hit a certain point.

He nipped her jaw, then inhaled the scent he'd recognize in a sea of a thousand other women. A little sweet, a little spicy, and all Hannah.

When she moaned, he caught her earlobe between his teeth and gave a gentle tug at the same time he tickled his fingers on her thighs along the hem of her dress. Hannah shuddered and gripped his sides. "Love when you touch me," she whispered.

"Mmm. How about we forget going out? I can take you to my room. Feed you there. Dance with you there. We can dance on my bed, against the wall, over my dresser. Fuck the club."

He was certain she was about to agree when a "Hell no, John Paul Benson. You are not messing up my night out to satisfy your penis," reached his ears.

With a groan, he turned his head to look at the intruder. Mickie stood with her arms crossed and a smug smirk on her perfectly made-up face. "You know you're evil, right?"

She shrugged. "Where's my man?"

"Probably hiding from you," JP grumbled.

Face even pinker than before, Hannah swatted his shoulder. "Play nice," she said.

He grabbed her around the waist and pulled her against him. "Pretty sure I was playing very nice until this one barged in." A well-placed play-bite on her neck had Hannah giggling.

"Ahh, young love," Mickie said. "Don't worry about me. I know my way around."

Keith had decided to shower and get ready over here instead of his own house. And decided meant he'd been forced to leave his home so Mickie and Ronnie could have their way with Hannah. Not that he was complaining. The result had been well worth not seeing her for the hours she'd been held captive by the ladies in his family.

"Now," he said when Mickie had disappeared. "Where were we?"

"Hmm." Hannah pursed her lips then tilted her head. "I believe you were right here," she said, tapping a red-tipped nail against her pulse point. "But I've been here a few minutes now and have yet to receive a proper kiss."

Damn, playful Hannah was fun.

"Well, shit. That oversight is entirely my fault. Let me fix that right now." He grabbed two handfuls of her ass and yanked her flush against him, making her yelp, then laugh. Or start to laugh, most of it he swallowed up with his hungry mouth.

He was betting tonight would end up being one of the best of his life.

Chapter Twenty-Seven

Dinner was a blast. They'd driven about forty-five minutes away to a steak house that had JP's mouth watering before they'd entered the building. The meat was cooked perfectly, sides hit the spot, and the two glasses of wine Hannah had consumed made her flirty and affectionate.

The perfect start to the night.

Mickie had handled all the evening's details. She'd booked the reservation, chosen the club, and driven since she no longer drank. That left JP and Hannah free to let loose and have fun. Something he hadn't done since before Kayla landed in his lap. Seeing Hannah chill and bubbly was a treat as well.

She'd made it clear she'd never been to a nightclub like this—an upscale venue with two lines at the door. One short line for VIPs and one for the rest of the world. With Mickie at the helm, it didn't take a psychic to predict which line they were cruising down.

Hand in hand, Mickie and Keith walked in front of him and Hannah. She clasped his hand in a vice grip, letting him know nerves ran below the put-together exterior.

"You good?" he asked. Women eyed him from their places in the general admission line. Though it made him sound like a douche, he was used to it and typically reveled in it. Most of the time, he had his pick of the pack. They loved his tattoos, his potty mouth, and his skill in bed. Ronnie called it is rough-around-the-edges-charm. Whatever it was, it worked for him. Tonight, however, he only had eyes for Hannah and wished the skimpily dressed women on the hunt would keep their gazes to themselves.

"Yeah," she said, squeezing his hand. "Just a little out of my element. And uh, you sure attract a lot of attention. Maybe you should have borrowed some of Mickie's magical coverup to hide your tattoos. I think they're making all these women stupid."

He let out a loud laugh, drawing even more attention. "Does that include you?"

"I'm probably the stupidest of all," she murmured.

"Hey." He stopped walking and wrapped an arm around her waist. Her soft curves molded against him in all the right places, making him want to back her against the side of the building and finish what he'd started back at the house. "Forget everyone else. Just you and me dancing tonight. Okay?"

"We've lived very different lives, JP."

"Maybe. But my life has changed since I became a father." The words still tasted so strange on his tongue. "Promise I'm only looking at one woman here tonight. Lucky for me, she happens to be the prettiest."

He kissed her.

"And the sweetest."

Another kiss.

"Kindest."

Kiss.

"Smartest."

She melted against him. "Okay. You win. We're in a bubble. Just us." Then she kissed him, slipping her tongue into his mouth for a deeper taste. His cock hardened against her belly. This night might kill him. Dancing against her, touching her, kissing her. Basically, an entire night dedicated to foreplay. Hopefully, he'd survive.

"Just us." He kissed her one last time, then winked and took her hand again. Had he been home, he'd press the heel of his hand over his cock to calm the thing, but that could get him arrested in public. Instead, he shifted as he walked. Beside him, Hannah snickered as though she sensed his growing problem.

"Not funny," he muttered. "You try walking with a lead pipe in your pants."

"Mmm. I'm too busy thinking about having that lead pipe in me later."

"Christ, woman," he groaned. "Two drinks, and you're talking like a phone sex operator."

Her loud laugh had more heads turning their way. He'd be lying if he claimed to not notice the feminine stares in her direction had grown a little colder while the guys looked with hungry eyes.

Fuckers.

Thankfully he seemed to have distracted her well enough to keep her from noticing. Elation radiated from her, and JP couldn't get enough of her energy.

By the time they'd caught up with Mickie and Keith, they were showing identification to the bouncer. The poor guy's eyes bugged the second he recognized Mickie.

Of course, the former actress was smooth as silk, holding up a hundred-dollar bill and whispering, "For you if you forget who I am and that I'm here."

He winked as he plucked the bill from her hand. "Sure thing, Miss run-of-the-mill person."

"Thank you." They followed Mickie into the club.

"Should we tell him he could probably sell a pic of you at a club for a few hundred times that c-note you gave him?" JP asked.

Keith scowled and took a mock swing at him.

"Now that I live a normal life, the media has mostly lost interest in boring old me, but once in a while, someone comes sniffing around looking for a scoop. Mostly wannabe entertainment reporters. No point in taking the risk." Mickie shrugged, then looped her arm through Hannah's. "Let's dance."

JP released Hannah's hand and watched as Mickie guided her into the crowded club.

"Damn, brother, you got it bad. Can't take your eyes off the woman," Keith said, slinging an arm across JP's shoulders.

He opened his mouth to argue but let the words die on his tongue. What the hell was the point? Keith wasn't blind. He picked up on the way JP slobbered after Hannah. "I do," he said to which Keith stopped in his tracks.

"No shit? Thought you were gonna give me hell for saying that."

With a shrug, JP said, "I don't know, man. She is on my mind every second we're apart. We have fun, I talk to her about shit I don't share with anyone, she's fucking amazing with Kayla as you've seen, and she fits in great with the whole fam."

"The sex?"

He narrowed his eyes. For the first time, he had no desire to share the dirty details of his sex life. What happened between him and Hannah was, well, between him and Hannah. "Best of my life."

A giant grin broke out across Keith's face. "Damn, JP. Sounds like you're in love." Keith slapped him on the shoulder. "Happy for you, little brother. I'll grab us some drinks while you keep an eye on the ladies. Let's have a few, then join them on the dance floor."

Love?

Love?

No way. Keith was out of his mind. JP didn't do love.

You also don't do children, a career, or stick with one woman for more than a night and yet...

But love? No. Love held no interest for him if it even existed. Besides, of all the women in the world, he couldn't be in love with Hannah. She was Mary Anne's sister, for fuck's sake. Kayla's aunt. Her parents thought his family was stealing their grandchild. Hannah lived across the freaking country and had no plans to stay in Vermont. And he had no plans to leave.

Yet as he watched her laugh and dance with Mickie, he couldn't help but admit he felt more for her than he ever had for a woman. And he got an ache on the left side of his chest when he imagined her returning home.

She brightened every day and heated every night. He couldn't deny waking up with her curled up beside him these past few mornings had been magical.

God, he sounded like a cheesy ballad.

Keith returned with two scotch and sodas. JP downed his in three gulps, much to his brother's amusement. The man sucked at hiding his laughter.

"Screw you," he said.

"What? I didn't say shit." Keith pressed his lips together, but the corners wouldn't stay straight.

"You didn't have to. That shitty grin on your face said it all for you. Smug bastard. Look, just because you found some lovey-dovey happily ever after garbage doesn't mean it's for everyone." It still baffled him how Keith could so easily play house with Mickie after living through a decade and a half of their parents' disastrous relationship. Being the first born, Keith suffered the abuse and utter unhappiness in their home for more years than JP had. Yet he still envisioned a forever kind of future with Mickie.

Mind-boggling.

"Maybe not," Keith said in that rational oldest sibling tone JP had always hated. Most of the time, he only busted it out when he was right, and the rest of them were wrong about something. Annoying as hell. "But that doesn't mean you haven't fallen for her."

Hannah laughed at whatever Mickie shouted to her over the electronic beat of the music. Her head tipped back, and those red lips parted. Her curled hair swayed and bounced along with her. She looked carefree, joyful, and happy. Only an idiot could resist falling under her spell. But that didn't mean he was ready to buy matching finger shackles.

"I admit I like her a lot," JP said. "We have a great time together. And yes, I care about her more than I have any other woman I've dated."

"You've never dated a woman."

He glared at his annoying brother. "But," he said as though talking to a child. "It doesn't have to mean anything more than that. Some of us don't need to attach ourselves to one person to feel complete. We can do that for ourselves."

With a snort, Keith supped his scotch. "You read that on a relationship blog or something?"

Flipping him off, JP turned his attention back to Hannah. Why waste any more energy on Keith when he could be watching his beautiful wom—uh, friend?

Hannah spun, and their eyes locked. "Here," he said, handing his glass to Keith. "Why the fuck am I talking to you when there's a gorgeous woman for me to dance with?"

Whatever Keith said in response disappeared into the pulsing bass and rushing in JP's ears. As he approached Hannah, Mickie backed away. Or maybe she went to find Keith. Either way, Hannah was his to dance with.

Her inviting grin grew with each step he took. Sure, the club was crowded with other dancers and hookup hunters, but he might as well have been Moses parting the Red Sea because he had a clear path to Hannah.

The song switched to something a little slower and sultry.

No words were spoken when he reached her. The volume on the dance floor left few options beyond screaming to be heard, so he slid an arm around her waist and pulled her in close. She smiled up at him with heated eyes.

As though they'd been dancing together for years, they fell into the rhythm of the music. Hannah was soft and pliant against him, allowing him to lead. Everything faded but the feel of Hannah against him and the magnetic draw of her gaze.

Was he in love with her? Is that what this was?

Was love the reason he didn't have a single urge to admire the other women in the club?

Was love why he'd rather be Hannah than anyone else?

Was love why he couldn't stop wondering what life would be like if she moved to Vermont?

Whatever it was, it had the power to make him think of his future. His and Kayla's. He'd been thinking in terms of jobs and housing for weeks, but now sneaky thoughts of holidays, traditions, and vacations spent with Hannah and Kayla were invading his brain.

Damn Jagger and Keith for prying into his private life and using words like love and relationship. They'd planted these seeds that were now sprouting into insane fantasies.

JP could blame his wayward ideas on his brothers' suggestions all he wanted, but deep down, he knew it wasn't them. No, these rogue musings came from one place and one place only.

The beautiful woman moving against him like a dream.

Chapter Twenty-Eight

The alcohol hadn't made her drunk, not by any stretch, but it relaxed her enough to act in a way she'd always wanted but been too self-conscious to allow. To let her hair down and embrace what was right in front of her without worry. She pushed away all the reasons she should hold back from JP and allowed herself to fully fall into the dance and the man.

She let her mind wander to places she hadn't permitted herself to travel to. To dangerous fantasies where she and JP threw birthday parties for Kayla. Where the whole Benson clan celebrated the opening of the resort. To long, passionate nights spent wrapped in each other's arms. To her own child. One with JP's dark hair and her blue eyes.

No!

She needed to squash that kind of thinking immediately. The only thing a future with JP would consist of was visiting Kayla for holidays. No togetherness, no family, no love.

Love?

Was she falling in love with the man?

As she gazed up into his hooded eyes, her stomach flipped.

Please don't fall in love with him.

She had to keep it what it was. Physical chemistry and friendship. It was the only way to keep from destroying her family.

That first part came easily as she'd never felt attraction like she experienced for him. She wanted him all the time. It was as if some perpetually sex-starved woman had taken control of her body.

The song ended, and another kicked up. This one was faster and with a spicy Latin beat. JP grinned, winked, then spun her out before pulling back in.

"You got some moves," she shouted over the music.

He bobbed his eyebrows. "Stick with me, baby."

She'd never danced to this type of music and had no idea what she was doing, but JP was a confident and skilled leader.

"It's salsa," he said against her ear. "It's a four-count, but only three steps. Watch my feet."

After watching for a few seconds, she mimicked his steps.

"There you go!" He grinned at her, and her stomach fluttered with pleasure. "Now, just keep doing that while I lead you around."

Right. She could handle that.

He twirled her around and led her across the dance floor with ease and skill. Hannah followed the best she could but stepped on his toes a time or two.

Or ten.

Not that he seemed to care, so she didn't stress over it either. In fact, she was having the time of her life. Everything about the night, from the food to the conversation at the restaurant to being in JP's arms, had been perfection.

The music slowed again, and he pulled her close once more. This time a sultry beat had their hips shifting back and forth in a near grind.

Her nipples tightened, aching in the way only JP could satiate. JP shifted his feet. One of his thighs nestled between her legs and pushed right against her sex. Her eyes closed, and she rocked against him, putting much-needed pressure on her clit.

God, it felt good, but she wanted more. She wanted to wrap her legs around his and ride his thigh until she came. Her thong was so soaked, she could feel wetness seeping out onto her thighs. The man was too sexy for his own good and drove her insane.

When she opened her eyes, she found him gazing down at her with a dark, ravenous expression. If it weren't for the other people in the club, she had no doubt he'd throw her to the ground and devour her.

And she'd beg him for it.

His hands slid down her back, landing on her backside. He squeezed, and she nearly moaned out loud. There they were in the middle of a crowded dance club, and she was seconds away from pleading with him to hike up her dress and take her against the bar.

What was happening to her? Whatever it was, she loved it and wasn't sure she wanted to give it up.

Ever.

Her breathing sped up along with her heart. Blood pounded in her ears, making her lightheaded. She licked her lips and thrilled at the way his eyes tracked the movement.

"Fuck," he mouthed as he drew closer.

She thought he was about to kiss her but instead pressed his lips to her ear.

"You are so goddammed sexy," he whispered, making her knees wobble. "I need you, Hannah. Now."

She needed him too. So much. And right then. But where could they go? The car? Outside? She wasn't exactly up for putting on a live sex show. But if they could find a private corner…

Who are you?

She was a woman discovering a new side of herself.

She gasped as an idea hit her. "Mickie said we have a private room. Something for VIPS," she said in his ear.

"Fuck. You're right." He grabbed her hand, and together they weaved through the dance floor. When he reached Mickie, he spoke to her quickly and nodded at what she said in return. Hannah didn't stand a chance at hearing, so she worked to pretend Mickie didn't know exactly why JP wanted the room. Mickie winked and gave her a thumbs up as she passed.

Maybe she should be embarrassed, but her sex throbbed, and her stomach coiled with need. Lust filled her brain, blocking out any room for embarrassment.

The further they got from the dance floor, the lower the music sounded. Before long, they were walking down a moderately quiet hallway with six doors. JP took her to the furthest on the left.

As soon as they stepped inside, he turned and shoved her against the wall. She barely had time to register the low mood lighting, the champagne chilling on a low oval table, and the plush, velvet seating before his mouth was on her neck. Then her jaw. Then her ear.

She had to lock her knees to keep upright as his lips turned her legs to jelly.

"It doesn't lock," he whispered against her ear, "but we'll be fine if I keep your back against the door." Then he pulled back, winked, and finally took her mouth.

It was a brutal kiss. No gentleness or soft lead-in like so many of their other kisses. JP attacked her mouth, and she permitted him to do anything he wanted. Their tongues met, dancing in the same way they had on the dance floor.

Pure foreplay.

Hannah's bones liquified as she gave herself over to the pleasure of his mouth and the hands wandering up under her dress.

He was hard against her stomach, grinding into her as he gripped the bare flesh of her rear.

"Jesus Christ, tell me you're not wearing panties under this sinful thing."

Sinful. Exactly how she felt right then, but in the best way. Like an ooey-gooey double chocolate lava cake oozing with delicious indulgence. Her lips curled against his. "A thong."

"Damn. Even better. I'm gonna have to get a very close look at that sometime tonight."

Suddenly the strong urge to tell him exactly how much he meant to her swelled. The words nearly burst forth, but she held herself back. Admitting she had fallen for him would be foolish. But deep inside, she wanted him to know how he'd changed her life, how overwhelming all these new and forceful feelings were, how he made her feel special. If she couldn't say the words, she could use her body to show him.

In a move that had his jaw-dropping, she spun them around and pushed him against the wall. She'd yet to be the aggressor with him, and the feeling of power washing over her was euphoric.

One of his eyebrows rose, and a smirk curled his mouth. "What are you up to, ma'am?"

Every time he spoke in a raw, primal way to her, a thrill zinged up her spine. Would he like the same? Could she do it?

One look at the prominent bulge in his jeans had her swallowing her apprehension. "I want you in my mouth," she said.

"Fucking hell." His head clunked against the door. "You know you don't have to, right?" he asked, though it seemed to pain him to be such a gentleman.

"I know." She licked her lips. "I want to."

White-hot lust stared down at her. "What? What do you want to do?"

Uncertainty crept in, nearly tying her tongue, but she forced it away. JP wanted her. Of that, she had no doubt. "I want to suck your cock," she said, sounding surer than she felt.

He cupped her chin then dragged his thumb across her lips. "You have any idea how hot it is to hear such dirty words coming from this sweet mouth? I'd give damn near anything to feel those pretty lips around my cock, baby."

That was all it took to have any remaining doubts flying out the window. Confidence surged, born only of the elemental knowledge of his desire for her. She sank to her knees at his feet.

With trembling hands, she reached for his button but stopped before touching it. When he nodded down at her, she worked it open. It took a few tries. Humiliation tried to burn its way to her cheeks, but when she risked a glance at him and found his chest heaving, his hands clenched at his side, and his nostrils flared, she let the negative emotion go.

He didn't give a crap if she wasn't practiced or skilled in seduction.

Next, she slid his zipper down. It wasn't as easy as she'd have expected due to the way his erection butted up against the teeth.

Once she had the jeans undone, she rose higher on her knees and shimmied them over his trim hips and down to his ankles. That left him in nothing but a pair of short, tight boxer briefs, the same dark gray as his top. He spread his legs, bracketing her thighs.

"Anything you want to do, Hannah. *Anything*. I'm at your fucking mercy."

Ho-ly God, that was the most erotic thing she'd ever heard anyone say, and she planned to take him at his word. With a gentle touch, she ran her fingers up the length of his fabric-covered erection. He hissed out a curse, making her grin.

She nuzzled her nose against him, breathing in his scent. Soapy, with a hint of the cologne she'd been getting drunk off all night.

"Jesus, save me," he whispered as she mouthed him through his underwear. Who knew where the impulse came from, but he seemed to enjoy it.

"You okay?" she asked in a playful tone.

"Who knew you'd take a little power and turn into an evil fucking tease?"

She giggled. The man was so much fun. "Sorry. Just investigating."

He grunted.

Still chuckling, she curled her fingers into the waistband of his underwear and drew them down over his ass to his knees. His cock sprung free, long and thick and *hard*. So hard the head was nearly purple. And so silky over all that rigidity that her mouth watered to feel it against her tongue.

So she did just that. Curling her fingers around the base, she held him right where she wanted him and tasted the tip. A few soft exploratory licks. His thighs flexed beneath her fingertips, and a low groan left his chest.

She wanted more.

She shifted, then wrapped her lips around the head of his hard-on and sucked gently. When he cursed and his palms slapped the wall, she sucked harder. He was smooth against her tongue and just thick enough to stretch her mouth.

A drop of salty precum hit her tongue. She curled one hand around the back of his tattooed thighs while the other still held him for her mouth. Then worked her mouth further down his shaft. When her lips reached her hand, he shouted a curse.

"Damn, that feels good."

She tried to smile but couldn't stretch her mouth any wider. Again and again, she worked her mouth up and down his erection.

JP didn't have a shy bone in his body. He shouted, he praised, he cursed, and moaned. After a few moments, when she had a rhythm going, she took her hand off him and held his other leg for support. She tried to take him deeper, all the way to the back of her throat, but at the same time, his hips jerked forward, making her gag.

"Shit," he said on a gasp. "Sorry. Lost control there for a second."

God, she loved that she could affect him enough to make him forget his determination to go easy on her. She didn't want easy. She wanted to make him crazy. Wanted him out of his mind. Wanted all of him.

Instead of pulling back, she relaxed her throat and tried again. Before long, she was sucking him for all she was worth and loving every filthy promise he shouted.

"Need to see your ass." He grabbed the back of her dress and yanked, hiking it over her hips and baring her bottom. "Fuck, that's a gorgeous sight. Damn, look at that ass shaking as you fucking destroy my cock."

Wetness flooded the tiny scrap of material between her legs. Could he tell? Had it soaked enough for him to notice?

A little devil spoke in her ear, making her shimmy her legs back and arch her spine as she swallowed around him.

"Fuck, fuck, fuck," he shouted. Thankfully the music in the club was loud as hell because they'd have heard that scream outside otherwise.

She swallowed around him again, and he growled. Literally growled like an animal. "I'm close, Hannah. Baby, I'm close. You need to pull off, or you gonna eat it all?"

Her knees burned, her jaw ached, and she was hornier than she'd ever been, but she'd die before backing off. She grabbed his ass, giving a squeeze as she tried to make this the best blowjob he'd ever had despite her inexperience and slightly sloppy technique.

His hands went to her head, but he didn't take control, just held on as his legs started to shake and his abs contracted. With a guttural curse, lurched forward and came in her mouth. She took it all as best she could, but some leaked out and ran down her chin.

"Too much, too much," he said after a few seconds.

Hannah sat back on her heels, wiping her mouth. She felt somewhat dazed by the rush of power and adrenaline that came with reducing JP to a swearing animal.

"You positive that was your first time?" he asked as he slid down the wall to the floor, still bare assed.

A satisfied smile curled her lips despite the fact she was seconds away from demanding he do something to make her come.

"I'm sure."

He cupped her face and gave her a dopey, blissed-out grin.

"You're fucking amazing, Hannah."

Her heart soared.

"Stand up?"

"Huh?" she said even as she did what he asked.

"It's my turn," he said with a devious wink.

He was on the floor, what did he plan to— "Oh!" she yelped as he grabbed her by her ass and jerked her to him.

Before she had a chance to process, his mouth was on her, licking and nibbling around the thong.

She gasped and braced her palms on the wall. JP ate her like a starving man. He yanked the thong to the side and speared his tongue inside her. She cried out and stared down, transfixed by the sight of him once again bringing her such ecstasy in such an intimate way. Blowing him had gotten her so worked up, this wouldn't take too long.

His tongue left her opening and traveled up to her clit. As she moaned, he slid two fingers inside. Immediately she clenched around them. That fullness felt incredible. And when he licked her clit at the same time?

Heaven.

Fucking her with his nimble fingers, he continued to flick his tongue over her clit. She thrust her hips in time with his efforts. Within minutes her legs were trembling, and her stomach had wound tight. Pressure mounted, needed desperately to escape.

"JP," she said in a needy, pleading tone she'd never heard from herself.

"Let go, baby. Come all over my face. Let me taste all that delicious juice."

God, his dirty mouth.

He curled his fingers forward and sucked her clit. Hannah couldn't have held off if she tried. Stars danced before her eyes. The VIP room disappeared, and all she knew was complete and total euphoria.

Just as she started to come down from the climax, he squeezed her ass and ran his tongue around her clit. She tugged his hair so hard he'd probably need plugs as a second orgasm ripped through her with brutal strength.

"JP!" She screamed. It was so all-consuming, she almost feared it.

"I got you, baby," he said, and even in the throes of a world-changing orgasm, she caught the smug tone of his voice.

Eventually, her body calmed. "I'm pretty sure I took flight," she said, panting as she rested her forehead against the wall.

"That makes two of us, babe." JP urged her down onto his lap. She straddled him, resting her head on his chest as he wrapped her in a sweaty embrace. There they sat, him with his pants around his ankles and her with her skirt rucked up around her waist, for long moments as they came back to earth.

He stroked his hands over the bare skin of her upper back. If Mickie and Keith had left them there, she could have happily stayed in that moment forever.

But of course, life didn't work that way. A phone buzzed from JP's pants where'd he'd been keeping them in his pockets.

"Hmm, think Mickie and Keith are getting restless?"

She laughed. "Maybe. Think it's yours or mine?"

"I'm gonna guess yours," he said. "Don't move. I'll get it."

She stayed right where she was as he rooted around for one of their phones.

"Yep, yours," he said as he held up a phone.

"Oh, it's not Mickie." He frowned. "Looks like it's your parents. Why would they be texting so late?"

"They're not very happy with me right now," she said as she straightened and reached for the phone. He handed it over with a concerned frown. "They were serious about me finding a way to help them get custody of Kayla."

"Fuck that. So what are they doing? Sending you guilt texts?"

"Pretty much." She opened her phone and pulled up the text. As she read it, her heart sank through the ground and all the wonderful effects of their spectacular night disappeared in a cloud of despair.

"Shit, babe, is it that bad? Your face just crumbled." JP put an arm around her. "May I read it?"

Her knee-jerk reaction was to stuff the phone in her pocket and keep it as far from JP as possible, both to protect her family and him. But this skin-tight dress didn't have pockets, and she was enjoying life out from under the heavy press of her parents' thumb. Plus, she wanted JP to trust her. After lying to him for so long, she had some ground to make up. So she swallowed the stark embarrassment and handed over the phone.

He read the text aloud. "Each day you stay in Vermont with those baby stealers, you dishonor your sister. You might as well have killed her instead of that horrible disease. You have betrayed your family. When you are ready to help us get custody of Kayla, you'll be welcome in our home again. Until then, you are no longer my daughter. Hannah, what the fuck? Has your mother been sending you shit like this all along?"

JP's horrified face did nothing to help the tightness in her chest or the crack that split her heart in two.

"It hasn't always been this bad. She's escalating," Hannah said. Tears threatened to spill down her cheeks. With one poorly timed text message, this went from being one of the most fantastic nights of her life to a complete disaster. A terrifying thought popped into her head. "JP, they have an attorney. What if they take you to court?"

He grunted. "Let them. What the hell are they going to say about me? I have tattoos? I'm unmarried? None of that matters in this day and age."

She worried her lip. There were things an attorney could focus on. His lack of full-time employment, Mickie's history, his father's imprisonment. Would those factors be held against him, or was she stressing for nothing?

"Babe, why didn't you tell me how bad it was?" The concern in his voice nearly broke her. She didn't want that from him. Didn't want to need it. Couldn't they just erase the past two minutes and return to post-sex bliss? But no. Reality had intruded, and she'd left her time machine back home.

"You're dealing with enough, JP. You don't need my family's drama."

"Hannah, we're a tea—we're close. Of course, I'd want to know. I'm so sorry she's doing this to you. You know she's wrong, don't you? You haven't done anything to betray your sister or your family."

With a sad smile, she glanced down at their half-naked bodies. "Haven't I?" she whispered.

"No!" He gripped her shoulders and forced her to look at him. "This is going to sound harsh, but Mary Anne and I were nothing to each other. Not a damn thing but one drunken night that resulted in a child. And while I wouldn't change that anymore, Mary Anne meant nothing to me, and she'd say the same about me. There is no betrayal here."

A choked sob ripped from deep within her, and she sagged against him. "I just want to do what's right. To keep my family from falling apart even more. But, JP, I don't want to lose this. It's…" She pulled back and looked at him. "It's the best thing that's ever happened to me."

He cupped her tear-stained face and pressed a soft kiss to her lips.

"Same, Hannah. Same."

And right then and there, she knew for sure she'd lost her heart to John Paul Benson.

Chapter Twenty-Nine

Hannah wore her sorrow all over her face, and it fucking killed JP to witness it. Flat eyes, downturned lips, pale cheeks. The opposite of the light that drew him to her. At the same time, he thanked the universe her phone had chosen that moment to chirp. If it hadn't, he never would have discovered just how toxic her family situation had become. She'd have kept her struggles to herself and continued smoothing ruffled feathers the best she could. Her family's wellbeing took priority at the expense of her own happiness. That's just the kind of woman she was.

Reliable, dependable, loyal, caring. She did so much for her loved ones including and sacrificing her own wants and needs. Whether that meant nursing her ill sister, moving across the country, caring for her niece, or placating her deeply grief-stricken parents, she did it without question because she loved them.

But she wasn't made of steel. A flesh-and-blood woman with her own unique set of desires, feelings, and needs lay beneath her mask. Who took care of Hannah while Hannah was attending to everyone else?

No one.

The excessive selflessness had to stop. Or at least find a healthier balance. It was time for someone to step in and see to Hannah's needs for a change. And JP was just the man for the job. In fact, he'd fight any asshole who blocked his path.

If anyone understood complicated family dynamics, it was a Benson. But he and his siblings also knew the power of blood relations as well. He'd do anything for his siblings and vice versa.

Anything.

And now that offer extended to Hannah. Without a doubt and without asking, he knew his siblings considered her one of the fold, just as they did with Mickie. It had nothing to do with her physical relationship with him or her connection to Kayla and everything to do with who she was.

They loved her for her.

"Hannah, I have an idea," he said as a seed sprouted in his mind. "I don't know if it will work, but maybe it can help nudge your parents toward healing and moving through their grief."

She straightened. Black eye makeup had smeared during the crying jag, and her hair stuck out from his wandering hands, yet she still stole his breath. "What are you thinking?" she asked.

He had her full and rapt attention. How had he never noticed how satisfying it felt to be valuable and important to someone beyond his siblings? "Do you think you can get your parents to take a call from you? Maybe a video call with Kayla?"

Her eyes widened as she nodded. "If I text them and tell them I have Kayla, I bet they will. But they'll probably think I found a way to get her away from you."

"That's okay," he said, letting his hand coast up and down her back. Touching her in an affectionate way felt so natural. Too natural. As though he couldn't *not* touch her when she sat so close. "What if I'm there too? We could talk to them together. Show them Kayla is happy and healthy. That I'm not the monster they think I am. Maybe if they get to know me in small doses while seeing their granddaughter, we can begin to come to an understanding."

Hannah gnawed her lower lip, clearly mulling over his idea. Those lips had been glossy when they got to the club, but he'd kissed the sheen clear off. Hell, he probably wore more of it than she did now.

"You'd do that for me?"

"Babe, I don't hate Mary Anne, no matter the circumstances surrounding how we met. Half of Kayla comes from your sister, which means your parents are every bit as important in Kayla's life as my family is. I'm more than happy for them to have a relationship."

"Really?" she asked with a small measure of hope in her expression.

"Of course. But…" He held up a finger. "But not if they are going to act toxic toward you or me and my family. That I won't tolerate. They don't have to love me, but they must accept me as Kayla's father. That means accepting my family as well. If they can't do that, if they continue to manipulate you or spew hatred toward you or anyone in my family, then they will not be permitted to have a relationship with Kayla. Protecting her from poisonous relationships—even within her family—is part of my job."

Hannah blinked. Slowly, a grin crept up her face, erasing the melancholy. "Well, John Paul Benson, you sounded very much like a father who loves his daughter more than anything just then, did you know that?"

He huffed. "Don't tell anyone. It'll ruin my rep."

"Thank you." She cupped his face and kissed him softly.

Quick as a flash, he gripped the back of her head and held her right where he wanted her. They kissed and kissed but kept it light, lazy, and more bonding than arousing. Instead of shooting a sharp bolt of desire to his dick as her kisses had done earlier, these settled in his chest, making him…squishy.

And that made him feel, well, pretty fucked in the head because it was becoming obvious whatever he and Hannah shared, it was enough to make him reconsider his entire life.

A sharp rap on the door made them both jump. When the jiggling door handle followed, Hannah gasped and practically flew off his lap.

"Keep your fucking panties on," JP called out as he climbed to his feet. He slapped a hand on the door just as it cracked open. "Not you," he said with a wink for Hannah. "You can take yours off anytime."

"Time's up, little horny rabbits," Mickie called out with a laugh.

JP rolled his eyes while Hannah straightened her dress then scrambled to smooth her hair back into place. "Oh, my God. This is so embarrassing. Do you think they gave us a time limit or something?"

Laughing, JP buttoned his jeans then stepped away from the door, which immediately burst open. Keith and Mickie tumbled into the room as though they'd been smashed up against the door.

"The hell are you two creepers doing?" JP asked as moved beside Hannah and slipped an arm around her waist.

"It's time to go," Keith said. "Now." He snapped his fingers. "Some group of fucking college girls recognized Mickie and have been trying to snap a clear photo of her for the past twenty minutes. I'd rather not be here when their horde of social media friends show up."

"Oh, fuck. Yeah, let's go." He'd been out with Mickie once shortly after Scarlett's whereabouts were made public, and it'd been a nightmare and a half.

Mickie and Keith were already halfway out the door. They had to deal with this bullshit from time to time, unfortunately. "Ready, baby?" he asked as he took his arm off her waist and held out his hand.

Hannah clasped it, and together they hustled from the room in time to hear someone scream above the music. "Look! There's Scarlett."

"Fucking fans," Keith growled.

It seemed as though every eye in the place turned their way. The mob of curious club-goers began to close in on them. People pointed, shouted for autographs, and bared body parts Mickie wouldn't have any interest in signing.

Or Keith wouldn't have any interest in her signing.

They had to get the fuck out of there before his grumpy older brother started brawling with every man leering at his woman.

"How are we gonna get through his crowd?" Hannah yelled.

"Like this." JP turned and hauled Hannah into a fireman's carry with a shoulder to her gut. She squealed, but it turned to laughter in a beat.

"You're crazy!"

"You can't run in those goddammed murder heels, so I'm carrying you. Leave no sexy woman behind, baby. You have no idea how psychotic a feeding frenzy of hungry Scarlett fans can get."

"Well then, giddyup, boy," Hannah said, laughing so hard he almost didn't hear the words. But he sure felt the smack on his ass.

"Oh, you're gonna pay for that." He sprinted for the door after Keith, who'd picked Mickie up in much the same way.

They made it to the car and out of the parking lot with minimal trauma. One fan threw himself in front of the car in some grand gesture of brainless adoration, but they hadn't counted on Keith, who'd mow them down without a second's thought. Especially if it was a man.

The poor guy ended up having to dive out of the way at the last second to avoid getting plowed down by Mickie's Audi SUV.

"Wow," Hannah said, glancing over her shoulder as Keith peeled out of the parking lot. One hand rested over her heart, which was probably beating as fast as his. "That was intense." Her voice lowered. "But kinda fun in an adventurous way."

Keith barked out a harsh laugh. "Tell me how fun it is when you have dudes leaving their used fucking boxers in your mailbox."

"Oh, ew." Hannah's nose wrinkled.

"I told him we could wash the ones that are his size so he could keep them, but he gets all growly when I suggest it,"

Mickie said with a shrug, craning her neck to face them.

God, his family was nuts, but he loved them.

JP smiled as Hannah rested her head on his shoulder. The plush leather seats cradled them in luxurious comfort. Within minutes her weight went slack, and her breathing evened. He kissed the top of her head and gazed out the window as a smile played across his lips.

What had he been so afraid of for so long? If this was what settled felt like, he just might be able to get used to it.

Around ten the next morning, Hannah sat cross-legged on her rented bed with Kayla in her lap. His daughter munched on these flower-shaped puffy baby snacks that basically melted o her tongue.

They were nasty as fuck—yes, he'd tried them—but Kayla couldn't get enough of the things. She was happy as could be, sitting with one of her favorite people and slobbering all over her favorite snack.

Hannah, on the other hand, could only be described as a nervous fucking wreck. She worried her bottom lip as she stared at the open video chat app on her computer screen.

"You might actually have to click something to get it to call them," JP said. He sat beside her with his second cup of coffee. Hannah had been cut off at one. The woman didn't need any help getting the jitters today.

"Yeah," she said, sounding so defeated, he was tempted to call the whole thing off. "I'm working up the courage."

"Hey, look at me."

When she turned those glum eyes on him, he grasped the back of her neck and kissed her. Once. Twice. The third one got a little out of hand. Only a squawk from Kayla when she ran out of puffs broke them apart.

"See," Hannah whispered. "There are much better ways we could be spending our time."

"Your parents are expecting your call. You know you'll regret it if you bail."

With a huff, she thunked her head against his shoulder. "I know. I'm just worried they'll be unkind to you."

God, this woman. Always thinking of everyone else. "Babe, I couldn't give two shits what they think about me. All I care about is how they treat you and Kayla, 'kay?"

She nodded against his shoulder. "Okay. Let's do this." Straightening, she gave Kayla another puff then hit the button on the laptop. The familiar ringtone sounded through the quiet apartment.

"My, baby!" Hannah's mother said soon as her face filled the screen.

JP did a shitty job of hiding his reaction. She looked so much like Hannah, he felt as though he were getting a glimpse into her future. Different from Mary Anne, who'd had darker hair and a lighter complexion.

"Hi, Mom," Hannah said. She gave Kayla her fingers to grip then said, "Can you say hi to Grandma?"

"Oh, my sweet girl. Look how big you've gotten." She straightened with a frown. "Hannah, should she be eating that? She could choke. Our attorney wants us to document any hazards we become aware of."

Beside him, Hannah stiffened but didn't react in any other way. "No, Mom. They're fine. They're designed for babies her age. See?" She held up the canister with the six-month-and-up label facing the computer's camera. "Actually, most of the time, they dissolve on her tongue before she gets a chance to swallow them."

The face her mom made would have had JP laughing if the situation wasn't so tense. "Sounds like they're full of chemicals. Figures they'd feed her—"

"Mom." Hannah's sharp tone dragged the woman's attention from the baby. "I'd like you to meet someone formally. This is JP. It was his idea to call you. He figured you'd love to see Kayla. JP, this is my mom, Patricia Briggs."

Way to try and give him a leg up, but from the looks of it, he'd need a whole soccer team's worth of legs to get in Patricia's good graces. He didn't want to admit it to Hannah and cause her more angst, but the attorney factor unsettled him a bit. Even if they had no grounds for obtaining custody of Kayla, they could make his life miserable with lawsuits and time in court.

Patricia's gaze shifted to him for the first time since the call began, and as though she hadn't realized he'd been present all along, her mouth opened and closed a few times.

"Nice to meet you, Mrs. Briggs." Might as well go for formal. She seemed the type to appreciate the gesture.

"What's going on? Hannah? Why is that man here?"

Maybe not.

"Mom, that man is Kayla's father. He wanted to meet her grandparents. To get to know you guys and reassure you that Kayla is happy, healthy, and in good hands. We thought—"

"David!" Patricia shouted in a nearly panicked tone. She gripped the edge of the computer desk as though she needed physical support. "David, I need you."

Hannah's dad appeared on the screen. "What's wrong, honey?" He looked older than his fifty-four years with thinning gray hair, dark smudges under his eye, and clothes hanging off his slim frame. Obviously, the stress of the past year had taken its toll on the man.

Losing a daughter and living with an unwell wife would drag any man down.

"Hi, Dad," Hannah said with a small wave.

He pressed his lips together as he peered into the screen. "What's the meaning of this?"

"I wanted you guys to get a chance to see Kayla. She's crawling all over now." Hannah's false cheer and overly bright smile broke JP's heart.

Kayla must have picked up on the tension in her aunt as well. She fussed and reached for him. Poor Hannah turned a distressed look his way. "It's okay, babe," he whispered. "She's fine. I'll take her."

The second he scooped his daughter onto his lap, Patricia called out, "No!" She pressed a hand to her mouth and stared at him with horrified eyes. "Put her down. Please don't hurt her!"

"Mom!" Hannah said with a gasp.

What the hell? He'd known the woman didn't like him and thought him unfit to raise Kayla, but actively freaking out when he picked up his daughter was taking it a bit far. He put a hand on Hannah's leg. The woman practically vibrated with suppressed frustration.

Once they finished this nightmare of a call, he had a few ideas on how to help chill her out.

"Mrs. Briggs, don't worry," he said in as benign a tone as he could muster despite wanting to reach into the screen and throttle the woman. "I've got her. I promise she's safe with me." Hopefully, appealing to reason and staying the calm, competent father he pretended to be would work in his favor.

"I will not be speaking to you!" she snapped. Instead of stepping in, her husband only stood behind her and rubbed her shoulders with a defeated frown. Was the man so beaten down by his own life he'd lost all fight?

"Mom, stop!"

"Hannah Briggs, how dare you. You led me here under false pretenses. I thought I was going to see my granddaughter, not be ambushed by some hoodlum."

With an exasperated huff, Hannah gestured to Kayla. "You are, Mom! She's right here. You're choosing to focus on everything but her."

"No! You did this." Patricia shook her head. If her frown got any deeper, her lips were going to hang below her chin. "You are hurting me every second you spend with them. I gave you a fantastic childhood, and this is how you repay me? With disloyalty? Do you know what happens to kids who go through the foster care system?"

Fuck this.

"Okay, let's take a step back," he interrupted.

He'd had enough of this bullshit. They could say what they wanted about him, he didn't give a shit, but Hannah's eyes had filled with tears, and he wouldn't stand by and watch her parents tear her down. Not when she worked so hard and gave up so much to keep them happy.

Not while she was his woman.

Chapter Thirty

Hannah's face burned with the fire of humiliation. Tears stung the back of her eyes and had her blinking up at the ceiling in a flimsy attempt to keep them at bay. She'd never be able to look JP in the eye after this disastrous video call. What had happened in the weeks since she'd been away? Her mother appeared to have lost her grip on reality and spiraled down so fast it made Hannah's head spin. And her dad looked like a shell of the man he once was, trampled by life and months of managing his wife's failing mental health.

"Do not tell me how to handle my daughter," her mom barked at JP. "You've been a father for ten minutes. You know nothing about raising children."

"That's true, ma'am. But I'm learning every day, and I'm trying my damn hardest." He looked to her with admiration shining from his eyes which only made her want to cry more. "Hannah has been a godsend. I have a tremendous support system in my siblings, too. Together we're providing Kayla a wonderful life full of love."

The man deserved an award for the calm and respectful response. Beneath his well-chosen words, his muscles vibrated with tension only she noticed. Including her as part of the crew raising, Hannah had a rush of warm fuzzy feelings flooding her veins despite the tension of the call.

"Your family?" Her mother snorted. "You mean that sleazy

actress?"

Hannah gasped and leaned forward, so her face dominated the camera lens. "Oh, my God, Mom! Stop, please."

How could she be so insulting to JP's face? The woman who raised Hannah had severe issues with anxiety and overbearing tendencies, but she'd been kind. She'd been fair. She'd never acted in a blatantly cruel manner. This unrecognizable woman left Hannah cold with a twisted stomach and heavy heart.

Her mother squared her shoulders, swiped the tears from her cheeks, then set her heartbroken gaze on Kayla before hardening her expression. She speared Hannah with a disgusted glare. "Hannah, he seduced our Mary Anne when she was at her lowest, and now it seems he's done the same to you. I warned you that you aren't welcome in my home until you distance yourself from him and the trash he calls family. Do not call us again until that happens. We won't answer next time, even if you use our granddaughter to manipulate us. You'll be hearing from our attorney soon."

"Mo—" The call ended, leaving her blinking at the quiet screen. "What the hell?" she whispered as hot tears escaped and rolled down her cheeks. Embarrassed didn't begin to cover how she felt at that moment.

The horror and revulsion that must be going through JP's head made shame wash over her. His family had been so wonderful. Welcoming, kind, fun. Even after they found out she'd lied. And there was hers, casting judgment and scorn when they'd been the ones to do wrong.

And Mary Anne had been the seductress.

They sat in silence for a few moments. All she could do was stare at the darkened video chat window. Facing JP seemed impossible. If only she could disappear and skip the awkward conversation to come.

"Hey," he finally said, placing his hand over hers clutched in her lap. The warmth of his skin seeped into her cold fingers but couldn't melt the block of ice in her stomach.

With a sigh, she looked up into the most non-judgmental face she'd ever encountered.

He squeezed her hands. "My mom died young, leaving us six kids with my dad. He's an abusive drunk who didn't give a shit about us for one second of his life. Not whether we ate, or had shoes, or heat in the frigid winters. Keith used to burn cereal boxes when our trailer got so cold our toes turned purple. Boxes from cereal he bought by recycling our dad's beer bottles. Sometimes it was all we ate for days in a row. Our bastard father is in prison now. Up until he got locked up, Keith was secretly funneling him money and dragging his drunk ass home from bars at all hours of the night just to keep his poison from leaking into the rest of us."

"JP…" Oh, how that sliced her in two. She'd known his upbringing hadn't been sunshine and roses, but wow. Her heart broke for the young JP who grew up in such an unstable home.

"I'm telling you this to show you that I understand families are complicated and sometimes just plain fucked up. Please don't be embarrassed on behalf of your mother." He took her hand and lifted it to his mouth, kissing each knuckle. "She's ill. I can see that. I understand how mental health issues can make someone say things or act extremely out of character."

She nearly melted into the bed. He'd been the one insulted by her mother's insensitive words. She should be comforting him. But there he was, being amazing, understanding, and just as handsome as ever. Hannah wanted to crawl into his lap and cling to him much the same way Kayla did. But she didn't have that luxury. As a grown woman, she needed to pull herself together and deal with her problems herself.

"You did nothing wrong, Hannah. You've tried to get her help, but she's an adult. What you need now are strict boundaries. You need to step away and stop trying to fix everything for everyone. Especially people who refuse help. They need to know you aren't going to be their whipping post any longer." He kissed her hand again, then set it down in order to adjust Kayla on his lap.

As much as it went against her grain to walk away from someone in need, especially a family member, he was right. Maybe time and space would help her parents work through their grief. All she could do was hope they came out on the other side better and stronger.

Still, it hurt that they'd never know Kayla because of their own biases and inability to open their hearts to the Bensons.

"I'm sorry about the things she said to you," she said, swiveling until she faced him so their knees touched while still sitting cross-legged.

"We're gonna make a rule here," JP said, with a half-smile she wanted to kiss into a full one.

Even in times of stress, she wanted him. Wanted to be close to him, touch him, and taste him.

"You are not allowed to apologize for someone else's words or actions, okay?" He rubbed his hand over Kayla's head as he spoke. The baby lay on her back in the space his crisscrossed legs made. Her eyes drooped with the heaviness of a child on the brink of sleep. Whenever his hand stroked her little head, she let out a small, contented coo that had Hannah smiling.

Why couldn't her parents see what she did? How kind he was? And generous? And what a fantastic father he was turning out to be?

All they saw were tattoos, a father in prison, and a relative with a public past. Nothing but imperfections. Full stop. As though they themselves were faultless.

Far from it.

Still, she felt responsible for subjecting JP to their vitriol, and leaving the guilt behind would be a mountain of a task. With a sigh, she said, "But I—"

"Nuh-uh." He held a finger in front of her face. "All I want to hear is 'Yes, JP. I will not apologize for other people's words and actions,'" he said as he tapped her lips.

A small laugh escaped as she rolled her eyes. "Yes, JP. I will try to stop apologizing for other people's words and actions."

"Try, huh? Pretty sure I didn't say it like that, but close enough." He gathered up a snoozing Kayla and settled her in the crook of his arm. "Well, well, someone found all this drama too boring to stay awake." As he spoke, he crossed the room toward the door. "I'm gonna lay her down. Don't go anywhere." With a wink, he was off to place Kayla in the small den where Hannah had set up a portable crib.

She used the few seconds of solitude to take a break and try to shake off the phone call. Time with JP was precious, and she wouldn't waste any of it stressing over something out of her control.

Or at least she'd work to stop stressing.

In less than twenty seconds, he was back and lingering in the doorway with his hands propped on the frame above his head. The move hiked the hem of his T-shirt, baring a strip of perfect abs.

"I was going to suggest we go grab a late breakfast, but it seems like Kayla had other plans." His lips curled into a wicked grin. "Whatever should we do to pass the time until she wakes?"

"Hmmm," Hannah said, rubbing her chin as she grinned. "You know I haven't scrubbed the toilets recently. You could help me with that."

"Ooo, yeah, that sounds like a blast." He stalked forward, keeping his hot gaze burning into her skin.

That was all it took for her to want him—one fiery look. Wetness seeped into her panties, preparing her for whatever he had in mind. He licked his lips, and her sex clenched. Whatever he was about to do, it had better include him inside her. And soon.

"Or, we could, you know, fuck ourselves stupid, then get lunch instead of breakfast, then put Kayla down for her afternoon nap, and fuck all over again." He reached her and bent to press his mouth next to her ear. "Then after she goes to sleep tonight, I'll spread you out on my bed and eat you for dessert.

All. Night. Long."

Her mouth opened and closed. *Sign me up.* The man was lethal. "Um, yeah, okay. Let's do that. Your plan. It sounds, uh, good."

Chuckling, he captured her earlobe between his teeth. Immediately goose bumps popped up all over, and she shivered as her skin felt more charged than a minefield.

"Just good, huh? I was hoping it'd be orgasmic." Warm breath tickled her ear, making her sigh in pleasure.

God, she loved this man. He made everything fun and focused on the positive. Didn't dwell in anger and negativity. Yes, she loved him for sure.

Oh crap.

"Uh, yeah," she said, clearing away the thickness in her throat as her insides went haywire. Love? What was she supposed to do with love? It hadn't been part of the plan. In fact, it was the opposite of the plan. Yet there she was. Smitten and head over heels in love with the father of her sister's baby. "Or—uh, orgasmic for sure."

"That's my girl," he said a blink before he descended on her mouth. Hannah kissed him back with everything she had. If she couldn't voice her love for him, she'd do her damn best to show him with her body.

His kisses were delicious. Deep, drugging, all-consuming sweeps of his skillful tongue that traveled all the way to her soul.

"JP," she whispered, as he kissed a path to her collar bone. Her head dropped back, allowing him full access to anything he wanted.

"Lie back," he whispered between kisses.

She did as he asked, lowering to the bed with his help. As soon as she'd settled, he pushed her simple T-shirt up. She lifted her arms and held, allowing him to disrobe her. Next went her striped cotton pajama pants. She hadn't bothered with panties, so he had instant access to her naked skin.

"Damn," he groaned as he kissed her inner thigh. "So fucking beautiful." Then he reared up and began to remove his own clothing. "I wanted to take my time. Drive you out of our mind with my mouth and fingers."

There went his shirt, somewhere over his head. She licked her lips as her favorite visual feast came into full view. Beneath his sweatpants, his erection stuck out, tenting the fabric as far as it would stretch.

With a sly smirk, he tilted his head. "You listening?"

"What? Huh?" Her cheeks heated.

"Fuck, baby, I love—" She sucked in a breath. Love? "your eyes on me. Eating me up. Lit up with excitement because I'm about to fuck you."

There wasn't time to feel any disappointment over the outcome of his statement. He shifted, pulling off his pants. A long, thick erection she'd grown quite friendly with jutted out so hard, the tip leaked with his desire for her.

Hannah's mouth watered, and her hands trembled. She reached for him. Maybe he'd let her play for a bit.

"Nuh-uh," he whispered, catching her wandering hand before it had a chance to wrap around him. "As I was saying. I'd love to take the time to drive each other crazy, but I'm the hardest I've even been in my fucking life. I can't even promise I won't shoot off the second I push into that wet pussy."

"Well then, I guess you better not waste any time, huh?"

"Brat," he said with a laugh. The man moved fast, diving onto the bed and flipping her on her side before she knew what hit her. He snuggled up to her back and bent his knees.

They fit together like two interlocking puzzle pieces, her more petite frame nestled into his much longer one. His hard length pressed against the seam of her legs, leaving a wet trail of precum.

When his hand slid up and over her hip to the place where she wanted him most, she didn't hesitate to open her knees like a clam shell.

"That's right, baby, let me in." He slipped his fingers into the slippery cleft between her legs. Within seconds, she was panting for release as he alternated between playing with her clit and fingering her opening. Rocking her hips, she aided him in hitting all the right spots.

"Shit," he cursed behind her. "I could fucking come just like this, humping your damn leg like a dog."

"Mmm." It was all she could muster. Her nipples ached to be pinched and pulled, but she didn't dare ask him to leave her sex. Instead, she touched herself, rolling the stiff nubs between her thumb and forefinger.

"Christ," he growled. "That's it. Can't wait." He hiked her top leg up and over his.

The next thing she knew, he was pushing into her. Nothing compared to the initial stretch and absolute bliss of that first thrust.

"Shit, shit, shit," he spat as he started to pull away before he'd bottomed out.

"No!" She reached back and grabbed his ass to pull him back.

"No condom," he said around his heaving breath.

No condom.

They should not be the hottest two words she'd ever heard him say.

"I'm clean," she whispered. "I have an IUD. Uh, I got it after Mary Anne found out she was pregnant. Just in case."

He remained silent, and she could have kicked herself. Of course, he'd be squeamish about taking her word for it. She'd been insensitive to think otherwise.

"I'm sorry. Forget it. I mean, it's the truth. I'd never, but—"

He nipped her shoulder in a sharp bite, making her suck in a breath. His tongue swiped over the spot a second later. "That's not it. I believe you. And I'm clean, too. Was tested recently. I just...you trust me?"

She craned her neck until she could see his dark eyes. This was a face-to-face conversation. "Of course, I trust you, JP. I-I love you."

His eyes flared wide.

Oh, God, she'd done it. Committed the cardinal dating sin and professed her love too early. Way too early. Forever too early. If she could have called the words back, well, she wouldn't. They were out there, and now, no matter what happened between them, he knew how she felt. How could she regret being honest with him after the way they met?

"Christ, Hannah, I love you too," he said in a rush.

It was her turn for the wide-eyed stare. "You do?"

He nodded. "Not gonna lie, baby, it scares the piss outta me. But it's true. I don't know how we'll—"

She kissed him long and hard. "Not now. We'll worry later."

He loved her!

"Fuck yes," he said as he captured her lips and pushed all the way inside her at the same time. She moaned into his mouth. Being full of both his tongue and his cock overwhelmed all her senses and nearly brought her to tears.

He kept the pace slow, almost leisurely, but deep. Now that they'd confessed their feelings, there was an intensity to his lovemaking that hadn't been there before.

"Jesus, Hannah," he panted after only a few moments. "Not gonna last. You with me?"

Was she with him? Her entire body popped and fizzled with electric pleasure, ready to come to a head. "So ready."

He kissed her again. Her neck ached from the twisted position, but she wouldn't change it for the world. JP picked up the pace of his thrust, pounding into her with intent. His fingers found her clit once again. As though they'd been together for years, he touched her in the exact way she craved. Seconds later, an orgasm so powerful her vision hazed slammed into her.

She ripped her mouth away, crying out his name.

He powered into her one last time, pinched her clit, and came deep inside her. His fingers still worked her clit, prolonging her climax all through his. When they finally calmed, plastered together, and breathing hard, Hannah grinned. She'd never been more satisfied or happier despite the problems waiting for her at home.

"Take a nap," JP whispered in a slurred voice, heavy with fatigue. "Love you."

Her grin grew into a full-blown smile. So she hadn't imagined it. "I love you too."

They dozed a short while until awakened by a hungry Kayla. After quick showers, they headed out for lunch and spent the day exploring JP's small town. Though they didn't do anything outrageous or exciting, Hannah couldn't remember a more perfect afternoon. That night, after putting Kayla to bed, JP fulfilled his promise. He worshiped her with his tongue until her legs turned to jelly, and she was begging for release.

All in all, Hannah was floating around on Cloud Nine. Even her dreams consisted of wonderful scenes and steamy imagery.

JP seemed just as happy as she was. They fell asleep that night, exhausted and wrapped up in each other's arms with smiles on their faces.

Until the phone rang at two in the morning, shattering any possibility of contentment for the foreseeable future.

Chapter Thirty-One

A cheerful ringtone sounded through the room. JP wrinkled his nose. What the hell was that? None of his phone's sounds were that upbeat.

Beside him, a gasp had his eyes popping open.

Hannah sat up with a hand over her heart and a furrow in her. She grabbed her phone off his side table and frowned at the screen. "Why is my dad calling at two a.m.?"

Shit. It couldn't be anything good. Who the hell called in the dead of night with good news? He sat up, rubbing the sleep out of his eyes. "Answer it, hon."

Nodding, Hannah swiped the screen and held the phone to her ear. He couldn't hear her father, but the way her face crumbled told him all he needed to know. The heaviness of dread settled in his stomach as he inched closer and rubbed a hand up Hannah's back.

"*What?*" she said, utter shock coming through loud and clear.

He tapped her arm and mouthed, "Speaker."

Nodding, she quickly pushed the audio button.

"—crashed her car head-on into a tree," her father said.

Oh fuck. He slid his arms around Hannah's shoulders and squeezed her close.

"How hurt is she?" Hannah asked in a frantic tone.

"Very bruised up. Broken nose and a mild concussion." Instead of scared, her father sounded resigned and exhausted.

"So they're keeping her in the hospital because of the concussion?"

When her father didn't answer, JP's stomach took a dive.

"Dad?"

"Um, no. They said she was intoxicated. I guess they did a blood test to see how much alcohol and it was right around the legal limit. Based on some of the things she's said since the ambulance brought her in, the doctor is worried she might be at risk for self-harm. They want to hold her in the psych unit she can be formally evaluated."

"What?" Hannah asked on a gasp. "Do-do they think she crashed on purpose?"

Beneath his arm, she began to tremble. He wrapped himself as tight around her as possible and began to rock her as he did Kayla when she cried. His heart broke for the woman he loved.

Damn her mother and her refusal to seek help.

"They do," her father replied with a weighted sigh.

"No," she whispered. "What...why?"

"It's too much, Hannah. Too much now that you are gone, too."

Wait just a fucking minute.

Hannah's head hung heavy. Tears fell from her eyes, plopping onto the phone screen. As JP was about to tell her father they'd call back later so he could make damn sure his woman didn't blame herself for this, she said, "I'll book the first flight out."

The fuck?

A few more words were exchanged, but JP missed them over the storm raging in his ears. She wanted to go there? What the hell for? To sit in the hospital and be chastised for something that wasn't her doing? To be criticized and fed poison about him and his family?

No. Hell no. He wasn't about to let her insert herself smack in the middle of this dysfunctional mess.

"Okay," she said. "I'm heading straight to the airport."

They shared a strained goodbye then Hannah practically

leaped from the bed. "I hate to have to ask this," she said as she searched the floor for her pants. "But could you give me a ride to the airport? My car is at my place, and I don't want to waste time going there first."

She didn't look him in the eye. Instead, she hopped on one foot while shoving the other in her pant leg. Because she knew he would disapprove?

"No," he said, then took a breath. Losing his shit now wouldn't help anything, but the thought of Hannah walking into that mess only to become the sacrificial lamb had his blood boiling.

She froze, bent over with one leg in her pants, then straightened. "What?"

JP climbed out of bed and strode over to her. When he reached her, he cupped her shoulders and looked her right in the eye. "I don't think you should go."

"What do you mean?" Confusion wrinkled her nose.

"I mean, I think you should stay here in Vermont with me. Hannah, you need to show them that you can't be manipulated. You need to stand firm and not let them control you. Do you know what's going to happen when you get home? They're going to blame you for shit that's not your fault because that seems to be your mom's method of choice. And you, being the kind, sweet, incredible person, you will take on that guilt and twist yourself into knots, trying to be what they want you to be." He almost had to bite his tongue to keep more from falling out of his mouth. With each word he spoke, Hannah's expression grew more incredulous. But he couldn't hold his feelings on the matter in. This was too important.

He loved her, and part of that meant wanting, needing to protect her from hurt, be it physical or emotional. And going home would hurt her heart in deep, bloody ways. That much he knew for certain.

Shaking her head, Hannah took a step back, out of his hold. "I can't believe what you're saying right now."

He stepped forward, but she held up a hand, warding him off. It felt like a punch to the gut. "Hannah, you're upset. Of course, you're upset. Anyone would be, but I think if you take a step back and then look at the situation, you'll agree with me."

"I'll agree with you," she said in a tone he'd never heard from her before. A combination of disbelief and disgust. "I'll agree that I shouldn't go see my mother, who is in the hospital after crashing head-on into a tree. That's what you're telling me?"

Shit, this was heading downhill fast. "I just mean—"

She scoffed and continued as though she hadn't heard him. "If Jag or Keith crashed their car and ended up in the hospital, I'm pretty sure you'd do anything to get to their bedside. I can't believe you right now. You honestly think I wouldn't want to go there?" She looked at him as though she'd never seen him before.

A sick feeling twisted his stomach. "No," he said, taking one step toward her. "I don't think that. I think you would do anything for your family. But I also think they know that, and I think your mom isn't above using the situation to her advantage. So I think you should stay."

"This is unbelievable." She gathered her hair up and secured it with a rubber band. Turning away from him, she found her sandals then sat on the edge of the bed to strap her feet in. "I'm going. I'll get myself to the airport."

"Hannah," he said as desperation began to claw its way into his chest. If she left, would she come back? "As scary and upsetting as this is, knowing she isn't critically injured… well, maybe this is for the best. Maybe this incident will be the start of her getting the help she needs."

A harsh, disbelieving bark of laughter left her as she stood from the bed. "Maybe my mother potentially attempting to end her life is a good thing?"

He swallowed. Shit. "I didn't mean—"

She snatched her purse off his dresser. "If this is your definition of love, no wonder you've never had a relationship."

He reared back, feeling those words slap across his face. Not once had he heard a nasty comment fall from Hannah's lips. To have her first harsh words directed at him broke something in him. He'd given her his heart. The one thing he'd kept locked away from everyone but his siblings. To have her throw it back in her face cut him to the core.

"Don't follow me out," she snapped before stomping toward the door.

"Oh, don't worry, sweetheart. I won't. Have fun being the whipping post. Again."

She glanced over her shoulder, and for no more than a heartbeat, he saw the devastation and loss flash across her face. Then she hardened her expression and blinked, but it was too late. One rogue tear rolled down her cheek.

"Screw you, John Paul Benson."

The she was gone, slamming the door behind her with enough force to rattle the house.

He stood there, shoulders slumped and arms dangling at his sides as he stared at the empty space where she'd stood only seconds before. If he could conjure her back with only his thoughts, she would reappear any time.

But she didn't. And he stayed there with his heart bleeding all over the floor. For him. For her. For Kayla. How had a day like yesterday, perfect in every single way, turned ugly with just one phone call?

The pounding of feet on the stairs had him holding his breath.

She'd come back. She hadn't left.

He took a step forward just as Ronnie called out, "JP? Are you okay? What the hell was that noise?"

His stomach took a nosedive as Ronnie burst into his room.

"JP?" She took one look at him and said, "Oh, no."

He nodded.

"I'm so sorry." Ronnie opened her arms.

What the hell was he going to do now that Hannah was gone? How would Kayla ever understand her sudden disappearance?

The reality of the loss became too heavy to bear, and he fell into his sister's outstretched arms.

She staggered back before catching his weight. "Jesus, JP, what happened?"

Not now. He shook his head. It was too soon to say it out loud. The shock, the pain, and the anger were too fresh.

Even the fear for what Hannah was about to endure lingered, screwing with his head. If he could spare her that pain, he would without thought, even as crushed as he felt.

Without saying anymore, Ronnie held him tight.

He'd been right to avoid relationships and a fool to let one woman change his entire way of thinking. If this pain in his chest was a broken heart, he never wanted to experience it again.

And he'd make sure he never did. He'd been so afraid of destroying someone else with his actions and genetic bullshit, he'd never even considered he'd be the one to have his heart pulverized.

Fuck love. He was done with that bullshit.

Chapter Thirty-Two

Hannah charged through the double doors and toward the main information desk.

If someone didn't call security and have her escorted out of the hospital, it'd be a miracle.

The stars had aligned, getting her on a five-forty-five a.m. direct flight to Colorado. She hadn't traveled with anything beyond her purse, and after hours on a plane followed by a forty-five-dollar Uber ride, she'd arrived at the hospital looking like she'd been dragged behind the plane instead of riding in it. That's what happened when she didn't even brush her hair or change her clothes before fleeing a man's bed.

God, she couldn't think about JP now. The tears would start again.

"Excuse me, hi," she said to the smiling gentleman behind the information desk. "Can you please tell me where I can find a patient by the name of Patricia Briggs? I'm her daughter Hannah Briggs."

"Let's see..." he said, shifting his attention to the computer. A few clicks later, he glanced at her. "Give me a minute. Our system is crazy slow today."

As he waited for the computer to do its thing, Hannah glanced around the lobby. Several visitors milled about, some on their phone, some waiting for who knew what. Even a few patients walked with visitors, dragging an IV pole along. In the center of the lobby, a tall fountain shot water in an arch that splashed into the shallow pool. An attempt to bring peace to a space that often symbolized stress and worry.

It wasn't working for her. Today not much would bring her peace. She'd spent the first half of her flight fuming and the second half hiding her tears by staring blindly out the window.

How could JP have been so insensitive? Where was the man she'd fallen in love with? The one who cared about family, made her laugh, and blew her mind?

Ugh, she promised herself she wouldn't obsess over him until she was safely behind her apartment door. Showing up in her mother's hospital room looking like someone who'd just had their heart broken wouldn't help anyone. She had to be strong, so she could help her parents through this trying time. Same as always.

Yet a nagging voice in the back of her mind wouldn't be silenced. It chastised her, calling her a fool and warning she'd fall right back under her parent's control as soon as she walked into the hospital room. Was the voice right? Would obligation, guilt, and responsibility crush her until she'd do anything to get out from under its heavy weight as she'd done her entire life? Was she doomed to a lonely existence making sure her mother didn't break down daily?

It was her comfort zone, after all.

More comfortable than opening your heart to a man.

She blinked. God, had she done it on purpose? Blown up at JP? Misconstrued his words because it was easier, less terrifying to remain in her small box than experience all life had to offer?

She pressed a hand to her stomach, shaking her head. Her mind wouldn't quiet, but she had to find a way to silence it because she was there now and needed to see this through.

"Okay, sorry about that. She is in on the psych floor which means you won't be able to go straight to her room. But it does look like you are on the list of approved visitors. I'll call up and let them know you're coming so they can bring your mom to the common room." He glanced up from the computer. "See those elevators over there?" he asked, pointing.

Hannah followed his finger to a bank of elevators beyond the fountain. "Yes, I see them."

"Those are the ones you want. Take them to the fifth floor. Make a left out of the elevator. Follow the hallway. It's going to take you through an enclosed bridge over to tower two. There's really only one way to go, so you won't get lost. They'll buzz you into the common room when you arrive."

"Left out of the elevator, follow the hall to tower two, get buzzed in. Got it. Thank you for your help." She tapped the top of the desk.

"My pleasure. Have a good one."

With a nod, Hannah was off. Funny how she could outwardly portray a calm person who wasn't dying inside when she felt one stiff breeze away from shattering.

"Breathe," she mumbled to herself as she pushed the up button on the elevator. Thankfully, she was the only one waiting and was able to catch an empty elevator. Making small talk with strangers wasn't high on her list for the day. At least when she was alone, she didn't have to smile and pretend life was good.

After a quick trip, the elevator doors slid open on the fifth floor. As instructed, Hannah followed the hallway across the bridge and to a set of locked doors. She pushed the button, stated her name and was admitted. A nurse pointed her to the common room and they said her mother was already waiting there.

"Thank you," she said to the nurse before making her way to the common room.

As she approached, her father's voice rang out from the otherwise quiet space.

"Patti, they aren't going to let you out until you speak with the psychologist. Please stop refusing so we can get you home."

"David, I don't need to see a psychologist. This entire thing is being blown out of proportion." Her mother's voice was riddled with annoyance.

A heavy sigh came from her father. "Sweetheart, you've been through so much lately. They found a mixture of medication and alcohol in your system when you crashed. They're worried, and quite frankly, so am I, that you may have done this with the intention of harming yourself. I can't lose you too, Patti."

Those words made Hannah's heart ache with fierce sadness. Her poor father. She should knock, let them know they weren't alone, but the desire to hear her mother's reply overrode her senses. Patti would never admit the truth in front of Hannah, but maybe she would when alone with her husband.

"Enough, David. I'm getting tired of listening to you parrot the doctors. It's tiresome."

"I'm only saying it because I love you."

"Look, it's just us right now. You can stop playing along."

"What?"

In her mind's eye, she could see her father's forehead wrinkle in confusion as it did whenever he was concentrating or solving a puzzle.

"You're really gonna make me spell it out?" her mother asked.

"Yes, Patti, I really am because I have no idea what you're talking about right now."

"Of course, I did it on purpose. But not with the intent of actually hurting myself. Give me a little credit, David, I know what I'm doing."

Hannah's jaw dropped. What the hell?

"I...but...what? I don't know what you're doing."

"I've tried everything I can think of to get Hannah to listen to reason. I've shown her who those Bensons are and how bad they are for Kayla, and instead of coming to her senses, she's dug her heels in. The stubborn child. I'd never have expected it from her. I thought for sure, cutting off communication would drive her home, but even that didn't work. Whether she's just being rebellious or she thinks she actually has feelings for that JP, it doesn't matter. I'm her mother. I know what's best for her. And

I'll do whatever I need to protect my child and my grandchild."

Holy crap! Hannah couldn't breathe. She couldn't even think. Her mother couldn't possibly mean what it sounded like she meant.

"I'm sorry," her father said in a tone she'd never hear him use. Measured, cold, detached. "Are you telling me you drove under the influence and crashed into that tree on purpose to get Hannah to come home?"

Please say no. Please say no. Hannah clung to the fading hope that she'd misinterpreted her mother's words.

"Brilliant, isn't it? You know how she is. Always needing to fix our family. I'm betting she hopped on the first plane without a thought for those Bensons."

Oh God, she'd played right into her mother's hands. Fallen for her sick plan exactly as she'd been expected to. Except for one thing. She'd sure as hell thought about the Bensons. But still, it hadn't stopped her.

She pressed a hand to her aching chest and sagged against the wall as her knees weakened. What had she done?

The sound of a chair scraping across the floor made Hannah jump. "Please tell me this is some kind of a sick joke," her father said with shock bleeding into his voice.

"No. It's not a joke. I'm sorry if I offended your delicate sensibilities, but some parents will do anything for our children."

She needed to decide. Go in the room and confront the situation or leave.

And go where? To a lonely apartment in a town that no longer felt like home? Back to Vermont to a man she'd hurt, and who probably hated her guts right now? Walking away from JP was the biggest mistake of her life.

"This has nothing to do with protecting Hannah. Or even Kayla. This is about you and your selfish need to control everyone in your life."

"David!" her mother shouted. "What the hell is wrong with

you? We always do what we must do to keep our family close. Think of all we've already lost. You should be thanking me."

Thanking her? The ridiculousness of that statement put the starch back in Hannah's spine. Straightening from the wall, she charged into the room to find her parents in a tense stare-off.

"Hannah!" Her mother cried, flopping back against the wheelchair as though more injured than she appeared. "You came! Oh, my sweet girl, thank you so much. I've been so scared." She trembled in an impressive display of acting.

Hannah trembled as well, but with a type of rage, she'd never experienced. How many times throughout her life had this happened? How often did she fall for garbage her mother spewed to get her way? And had Mary Anne been more observant? Did she recognize the destructive patterns Hannah missed and push against them?

"I just destroyed the most important thing in my life, so I could rush to your side because I was so sick with worry over the idea of you possibly harming yourself. I've been riddled with guilt. I ran from the man I loved and his child, who I also love, to be here for you. But you can't possibly understand the devastation you've caused me because you don't know how to love anyone but yourself. You're ill, and I hope you get the help you need, but I'm done."

She turned on her heel and took one step as her mother cried, "Hannah, wait."

Slowly, she faced her mom. One chance, she'd give the woman one chance to show remorse for her psychotic actions.

"Now that you're home, we need to start thinking of a way to get custody of Kayla. We can't possibly leave her with those people. Our attorney—"

"Your attorney?" Hannah blinked. "You crashed your car on purpose. Your attorney is out of their mind if they're telling you that you have a chance of getting custody after this stunt."

Her father also stared at her mother with utter disbelief in his gaze. This had gone beyond conniving and straight to delusional. Had her mother not heard a single thing she said?

"Well, that's why I need you now more than ever, Hannah. You can vouch for me. Tell them this is all a huge misunderstanding and nothing more than an accident."

Her laugh was harsh. "I won't be doing that, Mom. In fact, I will block any attempt you made to gain custody of that baby." She turned to her father, ignoring her mother's sputtering. "Dad, I hope you now see how much help she needs, and I hope you get her that help. Until that time, I won't be able to come around anymore."

Hot tears stung her eyes, and she marched out of the room, head held high. Losing her family and the man she loved all in one day just might break her, but she wouldn't back down. For the first time in her life, was free to do whatever she wanted without the looming shadow of her parents' worry hanging over her head. If only JP was waiting for her to return to Vermont.

"Hannah!" her father called out as she reached the elevator.

She watched him approach, taking in just how haggard he appeared. His clothes hung on his thinner frame, and his face had an almost greenish hue to it. Clearly, he hadn't been taking care of himself recently. "If you're here to make a plea on her behalf, just turn around. I'm done. I meant it."

He raised his hands as though surrendering. "I'm not. I'm here to tell you you're right. She needs professional help. I probably do as well. And I wanted to tell you I'm sorry. For all the pain we've caused you over the years, but mostly since your sister passed. I don't know if I will be able to get your mother help, but I've already scheduled an appointment for myself with a mental health professional."

Wow. She blinked at him, stunned by his words.

"I-I hope one day we can be a family again."

Part of her wanted to dive into his arms and beg her to tell him everything would be all right. But JP's voice sounded in her head, telling her she was strong. And that he had her back. Silly since he probably couldn't stand the thought of her by now, but still, his fictionalized support gave her the strength she needed to say, "I hope so too. Get yourselves the help you need, and maybe we can."

He nodded at her, sadness etched into the lines on his face. Then the elevator arrived, and she got in without a backward glance. Pride bloomed in her chest, settling next to the heartbreak. She'd done it. Finally taken a strong stand and made her demands known.

If only she had someone to share it with. If only she could call JP right now and tell him the news. Hear him say he was proud of her too.

And he loved her.

If only his strong arms were open and waiting for her.

But they weren't. All that waited was a lonely apartment thousands of miles away from the man she loved.

Chapter Thirty-Three

JP handed the full sippy cup to Kayla, who practically ripped it from his hands. He'd learned early on not to get between his hungry daughter and her formula. The girl would lay him out flat to get her chubby little fingers on her liquid meal.

She shoved the spout in her mouth and began to guzzle, making these adorable little hums every time she swallowed. He'd miss that sound once she outgrew it. Occasionally, he wondered about the things he'd never get the chance to miss. The things he hadn't had an opportunity to experience because she'd developed beyond them before coming into his life. When those thoughts popped in his head, he tried not to let them linger. Too depressing.

The formula kept Kayla from squawking in hangry protest as JP grabbed some baby yogurt out of the fridge for her breakfast. Hannah had purchased it for the first time a week or so ago. Of course, Kayla loved it. She wasn't exactly picky. If it could be consumed, his daughter would eat it.

With a sigh, he stared down at the unopened container of yogurt. Only two days had passed since Hannah left town, but he hadn't begun to shake the cloud of gloom hanging over his head. At least a hundred times, he'd been tempted to text or call to ask how she was holding up, but he held off. Anger resided in his soul, along with the crushing sense of loss.

When she'd said she was heading to the airport, he'd been

stunned. He'd wanted to grab her and shake her until the neurons in her brain aligned, and she agreed to stay away from her parents.

But then she'd left. Left him and left Kayla without thought of anyone but her own flesh and blood. Christ, he was such a fool. Letting his guard down, opening up to her, giving her access to his heart. A shitty childhood had taught him hard life lessons about the futility of romantic relationships and the myth of love. Yet all it had taken was one pair of hypnotic blue eyes, and a gorgeous smile sent his and his daughter's way for him to forget all he'd learned.

"Your own fucking fault," he muttered with a shake of his head.

He fetched a baby-sized spoon from the clean dishwasher then turned only to stagger back with a hand to his heart. "Christ, you two scared me."

Mickie and Ronnie stood behind Kayla's highchair with their arms folded across their chest and frowns on their faces. As usual, Mickie looked like she stepped right off the cover of a magazine with a designer sundress and coordinated heels even though it was seven in the morning. Ronnie, on the other hand, wore cutoff sweats and a wrinkled Van Halen T-shirt. Kayla stared up at her aunts with a huge grin and milk dribbling down her chin.

"What the fuck's with the creeper act?" he asked, though the question didn't need answering. They were there to butt their noses into his business. With a huff, he tore the top off the yogurt, pulled out a chair, and plopped down next to the highchair.

"We wanted to talk to you," Mickie said in a tone that had him feeling twitchy. No good ever came from that conversation opener. Hence why he'd been avoiding her for the past two days.

"I'm good, thanks," he replied, scooping up a spoonful of yogurt. Kayla abandoned her fascination with the ladies in their family and gobbled down the first bite.

"Don't be an ass," Ronnie said, tactful as usual. "Hannah is the best thing to happen to you in, well, like ever, and you fucked it up. We're here to find out how and help you come up with a plan to fix it."

He straightened and gaped at them. "I fucked it up? Excuse me, but what the fuck? Why would you assume I fucked anything up?"

Kayla made a near-growling noise accompanied by an aggressive arm-waving, clearly not impressed with the pause in her meal. "Sorry, baby." He held a full spoon up to her lips.

"Well, for one thing, you're a man," Ronnie said, holding up a finger. Her shitty smirk let him know she was enjoying his misery a little too much. "And two, you're a Benson man. That really says it all for us." Another finger joined the first, wiggling back and forth.

"Thanks," he said in a droll tone. "I feel better already. You really rock at this pep talk shit."

Ronnie flipped him off.

"Okay, okay, let's settle down. This poor child's first word is going to start with an f for sure." Mickie pulled a chair away from the table and took a seat. Ronnie followed suit. "We really are here to help, JP. You've been miserable the past few days. None of us want that. We love you."

He liked Ronnie's no-holds-barred approach better. At least he didn't feel like a dick for telling her off. When Mickie came at him with her sweet smile and talk of love, he looked like an ass for pushing her away. Guess he was stuck listening to them. That or listening to Kayla scream her face off if he cut her meal short and left the room.

"So what happened?" Mickie asked. She grabbed a napkin from a pile and wiped Kayla's chin. "That's better, messy girl."

He sighed. Both women watched him, waiting for an answer. Hell, they could probably wait him out all day if necessary. "Fuck." He gave Kayla another spoonful of yogurt then scrubbed a hand down his face. Lucky baby didn't have a damn clue what was going on. "Hannah's mom was in a car accident the other day. Nothing serious, but they are keeping her in the hospital because they're worried she may have crashed on purpose with the intent of harming herself."

"Oh, my God." Mickie pressed a hand to her stomach.

Even Ronnie looked a little stunned at his admission. "Poor Hannah. She must be devastated. Well, that explains why she took off so fast, but it doesn't explain why you've turned king of the sad sacks. Or why you didn't go with her."

They'd change their tune once they had more details about her mother's behavior. "She's not coming back." He shrugged. Hopefully, they wouldn't see behind his façade to truly how shredded he was. "I told her not to go. We fought about it. She left. It's done. That's that."

"Whoa, whoa, wait up." Mickie lifted a hand. "Let me make get this straight. You told her not to go see her mother, who is in the hospital, injured and potentially suffering from a mental health crisis?"

The censure in her voice made him feel two inches tall. "Um, yes?"

"Jesus Christ," Ronnie said with a shake of her head. "You really are an idiot."

"Hey! You two have no idea how horrible her parents were to her. To us. They told her she wasn't welcome in their home until she walked away from all Bensons and was willing to help them fight to gain custody of Kayla. They're toxic and completely dysfunctional." He set down the yogurt despite Kayla's protests. "I wasn't trying to be a dick. I wanted to protect her from the pain I know they will inflict on her. They'll blame her, and she'll take it on. For fuck's sake, I love her and can't bear to think of her being treated that way." He snatched up the yogurt and resumed feeding Kayla, who remained oblivious to the riled-up adults around her.

Ronnie gawked at him, wide-eyed.

"You love her?" Mickie asked in what could only be described as a mushy tone.

JP's shoulders sagged. "I do." God, how he missed her. Missed her laugh, her smile. The way she'd grab Kayla from him without him asking as though she sensed when he needed help. They were connected in a way he'd never experienced and hadn't believed possible. Maybe that was part of the reason he'd felt so ill the past two days. He was suffering right alongside her, knowing full well her parents wouldn't treat her kindly.

"Well," Mickie said, glancing at Ronnie. "At least he got it half right."

"Yeah, his heart was in the right place. Too bad he's too dumb to know what he did wrong."

JP frowned. His sister was having way too much fun at his expense. "Just wait until you fall in love, Veronica. I'm gonna rub your nose in every damn mistake you make."

She snorted. "After growing up with five brothers, do you really think I'm itching to shackle myself to a man? Hell no. Not for me."

Giggling, Mickie added, "You'd walk all over the beta males, and I can't even begin to imagine you with an alpha."

Ronnie shuddered. "Perish the thought. I'll stick to sex-only hookups, thanks."

Ugh, gross. Snapping his fingers, JP rolled his eyes. "Hey, could we get back to me here? I'm the one who hasn't slept or eaten in two days."

Mickie's expression softened. "Okay, I'm going to ask you a question that I want you to really think about. Don't just give me a knee-jerk reaction."

Nodding, he scraped the last bit of yogurt out of the container, fed it to Kayla, then focused on Mickie. "Okay."

"May this never happen, but let's say my friend Ralph died tomorrow." She winced as though the thought of losing her best friend physically hurt.

"Okay…" Where the hell was she going with this?

"I think it's pretty safe to say I'd be devastated. Ralph is so much more than simply a friend to me. Before I met Keith, he was all I had. My only family. The only person who'd stuck with me through all of my ups and downs."

"Mickie, I know all this."

"Shh, just listen. So, imagine Ralph passes, and I fuck up. I get wasted. Totally blackout drunk."

"You wouldn't—"

She lifted a hand. "I might, JP. I'm a recovering addict who used alcohol and drugs to mask emotional pain. The threat is always there. Losing Ralph would be traumatizing for me. It'd shake up my entire world, flip everything I know upside down. I'm not sure I'd be strong enough to handle something that horrifying."

Frowning, he leaned back against his chair and really gave Mickie's words a chance to set in.

"You guys didn't know me when I was using, but trust me, you wouldn't even recognize me. I was mean, hurtful, toxic to everyone around me. I used people, did things that I'll forever be ashamed of, and spit in the face of everyone who tried to get me to admit I needed help. So let's say I became that woman again. I'm awful to all of you. Damn, near abusive. Then I'm in an accident, and you get the call. What would you do?"

The urge to immediately tell her he'd do anything for her sat on the edge of his tongue, but she held up a finger.

"Think before you answer."

So he thought. He thought of how much he loved his siblings, Mickie included. He thought of all the shit they'd been through and how they depended on each other. He thought of how distraught Keith would be to see Mickie suffering in such a way. And he discovered that no matter what, no matter how destructive Mickie became to herself or others, he'd always try to help her. No. Matter. What. As he'd do for any of his family members.

"Shit," he said as the weight of his mistake crashed down on his shoulders. "There isn't anything you could do that would keep me from rushing to your bedside."

"Exactly," she said with a soft smile as she sat back in her seat. "What Hannah is going through with her parents isn't the same as how things are with your father."

"That's for damn sure," Ronnie added. Something flashed in her eyes. A sadness JP had never seen before. "I think we're all a little screwed up about relationships because of him. Quick to walk away when something goes wrong, or afraid to even dive in because we're terrified of being trapped in a toxic situation like we were as kids."

Huh, he'd never thought about it quite in those terms.

"But it's not the same for Hannah," Ronnie continued. "Her parents are struggling, suffering, and spiraling out of control. They need help. And sometimes, when family needs help, you step up, even if you know it's going to be painful for you. Our father is irredeemable. He's never been more than a piece of shit. Hannah's parents were loving and raised her the best they could. Not perfect, no, but flawed humans like all of us. They're drowning in grief and despair. Hannah isn't the type to turn away from them because helping will be uncomfortable. If you ask me, that's a pretty damn admirable quality."

It was admirable. That loyalty was one of the qualities he loved about her.

As the baby of the family, sometimes he and his brothers forgot Ronnie was an adult like the rest of them. Hell, probably more mature than the lot of them combined despite her brash attitude and sailor's mouth. "You're pretty smart, you know that?"

She rolled her eyes. "Yeah, I know it. You guys are just too dumb to notice most of the time."

Well, she had him there.

"You know," Mickie added, "things aren't going to be perfect between you guys. You'll mess up, she will too. You'll hurt each other, maybe try to push each other away sometimes. But in the end, if you've made a commitment, then you've made the conscious decision to work through the bullshit and come back to each other. Doesn't mean it's a bad relationship or hopeless."

"So you're saying there's hope for us?"

"Does she know you love her?" Mickie asked.

"She does." And if she gave him a second chance, he'd make sure he told her every day. Multiple times per day. Hannah would never doubt his feeling for her.

"And do you know how she feels?"

He warmed at the memory of Hannah telling him she loved him. God, he hoped she'd meant it.

"That dopey grin says it all." Mickie winked. "Yes, JP, there is hope for you two. I bet she'd appreciate some support right about now. Maybe in the form of her boyfriend showing up for her."

He'd just been thinking the same thing. He could snag the next available flight out and be in Colorado by evening.

"We're happy to keep Kayla for you while you go get your girl," Ronnie said, blowing kisses at her niece, who'd gone back to her formula.

Hmm, it would be easier to travel without an infant, that was for damn sure, but an idea started to brew. One he'd need Kayla's help for.

What if he could do more than just show up for Hannah? What if he could prove himself and his love for her by helping to alleviate her greatest stress?

What if he could help her parents begin to heal?

"Nah, I'm gonna take her with me. But could you watch her for a bit while I pack?"

"Of course," Mickie said. "There's no one else I'd rather hang out with. Is there, pretty girl?" she cooed at Kayla.

JP jumped to his feet, pulled the baby out of her highchair, and blew a loud raspberry on her cheek. She giggled as he handed her off to Mickie.

It hit him then. He'd be seeing Hannah that night.

Holy shit. A bark of laughter left him. It'd been days since he felt this light and excited about life. "I'm going to get Hannah!" he shouted, making Ronnie roll her eyes and Mickie whoop in support.

He grabbed Mickie's face between his palms. "Thank you." Then he kissed her cheek.

"Hey! Get your fucking lips off my woman!" Keith hollered as he lumbered into the kitchen.

JP rolled his eyes and planted another loud smooch on Mickie's cheek. Next, he made his way toward Ronnie. "Oh, hell no!" she said, hopping out of her chair. "You know I hate that affectionate shit." She backed away as he advanced on her. "Seriously, JP. Don't you dare hug me. Ah!" She took off in a run, and he gave chase.

When she reached the couch in the living room, he launched himself at her, and together they crashed onto the sofa.

"Thank you, sis," he shouted in her ear right before smacking a big kiss on her forehead.

"God, get off me, you disgusting brute. Go get your woman back."

"Oh, I plan to." And once he got her back, he intended to hang on to her forever.

Chapter Thirty-Four

Hospitals sucked. JP didn't have many memories of his mother, but most of them took place in a hospital. Since her death, he'd only been in hospitals when his father had been brought in on suspicion of alcohol poisoning. Also, shitty memories.

And there he was now, about to speak with a woman who hated him. The mother of the woman he loved. Grandmother of his daughter. Not to mention Hannah had no idea he'd hopped on a plane and traveled across the country.

Did it get more fucked up than that?

Kayla flapped her arms and babbled from the baby carrier strapped to his chest. He'd brought a stroller but found this much easier. Plus, she loved it. He kept her facing out, and she flirted with everyone who walked by, giving them her charming smile. It'd saved his bacon during the long layover in Chicago. Thankfully she'd passed out five minutes into the first flight and remained calm on the second. Traveling with infants was no joke.

He took his time following the hallway he'd been instructed to take to get to Patricia Brigg's room. She'd been transferred from the psych ward to a standard room, which allowed visitors. Despite hours of air travel, he still wasn't certain what he planned to say. Just that he had to find a way to get through to Hannah's parents. Hopefully, having Kayla with him would soften their hearts. Mostly, he hoped meeting him in person, without Hannah around to absorb their anger, he'd be able to ease their hatred.

Guess they were about to find out.

After softly knocking on the door, he heard a "Come in," and entered. The first person he saw was Hannah's father, sitting in a chair in the corner of the room. His eyes widened, and his mouth formed an 'O' shape.

"David, who is it?" Patricia asked.

"It's, um, it's…"

JP continued into the room.

"Well, see for yourself."

He rounded the curtain and stood at the foot of Patricia Briggs's bed.

"You," she said with disgust in her voice. "What are you—"

Kayla giggled and flapped kicked her legs.

Patricia gasped. "My baby." Her entire demeanor changed, softening and becoming about a hundred times more animated. She pressed a hand to her mouth, blinking rapidly. "My God, you've gotten so big."

JP remained quiet, allowing the couple a minute to absorb the shock of Kayla's presence. They'd been so fixated on seeing her again, this had to be blowing their minds.

After a few moments of oohing and aahing over the changes in Kayla, Patricia shifted her attention back to him. "She sent you, didn't she? She thought this would make me do what she wants."

Shaking his head, JP said, "No, Mrs. Briggs, she didn't. In fact, she has no idea I'm here."

David frowned. "So she didn't tell you?"

JP raised an eyebrow. "Tell me what?"

"Nothing!" Patricia averted her gaze, and he could have sworn he saw a flash of shame cross her expression before she hardened her mask of hatred back in place,

"Well, I'm not here to play games, so if you won't tell me, I guess I'll be going." He turned toward the door and took two steps before—

"Wait!" The panic in Patricia's voice seemed to be the first genuine emotion he'd heard from her.

Gotcha.

Slowly, he spun back to face her.

"Wait," she whispered.

They stared at each other for a few long, heavy seconds until Hannah's father finally spoke up.

"The crash wasn't an accident. Patti knew it would bring Hannah rushing back."

His blood ran cold. That couldn't possibly be true, but one look in Patricia's eyes and he knew to the very depths of his soul that she had, in fact, sunk so low in order to manipulate her daughter.

"What did Hannah say?" he asked, surprised by how even he managed to keep his tone. Kayla often picked up on tension in his body, so he worked to keep from setting her off as well.

She looked everywhere but at him. "She said she was done. With us. And she left." Her voice was thick with unshed tears.

"I see." Suddenly, he knew exactly what to say to handle this situation in the best way for Kayla, Hannah, and himself. He walked forward, then placed his hands on the foot of the bed. "By the look on your face, I don't have to tell you how messed up that is, do I?"

Patricia's eyes narrowed, but then her gaze shifted to Kayla, and she shook her head. "No," she said in a small voice.

"Good. So this is how things are going to proceed from here on out. You are going to get help. Not a once a month visit to a therapist, but serious psychological help. Both of you." He glanced over his shoulder at Hannah's father, who wore a look of relief and nodded immediately. "Until your psychiatrist is convinced and can assure me you will not be a danger to yourself, your daughter, or your granddaughter physically or emotionally, you will not have access to either."

Hannah would have his ass if she heard him, but he refused to let them hurt her one more time. If he knew his girl, and he did, she was sitting in her apartment beating herself up for everything that happened since the day he met Mary Anne.

"You can't tell me—"

"I can, and I am," he said, holding up a hand. "Kayla is my daughter. It is my job to protect her from any harm. And right now, you both are harmful. I don't want my daughter to grow up without grandparents. You and Hannah are the only links she'll have to her mother. She deserves so know her mother through your memories. But if you want a relationship with Mary Anne's daughter, you'll stop denying the truth and get the help you need to be happy and healthy."

Yes, throwing Mary Anne's name in the mix was a low blow, as evidenced by Patricia's flinch. But something needed to be done to snap these two out of their denial. He wasn't above using their daughter's name to make that happen.

"You and Hannah…" David spoke from behind JP.

He glanced at the man who appeared to need a week of sleep straight. "Hannah's and my plans do not concern you."

David's eyebrows drew down. "Excuse me?"

His lips twitched at the fatherly display of concern. Finally. "As I said, she has no clue I'm here. And I'm not about to get into our business with you, but I'm heading to see her next."

"You won't keep Kayla from us?" David asked.

"If you're safe, healthy, and I can trust you, then no. I won't. You have many misconceptions about my family and me. Family is extremely important to me. Keeping Kayla from her brings me no joy. But I also have no problem doing what I must to make sure she has a childhood that far exceeds what mine was."

Biting her lower lip, Patricia nodded. "You aren't what I thought."

"I know that, ma'am. Remember that when you're working through your issues. It won't be easy, but it will probably be the most important thing you ever do. Both for yourselves and the sake of your family. Now, if you'll excuse me, I'm about to crawl out of my skin with the need to see your daughter." Christ, how he wanted to be near her.

"Take good care of them," she whispered.

"I promise you, I will."

He had the sense she wanted to say more. Maybe explain herself, or say sorry, but today wasn't the time. Hannah's parents had so much to work through. Trauma that stemmed back to their own childhood. There'd be plenty of time for explanations and apologies in the future. Today, his mission had been accomplished. They knew he wasn't going anywhere and would remain Kayla's primary caregiver. They knew Hannah wouldn't put up with their bullshit any longer. And they knew they could have a bright future that involved both their daughter and granddaughter.

If they followed his terms and put in the work. He had no illusions it'd be all rainbows and sunshine from here on out. There'd be hard times and tears ahead. Probably some progress followed by setbacks, but that didn't scare him.

What scared him was the prospect of losing Hannah.

Which led to the second part of his plan.

Win Hannah back.

EVERY MOVEMENT FELT as though it took a hundred times more energy than normal. Even lifting her hand to push a stray lock of hair out of her eyes seemed a Herculean task.

She'd lost her family.

Poof, all gone.

Her sister died.

Poof.

She'd left her niece in Vermont.

Poof.

She couldn't be around her parents in a healthy way.

Poof.

All. Gone.

Yet all she could think about was one man. Being without JP

was tearing her up inside. She'd read poems about love and loss where the poets talked about the sun no longer shining, food no longer having flavor, and life no longer holding joy when referring to lost love. She'd always assumed it was hyperbole; over-the-top words to paint a vivid picture.

Now she knew better.

The consuming agony of a broken heart was all too real.

And she was living it.

At some point, she'd need to collect herself off the couch, throw away the empty ice cream cartons, and find a way to move forward. But not today. Today was for wallowing and more ice cream.

A knock at the door had her groaning.

If she mustered the energy to open it only to find one of her parents standing on the other side, she'd likely lose it. What a waste of her entire day's worth of motivation that would be.

Another knock, this time more insistent.

"Coming," she yelled out without moving from where she lay sprawled on the couch.

Blowing out a breath, she forced herself to sit up.

Part way there. *Way to go, Hannah!*

Next step, stand. She did, creaking and cracking the whole way. Crap, she was way too young to be feeling this ancient. Maybe lying around the house for so long hadn't been the wisest idea.

She managed to put one foot in front of the other enough times to get her to the door to her apartment. After unlocking the four—yes four—deadbolts her father had installed, she pulled the door open.

"If you're selling something, I'm not"—time stood still as her gaze encountered JP's— "interested."

Her heart pounded so loudly that if he said anything, she missed it. "Y-you're here," she said as though he wasn't aware of where he stood. "With Kayla." She sucked in a breath. "Oh, my God, is everything okay?" If something had happened to Kayla after she left, she'd never forgive herself. But the baby looked beyond happy to see her, squirming and making the cutest coos of delight.

"It is now," JP said. "It is now."

"What?" She shifted her gaze back up to him.

He chuckled. Why was he there? How was he there? At her door. In Colorado. With Kayla.

She blinked. Maybe she was dreaming. Maybe she fell into a sugar coma and was now dreaming the sweetest fantasy.

He laughed again, snapping her out of her stupor. "I'm sorry. I'm just…stunned. What did you say?"

"Can we come in?" He raised an eyebrow. Any anger or frustration with her seemed to have dissipated since she'd last seen him.

"Yes, of course. Please." She stepped back, allowing them in.

God, he looked good. The sun shone to the side, giving his skin a golden glow and making his ink stand out even more. Was it possible for him to have gotten hotter in the three days since she'd last seen him? And she swore Kayla grew an inch.

"Can I, uh, can I get you anything? Water? Beer? A snack? Not ice cream though, I seem to have eaten all of that." A nervous laugh bubbled out of her. God, she needed to shut up. Having JP in her apartment was making her stupid. Well, having JP in her apartment and not knowing why had her in a tizzy.

"Hannah," he said, calm and cool as ever.

"Yes?"

"We're fine. Sit with me?"

Nodding, she walked over to the couch where he'd already sat. With a few practiced movements, he had Kayla out of the baby carrier and onto the carpeted floor. She immediately started cruising around on all fours, exploring the new territory. Hannah's heart squeezed as she watched her niece crawl over to a stack of paperbacks and knock them down.

"Oops, Kayla," he said as he started to move from the couch.

Hannah put a hand on his knee. "She's fine. I don't mind if

she plays with them."

His skin was warm and strong beneath her hand, reminding her of everything she'd missed so badly over the past few days. But he was there. Within reach once again. Why?

When she went to move her hand, he placed his over it. Oh, those calluses. She almost groaned at the feel of them. She wanted them touching her anywhere, everywhere. Her face, her belly, her breasts, her thighs, inside her.

God, was he here to punish her? Torment her? If this was all she'd get of him, it would be torture. But JP wasn't that kind of man.

"So, how are you?"

"I'm an idiot," he said at the same time.

Her heart skipped a beat. "What?"

"I'm an idiot. For how I acted the other day."

Shaking her head, she scooted closer. "No. JP, no. I'm the idiot. I—"

He stopped her with a hard kiss. She almost wept at how good it felt. But it was over too fast, leaving her pressing a hand to her lips to capture the feeling.

"I understand why you came home. You should have come home. You wouldn't be you—the amazing, kind, compassionate, loving woman I fell in love with—if you didn't take care of your family. God, Hannah, I'm so sorry."

"No," she said, shaking her head as sadness won over the elation of having him there. "You were right. I shouldn't have come. Actually, it was worse than you or I thought it would be."

"I know," he said, cupping her face between his palms. "Your mom told me."

"My mom—wait, what?'

"I said I know, baby." He kissed her again. "I know what she did." Another kiss. "I went to the hospital."

He went to the hospital.

Another kiss landed on her lips, this time longer and hungrier.

"Wait," she said, pulling back as far as she could with him still cradling her face. "I can't think when you do that. All I can concentrate on is wanting to rip off your clothes."

He groaned. "Yes, let's do that." He moved in to kiss her again.

"JP!" she said with a laugh as she covered his mouth with her palm.

He peeked at Kayla, who was happily playing with the books, then sighed. "Talk first, make-up sex later."

That sounded like he planned on sticking around for a bit. Her heart soared.

"I can't believe you're really here," she said.

He kissed her one last time, softly, before lowering his hands to her legs. "Hannah, I missed you like I'd miss a limb. It literally felt as though you took a part of me with you when you left, and it's because you did. Cheesy as it sounds, you took a huge piece of my heart. I'm here because I don't want to be without you." He glanced at Kayla, then smiled. "We don't want to be without you for another day."

Tears flooded her eyes, blurring her vision. "JP," she whispered. "I miss you so much. I feel like I can finally breathe now that you're here. Why did you go to the hospital?"

"Because I love you, Hannah. You've shown me what I'm missing. What a real family can look like. You and Kayla made me want things I'd always been afraid of. But I'm not afraid anymore. I'm not my parents, and you aren't yours. I want breakfasts with you. And I want to comfort Kayla with you in the middle of the night. I want to decorate a Christmas tree with you. I want long, passionate nights driving each other insane with pleasure. I want everything. When I think of the future, I imagine the three of us together. Everyday."

Was this real? Did he want all the same things she did? "JP—"

"Wait. Let me finish." He laid out what happened during his visit to her parents. With each word out of his mouth, her jaw dropped lower until he practically had to scoop it off the couch.

He'd gone to her parents and demanded they get the help

they needed. For her. Her heart was so full, it felt as though I'd burst right through her ribcage. "I can't believe you did that."

"Then I've done a really shitty job of showing you how much I love you. And I plan to never make that mistake again. You deserve to know how much I love you every single minute of every day. And I mean it, Hannah. I have no intention of keeping Kayla from them. It's important for her to have that connection to her mother. But only if they follow through."

"Thank you," she whispered as the emotion clogging her throat stole voice. "JP, I love you too. So much."

"We'll figure everything out, and we'll make it work. I'm not losing you, Hannah."

This time, she kissed him, grabbing his shoulders and yanking him to her. If she had her way, they wouldn't come up for air for the rest of the day. Maybe a few days.

A light smacking sound penetrated her lust-filled brain. What the...

She glanced over her shoulder to see Kayla staring at them and whacking her little palms together in an uncoordinated clap. She grinned her toothless smile and giggled.

"Oh, my God," Hannah said. Heat rushed to her face. "I forgot she was there. I was about to...well, do things she shouldn't see. How could I forget about her?"

JP laughed. "I have that effect." He laughed again as Hannah slapped his shoulder. "Hey!"

She looked up into his heated gaze. "Yeah?"

"Come back with me tomorrow. Stay with me. With us. For good. Be my family."

Hannah peeked at Kayla, who'd gone back to stacking books. Her entire life had changed since she got on a plane to Vermont. She'd changed inside. Finally allowing herself to break free of her parents' chains had brought magic to her life. Nothing was guaranteed, and as everyone in her family knew, situations could turn on a dime. Never again would she let life pass her by because of fear, guilt, or anxiety. She would grab every experience with both hands and hang on tight.

She gave JP her full attention.

"There's nowhere else I'd rather be than with you and Kayla."

This time as they kissed, she swore she heard Mary Anne clapping right along with Kayla, and she sent thanks to her sister for bringing JP into her life.

Epilogue

Hannah smelled like sugar and vanilla. A mouthwatering combination JP couldn't resist. Especially when he knew how it tasted on her skin.

"JP, quit it," Hannah said, giggling as she swatted his forehead with her spatula.

"Mmm." He nibbled up the side of her neck to her ear. "I can't stop. You're too delicious." As expected, she shivered as soon as his teeth grazed her earlobe.

"Well, um, you, uh need to stop," she said in a breathy tone that told him he was winning, and she'd be forgetting all about frosting the cake in a few seconds. "I have to finish—oh, screw it."

She dropped the spatula on the counter with a clatter, then turned and threaded her arms around his neck. Her lips found his, and he dove into the sweetest treat of all.

"Oh, for fuck's sake," Ronnie grumbled from somewhere off to the side.

Hannah jerked in his arms then pulled away, face flushing. "Sorry, Ronnie. Blame him. He distracted me." She spun back around and resumed frosting the cake she'd baked, then tossed, then re-baked no less than three times.

"Yes, Ronnie," he said with a scowl for his annoying sister. "Blame me for distracting my girl who is currently freaking the fuck out about her parent's first visit."

His sister had the good grace to wince. "Shit, sorry, I forgot. I have an interview with a chef tomorrow that's got me all up in my head."

"You're nervous about that?" Hannah asked, setting down her utensils. Well, if his mouth couldn't distract her, at least something could. Her parents scheduled this visit a few weeks ago, and Hannah had been a ball of nerves ever since. In the six months since they'd left Colorado together, Hannah had only spoken to them a few times by phone. Her mother had ended up checking herself into an intensive inpatient therapy program while her father began outpatient visits.

According to both their psychologists, they'd made marked improvements, had a stable medication regimen, and were ready to visit.

They would arrive tomorrow morning. Hence Hannah's baking, mad cleaning fits, a shopping spree for Kayla, and nerves. For his part, he'd done his best to de-stress her with as many orgasms as possible. Soon as he could pry her away from this damn cake, he'd be getting back to that strategy.

"The guy seems like a dick," Ronnie said with a roll of her eyes. She leaned against the counter and accepted a cupcake that didn't make the grade from Hannah. "Thanks. I know he's supposed to be this cultured, fancy, world-class chef, but is it a requirement for him to be an arrogant ass? I mean, we haven't even done the interview, and the guy thinks he runs my kitchen already."

"Is he hot?" Hannah asked.

"Hey!" He swatted her ass, then pulled her into his arms, pressing her back to his front. Her ass nestled into his crotch, nearly making him groan. How fast could they get rid of Ronnie?

Giggling, she shrugged then glanced up at him. "What? It's a valid question."

With a snort, he wrapped his arms around her to keep her from moving. If he couldn't get her naked, at least he could hold her. They had to get their own place. It was hard enough with Kayla around to get as much skin time with Hannah as he'd like. Throw in a sister and brother living in the same house and another across the street, and spontaneity went out the window. The few times he'd tried to get her naked in this very kitchen, they'd been interrupted within minutes.

Damned annoying siblings.

Still, they'd been able to save a ton of money, and with him working and taking classes, having so much family in the house made life a million times easier. Even if privacy was almost nonexistent.

"Hot doesn't begin to describe him," Ronnie said around a bit of cupcake. "Which makes it more annoying. It's like he knows just how gorgeous he is and just how good a chef he is. And he knows we'd be lucky to have him." With a low growl, she shook her head. "This is going to turn into him interviewing me, not me interviewing him. I just know it."

"Yeah, you might not be the best one for that task, sis," JP said. He dodged a chunk of flying cupcake as Hannah laughed. "What? You're not exactly shy and demure. I'm more worried about you ripping off his balls if he pisses you off than whether or not he gets the job. Why don't you have Mickie do it?"

"Ugh." Ronnie's head fell back on her shoulders. "She can't. She and Keith are heading to Boston for the weekend for a buying trip."

"Sorry, sis. Sucks for you. Now, if you'll excuse us. Kayla is asleep, I finished my course work for the day, and both Hannah and I are awake. That means we should be fucking."

"Seriously?" Ronnie threw her hands in the air. "Isn't it about time you two get your own place so you can do your rabbit imitation whenever you want, and I don't have to hear about it? Or hear *it*."

With a playful growl, JP bit the side of Hannah's neck. Her knees wobbled, making her sag in his arms. "Good idea, Veronica. But for now, I'm taking my woman downstairs. Grab your noise-canceling headphones."

"JP!" Hannah said, but the reprimand sounded way too needy to be scolding.

He scooped her up damsel-in-distress style and ran them through the house, down the stairs, and into his bedroom, where he tossed her on the bed.

She landed with a bounce and a smile. "You're crazy."

"Crazy about you."

"Cheesy, too."

He winked as he tugged his shirt up and off his head. "Get naked, babe. You iced a batch of cupcakes this morning. What happened to those?"

"Um." Her eyes fell to his chest as she wiggled out of her sleep pants.

Last month he'd added to his ink. A compass now resided over his heart. Instead of an *N* in the north position, an *H* had been inked in its place with the arrow pointing to it.

"Let me see it," he said, breathless.

Her smile turned sly, and she ever so slowly pulled her T-shirt up. A matching tattoo had been inked above her left hip with a *J* for her north. The perfect symbol for their relationship. No matter what had happened over the months they'd been together, parental drama, job changes, teething, and various other stressors, they were guided to each other through it all.

Stronger and better together.

"So," he said with a wink. "About those cupcakes?"

"Oh, um, they didn't look right. I gave them to a neighbor."

Sighing, he braced himself on his arms, hovering above her. "Baby, you're going to worry yourself sick over this visit. I can promise you they don't give a shit if the cupcakes are perfect. Or if the pillows on the couch match the curtains. Or if the house is spotless."

She shifted her gaze away, but this time he wasn't having it.

"Hannah, honey, look at me."

When she met his eye, hers were shiny with unshed tears.

"Talk to me, babe."

"I-I just want this visit to go well. I want them to be better. I want them to know you and Kayla. I want my family back." Tears leaked from the corners of her eyes down to the pillow beneath her head.

It killed him that he couldn't guarantee a positive outcome for her. But there were a few promises he could make to ease her mind before he worked the tension out of her body. "Hannah, they've been working their assess off to get healthy since I gave them the ultimatum. They're dying to see you and Kayla. Their therapists have told us they feel this is the right time for a visit. Right?"

"Yes."

He wiped the wetness from her cheeks. "Then you need to trust in that. And trust in me. I will not let things escalate. I will not tolerate anything that hurts you."

Her smile was small but unmistakable. "That's the part I have no doubts about."

Fuck, still, months later, words like that hit him right in the feels. How he'd gotten the unconditional love and trust of this amazing woman still baffled him, but he didn't take it for granted. Not once.

"And you're right." She blew out a breath. "I need to chill and trust in the effort they've put into themselves."

"That's my girl. And if nothing else goes right tomorrow, at least we'll get to hear the story of how Ronnie gets her ass handed to her by a cocky chef." He winked.

That had Hannah laughing out loud, but then her face grew serious. "Thank you. You always know just how to make things right again." She stroked a finger across his lips. "You know I love you, right?"

After kissing her fingertip, he nodded. "Baby, that's the part I have no doubts about," he said with a smile, giving her back her words.

She huffed a small laugh. "Smartass. You're lucky you're hot."

Laughing, he rolled his hips, grinding his cock against her wet sex. "I'm lucky you think I'm hot."

Hannah moaned. "Can we be done talking now? I'm ready to have my world rocked."

"Just one more thing." He let his weight settle on top of her and spoke with his lips brushing hers. "I love you."

"Love you," she said as she kissed him.

They took their time loving on each other. With Kayla asleep and nothing to do until morning, they had the whole night for nothing but each other. Kisses, touches, licks, sucks. They did it all until sweat glistened, muscles shook, and throats cried out.

And when he finally surged into her, sometime in the night, he kept her as close as possible. Chests molded together; their hearts beat as one. Their breath mingled, and sighs were swallowed by panting mouths.

They came together, clinging tight and sharing the pleasure.

As they'd share the rest of their lives.

Maybe one day get married.

Give Kayla a few siblings.

His life was unrecognizable from last year.

And all because of a girl named Mary Anne.

She gave him Hannah and Kayla.

She'd given him everything.

Hours later, in the dead of night, he lay awake next to Hannah, enjoying the feel of her as he reviewed the success of the day. She shifted in her sleep, nuzzling deeper into his embrace. As he kissed the top of her head, he closed his eyes.

For so long, he'd been terrified of this very thing.

But now he understood how wrong he'd been.

Because life with Hannah was more perfect than he could have imagined.

Thank you so much for reading **SHOCK AND AWW**. If you enjoyed it, please consider leaving a review on Amazon or Goodreads.

Other books by Lilly Atlas

No Prisoners MC
Hook: A No Prisoners Novella
Striker
Jester
Acer
Lucky
Snake

Trident Ink
Escapades

Hell's Handlers MC
Zach
Maverick
Jigsaw
Copper
Rocket
Little Jack
Joy
Screw
Viper
Thunder

Hell's Handlers Florida Chapter
Curly
* * *

Blue Collar Bensons
First Comes Loathe
Shock and Aww

Audiobooks
Audio

Join Lilly's mailing list for a **FREE** No Prisoners short story.
www.lillyatlas.com
Facebook
Instagram
TikTok
Twitter

Join my Facebook group, **Lilly's Ladies** for book previews, early cover reveals, contests and more!

About the Author

Lilly Atlas is an award-winning contemporary romance author. She's a proud Navy wife and mother of three spunky girls. Every time Lilly downloads a new eBook she expects her Kindle App to tell her it's exhausted and overworked, and to beg for some rest. Thankfully that hasn't happened yet so she can often be found absorbed in a good book.

Made in the USA
Columbia, SC
11 June 2024

37032921R00187